Praise for Elmer Kelton

"One of the best of a new breed of Western writers who have driven the genre into new territory."

—*The New York Times*

"Kelton is a genuine craftsman with an ear for dialogue and, more important, an understanding of the human heart."

—*Booklist*

"*The Smiling Country* is a superb Kelton—a warm, non-violent tale with captivating characters, a sweet love story, the flavor of a better time that has sadly passed."

—*Rocky Mountain News*

"You can never go wrong if you want to read a good story with realistic characters and you pick up a title by Elmer Kelton. In the case of his newest book, *The Smiling Country,* the guarantee is as good as gold. . . . Kelton's characters jump off the page, they are so real. This is another fine title from the man named the Greatest Western Writer of All Time in a 1995 survey by the Western Writers of America."

—*American Cowboy*

Forge Books by Elmer Kelton

After the Bugles
Badger Boy
Barbed Wire
Bitter Trail
Bowie's Mine
The Buckskin Line
Buffalo Wagons
Captain's Rangers
Cloudy in the West
Dark Thicket
The Day the Cowboys Quit
Donovan
Eyes of the Hawk
The Good Old Boys
Hanging Judge
Hard Trail to Follow
Hot Iron
Jericho's Road
Joe Pepper
Llano River
Long Way to Texas

Many a River
Massacre at Goliad
Other Men's Horses
Pecos Crossing
The Pumpkin Rollers
The Raiders: Sons of Texas
Ranger's Trail
The Rebels: Sons of Texas
*Sandhills Boy: The Winding
    Trail of a Texas Writer*
Shadow of a Star
Shotgun
Six Bits a Day
The Smiling Country
Sons of Texas
Stand Proud
Texas Rifles
Texas Standoff
Texas Vendetta
The Time It Never Rained
The Way of the Coyote

Lone Star Rising
(comprising *The Buckskin Line, Badger Boy,* and
The Way of the Coyote)

Brush Country
(comprising *Barbed Wire* and *Llano River*)

Ranger's Law
(comprising *Ranger's Trail, Texas Vendetta,* and
Jericho's Road)

Texas Showdown
(comprising *Pecos Crossing* and *Shotgun*)

Texas Sunrise
(comprising *Massacre at Goliad* and *After the Bugles*)

Long Way to Texas
(comprising *Joe Pepper, Long Way to Texas,* and
Eyes of the Hawk)

THE
GOOD OLD
BOYS

—and—

THE
SMILING
COUNTRY

Elmer Kelton

A TOM DOHERTY ASSOCIATES BOOK | NEW YORK

THE GOOD OLD BOYS AND THE SMILING COUNTRY

The Good Old Boys copyright © 1978, 1985 by the Estate of Elmer Kelton

The Smiling Country copyright © 1998 by the Estate of Elmer Kelton

All rights reserved.

A Forge Book
Published by Tom Doherty Associates
175 Fifth Avenue
New York, NY 10010

www.tor-forge.com

Forge® is a registered trademark of Macmillan Publishing Group, LLC.

ISBN 978-0-7653-9197-1

Our books may be purchased in bulk for promotional, educational, or business use. Please contact your local bookseller or the Macmillan Corporate and Premium Sales Department at 1-800-221-7945, extension 5442, or by e-mail at MacmillanSpecialMarkets@macmillan.com.

First Edition: November 2016

Printed in the United States of America

0 9 8 7 6 5 4 3 2 1

CONTENTS

THE GOOD OLD BOYS   1

THE SMILING COUNTRY   295

THE
GOOD OLD
BOYS

This book is gratefully dedicated to:

Jim Long	Son Guin
Wes Reynolds	Raymond Glasscock
Elliott Moore	Bill Lucas
Carroll and John D. Holleyman	Manerd Gayler
John Patterson	Chuck Olson
George Teague	Brown Fisher
Tommy Cameren	P. O. "Slim" Vines

and the other old-time Jigger Y cowboys of fond memory.
Their boots have tracked all through these pages.

INTRODUCTION

In several ways *The Good Old Boys* is a very personal story to me. Shortly after I began writing it, my father—a cowboy and a rancher all his life—suffered a stroke. My brothers and I took turns staying with him in the hospital. To help pass the long hours, I encouraged him to retell many of the old stories I remembered from boyhood.

Parts of *The Good Old Boys* were written in longhand on a note pad while he slept. Though few if any of his stories actually were incorporated into the novel, their infectious color and spirit became the heart and soul of it.

Writing the book was therapy of sorts and helped me come to grips with the personal tragedy. The first chapters were difficult. The words came slowly and painfully, and much of the opening section was written over and over again. Suddenly the dam broke, and the story came pouring out, much of it unplanned and seemingly spontaneous, from some deep part of the subconscious. I would stare in amazement at words on the paper, wondering where they had come from.

The Good Old Boys is probably the closest I have ever come to writing from sheer inspiration. Hewey Calloway and the other characters took hold of the story like a cold-jawed horse grabbing onto the bit, and about all I could do was hang on for the ride.

Few people except other writers ever completely understand when I tell them about fictional characters becoming so real that they take over the narrative almost by force and carry it off into directions of their own. This has happened to me many times, but never more so than with Hewey, Eve and the Calloway boys.

To some degree the novel was drawn from life. Hewey Calloway, the footloose cowboy, was derived from several I knew in my boyhood. I simply moved them back about thirty years in time. My father, Buck Kelton, was foreman of the McElroy Ranch near Crane, Texas. Cowboys frequently came to the ranch looking for a job. In the 1930s they were likely to be driving a battered old coupe, but in spirit and outlook they were no different from the horseback Hewey.

For the characters of Walter and Eve, Hewey's brother and sister-in-law, I borrowed more than a little from my grandparents, the Bill Keltons, who went to the Midland area about the time of my story and took up a homestead. Granddad worked "outside" for cowboy wages because the homestead would not make a living for the growing family. That homestead served as model for the Calloway place, though for story purposes I moved it south into Upton County.

In real life, as in the book, freighters used to camp in a little grove of hackberry trees below the house, bringing their horse and mule teams up to water at my grandparents' windmill. Granddad would not accept payment for the water, but the freighters usually left some feed at the campgrounds. Mornings, Dad and his sisters would pull a little red wagon down there and pick up the feed for the family's own horses and milk stock.

That grove of trees still stands north of Midland at the edge of a highway built along the same lane the freight wagons traveled eighty years ago.

Snort Yarnell, Hewey's free-spirited sidekick, owes part of his existence to a Midland cowboy known as Bellcord Rutherford, truly a legend in his own time. Unfettered by society's ordinary restraints, Bellcord lived by his own rules and changed those rules as easily as he changed his socks.

A little of Snort's character is also drawn from the great steer roper, Bob Crosby, whom I once met on a front porch during a rodeo in Midland when I was ten or twelve. I could not have been more awed if he had been president of the United States.

The only character drawn entirely from real life, however, is Boy Rasmussen, the senile old drifter who serves as a harbinger of Hewey's future. Basically, the only major change I made was in the name, and in moving him back to 1906. The prototype for Boy used to drift by my grandparents' little ranch, a grizzled old man hard-used by life. He rode an old horse as hard-used as himself. He would bum a meal, and perhaps a bed, before moving on. Granddad always treated him as an old friend, while my grandmother tried to feed him on the open porch, from the upwind side.

As a boy, I thought him a romantic figure, riding free as in the horseback days of old. Years later, looking back, I could see the pathos of his aimless chuckline-rider existence. As in the book, he died a few miles from my grandparents' place, a heart attack killing him as he stepped down from the saddle to open a gate. He had lived his life alone, and he died alone, out on the prairie.

The Good Old Boys was written on two levels. On the surface it is intended to be a humorous and good-natured look at West Texas country life of that period. Most reader comments have been about the humor. But on another, less obvious level, I wrote in sadness, a lament for a less-pressured time and a simpler way of life that had died, as my father was dying.

Hewey Calloway tries to live a life that is already out of its time. He attempts to remain a horseback man while the world relentlessly moves into a machine age. He tries to hold to the open range of recent memory even after that range has been cubed and diced and parceled by barbed wire. He lives in an impossible dream, trying to remain changeless in a world where the only constant *is* change.

Though the story is set in 1906, the problem of dealing with change has intensified with every succeeding generation. Technological and social upheavals have outpaced our ability to adjust. We find ourselves under constant challenge to come to terms with a new and sometimes frightening world we cannot entirely understand.

Hewey is regional, but his problem is universal.

Hewey, like all of us, faces the necessity of painful choices, knowing that every choice will bring sacrifices. He knows, as we all know, that we cannot have everything we want in this life. To fulfill a wish we often must give up something of equal or nearly equal value. Hewey feels drawn to the life his brother Walter has found: a home, a family, a piece of land that is his own. But to have these he knows he must give up his freedom to go where he pleases, when he pleases, to travel his own road without considering the needs of someone else.

He cannot have it all; nobody can.

In this respect, Hewey Calloway is all of us.

ELMER KELTON
San Angelo, Texas

1

For the last five or six days Hewey Calloway had realized he needed a bath. Now, in the final miles of a long horseback trip, it was a necessity no longer to be denied. By nightfall he would be eating hot biscuits and brown gravy at his brother's table. Sister-in-law Eve Calloway was not inclined to generosity regarding the social graces.

Ahead of him the red wooden tower of an Eclipse windmill stood almost astraddle the wagon road which meandered casually among the gentle hills and skirted respectfully around the scattered stands of low-growing mesquite trees. The leaves were still the fresh pale green of early spring. Tall above those trees, the mill's white-painted cypress fan turned slowly in the warm west wind which had stuck Hewey's old blue shirt to his skin much of the morning. A vagrant white puff of cumulus cloud drifted over him, yielding a few minutes of pleasant shade before the sun broke free again in the full heat of early May.

The more he thought about it the more he began to look forward to that cool bath, but he didn't want to push Biscuit into a trot. The brown horse was favoring his right forefoot a little. If it got any worse Hewey would have to walk and lead him.

Hell of a note, going lame the last day out. But better here than where they had started the trip three weeks ago in the melting snows of New Mexico high country.

He had known this region for years, and the sight of the red and white windmill confused him a little. Those colors were the trademark of the Two C Land and Cattle Company, old C. C. Tarpley's outfit. Hewey would take a paralyzed oath that the place just ahead belonged to a four-section bachelor homesteader, a former cowboy who had always been glad to provide Hewey a meal or two and let him roll out his blankets on a hard and civilized wooden floor instead of the soft and uncivilized ground.

The red towers and white fans scattered from here halfway to Midland were sign to a traveler that he was crossing Two Cs land, and welcome to it so long as he shut all the wire gates behind him and didn't run the cattle. He was welcome to camp a night anywhere but never two nights in the same place unless he had a broken wheel. One night was traveling; two nights was squatting.

Gradually Hewey realized he had been right about the homesteader. He recognized the layout of the place, the fallow field, some faded, rotting stalks where last year's hegari crop had grown, and last year's cane. By now a good farmer should have plowed it up and started planting anew. The crude shed stood where Hewey remembered it, but the little frame house was gone. Nothing remained but stubby cedar posts that had been its foundation, and a weather-bleached four-by-four privy thirty feet from what had been the back door, a short run on a cold wet night. Somebody had dismantled the house for the lumber, more than likely. By the windmill's color, that somebody had to be C. C. Tarpley.

Old C. C.'s still spreading out, Hewey thought idly, begrudging him nothing, curious as to why he hadn't taken the privy too. It looked lonesome standing there by itself.

C. C.'s water would be as wet as anybody's. Hewey looked up at the Two Cs brand painted in red on the mill's white tail, which automatically held the fan into the west wind to keep the maximum driving force on its angled wooden fins. The slow turning activated a sucker-rod which clanked and shuddered down the center of a pipe reaching deep into the ground. Each stroke of the rod brought up cool water from the dark depths of the earth, rhythmic gushes pumping it into a big dirt tank which long hours of man and mule sweat had scooped from the ground.

Hewey swung his right leg across Biscuit's rump, holding the leg high to clear the rolled blankets and the "war bag" of miscellaneous cowboy accumulations tied behind the high cantle. Over that cantle was stretched a dried rattlesnake skin, supposed by many to ward off rheumatism, which became a mark of the trade for cowboys who survived the other hazards long enough to acquire it. Some said it also helped prevent hemorrhoids, another ailment common to the horseback profession.

Hewey doubted that, because he had them.

He stretched himself and stamped his feet to stimulate the blood and to steady his saddle-cramped legs. He unbuckled the girth, slid the saddle from Biscuit's back, then led the horse down to the water's edge to let him drink. Not until Biscuit had taken his fill did Hewey tie him to one of the tower legs and prepare to get a drink of water himself. He laid down astraddle the heavy pipe which extended from windmill to tank. He pushed carefully out to the end of it. The pipe was pleasantly cool. He held on with both legs and his left hand, cupping his right hand just under the mouth of the pipe. He drank thirstily from the hand as the water pumped out in time to the mill's even strokes.

It was good water, carrying only a faint suggestion of the gyp common to much of West Texas. Water was a thing to be cherished in dry country. A man prized a good sweet well the way he prized a fine horse. Hewey finally took some of the water up his nostrils and choked. He decided that was enough for a while.

He inched his way back along the pipe, misjudging where to step off and sinking his left boot into the mud. He talked to the boot the way he was accustomed to talking to his horse. "Won't hurt you none. Damn little mud you'll ever get on you in this country."

Inside a small plot which had been the homesteader's garden, green grass was coming up between last year's plowed rows and the fence. Hewey led Biscuit there and turned him loose, fastening the sagging wooden gate to keep him from straying off. He watched the horse roll in the soft dirt, taking up the sweat where the saddle and blanket had been.

Hewey was vaguely disappointed. He had counted on a noon meal from the homesteader, even if only some rewarmed red beans and hogbelly. Well, at least the horse could graze awhile. Hewey would make do with a cold biscuit and dried-out bacon brought from the Two Cs line camp, where he had stayed last night with old cowpuncher friends. He might brew himself a can of coffee too, after a while. Right now he wanted to test the water in that tank.

He emptied his pockets and piled their contents on the bare tank dump. They didn't amount to much . . . a couple of silver dollars and some smaller change, a Barlow knife, a sack of Bull Durham smoking tobacco and a book of brown cigarette papers, a wallet containing his life's savings of twenty-seven dollars. He set his boots beside his treasure. On them jingled a set of scandalous "gal-leg" spurs, the shank shaped like a woman's leg, silver-mounted to show the high-heeled dancing shoe, the stocking, the garter on a plump thigh. It took a sport to wear such as that. He clutched his sweat-stained cotton socks in his hand and waded off into the tank with the rest of his clothes on.

The deepest part came up barely past his thighs. He took off his faded jeans and washed them out, then his shirt and finally his long-handled cotton underwear that once had been white. Naked except for the hat, he walked out with the wet clothing, squeezed as much water from it as he could, then hung it piece by piece to dry in the sun on the bottom brace of the windmill tower. That done, he waded back into the tank until the water was to his knees, then sat himself down shoulder-deep.

If a bath always felt this good, he thought, *I would take one every week or two.*

He sat soaking, only his head and his battered old felt hat above the water. By and by half a dozen cows and their calves came ambling out from a thicket, bound for a cool drink of water and then a long, lazy afternoon shaded up beneath the mesquites, chewing cud. The cow in the lead made it all the way to the top of the earthen dump before she noticed Hewey. She stopped abruptly, her head high in surprise. Her calf spotted him at about the same time and turned to run off a little way, its tail curled in alarm. The cow stood her ground but advanced no farther. The other cows came up even with her and joined her in consternation.

Hewey spoke gently, "Don't be afraid, girls. I'd scare you a lot worse if I was to come up out of here."

The voice was not reassuring. Hewey held still, and one cow's thirst overcame her timidity. She moved cautiously to the water, lowered her head for a few quick sips, then jerked it up again to study Hewey critically, the water drops clinging to the hair under her chin. Gradually she decided he posed no threat as serious as her thirst, and she settled down to drinking her fill. The other cows, followers all, took this for a clearance and moved on to water. Hewey watched, knowing that curiosity would sooner or later lead one of the cattle to investigate his boots and his pocket possessions. When a calf warily started toward them, Hewey brought up a handful of mud from the bottom and hurled it at him. All the cattle ran. But in a few minutes they trailed down to the water again. Hewey held still. It was a cardinal principle not to disturb cattle unnecessarily, especially when they were watering. A cow had to drink plenty of water to make milk. She had to make milk to wean off a healthy calf. Motherhood—human or bovine—was a sacred thing.

Eventually the cattle trailed away to the thicket and lay down in the shade to relax away the warm afternoon and rechew the grass they had packed into their paunches all morning. Hewey began to think he ought to be fixing himself a little coffee and moving on, but the water felt good. He sat lazily watching a hawk make slow circles above the thicket, screaming a vain protest at the cattle. She probably had a nest in one of those big granddaddy mesquites. The cattle ignored her.

Too late he heard the rattle of chains and then the clopping of hoofs and the sand-slicing sound of narrow iron rims along the wagon road. A desperate thought came to him: these might be womenfolks, and they were going to catch him in this tank barefoot all the way to his chin. He weighed his chances of making a dash for his clothes without being seen. They were poor. He sat where he was, stirring the muddy bottom with his hands to make sure nobody could see through the water. The move was unnecessary; there had never been a day when this tank was that clear.

Up to the windmill trotted two matched dappled gray horses pulling a buggy. Two men sat on the spring seat. Hewey's attention went to a gaunt old man with sagging shoulders and sagging mustache. Sawing on the lines to pull the horses to a stop, the old man stared at Hewey with about as much surprise as the cows had shown. He reached instinctively under the seat, where he probably carried a rifle.

Finally he found a brusque voice. "Are you alive out there, or have I got a drowned man on my hands?"

Hewey grinned, relieved that there were only the men. "How's the womenfolks, C. C.?"

"Just barely tolerable. That you, Hewey Calloway?"

"It's me. I'm comin' out, C. C."

His surprise gone, the old rancher watched with a measure of tolerant humor. "Damn if you ain't a pretty sight! I don't believe I ever seen a man take a bath with his hat on."

"I sunburn easy, C. C."

Hewey waded out, following a patch of bermuda grass along the water pipe to keep his feet from getting muddy.

He felt his clothes, found them mostly dry, then began putting them on over his wet skin. His body was almost white. His hands and neck and face were browned, but the rest was customarily never exposed to the sun. Even his loose collar would usually be buttoned to keep the sun out. The last thing he did was to rub the sand from his feet, then put on his socks and boots.

The other man had never spoken. Hewey decided he probably wouldn't. He was a generation and a half younger and fifty pounds heavier than C. C. Tarpley. His name was Frank Gervin. Behind his back, people referred to him by a boyhood nickname, "Fat," but the tactful and prudent never called him that to his round and ruddy face.

Hewey said, "Howdy, Fat."

Fat Gervin winced and slumped a little deeper in the buggy seat. He gave no more than a nod, a very small and tentative recognition of Hewey's existence, and then he looked away, his eyes resting in the direction of home, shade and cool water. Fat had worked as a cowboy on many West Texas ranches, usually for only a short time at each place. He tended always to be lost on drive or to be sitting his horse in the middle of the gate when other hands were trying to put cattle through. Evidently he was better as a lover than as a cowboy, for he had somehow swayed and won Tarpley's only daughter while the old man's attention had been directed to more important things. This gave him a hold on the Tarpley inheritance, provided the old man did not decide at the end to take it all with him.

Hewey gave Gervin no more of his attention. He said, "I had it in mind to fix me a little coffee. Join me, C. C.?"

It would amount to nothing more than some water boiled with coffee grounds in the bottom of a smoke-blackened can and drunk directly out of that can. Hewey didn't even have a cup. But C. C. Tarpley, biggest cattleman this side of the Pecos River, said he wouldn't mind if he did, and he climbed down. Fat didn't say anything; he kept his seat in the buggy.

C. C. didn't look like a big cattleman was supposed to. If anything, in his frayed old clothes and run-over boots he appeared as if he might have a hard time holding down a swamper's job in a saloon. His wrinkled shirt was pockmarked by tiny tobacco burns. He didn't have to dress up to impress anyone; everybody in this country knew him. If he went somewhere else on business, nobody knew him, so he didn't dress up for them either.

The two men squatted on opposite sides of an economical fire and watched while the water stubbornly refused to boil. Tarpley said, "Boys at the Tule camp told me you spent the night there. I'd decided you left this country for good."

Hewey shrugged. "I've got kin here. Walter and Eve and their boys. I got lonesome to see them."

"How long since you left here, two years?"

"One year, ten months and twenty-odd days."

"I reckon you got lots of money, Hewey."

"Money?"

"I recollect you ridin' away on old Biscuit, leadin' a packhorse with all your stuff on it, sayin' you wasn't comin' back till you was rich and famous. I ain't heard a word about you since, so I don't reckon you're famous. How rich are you?"

Hewey grinned sheepishly. "Had twenty-somethin' dollars, last time I counted."

"What come of the packhorse?"

"Sold him."

C. C. turned his head and took a long look at the brown horse. Hewey was glad it wasn't apparent that Biscuit was trying to come up lame. Tarpley said, "Well, if you ain't famous, and you ain't rich, maybe you've come home two years smarter. Ain't you about worn the itch out of your feet, Hewey? Ain't you ready to light someplace?"

Hewey looked at the coffee. "I believe it's finally about to come to a boil."

"Ain't you ever found anywhere you wanted to stay?"

"Just about every place, at first. Then directly I get to thinkin' there might be somethin' better down the road."

"But it's never there, is it?"

"It's *always* there, for a little while." Using two big sticks as a clamp, Hewey gingerly lifted the can from the fire and set it off onto the ground. "Ought to be ready to drink in a minute. You're company, you can have the first sip."

"No, you're company. This place is mine. I bought out Sam Gentry as soon as he got it proved up."

Sam Gentry. Hewey had been trying for an hour to remember the homesteader's name. Sad, how quickly a man's name got lost. It was hard to make a big-enough track that your name was long remembered.

People here would remember C. C. Tarpley for a long time, of course. He had done well for himself the last twenty-five years, since he had stretched a castoff army tent on the Pecos River in 1881 and had turned loose his thirty-three spotted cows and one droop-horned bull. If that bull hadn't made the first winter, C. C. wouldn't have survived either. But the cattle had been prolific. People used to say that on the Tarpley place even the bulls had twin calves. It was also said that C. C. Tarpley could find and put his brand on more unclaimed mavericks than any three men on the Pecos. In his prime he rode fast horses and carried an extra cinch ring tied to his saddle so he could stop and brand any animal he came across that didn't already have a claim burned on it. That sort of ambitious endeavor was occasionally fatal to other men, but C. C. was tough enough to make it stick.

Now, six years into a new century, if anyone were to gather the whole Two C herd from where it was scattered over four hundred square miles of mesquite and catclaw and greasewood country, he would probably tally out five or six thousand mother cows plus no telling how many yearlings and two-year-olds. All that in twenty-five years from thirty-three cows and a bull.

Hard work and attention to business were the key, C. C.

had often preached. But he had always said he was not greedy. All he had ever wanted was that which rightfully belonged to him, and that which adjoined it.

The hard years of acquisition had not let him run to fat. He weighed no more now than when he had first come here. He rode in a buggy more than on horseback, a concession to rheumy bones, but the fire of ambition still glowed in coffee-brown eyes.

C. C. said, "I reckon Walter sent for you to help him out of his trouble?"

Hewey looked up quickly, surprised. "Trouble? I never heard about no trouble."

C. C. had the coffee can, carefully holding his fingers high up near the rim where the heat was not enough to blister. The coffee was only a minute or so past a full boil, but he drank it without flinching. He had always been a man in a hurry.

Hewey waited impatiently for an explanation, but C. C. was busy with the coffee. Hewey demanded, "What kind of trouble is he in?"

"Same as all these nester operators . . . money. He's stretched thinner than a cotton shirt in a cold norther. Come fall, I figure he'll have to fold up and quit." C. C. stared quizzically at Hewey. "You sure he didn't send for you?"

"I ain't even heard from him since I left."

C. C. shrugged. "Not much good you'd do him anyway. You won't stay lit in one place long enough to wear out a change of socks." The statement was made matter-of-factly, not in an insulting way.

"I reckon you could help him, C. C., if you was of a mind to."

"I've tried. I offered to buy him out, same as I done with Sam Gentry. Walter ain't goin' to do any good on a little greasy-sack outfit like that. He'll just starve that good woman and them kids of his to death. I told him I had his old foreman's job waitin' for him any time he wants it back.

When a man's been as good a cowboy as Walter is, it ought to be a penitentiary offense for him to ever take hold of a plow handle."

"What did he say to the offer?"

Fat Gervin had finally climbed down from the buggy. He put into the conversation, answering for Tarpley. "Said what all them shirttail nesters say, that he'll make it all right. But he won't. Best thing that can happen to this country will be when all them nesters starve out and leave it to people that know how to run it."

Hewey didn't look up at Fat. C. C. Tarpley gave him a sharp glance back over his shoulder, a look that told him to shut the hell up. He turned his attention back to Hewey, closing Fat out of the conversation. As if Fat had said nothing, Tarpley answered Hewey's question. "He said he'll make it."

Hewey frowned at the hot coffee. "But you hope he *don't* make it?"

"I got nothin' but his best interests at heart. I like Walter Calloway; I always did. I wouldn't do a thing to hurt him."

"But you wouldn't do anything to really help him."

Tarpley's eyes narrowed. "Best help for your brother would be to get him onto a steady job where he could do some good for himself and be of use to somebody else too. I never could understand what a man wants with one of them little old starve-out places."

"You started small, once."

"That was a long time ago. There was room in this country then. Now it's gettin' so crowded up that you can't breathe, hardly. You're apt to run into somebody's house every five or six miles. Nowadays everybody wants somethin' for nothin'. That's what's behind all these homesteaders, a hope they can get somethin' for nothin'. Everybody ought to pay his own way, is how I see it."

C. C. hadn't paid anybody for the use of the land here in his beginning years. Nobody else was claiming it, at least nobody as tough as C. C. It was too far from Austin for the state authorities to come out collecting. By the time they started charging lease, C. C. had had many years of free use and was strong enough financially that he could afford to pay. Even so, he had snorted and raised hell.

Hewey said, "Lots of people—I never was one myself—want to own somethin' even if it's small. They see honor in havin' a place they can stand on and say, 'This is mine.' "

"There's honor in bein' a Two Cs cowboy, too, if you're a good one." C. C. studied Hewey with keen brown eyes. "I've still got a place for you, too, if you're ready to settle down."

"Still payin' the same wages you used to?" C. C. had always advocated a high sense of morality among his ranch help. Too much money being a threat to that morality, he had seen to it that they were never seriously challenged.

Tarpley frowned. "Times've been a little tight. I've had to cut expenses. But I've always paid a fair wage."

Fair but not good, Hewey thought. He said nothing.

Fat Gervin took that silence as a challenge to C. C.'s generosity. He said righteously, "The man that's payin' the money is the one to say what's fair and what ain't. Trouble with the laborin' class is that it's always askin' for more than it's worth."

Fat had been born into that class, though he had labored little. He had started at the bottom and married up. He stood with his round shoulders back and his belly out, inviting Hewey to contest his studied judgment. To his disgust, Hewey ignored him. As the probable inheritor of the Tarpley power, Fat had tried diligently to copy C. C.'s gruff mannerisms, his toughness, his sureness of self. But he bore no more resemblance to the old man than the reflection in mossy water bears to the battle-scarred stallion.

C. C. turned on him irritably. "Fat, I wisht you'd take and water the horses."

Color flushed the big man's face. He turned and started to lead the horses to the tank, pulling the buggy. Tarpley said, in the same impatient tone he would use against an errant hound, "Unhook them first."

He and Hewey then hunkered in silence, passing the blackened can back and forth, offering none of it to Gervin. A stranger, if told one of them had six thousand cattle and the other had twenty-seven dollars, would have had a hard time deciding which was which. More than likely he would simply have doubted the statement. They were alike in as many ways as they were different. They had come from the same sun-warmed Texas soil. Though they had taken different forks on many roads, their roots gave them a kinship of sorts. They had a respect and a regard for each other that transcended the vast differences in their individual codes, their personal goals and their financial status.

C. C. Tarpley had been orphaned at an early age and cast out on his own in a world where orphans scratched or starved. A few years ago, in an uncharacteristic surge of emotion, he had contributed four hundred dollars toward the building of an orphans' home in Fort Worth. The word had spread and earned him a reputation as a philanthropist among those who did not know him well. Hewey Calloway, who had never owned more of the world's goods than he could tie on a horse, gave freely of whatever he had when he had it. Last fall he had given up a well-earned spree in town before it had fairly begun and contributed his only thirty dollars to a collection for a newly widowed nester woman and her four children. No one ever knew of it except Hewey and a half dozen other cowboys who had volunteered in like manner from their own pinched pockets. Reckoned on a percentage basis, Hewey was by far a more liberal philanthropist than C. C. Tarpley.

C. C. said, "You tell Walter I'd sure like to have him back. I miss him over at the ranch. God, Hewey, you've got no idea how hard it is anymore to find decent help. Just the other day I had to go all the way to Sweetwater to get me two good cowboys."

Remembering what C. C. paid, Hewey was not impressed. But he said a noncommittal, "Well, I'll swun," which C. C. could take for sympathy if he wanted to.

C. C. continued, "I miss that little woman of his too. When Eve was cookin' for the hands I used to like to go by there every so often and debauch myself on her cobbler pie. My wife never could cook worth doodly squat."

On the Two Cs Eve had been expected to cook for the regular bachelor cowboys, plus any extra help, plus any company that happened along. She wasn't paid for it; it was simply part of the honor of being the foreman's wife. That was one reason she had clung so tenaciously to the little homestead, poor as it was. She probably worked as hard or harder there than ever before. But she cooked for her own family and nobody else.

C. C.'s eyes narrowed. "You got an ugly mark across your jaw, Hewey. Fresh, too. Where'd it come from?"

Instinctively Hewey brought his finger up. The place burned beneath his touch. He didn't look C. C. in the eye. "Horse," he said.

C. C grunted. "How old are you, Hewey?"

Hewey had to figure; he hadn't thought about it in a while. "Thirty-eight. Thirty-eight the fourteenth day of last February."

Tarpley mused. "You sure ain't no valentine. I'll bet by now you're beginnin' to feel the arthritis settin' in. About time for the gray hair to start takin' over too. And all you've got is a brown horse past his prime, an old saddle and maybe twenty dollars. Ain't much to show for them many years, is it?"

Hewey thought before he answered. "I've left a lot of tracks and seen a lot of country. I've worked down to the border of Old Mexico. Been to Cuba for Uncle Sam. I've worked cows from the San Saba River plumb up to Wyoming and Montana. I even went north once into Canada and seen the glaciers. You ever seen a glacier, C. C.?"

The old man just stared at him. He probably didn't know what a glacier was. "What's it ever got for you?" he demanded. "Them places are too far from here to ever amount to anything. The man who gets ahead is the one who stays put and tends to business, not the one always fidgetin' around to go, like a horse in an antbed. You've seen all of that country, but how much of it do you own?"

Hewey pondered the question. "In a way, I own it all."

Old Tarpley didn't understand that. Hewey had found a long time ago that most people never did.

After C. C. and Fat had gone, Hewey squatted to finish the coffee. The wound on his jaw still burned where he had touched it, and he couldn't help touching it again. He had lied to C. C., because this was something else C. C. wouldn't have understood.

He would have to keep on lying about it, for he would not be able to explain it to Eve, either. She was not always an understanding woman. She would not be tolerant of the truth in this case. He had never seen harm in an occasional small liberty with the facts, provided the motive was honorable. The motive in this case would be to keep Eve from raising hell and later regretting her lapse from grace. It had always been his policy to protect her from herself.

The mark on his jaw represented the only bad incident Hewey had encountered on his ride home from New Mexico. He did not consider the morning he had ridden Biscuit off into a snowdrift and had almost smothered them both. That had been a natural hazard, the kind of thing a man had to expect. What he had never been able to understand were human obstacles; they seemed so unnecessary.

He had ridden a little out of his way to pass through New Prosperity, a Panhandle railroad town, thinking he might find something there wetter than windmill water. It seemed natural enough to take a shortcut down a nice wide street where all the houses appeared to be owned by bankers and merchants because every one of them had two stories. Most were decorated by gables and bay windows, and by ginger-bread and scallop trim that reminded him of a good brown-topped apple pie. The thought of having to live in one of those houses and take the responsibility for it would have scared him half to death, but they were pretty to look at. Damn few ranches and no cow camps at all had anything like that.

At a corner stood a man who hadn't missed a meal since the winter of '89. He waved his hand sharply and hollered at Hewey, "Hey, you! Come here!"

Hewey reined up in surprise and looked behind him, thinking the man might be shouting at somebody else. He had the street to himself. He sat there in the middle of it, wondering why anybody in this town could be mad at him. He had never been here before.

The man kept yelling, and Hewey kept sitting. Unlike Fat Gervin, who was big all over, this portly gentleman ran mainly to belly. When he tired of straining his voice he walked out toward Hewey, working tolerably hard at his short, choppy steps. The sun flickered off of a small badge on his black vest and called Hewey's attention to the fact that he represented the full majesty of New Prosperity law.

"Cowboy, I told you to come here!"

"I am here."

"What's your name?"

Hewey had heard that tone of voice a right smart in the Army, while he was in the Cuba campaign. It was one reason he had not chosen to remain in the service. "Hewey Calloway."

"This is a residential street, cowboy."

Hewey nodded. "Yes sir, and a damn nice one too."

"You're on the wrong side of the tracks."

"I was figurin' to cross over, soon as I get to them."

"Transients ain't allowed on a residential street. The only

people who use this street live here or have got business here. One look tells me you ain't got no business here, Holloway."

"Calloway."

"The name don't mean anything to me. You're just another saddle tramp, and you're ridin' where you ain't supposed to."

Hewey's face turned warm. "I ain't never been no saddle tramp. I've got money in my pockets."

"How much money?"

Hewey didn't see that as anybody's business. It was impolite to ask a man how much money he had or to volunteer how much you had. The latter was usually either a brag or a complaint, and nobody wanted to listen to it. Money was no yardstick of a man's worth. Anyway, Hewey hated to admit how little was left to show for a cold winter's work. He inflated it. "Fifty dollars, maybe."

"Just about enough to pay a fine for trespass. You get off of this street right now, and I don't mean in a walk, cowboy. I want you to run that horse." The city marshal placed his hand on his gun butt to punctuate his order.

Hewey prided himself on tolerance, but there was a limit to all good things. He regretted the occasional necessity of giving one man authority over another because some people enjoyed that authority too much to be entrusted with it. They tended to be easily misled into a gross overappraisal of their importance. It seemed to him that when a man was too thick-headed and too low-down trifling to hold an honest job, he was usually able to find some other damn fool willing to hand him a measure of jurisdiction over the lives of his betters.

Hewey said, "I didn't see no sign that said to keep off."

"You see me!" By now the officer was swelled up like a toad at a water tank.

Hewey touched his spurs lightly to Biscuit's sides and

started moving in a walk, a very slow and defiant walk. He was afraid his hatband would split in two from the pressure his anger pushed against it.

"Cowboy!"

He looked back. The officer had the pistol in his hand, pointing it at him. "I don't let nobody smart-aleck with me. You get down off of that horse or I'll shoot you off of him!"

The sight of the pistol brought a cold chill. But Hewey sat looking at the marshal a minute, the way he would look at a cull just before he cut it out of the herd. He swung his leg slowly over Biscuit's rump and touched his right foot to the ground, making it a point not to hurry his compliance. While Hewey was still off balance with his left foot in the stirrup, the officer swung the pistol barrel at his head. Hewey dodged. The barrel struck him a glancing blow along his jaw and then hit hard on his shoulder. He saw a shower of bright lights.

It was the mark of a cowardly law to pistol-whip a man at the outset and eliminate any resistance. The marshal never had another chance. The move startled Biscuit. The horse lunged, striking the man with his heavy foreshoulder, sending him stumbling back. Hewey swung his fist with all the force he had. The man's soft nose crushed like a cantaloupe. Hewey saw blood on his knuckles when he rubbed them and hoped it wasn't his own. The officer lay flat on his back, spread-eagled with that big stomach sticking up like a washpot turned upside down. Hewey started to go off and leave him but thought of the pistol. The marshal could easily shoot him in the back as he rode away, and he might if he could clear his eyes. Hewey picked up the pistol and shoved it in his waistband.

He rubbed his jaw and then his shoulder, both aching from the blow. He said, "You've cost this town my business. I reckon I'll save my money till I find me a friendlier burg."

He doubted the officer heard him very clearly. It didn't matter.

He made it a point to stay on the residential street and to ride in a slow walk until he passed over the tracks. He paused to pitch the pistol into a wooden water trough. He had never liked to carry one around. He kept Biscuit in a walk until he passed the last Mexican shack on the south side of town, then pushed him into a trot.

The swelling had gone down in the days that had passed, but some of the rawness remained. Hewey washed his jaw again in the dirty tank water.

Biscuit's limp became worse as the afternoon wore on. Hewey carefully looked over his right forefoot two or three times, trying to find some physical sign of the trouble. More than anything else, probably, Biscuit needed a rest. Even at Hewey's chosen leisurely pace it had been a wearisome trip down here from that cow camp where the two of them had spent the winter in the Sangre de Cristos. He knew that in most people's sight he was probably working the whole thing backward, wintering in the New Mexico snow and summering in hot western Texas. But he had always drifted as the fancy struck him, and the long winter's solitude had given him lots of time to think about his few kin. The urge to see them had grown beyond resistance.

About midafternoon he came upon a band of grazing sheep, scattered for half a mile up and down a wide draw where good moisture was bringing up the spring weeds. He was surprised to see the Two Cs paint-branded on their woolly backs. Old C. C. had always prefaced the word "sheep" with a couple or three pungent adjectives. But maybe the wool market had turned strong and the cow market had soured. To C. C., like lots of ranchers, nothing could be all bad if it paid a dividend.

Hewey hunted up the herder to auger a little. He was seldom in such a hurry that he wouldn't take time to visit. But the herder was a ragged, graying old Mexican who didn't seem to know three words of English. The only Spanish

Hewey knew was a few cuss words, and those seemed in-appropriate. Efforts at communication came largely to nought. The herder was too far from his tent camp to offer coffee, so Hewey didn't stay.

Shortly afterward he saw a wagon moving to intersect his line of travel. He could see two men on its seat. They had a considerable load of goods in its bed. One of the men tilted his head back and took a long drink from a bottle just before Hewey came up even with him.

"Hey, Alvin!" Hewey shouted. "Alvin Lawdermilk!"

The wagon driver was a young Mexican whose growth had stopped at just a little more than five feet. He brought his four young Spanish mules to a stop. A couple of them fidgeted and stomped up dust, showing they were not yet well broken to the harness. Among other livestock, Alvin Lawdermilk and his wife, Cora, raised mules. Their place had a reputation for being Western when raw mules were introduced to collars and hames. It was also known to get Western when Cora caught Alvin drinking. She seldom caught him.

Lawdermilk twisted his face and tried to bring Hewey into focus. Hewey heard him ask the Mexican, "Hooley, who is that?" When the Mexican answered, Lawdermilk shouted happily, "Hewey Calloway! I thought you'd wandered off the edge of the earth and fell to your doom."

Lawdermilk tried to climb out of the wagon and almost fell to his own doom. The Mexican quickly caught his arm and pulled him back to safety, somehow getting him settled squarely onto the seat and grinning apologetically at Hewey.

Hewey said, "You better stay put, Alvin. That wagon is pretty bouncy." It was standing still.

He rode up beside the left front wheel and pumped Alvin's hand. He reached across to the Mexican. "Howdy, Hooley. I'm surprised you're still puttin' up with Alvin." The Mexican's name was Julio Valdez, the *J* pronounced like an English *H*. The Anglos had corrupted it. Hooley had a reputation as a great hand at breaking mules. Though short in stature, he was quick. Hewey respected other people's proficiences, whatever they were.

Alvin Lawdermilk's pudgy red face seemed always to be smiling, even when he was sleeping off a lost bout with a bottle. Hewey had never seen him really angry at anyone except his wife, and never in her case where she could see it. Alvin knew how to handle wild broncs, but Cora knew how to handle Alvin.

Alvin's smile was exaggerated by false teeth that were too white and too perfectly shaped, pushing his upper lip out more than was natural. He said exuberantly, "Damn, Hewey, it's good to see that ugly face of yours again, though I can't say it improves with age. Where you come from?"

"New Mexico. Spent the winter hayin' cows in the Sangre de Cristos."

"Wonder you didn't freeze your butt off."

"I did. It'll take me half the summer to thaw the ice out of my blood."

"A wee drop of kindness will build a fire for you." He handed Hewey the bottle. Hewey rubbed his hand across the mouth of it, for he knew Alvin to be a tobacco chewer. He had no objection to following somebody on a bottle, but secondhand tobacco juice took a broad mind. Alvin grinned in shared pleasure as he watched Hewey take a Texas-sized drink and wipe his wrinkled sleeve across his mouth. Alvin said, "What this old world needs is a lot more kindness."

"Truer words was never spoke." Hewey handed the bottle back, enjoying the warmth of the whisky making its slow way down to his stomach. "You ain't buyin' the cheap stuff."

"When they tote me off in that big black wagon, I want it said that I died of the best." Alvin passed the bottle to Julio, who took only a modest sip and handed it back. Somebody had to stay sober for the mules.

Hewey glanced at the goods stacked high in the wagon bed . . . flour, potatoes, Arbuckle coffee, a keg of steeples, several spools of barbed wire. Beneath the seat, where nothing could fall on it and cause grievous damage, was a new wooden case full of whisky bottles. "Looks like you went and supplied yourself for the summer."

"Only the necessaries. You'll never catch us Lawdermilks throwin' good money away on things we don't need. Waste not, want not."

Hewey knew Cora Lawdermilk. She would inspect every item as it was unloaded, and woe unto all within hearing if anything came up short, or if she found anything on the wagon which she had not ordered or approved. The case of whisky would not be there when she checked the rest of the goods. Alvin would unload it in some safe place before he reached the house. Then, as the opportunities arose, he would carry the individual bottles to secret places for ready accessibility in time of need. There was not a windmill on the Lawdermilk ranch where Alvin did not have a bottle cached to help heal some inner misery, or to cut away the taste of gyp in the water. He kept one at his milking shed, two or three in the barn and one at the corner post of the field where he raised hegari and redtop cane as feed for his horses and mules, and where he trained the young ones to work. No emergency, anywhere on the ranch, ever caught him unprepared.

Yet, with it all he was a successful rancher as success was measured in this country. A successful rancher was one who had not been broke, lately. Though Alvin did not rival C. C. Tarpley and had no such ambition, he was no shirttail nester. If the sheriff came down his road it was to electioneer, not to post a notice of foreclosure.

Hewey said, "How's my family, Alvin?"

Alvin stared at the bottle in his hand. Hewey got the quick impression that he was uncertain how to answer. Alvin said, "I see them two buttons every day, almost. They've growed like weeds."

Hewey waited until he decided that was all Alvin was

going to tell him. "I had a visit with C. C. He talked like Walter is in trouble."

Alvin looked out across the pasture, framing his words with care. He looked sober, all of a sudden. "C. C. give you any details?"

"Just said there's money trouble."

"I reckon that's so."

"Is Walter fixin' to lose his place?"

Alvin didn't answer, not directly. "Hewey, I'm concerned about him. Walter labors from lantern light to lantern light. You got to tell him he's workin' too hard. Each man to his own way of dyin', but I'd hate to think mine was to be from overwork."

Hewey felt increasingly uneasy. It was Eve's doing, sure as anything. She was always pushing for better than she had. Times, just for a minute or two, Hewey would get to thinking Walter might have been better off if he had never met her. But then, he wouldn't have had those boys.

Alvin said, "A woman has got a right to a certain amount of ambition, but not to excess. A man ought to keep her under control, like I do with my Cora. I don't do nothin' on my place unless I want to."

Julio looked quickly away, studying the flight of a scissortail; its presence meant spring had come for sure.

Hewey's conscience began to stir. He should have written, should have kept the family posted so they could write and tell him if anything was wrong. It was something he had always intended to do, but writing a letter was harder work for him than breaking a bronc or digging a string of postholes. His formal schooling had stopped just shy of the last pages in McGuffey's third reader.

His rump was prickling now in his anxiety to go. "Alvin . . . Hooley . . . it was sure nice runnin' into you-all. I reckon I better be seein' about the family."

Alvin said eagerly, "You lookin' for a job, Hewey? There's a right smart more work over at our place than we've been able to get done. If you take it in mind to light someplace awhile, we'd be tickled to have you." Alvin extended the bottle again. "Better have one more. It'll make the country look greener."

Hewey shook his head. "One's enough, I reckon. Eve'll smell it on my breath. She don't hold with drinkin'."

"Neither does my Cora. Ain't nothin' like a righteous woman to drive a man to sin." Alvin reached into his shirt pocket and brought out a plug of tobacco, only a little of it bitten off. He took a pocketknife and carved a generous slice, holding it toward Hewey. "Take a chaw of this just before you get there. It'll kill the scent. Even if it don't, the sight of a little tobacco juice runnin' down the chin will keep a woman at a distance; she won't smell the whisky."

Hewey had no intention of chewing the tobacco, but he accepted it as hospitality freely offered. He also accepted one more drink from the bottle. He said, "You watch Hooley now, Alvin. Don't you let him drink too much."

The little Mexican smiled and flipped the reins. As the wagon pulled away, Alvin turned in the seat and shouted back, "Bunch of us will be over tomorrow and help Walter raise a windmill. I'll want to visit with you and hear all your yarns. Ain't many of us poor devils ever gets to travel all over the world."

The words soon became unintelligible, but Alvin kept shouting back, and Hewey kept nodding as if he understood and agreed. He watched the wagon lumber on down the trail toward the Lawdermilk place, thin gray dust drifting off and settling slowly on the grass standing shin-high and green from the spring rains. It didn't take a trail long to dry out. Hewey touched a spur gently to Biscuit's side. "Come on, old friend, we still got a ways to go."

The prickling came back as he picked up landmarks that told him he was nearing Walter's land. He stared at a small flat-topped hill with an abrupt rimrock edge running along its north face. People here called it a mountain, which in a strictly local and relative sense it might be. But Hewey had seen real mountains, so he regarded this as simply a hill. Beneath it was a dry, water-hollowed place that appeared to be a wet-weather spring, though he had never been here in a time wet enough to see it run. Indians had camped here. Many times Hewey had come with Walter's two boys to help them hunt for arrowheads. They had probably collected a bucketful. To the boys these were a treasure left from a mysterious time they had never known. Hewey had seen Indians in the Territory and up in the mountain states. To him they were not mysterious or remote; they were real.

He edged Biscuit across the old campsite and leaned low in the saddle, watching the ground. It would tickle the boys if he brought them a couple of good points. But if any arrowheads were left, the new grass was hiding them.

He came presently to a fence and reined up, surprised. He knew this was more or less the boundary of Walter's four sections, but the last time he had been here Walter hadn't yet accumulated the money or the credit to put a fence around it and keep C. C.'s cows from helping themselves to the grass, crowding Walter's own little herd. The fence had only three strands of barbed wire, still shiny from the factory, not yet dulled or rusted from standing exposed to winter blizzard and summer sun. Three strands were the mark of a nester, poor as a whippoorwill. A real rancher like C. C. would put up four wires. Anything less was unprofessional and farmer-looking.

Cedar posts were best for fencing; they lasted longer. They cost money, though, and had to be freighted in by wagon from the hill country south and east of here. Mesquite posts would not stand as long, but a man could chop them himself, close to home. They cost him only his time and sweat. These posts were all mesquite. Hewey knew how Walter had spent the winter.

He started down the fence, looking for a gate or a drop-gap.

Until recent years this gently rolling rangeland had been a haven for massive herds of buffalo driven south each fall and winter by the chill winds howling across the high and open plains. They could find shelter here in the scattered stands of mesquite which fringed the wide draws and wet-weather creeks, and on the lee sides of the little bluffs and breaks which marked the southernmost fringe of the great caprock. As recently as thirty years ago the plains Indians had roamed here, following the buffalo, hunting the deer but settling sometimes for rabbits and rattlesnakes when times were lean.

Much of this land was unsuited to cultivation, and the man who sank a plowpoint into the sod would have ample cause to regret it. Yet there were wide deep-soil flats which could be farmed if a man had patience enough, and faith. The average rainfall was less than twenty inches a year, and the actual amount in a given year could be far, far less than that. The ranchers, already here, made it a point to tell every prospective land seeker about those worst years if they could find a way to reach him in time. The town promoters and boomers told him only of the best years, those infrequent periods when rains were generous and corn made heads bigger around than a man's fist, kernels as big as cats' eyes.

Given any chance, this virgin land usually made big crops the first time or two, using up nutrients stored by the grass roots for thousands of years. Few people had farmed here long enough yet to know how poorly the land might yield when it became tired of bearing crops Nature had not intended.

Because of its shortcomings, this region had been among the last to draw the farmers and small settlers. It was among the last large stretches of state-owned land that Texas had taken out of grass lease and had thrown open for homesteads of up to four sections—twenty-five hundred acres—per claimant, to be lived on and proved up in three years. Texas was more generous in its homestead programs than the federal government had been in other western states, possibly because its legislators lived nearer to the land involved and realized its limitations. They knew a man could starve to death in a year on a hundred and sixty acres. On four sections it took longer.

Hewey found a wire gate half a mile from the point where he had struck the fence. He dismounted and led Biscuit through, flinching as he touched the sharp barbs. Though it belonged to his brother, the fence stirred a latent resentment in his free-roaming spirit. This great open land had given him a kinship of sorts to the nomadic Indian. He could remember when a horseman might ride two or three hundred miles and never encounter a barbed-wire fence. Now he was lucky to travel twenty without having to look for a gate or to pull steeples out of the posts and push down the wires to cross over.

He recognized the fence as a necessity for the small settler's survival, but it was not a thing he could accept without regret at the passing of a freer and more open time. A fence—any way you looked at it—was an obstacle. It shut you out or it shut you in.

He rode down a familiar wagon road, his heartbeat quickening. He had been here when Walter had taken up this little piece of land. Though Hewey had no liking for a plow, he had helped Walter break out his first field and build the small, ugly-plain frame house that would meet the legal requirements of the state and the shelter requirements of a wife and two sons. Walter had wanted a few cattle; that was the cowboy in him. Hewey had gone east to San Angelo and had bought him thirty cows of the upgraded type, the red body and white face of the Hereford blood showing stronger than the stubborn lean base of Longhorn. Three of the cows had calves on the trail; by the time they had reached here Walter owned more cattle than he had paid for. That had pleased Eve. She had an instinct for acquisition.

Walter had tried at the time to persuade Hewey to take up a homestead for himself. The temptation had been strong—for a couple of days. But Hewey contended that land ownership worked two ways. A man might own the land, but the land also owned *him*. Anyway, he had told himself, the state of Texas held all the best cards. It was betting a man a piddling parcel of land against three good years of his life, and the odds were against the man. Hewey had no wish to be tied to one place so small that a horse would hardly break a sweat loping across it in trade for his freedom of the whole West from the Rio Grande to the Canadian border.

All Walter owned was this one little piece of land. Hewey owned it all.

He came presently to the edge of the field and noted that it stretched farther than he remembered. Walter had added to it gradually until it took up just about all the deep soil that promised an affinity to the plow, and also some that didn't. It was farmer nature, Hewey thought, to overreach oneself.

Walter had not been a farmer by inclination. Necessity had forced him to it, necessity and a woman. In his growing years Walter had been much like Hewey, a cowboy at heart, unfettered of spirit, ready to ride anywhere he had not already been, ready to try anything he had not already tried. Motherless, they had roamed with their restless father through the years of their boyhood while the elder Calloway sought in vain for an ideal land that existed only in his mind. When Hewey was fifteen and Walter barely fourteen, they had buried their father on a grassy Kansas upland above a river where he had waited with other "boomers" for the anticipated opening of the Indian lands across the deadline in Oklahoma. This was to have been the last great bonanza. But two underage boys were not eligible to try their luck in the big land run, so they had moved on. They had worked steers for Texas cattlemen leasing grass from the Osages and the Cherokees, then moved back across Red River into the land of their beginnings, searching vainly for roots hopelessly lost during their wandering years. The place of their birth had been taken up by strangers. Whatever kin they might have had was gone, scattered like tumbleweeds in a long winter wind. So they went drifting as their father had drifted, never knowing truly what they searched for, or how they would recognize it if they found it.

Walter, at least, had been able to compromise. When he married Eve, the daughter of a poor San Saba County farmer, he had tried awhile to continue the footloose ways of former years. But Eve had a strong instinct for the nest. She had pressured Walter to light in one place, old C. C. Tarpley's ranch. She had seen to it that Walter stuck to one job while Hewey was working at a dozen. She had made Walter smoke little, drink nothing, wear boots twice resoled and clothes that had patches on the patches. She had seen to it that Walter saved every possible dollar, while Hewey was spending his much easier than they had come.

When parts of this land were finally taken from the grass-lease ranchers like C. C. and thrown open for claiming, Eve's time of fulfillment had arrived. Walter was at the head of the pushing, shoving, shouting line of men scuffling at the front door of the county courthouse. Hewey had hunkered with his back to the white picket fence on the courthouse square, ready to go to his brother's aid if any of the toughs and the hungry and the desperate tried to throw him out of his place in the line. But Hewey had not the slightest inclination to join that line himself. He found something offensive and dehumanizing in the system, something that robbed a man of pride and dignity, pitting friends against each other, bringing ugliness and greed and violence rising to the top like sour cream on spoiled milk.

Many of the men who homesteaded these places were cowboys for the big outfits and tacitly agreed that when they had finished living out their claims they would sell them to the ranches they worked for. C. C. Tarpley had expected all along that he would get Walter's parcel and put it back into his original holdings for perhaps the price of a good horse and a new R. T. Frazier saddle. But he had reckoned without Eve. Anything she once acquired, all hell would not prize from her grip.

Across the field Hewey could see two teams, each pulling a walking plow. It was too far to recognize the plowmen, but one would almost certainly be Walter. The other was probably one of his boys unless Walter had become flush enough to hire help. Hewey doubted that. Hiring help was wasteful if you could do the job yourself, Eve always said. Eve always said a lot.

Hewey rode down the field fence until he came to the corner gate. He found it open, marked by fresh tracks of the teams moving in and out. This early in the season the field held nothing for the cows to get into and ruin. Hewey rode up the turnrows a way, then dismounted, squatted on his galleg spurs and rolled himself a cigarette while he waited. He had no intention of riding or walking across that newly plowed, violated ground.

He watched a black dog following behind one of the plows, waiting to catch a rabbit or chase after a ground squirrel if one was scared up. As the plow neared, the dog trotted around it and hurried out in front, barking a challenge at Hewey.

Hewey had time to finish his cigarette before the plow hand began to shout at him. "Uncle Hewey! Uncle Hewey!"

A young boy reached the turnrow and reined the team to a stop; the two gray mules had no objection. He tipped the plow over on one side and ran across the plowed earth, the dog beside him, barking. When the boy reached the grass he shouted joyously and threw his arms around Hewey, hugging him with a surprising strength. Hewey danced, swinging the lad off his feet. Biscuit took a couple of steps backward, startled at the exuberance. The black dog kept barking, afraid Hewey was hurting the boy, but it took no other action.

"I'll swun, Cotton," Hewey exclaimed, "you've growed a foot."

"I'm not Cotton. I'm Tommy."

Hewey held the boy away at arm's length and took a long look. "You *are* Tommy. Boy howdy, you've growed *two* feet. They been feedin' you Tarpley beef?"

"You just been gone a long time."

"I didn't realize how long."

"We missed you, Uncle Hewey. Have you come home to stay?"

Hewey had no honest answer. "Maybe awhile. We'll see." A thought struck him. "How come you're not in school?"

"This is Saturday."

"Saturday?" Hewey blinked, trying to calculate. "Funny, I thought it was Wednesday." He stared at Tommy, and the boy stared back at him until the two broke out laughing again for no good reason either could have named.

Tommy said, "We got us a fishin' hole now, Uncle Hewey. I'll take you there. We'll catch us a perch."

Hewey nodded, still not able to accept how much the boy had grown. "If you're this big, how big is Cotton?"

"About grown. He's comin' on sixteen, you know."

Sixteen. Hewey knew it, yet he could not quite accept it, either. It didn't seem possible that so many years had drifted by so quickly. "You're almost a man yourself, Tommy. Couple more years . . . Which one of you is the best cowboy, you or Cotton? Tell me the truth now."

"I am. All Cotton wants to do is build things and tinker around with tools and wrenches all the time."

Hewey kept grinning. "I was thinkin' maybe when school is out I might take you two buttons with me and find us a cowboyin' job for the summer out west of the Pecos. Good chance for you-all to see a little country."

Tommy's blue eyes flashed in quick pleasure. But his smile faded as he thought about it. "Mama and Daddy will need us. We've got more land to take care of now."

Hewey didn't know whether to be glad for them or to sympathize. "How'd that happen?"

"Grat French finished provin' up his four sections that adjoined us. Mr. C. C. tried to buy the place, but Mr. French was peeved at him and didn't want him to have it. He offered it to Daddy and Mama instead. They took out a mortgage on everything we own. Except maybe my dog."

Hewey let a slow dry whistle pass between his teeth. "I'll bet old C. C. busted a gut."

"No, it was him and his bank that loaned us the money. Mama says he wanted the French land and ours too, and he figured this way he would wind up gettin' them both. She says we're goin' to fool old Mr. C. C." Tommy frowned. "But I don't know. Last year we come up shy on the crops, and the cattle market was kind of poor on our yearlin's."

Hewey saw worry in Tommy's eyes. It wasn't right, he thought, for a fourteen-year-old boy to carry a burden like this. "Well, it's just a piece of land," he said, trying to make the best of it. "There's land everywhere, most of it better than this."

"But this is *our* land. This is home."

He stared at the boy, looking at those features that marked him as a Calloway. But Tommy was Eve's son, too, and that was a side of him Hewey would never fully understand.

Land. It was a pleasant thing to ride across but a demanding thing to own. So now Walter and Eve owned eight sections of it and stood a considerable chance of losing it all. Maybe in the long run it was just as well. It would probably cost eighty years of hard labor, first for them, then for their kids and eventually for their grandchildren. Chances were that in the end none would ever feel any richer than Hewey had felt all his life.

But it bothered him, thinking that after all their planning and all their work it might fall into the open hands of C. C. Tarpley like a ripe peach falls from the tree to be grabbed up by an orchard boar. Other land-hungry men had used more direct methods; they had burned out fields and barns, run off homesteaders' cattle, even killed. C. C.'s brand of avarice ran in a subtler vein, infinitely more patient.

Hewey frowned, watching his brother working his way across the field with his plow, a mismatched horse team laboring to break new rows in the damp and grudging earth. He pondered darkly on how a man is brought down from being a hawk in flight to a slave in chains.

This was a long way from the Osage.

2

The first thing to strike Hewey about his younger brother was that Walter was wearing bib overalls. In olden times he had rather have ridden stark naked down a cow-town street at high noon than be seen in overalls. The second thing to strike him was that Walter looked like the older brother, not the younger.

He was a little slow setting the plow over. He gave Hewey a tentative and apologetic wave as he paused a moment, stretching his stiffened arms and rubbing his right shoulder. But he grinned with his whole face. Hewey forgot about the plowed ground and walked out hurriedly to meet him. They shook hands, but that wasn't enough, so they threw their arms around each other. Happy tears ran unashamed down Walter's dusty cheeks, leaving little tracks of mud across what looked like weathered leather.

"The prodigal son," Walter exulted, "finally come home. And there's not a fatted calf on the place."

"I'd settle for a wing from a drouthy quail."

"You may have to." Walter stepped back for a good long look at Hewey, from his face to his thorn-scarred boots. "I'd about decided you'd finally found a bronc you couldn't ride or a cow you oughtn't to've roped. Thought they'd buried you someplace without us knowin' it. You had three years of schoolin'. Didn't you learn to write?"

"Not to where you could read it."

Walter's overalls were old and thready, both knees patched with newer material that stood out darker than the faded blue. His old hat was shapeless, the brim flat, showing none of the flair that had been a trademark of the Calloway brothers in their wilder years. The hat now was strictly for business, to keep the sun from his face; the flatter the brim the better it did that job.

Even in a winter bachelor camp where nothing could see him except three horses and a bunch of hungry cattle, Hewey had taken care about the shape of his hat. He watched his shadow sometimes as he rode. Even the shadow had style.

The two brothers, over the first flush of joy, stood back at arm's length and regarded each other critically, neither altogether pleased by what he saw.

Walter accused, "You ain't been eatin' regular."

"I never did. But I'll bet I look better than *you* do. You been drivin' yourself, ain't you?"

"Hard work never killed anybody."

"Neither did hard liquor, taken in moderation. But I've seen men that could get drunk on work and business, same as on whisky. You sure you ain't turned into one of those?"

Walter passed the question without an answer. He demanded, "What's that mark along your jaw?"

Hewey lied, "Got pawed by a bronc. Only grazed me, kind of."

"Don't you think you've come to an age where you ought to stop messin' with them bad horses? They'll kill you one of these days."

"Age? I ain't but thirty-six."

"Thirty-eight, and in some danger of never seein' thirty-nine. Don't try to hooraw me, Hewey. I got a memory for dates and figures."

Tommy watched them nervously, unsure if he should stay or quietly return to his plow. He couldn't tell whether his father and uncle were in jest or really quarreling.

Hewey wasn't sure either. There had always been a fine line between the two, and he had never been able to discern just when they crossed it. He looked at the worried boy. "Better slack up, Walter. Tommy'll think that brothers argue all their lives. That don't give him and Cotton much to look forward to."

Walter broke into a long grin that lifted ten years from his face. He said to Tommy, "We ain't arguin', son. You ought to remember; this is the way me and your Uncle Hewey always carried on. We don't mean nothin' by it."

Hewey wasn't sure about that, but he nodded agreement. "We never used to fight, your daddy and me. We never disagreed in our whole lives, did we, Walter?"

Walter glanced at Biscuit, then turned back to Hewey. "You said you're hungry. You ride on down to the house and get Eve to fix you somethin' to eat. Me and Tommy, we'll be in about dark."

The sun was still two hours high. "Dark?"

"We need to finish gettin' this field broken and planted. A spell of wet weather has throwed us late."

"Two hours won't make that much difference in a whole year's crop. You could quit early, just this once."

Walter appeared tempted. "Two hours wasted is two hours gone forever."

Two hours. Hewey could remember one time he and

Walter had camped for two *days* outside a coyote den hoping to get a shot at a calf-killing bitch as she came out.
When she finally did, they both missed her.

Walter repeated, "You go on in, Hewey. Eve'll be tickled
to see you."

Like a case of the measles, Hewey thought. He remembered that she had usually been far more tickled to see him
leave than to see him arrive. He said, "Where's Cotton?"

"Over on the French place puttin' a windmill together."

Hewey was incredulous. "You let that little boy climb a
windmill, all by himself? What if he falls?"

"That *little boy* is damn near grown. Anyway, he's puttin' it together on the ground. A few neighbors are comin'
over tomorrow to eat fried chicken with us and help us raise
the mill."

Hewey loosened some. "I been itchin' to see that boy.
How'll I find him?"

Walter's eyes narrowed. "It's a ways over there. Cotton'll
be home directly, and you can see him without tirin' your
horse out so bad."

Hewey shrugged. "Maybe I could be some help to him."

Walter shook his head knowingly. "You never used to be
afraid of anything, Hewey, but you're scared to go down to
the house and meet Eve all by yourself. She don't bite."

"She don't bite *you,* maybe."

"I never did understand what got wrong between you
two, but that's been a long time ago, and long forgotten
about." Walter kept looking at Hewey, knowing he wasn't
convinced. Finally he shrugged, giving up. "Hell, it's Saturday, and tomorrow's the Sabbath. The Lord won't condemn
us for sloth just this once. We've got company to celebrate.
Tommy, let's unhitch the teams."

He didn't have to say it twice. Tommy was already at his
plow before his father had taken three steps. Hewey went
to help Tommy. They left the plow where it stood in the
newly turned earth at the end of the row, ready for a fresh

start on another day. Tommy gathered up the lines and jumped easily onto the bare back of a gray mule.

Hewey smiled. "Mind if I ride the other one and lead Biscuit? He's kind of wrung out."

"Hop on."

Hewey grasped the mane and bent his knees, then sprang up, throwing his belly across the mule's broad back. That part wasn't so hard, but dragging his right leg up and over seemed to take about all the strength he had. Funny, didn't seem like it used to be so hard to mount bareback. He guessed it was just that he hadn't done it in a spell. It wasn't a thing that came up every day in his normal routine. He swung the mule around so he could gather up the bridle reins and lead Biscuit.

He watched Walter struggle to get onto one of the horses bareback. Maybe he was just tired. Plowing a half-wet field was hardly restful.

Hewey quickly discerned why Tommy had chosen the other mule. This one had a trot that would jar the innards out of a seventy-dollar pocket watch. Hewey pulled his hat down tight and made it a point not to look at his shadow.

Walter said, "You can ride this other horse if you'd rather."

Hewey had much rather, but he did not wish to back down in the sight of his nephew. "I'm doin' just fine. I ain't used to no rockin' chair." He wasn't used to a sledgehammer, either.

Three trees were beginning to reach up well beyond the roof of the plain frame house. Hewey found it hard to believe they had grown so much. He turned to Tommy and pointed. "Those can't be the chinaberries we set out that time, me and you two buttons?"

"It's them," Tommy said with pride. "Three of them just like we said when we did it . . . one for me and one for you and one for Cotton. You promised that when they got big enough we'd climb up to the tops of them, the three of us. They're big enough now."

"I said that?"

"You sure did. You made a promise and took the oath of a Cherokee chief."

The oath of a Cherokee chief? Hewey frowned, unable to remember. Some wild idea he had thought up on the spur of the moment, probably. He had always done that with the two boys, and with other boys he came across in his travels. If they wanted a story and he didn't have one to fit, he made one up as he went along, indulging in wild fancies that seemed to drift effortlessly to him out of the clouds, and as effortlessly return there, quickly forgotten.

He was going to have to quit that. The boys were older now and had good memories.

Tommy said, "I've climbed up in them. I want to see you clear at the top, Uncle Hewey."

Hewey shook his head. "I can't do that kind of thing anymore, button. Doctor's orders."

"Doctor's orders?"

"I ain't supposed to go up high anymore. Makes my blood get thin."

Tommy didn't accept that. "How come?"

Hewey never knew where the inspirations came from. All of a sudden the yarns would be spinning and he had no real idea what the source was, or even how they would end. "Well, it was when I was up in Colorado, up in the high country. There was a boy I met up yonder . . . same age as you, looked a whole lot like you, only his name was Timmy instead of Tommy, and he had built him a great big kite, big as a haystack. He wanted me to help him get it started. Well sir, a little breeze came up, and I taken out runnin' with it to get the kite started, and somehow I got my arm tangled up in the string, and one of them big winds come along the way they do sometimes in that country. It picked me up with the kite and sailed me way up high. Just like a bird, I was, with the prettiest view of that valley down there a thousand feet under me. I just went sailin', nice and free as you please, higher and higher up into them mountains, till I got all the way to the top. Then the breeze died down, and I floated to earth on the peak of the very highest mountain there was. I could look down in all four directions and see a hundred . . . no, two hundred miles.

"I can't describe it to you, button; I ain't got words big enough. It was the most beautiful sight ever I seen in my life, big tall pine trees and big blue lakes stretchin' off out yonder as far as an eagle could see. A little bit like it must look to God, I reckon, sittin' way up high. I sure did enjoy it. But I got to thinkin' about my little friend Bobby down there at the foot of the mountain, cryin' for his kite, maybe figurin' I had stolen it from him. So, there wasn't nothin' for me to do but start down, walkin' all the way. It was summertime, but it gets cold up in them mountains. The longer I walked the colder I got, and when I come down finally to the valley where it was warm, I was still cold. I gave Johnny his kite and then went to the doctor. He told me the chill had thinned my blood too much, and I had to get it thickened up again. You know how I done that? I done it eatin' syrup. Blackstrap molasses, the thicker the better. I reckon I must of eaten a barrel of it before my blood stiffened up to where I wasn't cold anymore. Doctor told me I couldn't afford ever to go to high places again. So that's why I can't climb trees. I reckon that's a pleasure I'll have to give up for the rest of my life."

Tommy rode along in silence, digesting all that. At length he asked, "Uncle Hewey, I don't reckon you saw God while you was way up on that mountain?"

Hewey shook his head. "No, I didn't."

Tommy nodded. "He'd of told you where He sends people who tell stories like that."

Riding in to Walter Calloway's little headquarters from its back side, Hewey couldn't see that much had changed. The barn was a box-and-strip building, not one foot larger than it had to be to house his saddles and harness, some sacked stock salt, scooped from the edge of the big Juan Cordona Lake, and the assortment of livestock medicines and liniments which gave off a smell that reached beyond the door and struck a man squarely in both nostrils before he touched the latch. On one side was a lean-to roof with a trough and a hayrack where the work stock could be fed dry during infrequent rainy weather. On the other side was another rude lean-to, walled only on the north, sheltering a forge and an anvil where Walter and the boys could do whatever blacksmithing was necessary. Most horses and mules in this country went unshod. The hoofs were simply kept trimmed so they wouldn't break or split and cause lameness.

Next to the barn stood a wooden windmill tower, topped by a twelve-foot Eclipse wheel turning in the warm afternoon breeze. Its sucker-rod clanked with a steady rhythm in the pipe. Its water flowed first into a big wooden barrel, the mouth of the pipe set high enough that a bucket could be placed under it to fill with clean drinking and cooking and washing water for the house. From the barrel the water passed through a short pipe into another frame building even smaller than the barn. Hewey looked at his brother.

"There's somethin' new. You built Eve a milk-house?"

Walter proudly held the door open for Hewey. Hewey saw that the water from the pipe flowed into a slanted open concrete trough into which Eve had set several cloth-covered milk and cream jars to keep their contents from souring too soon. The water fresh from the ground was always cool.

Walter said, "We built the trough with just enough slope to keep the fresh water runnin' through and out the far end."

Hewey saw scratched into the cement before it had hardened "Cotton—Tommy '05."

Walter said, "It was Cotton laid it all out." The water gurgled as it eddied into another pipe which led to a big open-surface tank. There it was available to the livestock after the people had finished with it. There was no water in the family house except that which somebody carried in a bucket. The windmill supplied all the water for man and beast. Without it, or another of its kind, life could not long be sustained here. Nature had not provided it at the surface, free for the taking; it had to be worked for. That was the reason this part of Texas had been slow in settling up, the last to be claimed other than by the free-sprawling cattlemen such as C. C. Tarpley. The real enemy here had not been Indians or the thin scattering of outlaws; it had been the lack of water. The windmill had done more for settlement than all the cavalry and all the sheriffs since the Civil War.

Hewey looked up at the family's meat supply, beef wrapped in a protective tarp to keep the flies off. It was hanging from a steel hook attached to the end of a lever. Walter reached over to a peg and untied a short length of rope. Running up through a pulley, it freed the lever so that the quarter of beef was lowered by its own weight to about shoulder level. Walter pulled on the rope. The lever moved up, raising the meat back almost to the ceiling.

"Cotton's idea too," Walter said. "He designed it to make more workin' room and still keep things easy for his mother."

Moving out, Hewey stepped to the side of the barn and ran a thumbnail along a plank, testing the peeling paint. He had helped Walter put this barn up; he hated to see it looking this way. "Needs paintin'."

"First things first. We've had other things more in need."

"I'll paint it for you if you'll fetch some red paint first time you go to town." Red paint was the cheapest; its color was dark enough that even a cheap grade would cover.

"Paint don't come cheap. Barn won't fall down if it goes another year without new paint. Eve's gone *two* years without a new dress."

Hewey frowned and said nothing. The whole barn wouldn't take but a dollar's worth, maybe two. Many a time he had put a dollar's worth of whisky down his throat between two breaths and never begrudged the money. A dollar had never meant much to him, beyond whatever pleasure it might bring to him or to somebody whose company he enjoyed. Want of money was a thing he never experienced and never understood. He had been broke often, but he had never been poor.

He had never had a wife to support, of course, or two sons, or a homestead to prove up. He guessed to Walter a dollar bill must look as big as a saddle blanket, and as scarce as July rain.

Walter had added no new corrals that Hewey could see; four sections of land wouldn't carry a great many cattle, not in this part of the country. Hewey had helped him build all the pens he needed several years ago. They had used mesquite timber, stacked horizontally between pairs of heavy posts, making a fence tight enough that a kid goat couldn't crawl through. They had cut rawhide strips to tie the pairs of posts at the top instead of buying wire. They hadn't used five dollars worth of bought materials.

They hadn't had five dollars to spend.

Tommy dipped a tin bucket into an oat bin. The oats, cut last May or June and almost a year old now, had a dry and dusty smell as he spread them along the bottom of a wooden trough. The two work horses and the mules went straight to the feed. Biscuit had stood apart from the other stock, a little superior in attitude, his custom among strangers. But when he heard their teeth grinding the oats, he turned democrat and joined them at the trough.

Hewey said, "I wouldn't want to spoil him. He don't get this style of treatment everywhere."

Walter said, "He won't get enough of it here to do him any harm. You wouldn't believe, Hewey, what a bushel of oats is worth these days."

Tommy said, "We gather up most of these down at the freighters' campground, what they spill when they feed their stock."

A freight-wagon road ran nearby, a couple of hundred yards below the house. For years freighters had made a custom of camping in a grove of wild chinaberry trees and had led their horse and mule teams up to the corrals to water them from Walter's tank. It was a point of pride with Walter not to charge them for it because the Lord had provided the water. The Lord had not provided the windmill, however, except in an indirect manner. The freighters recognized this fact and usually made it a point to waste some feed that the boys could gather up in a sack.

From somewhere appeared a droop-eared burro, its brown hair still ragged with unshed winter growth. It pushed in beside Biscuit and shoved its nose into the oats. Biscuit, nettled by the uninvited familiarity, bared his teeth and took a nip at the burro's flank. The burro wheeled, showed his backside and kicked Biscuit squarely in the stomach. His point made, he went back to the oats. Biscuit stood to one side, surprised and shamed. Finally he turned back to the trough but kept one of the work stock between him and the burro.

Hewey grimaced, sharing Biscuit's shame at the hands of an inferior. "He ain't met many burros. He's got a right smart to learn."

Tommy said, "He'll learn it if he stays around this one. The burro's Cotton's. Alvin Lawdermilk gave it to him for helpin' him work some bronc mules." Many ranchers used burros to teach young broncs to lead and obey the rope. They would simply tie the burro and the bronc together. The stubborn burro would go where he wanted to and make the bronc come along whether it suited him or not. Size and weight counted for little. The burro almost always won.

"Every boy ought to have him a dog and a burro," Hewey said. "What do you call him?"

Tommy glanced quickly at his father, then back at the animal. "Mostly just 'Burro,' or 'Hey, you!' He don't answer to a name. He just answers to feed."

Hewey watched the horses and mules and the burro eat, a thing that had always given him pleasure. He had heard few sounds in his life that he liked better than a strong set of teeth grinding at a bait of oats, unless it was a good rain beating upon a tin roof in a dry country that needed it. He noticed finally that Walter was waiting for him, holding the gate open. Hewey walked out so Walter could shut the gate behind him. Walter said, "Tommy, you can milk the cow before supper."

"It's Cotton's turn."

"Cotton's still out workin'. I let you quit early."

The argument was over; neither Walter nor Eve stood for it from the boys.

They all started walking toward the house. Hewey's skin began to prickle. He never knew what kind of reception Eve would have for him on any given day. He remembered a couple he wouldn't wish on Fat Gervin. "You better go on ahead and tell her I'm here, Walter."

"She'll know it when she sees you. Come on." Walter scraped his boots on the edge of the step at the kitchen door, in case he had set foot into something he hadn't noticed. Eve would notice it; that was certain. Tommy grinned in anticipation of his mother's happy reaction. Hewey wiped his feet with even more care than Walter had taken and rubbed the toes of his dusty boots on the backs of his legs, not removing any dust but moving it around. He wished he had taken longer in Tarpley's water tank.

He heard Eve's voice, tinged with concern. "You're home early. Somethin' wrong?"

"Nothin' wrong," Walter replied. "Everything's right."

"It's still daylight. I haven't got supper fixed yet. I didn't figure on you-all till good dark." Hewey imagined he could detect reproach, but he knew he was probably giving her the worst of it.

"We had good reason to quit. Come on in here, Hewey." Hewey took a slow, deep breath and pulled the kitchen screen open. He stopped just inside, letting it bump against his backside as the spring pulled it shut. He held his hat in both hands and was ready to hit the screen running if need be. Shifting his weight from one foot to the other, he finally managed, "Howdy, Eve." Nothing else came out.

Eve Calloway was well into her thirties, no longer really young but not yet reconciled to pass over that one-way threshold into middle age. She was at a time in her life when with the right clothes and activated by the right mood she could still seem girl-like, years younger than her actual age. Or, if tired and irritable and taking no care for her appearance, she could look years older than she was. Hewey had seen her both ways so many times he never knew which to expect. At this moment, she seemed more inclined toward the latter.

She stared at him with wide eyes. Other than surprise, he could see no readily identifiable emotion in her face. He kept his back against the screen. Waiting vainly for a reaction, he finally blurted, "I ain't stayin' long, Eve."

Walter watched his wife, waiting for her to give his brother a joyous welcome. When she didn't, he became as nervous as Hewey. He walked to the woodbox and glanced perfunctorily inside. "Low on wood. I better chop some more before supper."

Hewey quickly volunteered, but Walter cut him off. "You stay here and visit with Eve. She's anxious to know where-all you've been." He pushed past Hewey and went out the screen door, pausing to lift a milk bucket from its rack beside the steps. Outside, he was telling Tommy to get on with the milking.

Alone, Hewey and Eve stared at each other across the width of the little kitchen, neither moving.

"Well, Hewey . . ." she said at length, and let it drop there.

"Well, Eve . . ." he replied, and didn't pick it up.

When the tension between them became too heavy for her, she turned to the Majestic iron cookstove, removed the round front lid from its place, did momentary violence to the red coals with an iron poker, then shoved in a couple of chunks of dry mesquite from the woodbox. Hewey suspected it was not a thing she especially needed to do; it was something to busy her hands. Not looking at him, she said, "You'd just as well sit down and stop blockin' the door. And you'd better pitch that hat into a corner before you twist the brim plumb off of it."

Hewey dropped his hat on the floor, took one step sideways and hunkered down campfire style, his back against the flower-papered wall. The paper helped keep the wind out; the box-and-strip siding—one-by-twelve planks and one-by-four strips nailed over the joints—did not seal.

Eve tentatively touched her fingers against the coffeepot, testing its warmth. She pulled the hand quickly away. Hewey remembered it was her habit to keep the coffee drinkably warm all day. Like most farm and ranch wives of her place and time, she had rather have faced the devil in her nightgown than to be caught smoking a cigarette or drinking whisky. But she drank more coffee than Walter did. She fetched a flat-bottomed gray enamel cup from a plain open-fronted cabinet nailed to the wall. She turned with the coffeepot in her hand. She stopped at the sight of Hewey sitting on his spurs. "You're just like every cowboy I ever saw in my life," she scolded. "If I had a dozen rockin' chairs in the room, they'd still squat on the floor. You get up here and sit at the table and try to act like company! This is a house, not a cow camp!"

Hewey was quick to do what she told him. She spilled a little of the coffee in her nervousness. Instinctively Hewey rubbed his hand through it to wipe it up, then didn't know what to do with the wet hand. He dried it on his trousers, under the table and out of sight.

Eve poured herself some coffee but didn't sit at the table with him. She stared at him from her position in front of the stove. The mesquite wood was starting to crackle a little, though Hewey imagined the sound might be coming from Eve herself.

"Look, Eve," he said finally, "I got a little homesick. The boys got to weighin' on my mind. I just felt like I had to see them. A day or two, that's all, and I'll be gone."

Her blue eyes reminded him of a diamond, cutting glass. "You're lookin' thin, Hewey. Haven't you eaten regular?"

"I'm all right. I been batchin' all winter."

"Batchin'? No wonder. There's not many men can cook fit to feed a hound dog, and you're sure not one of the few. It'll take me a month to put some flesh on you."

"I don't figure to stay that long."

Her eyes lost their cutting edge. Though he knew it was unlikely, he thought he saw the beginning of a smile start pulling at the corners of her mouth. If so, she quickly got the situation under control. "You're here, Hewey, so you'll stay." It sounded like an order.

Hewey didn't know what to say, so he kept his mouth shut.

She demanded, "Where in the world did you go, Hewey? Leavin' like that, in the middle of the night? We just got up in the mornin' and found you gone. The boys cried, both of them. Walter didn't know what to think."

"You know why I left."

"You've made me live with a bad conscience. I knew you left because of what I said to you, and I couldn't tell them."

"What you told me was true, every bit of it. I didn't have no part in what you and Walter was tryin' to do here. Only thing for me to do was to leave and not come back." He looked down at his coffee cup, lifted it partway, then set it on the table again. "I stayed away as long as I could."

She took a couple of steps toward him. "Hewey Calloway, look at me!" He did. He had been watching her ever since he had come into the house. She said, "You helped us get this place. You helped us build this house and a lot of what else is here. You've got a right to stay as long as you want to."

He blinked. "That's not how you sounded when I left here."

"I was mad."

"I ain't changed any. You'll be mad again if I stay long."

She took another step. "I know. You can be an exasperatin' man, Hewey. I'll bet there's not three things in this whole world that we agree on, you and me. But the next time I get mad, you just go off out of my sight awhile and give me a little time. You don't have to stay gone for two years."

He sipped the coffee and found it bitter; it had been heating too long. But it was coffee, and that was the staff of life around most cow camps he had ever stayed in. He looked up at her. "I'll try not to make you mad atall. I'll try to keep my mouth shut."

She shook her head, a smile breaking across her face. "I wouldn't ask that much of Nature. I would as soon ask the snow to come in July and the sun to rise in the west." She leaned across the table and reached toward him. He flinched, not knowing what to expect. She took hold of his chin and turned his head a little, looking at the wound on his jaw.

"Just got it from a bronc," he lied before she could ask him. "It's a long ways from the heart."

"One of those broncs will kill you someday. It's time you settled down to somethin' steady and admitted your age."

That was what had started the quarrel the last time, and most of the others he could remember. Eve was always lecturing him about settling down, about responsibility, respectability, always trying to change him. The way Hewey saw it, the Lord had purposely made every person different. He could not understand why so many people were determined to thwart the Lord's work by making everyone the same.

He said, "I've never let a bronc kill me yet."

"*Yet.*" She repeated the word firmly for emphasis. "Let me see your hand . . . your right hand."

He extended it uncertainly. She took it, turned it over and

looked at the palm, then gave his wrist a vigorous shake. "Well, it's not broken after all."

"What made you think it was?"

"You never did write a letter. For all anybody knew you could've been dead and buried somewhere."

At last Hewey began to relax, and he felt the birth pangs of a grin. "If I ever die, you'll know it right away. The Lord'll lift a heavy weight off of your soul, and you'll know I've flown."

"*Fell* is more like it. You hungry?" She answered her own question. "Of course you're hungry. You're always hungry. Well, you'll have to put up with stew tonight. Tomorrow's Sunday. Maybe I can fill you up on chicken."

"I'll be obliged for anything. You know me . . . there ain't much I won't eat."

"That," she said, "is gospel fact."

She started to turn away from him but stopped, looked intently at him, then leaned across the table and kissed him on the cheek. "Welcome home, Hewey."

His jaw sagged. If he lived to be a hundred and six, he would never figure out his sister-in-law. She could change quicker than the wind.

Occasionally on a cold winter night when he was being honest with himself, Hewey knew that if he had been the marrying sort, and if Walter hadn't seen Eve first, he might have married her. She had been pretty then, and sweeter than a fresh-stirred batch of wild-plum jelly. She still was, now and again, when she wasn't being overly protective of home and brood. At such times, if he didn't watch himself, his old feelings about her would rise up to confuse and discomfit him.

Fortunately he always got over them the first time her eyes snapped.

Eve opened one of the big warming ovens which extended forward over the cooking surface of the iron stove, taking their heat from the chimney that ran up through them.

Inside, stacked on a tin plate, was leftover cornbread. "I can fix you some cornbread and sweetmilk right now if you'd like."

He shook his head. "I'll wait and eat with the rest of you. Wouldn't want to cheat Walter and the boys. They been workin'." He began to feel more at ease. He listened to the ax chopping wood and was glad Walter hadn't let him take that quick and easy way out.

A fat old gray tomcat wandered into the kitchen from one of the tiny bedrooms, pausing to stretch himself in the doorway, then studied Hewey with a look that came near being disdain. He ambled over and examined Hewey's hat lying on the floor, smelled around Hewey's boots, found nothing of particular interest and wandered back toward the open doorway again, pausing for one long backward look which confirmed his earlier low appraisal.

"I see you've still got the same independent cat," Hewey observed.

"Nothin' changes around here. We just get a little older, is all."

Hewey looked around the little kitchen, trying to find signs of anything new since he had left here. Everything seemed the same. Any improvements the family had made had been out on the place, not in the house they lived in. The table and chairs were plain and had already been old when Walter had bought them. The black iron stove had come out of a ranch's cow camp after the state had terminated the lease and put the land up for homesteading. The pots and pans, the utensils, the cheap porcelain dishes were remnants of a well-used set Eve had brought with her into the marriage. So far as Hewey could see, the only thing new was Eve's patent-medicine calendar advertising a remedy for woman's complaint. He wondered about that; he had never seen a medicine that stopped a woman from complaining. He noted one date—he had lost track and didn't know how long ago it was—pencil-marked with a small feminine X. He wondered idly what that was for.

Eve hadn't gained a pound of weight. She worked too hard to get fat, he had always thought, ignoring the fact that he had seen other country women who worked just as hard and got to weigh two hundred pounds by middle age. She wore a plain cotton dress she had made for herself from a large bolt of blue and white tiny-checkered cloth. She had bartered for the cloth years ago, trading some eggs and old boiling hens. She had been sewing dresses off of this same bolt for six or seven years to Hewey's certain knowledge. They always looked alike, differing only in age and extent of wear.

Wind and sun had been unkind to Eve's complexion, though she wore a big slat bonnet to protect her face when she went outdoors. That faded bonnet, ribbed with long thin strips of cardboard and made from the same cloth as the dress, was hanging from a nail near the door. Despite the sun's work on her skin, Eve's features were still small and fine as they had been the day she and Walter had married.

He said, "That Tommy has growed like a weed. I thought he was Cotton when I first seen him. He looks finer than a Morgan colt."

"He's a good boy," Eve replied, stoking the burning wood and putting in another chunk of mesquite. "I don't say that just because he's mine."

Hewey looked out the window, hoping. "I can't hardly wait for Cotton to get here. How's *he* been?"

Eve didn't answer for a minute. "Fine. Just fine." When she turned he saw that her lips had tightened.

Uneasy, he demanded, "Somethin' the matter with Cotton?"

"Nothin'," she said, suddenly defensive. "He's fine." Hewey stared at her, unsatisfied, until she shrugged and sat down across the table from him, her shoulders pinched. "I don't know. There's probably nothin' wrong with Cotton; it's probably somethin' wrong with *me*. I just don't understand him anymore."

She picked up her coffee cup, but she set it down again, the coffee untouched. It was probably cold anyway. "I thought all we had to do was to raise the boys in a good Christian home and they'd turn out just like us. But Cotton has gotten away from us somehow. He's different."

Hewey frowned. "You tryin' to say he's like *me*?"

Eve stared back at him. "He does have some of your ways. He's restless and all . . . enough to scare me, rememberin' *you*. But he's got other ways that are his own. He's not the same as us and not the same as you either. He's *Cotton*."

"He been in trouble?"

"No, nothin' like that. He works hard, never troubles anybody but us, and he doesn't intend to do even that. He did run off once for a couple of days . . . talked the freighter Blue Hannigan into givin' him a ride to Midland . . . told him he was on an errand for us. He came back on his own. Never explained much . . . just said he wanted to go and see one of those automobiles he had read about. Said he didn't ask us because he figured we'd say *no*."

"Would you have?"

"Certainly. A boy has got no business runnin' off to a big city like Midland by himself. Must be two . . . maybe three thousand people livin' over there. No tellin' what kind of sinful goin's-on a boy might see."

Hewey agreed. "Sure is a big town, all right."

"He said you told him once you'd seen an automobile in Midland."

"I did?" Hewey frowned again, looking for criticism but unable to read the thought behind her eyes.

She said, "I blamed you at first, fillin' the boys' heads with a bunch of foolishness. That was easier than to blame myself. I likely bore down on him too hard, too many times. It's a thing I do too easy, and then I don't know how to back away." She looked intently at Hewey. "Maybe it's good you came when you did. You always had a special touch with the boys. You could always reach them in a way that I couldn't, or their daddy couldn't."

"I'll talk to him."

"It'd be better if you got *him* to talk to *you*. Cotton doesn't open up to us much anymore."

The wood-chopping stopped. Walter came to the door, carrying an armload of dried mesquite cut to stove-burning length. He glanced in before opening the screen, then stopped again for a moment just inside before proceeding to the woodbox and dropping the wood carefully so that it lay lengthwise, not in a scrambled manner. He turned and studied his wife and Hewey with a little apprehension. When he saw no quarrel between them he began to smile.

"See there, Hewey? I told you she wouldn't bite."

Eve built up the fire. She pulled a pot of stew and another of beans out onto the stove's flat top to warm for supper. The heat of the kitchen became oppressive. Hewey pushed the screen door open, walked down the steps and paused to stretch the kinks out of his arms and legs. He rolled and lighted a cigarette, his first since he had gotten here. Looking to the barn, and beyond, he saw that Tommy had turned the milk cow back into the pasture for the night. This late, she wouldn't stray far before bedding down. She would be at the gate long before milking time in the morning, bawling plaintively for her recently born calf, kept separated from her in a small pen so it wouldn't take all the milk. The work stock had also edged away into the pasture and were cropping the green spring grass they had missed all day in the field. Biscuit followed them but remained to one side, a little aloof, especially from the burro.

Hewey heard the rattle of trace chains and looked to the northwest. In the dusk he made out the shape of a wagon. The black dog heard too. He came out from under the house, gave Hewey another tentative check, for he hadn't accepted him as belonging, then went trotting to meet the wagon, his tail busy. A country dog of any intelligence knew the sound of his own people's wagons and could usually tell when a strange one was coming. The same was true for his people's horses, the ones they rode most often. A dog was usually either wagging its tail or barking while humans still strained their eyes, trying to see who was coming.

It was too small for a freight wagon, so this had to be Cotton; he was the only one still out. Hewey strolled slowly to the barn, timing his pace to get there when the wagon did. He found it difficult to believe that tall boy on the wagon seat was his nephew. Lord, what a difference two years could make! Hewey exclaimed, "I'll be damned!" Talking to oneself was a habit many a cowboy developed when he was alone a lot. The sound of a human voice was a reassurance of sorts, even one's own.

Cotton didn't see him at first; he was busy maneuvering the wagon under a brush arbor where it was kept for some protection from the elements. Hewey glanced up at the darkening but cloudless sky and saw no reason to expect any trouble from the elements tonight. Shedding the wagon was a good habit to instill in a boy, though; it taught him responsibility. If he shirked the chore when he saw no need in it, he might find it easy to shirk when the need arose.

The boy handled the two mules with firm hands, backing them carefully to put the wagon into place. They were young mules—green broncs, really—and required a lot of patience. Cotton talked to them, alternating between soft approval and sharp words of scorn that Hewey hadn't heard him use before. Twice the wagon hubbed a post, and Cotton had to move the mules forward, then back again. They worked with much twitching of long ears, much chomping at the bits. Hewey guessed they belonged to Alvin Lawdermilk, and that Cotton was training them for pay or trade. He watched with satisfaction as the wagon at last rolled into its proper place. Cotton had always had a special aptitude at anything done with the hands, whether the tool be a wrench or a pair of leather reins. From the time he had been seven or eight, he could take a little lumber, a bucket of nails, a saw and hammer and build anything he set his mind to.

Hewey would not have admitted it to the Lord Jesus, should He come and ask, but Cotton had always been his favorite of the two boys by just a thin edge. Perhaps that was natural, Cotton being the first-born, the lone recipient of a bachelor uncle's adoration and hopes for two full years before Tommy showed up. By virtue of his extra age, Cotton had been the first to try almost everything—the first to ride a horse, the first to pick up a rope, the first to fall off of the barn. By the time Tommy came along to do the same things, the new was gone.

The boys had no grandparents to spoil them, so Uncle Hewey had served that function. Riding in at intervals, doing his mischief, telling them stories that would never have stood the scrutiny of a court, playing hell with family discipline, he would then ride cheerfully away to greener pastures without having to assume any responsibility for the chaos he had wrought. He had all the privileges of a grandparent but was saddled with only half the age.

Hewey spoke as the boy hopped down. "Howdy, Cotton."

He expected Cotton to come running with open arms, as Tommy had done, and he braced himself for the jolt. He saw the surprise, the quick flash of an unguarded smile. But suddenly, unaccountably, the smile was gone. Cotton stood by the front wheel, holding the lines uncertainly. His face was sober and reserved.

"I see you finally got home."

Hewey had always found it easy to talk to the boys. It had always seemed to him that their thoughts and his ran along the same trail, possibly because they hadn't had time to grow up and he hadn't had the inclination. He stared non-plused at his nephew and could not bring up an intelligent word to say. "I'm home," he replied, like an echo. He waited in vain for Cotton to come to him.

Always before, Cotton had come running, joyously, unrestrained, with laughter and shouting and love. Now it was Hewey, finally, who went to Cotton. He was unexpectedly nervous, as ill at ease as he had been with Eve. He wanted to put his arms around Cotton and hug him as in other times. He held back, watching for some sign in the boy's eyes.

All he got was that stare, not hostile but not warm. Hewey awkwardly thrust out his hand, as he might do in meeting a stranger. "It's good to see you, button."

Cotton took his hand. His grip was strong, and hard, but it was also polite and somehow formal.

"I'd better unharness the mules, Uncle Hewey."

Hewey watched him in uncertain silence, wishing to help but not sure his help was wanted. He leaned his back against the wagon wheel. For a moment or two he felt cold, like in that lonesome shack high up in the snows of the Sangre de Cristos.

Walter came to the barn as Cotton was pouring out oats for the mules. "Daddy," Cotton said, "I didn't finish. Those mules kept runnin' away. I thought sure they'd wreck the old wagon."

Walter frowned. "I'd hoped . . . well, we can't help it now. We'll need everything to be ready for them folks when they come tomorrow afternoon. Your mother won't like it, but I reckon you'd best stay home from church and finish the job in the mornin'. You ain't so sinful that missin' church one Sunday will condemn you to the fires."

Hewey spoke up. "I'll stay and help Cotton. I don't think the Lord will miss me."

A smile tugged at Walter's mouth. "Miss you? If you showed up in church the Lord would probably wonder who in hell you are."

Cotton said, "I can handle it myself. I'd be through already, only those mules . . ."

Walter replied, "I know you could do the job alone. But let Uncle Hewey help you; it won't take you much longer. It'll give you-all a chance to visit."

Hewey nodded eagerly. "We got a lot to talk about."

Cotton said nothing, but his eyes indicated that he doubted it.

A month earlier it would have been too cold to sit in the front yard and talk in the full moon's light. But the slight nip of the May night was invigorating after the heat of the afternoon. They had carried chairs out from the kitchen and set them on the ground because there was no porch. A porch was often a luxury, added to a utilitarian frame house in this part of the country only when the family reached a modicum of financial security and the wolf no longer howled by the door. The breeze was light, barely enough to rustle the new leaves of the big chinaberry trees under which Hewey rocked the straight-legged chair, flirting with a backward fall.

Walter asked Hewey about various people they had known in years past, people he hoped Hewey might have seen. Hewey told him of those he had encountered, repeating and embellishing a little on any wild gossip he had heard. Tommy asked question after question about the towns Hewey had visited, the wild cattle he had chased, the wild horses he had ridden. Hewey's answers were patterned to fit what he thought Tommy wanted to hear. The cows ran faster and the horses pitched harder than had ever been known by most mortal men.

Eve asked him about the clothes the women were wearing in the towns, and Hewey was stumped. "They was wearin' dresses," he acknowledged. "If they hadn't been, I reckon I'd of noticed."

"But what kind of dresses? What did they look like?"

"Well, they was of all colors, and long enough to cover. That's about all I can tell you."

"What about the hats?"

"Well, all the hats I seen were on top of their heads. Had feathers, some of them. Bird feathers."

Every so often Hewey glanced at the yellow glow of lamplight in the kitchen window. Cotton sat in there by himself, reading a book at the table. Hewey kept thinking he would eventually come out in curiosity to hear the stories, but he didn't.

Walter said, "I didn't think to tell you, Hewey, but old Snort Yarnell came by last summer, hopin' to find you here."

Hewey sat the chair down abruptly, smiling as a hundred pleasant memories came flooding over him. "Old Snort! I wisht I'd seen him. How'd he look?"

"Same as ever. He gets a little older along, and that's the only change."

"Still wilder'n a peach-orchard boar, I expect. He sure is a good old boy."

Eve put in sharply, "Good for *nothin'* old boy. A tramp, a chuckline rider. I'll bet in his whole life he never did three honest days' work hand-runnin'."

"But he knows how to enjoy life. That's more than most people do. Old Grady Welch used to run with him a lot. Was Grady with him?"

Walter looked at the ground. "I don't reckon you've heard. Grady Welch is dead. Horse throwed him off and stepped on him."

The moment of happy memories passed. Sadness pressed down on Hewey. "You sure about that, Walter?"

Walter nodded. "Snort was with him when it happened, out in the Davis Mountains. He helped bury him."

Hewey shook his head. "Damn, but I hate to hear it."

Eve said, "It gets them all if they stay out there and court it long enough. That's why I wish you'd find a place and settle down, Hewey."

Hewey didn't answer. At length he asked, "Eve, you still got some coffee on the stove?"

"Yes, I'll go get you a cup."

"No, you stay where you're at. I'll fetch it."

He walked into the kitchen and stopped to look at Cotton, sitting at the plain pine table, the lamplight falling on an open book. Cotton nodded but said nothing. Hewey ventured, "I've done a right smart of readin' myself. You get lots of time for it in a batchin' camp. Have you read *Ivanhoe* yet?"

Cotton shook his head.

Hewey said, "It's got lots of good fightin' and killin' in it. You'd enjoy it."

He received no response. He stepped closer, trying to read over Cotton's shoulder. "What's that you're so interested in?"

"The theory of internal combustion."

Hewey blinked. "What you goin' to bust?"

"Internal combustion is what makes automobiles run."

Hewey blinked again. "Do you understand that stuff?"

Cotton didn't look up from the book. "No, but I'd like to."

Hewey poured an enameled cup full of coffee. He stalled a little, hoping Cotton would volunteer to say something. But Cotton kept reading. Hewey went back outside and sat down in his chair again, rocking it faster than before.

Walter said, "I been thinkin' about old Homer Ganss, up in the Territory, and some of the wild stunts he used to pull. He was a lot like Snort and Grady . . . and you. I don't reckon you came across him by some accident?"

Hewey slowed the chair and warmed to the conversation. "Not by accident. I made it a point to go and stay with him a couple of weeks last year. Salty as he ever was; ain't changed a particle, only his hair is thinner, and he's short a couple of front teeth, and he's got a stiff leg where a horse rolled on him. Gettin' a shade fat, too. Ain't changed a bit. You'd know him a mile off." Hewey launched into a story, only modestly exaggerated, about their riding into a Territory town with a string of Homer's green-broken ponies to trade to the Indians. They had gotten into a horse-race bet and lost all the ponies but had such an up-roarious celebration with the Indians that it had seemed cheap at the price.

Eve was incredulous. She had heard plenty of Hewey's stories, but this one was outrageous enough to be true. "You're tellin' us that he threw away a whole year's work, just like that, on one horse race?"

"He didn't throw it away, he *bet* it. He'll have another string of ponies to sell this year. And you ought to've seen that horse race!" He began to describe it in all its thrills and spills, adding two or three to bring them up to even measure.

Walter laughed and slapped his knee. "I swear, Hewey, that sounds just like you and old Homer. I wisht I could've been there."

"I wisht you had been too. I tell you, Walter, you're goin' to have to take yourself a vacation off of this place and go on a trip with me one of these days. It'll do you a world of good."

"I know it would, and I'm just liable to do it."

Eve cut a sharp glance at her husband, then back at Hewey. "Walter," she said firmly, "we've got a long day ahead of us. I think it's high time we all went to bed."

3

Cotton hadn't said three words since he and Hewey had hitched the half-broken mules in the first light of a cool dawn and had set out over the hill for the recently acquired French place. In the bed of the wagon rattled the carpentry and digging tools Cotton had judged he would need to complete restoration of the windmill and have everything ready for the raising. Also carried were heavy wrenches and grips, well ropes, block and tackle.

Windmilling was not a horseman's type of work.

Daylight and the fresh dampness of the May morning had brought the cattle out to graze. They were gentle, a far cry from the twistified cattle Hewey was used to. They paid only momentary attention to the creaking wagon. A calf approached in curiosity, then turned tail and ran back to its mother as a wheel dropped into a hole and made everything in the wagon bed clatter in protest.

Hewey tried to bait Cotton into conversation but had only sporadic and short-lived success. He pointed to a mottley faced cow whose horns were beginning to show rough circles at their base, an indication she was moving past what might charitably be termed middle age. "I remember that old sister. She was in the bunch I brought out for your daddy from over on the Concho."

Cotton only nodded. Hewey went on, "I remember she had a good heifer calf, kind of a roan with a white face. She still in the herd?"

Cotton made the longest speech Hewey had drawn out of him all morning. "We've still got her."

"She raise a calf every year?"

Cotton nodded.

Hewey could see he was losing ground. Cotton kept his gaze on the dim trail of wheel-crushed dry grass from last year; the new green grass was attempting to heal it over. Hewey gave up awhile and studied the open, rolling country. It wasn't the best grassland he had ever seen, by a long way, but he knew it was deceptive. Here just to the east of the Pecos River the land seemed to suffer for rain more often than not, and grass tended to be of the short varieties, not the tall, thick growth that dominated farther east in Texas or up in the Indian Nations, especially the Osage. But this was strong grass. In a hard year a cow might walk herself half to death trying to find enough to fill her belly, but what she found was well supplied with minerals and nutrients. If she never got fat, at least she stayed hardy. Back east he had seen cows starve with tall weak grass tickling their bellies.

Farming, now, was a different game of poker. They ought not to allow a plow within a hundred miles of here, he thought, unless it was passing through on a freight train with the doors sealed. He had heard it said that when a man traveled west in Texas he lost an inch of average annual rainfall for every fifty miles. If this figure was correct, he could be in the red by the time he made El Paso. It seemed to Hewey that God had already put this country to its proper use without anybody's help. Grass was what it raised best, and it ought to be left that way. But this was not a popular time to be expressing such a sentiment. In fashionable circles it was considered nonprogressive, the outmoded defense of the old-line free-range cattlemen like C. C. Tarpley who didn't want to give up private possession of land that rightfully belonged to all the citizens of Texas. Anyone who spoke such a sentiment was allying himself with the forces of monopoly and greed, the reformers shouted. He was setting himself against progress and the uplifting of the common man. He was to be shunned by all good Christian soldiers dedicated to God's work.

Hewey had already seen many of God's good common men starve off of the plow and desert the land they had broken out in His name. The dried fields would scour and blow away in the hot west wind, leaving a sore that wouldn't heal in a hundred years.

"You oughtn't to ever plow it," he said, unintentionally putting his thoughts into words.

Cotton was caught off balance, his thoughts elsewhere. "Hunh?"

"The homestead law . . . I say it's wrong to make a man plow out a field to hold his claim. He ought not to rip up land that God has already planted to grass and handed to him as a gift."

Cotton's shell seemed to crack a little. "You better not say that where Mama can hear it."

Hewey nodded. "There's a lot she don't agree with me about."

"She says leavin' good land in grass is slothful, that the Lord wants us to cultivate it and make it blossom like the rose."

Hewey grunted. "Lots of people talk about what the Lord wants. Wonder how many has ever asked Him?"

"You could've asked Him yourself if you'd gone to church with the rest of them this mornin'."

"I don't have to go to church to hunt for Him. I see Him around me every day, everywhere I look."

Cotton studied his uncle with a growing interest. "That sounds like pantheism, like the preacher is always warnin' us about."

"Is that somethin' like the Catholics?"

"Must be pretty bad, because the preacher is sure down on it."

"Only religion I ever had was the same as yours. I was ducked for a Baptist. But the water didn't soak very deep. I taken up my old and willful ways again pretty soon."

"Some churchgoin' might be good for you, then."

"I always liked God better when I found Him outdoors. He always seemed too big to fit into a little-bitty cramped-up church house."

Cotton fell silent again. Hewey changed the subject, talking about things he understood far better than religion, but he seemed unable to draw Cotton far out of that protective shell. He tried to make it appear he was watching the country, while his eyes kept cutting back to Cotton. At length he said, "We used to understand each other pretty good."

"I've got a little older, Uncle Hewey."

"So have I."

"On you it don't ever seem to make any difference."

Hewey felt a cutting edge in Cotton's voice, a reproach he could not understand. "Button, if I've said somethin' that hurt you . . ."

The boy shrugged and turned his attention back to the bronc mules. "It's been a long time. You probably forgot what you said as soon as you were done sayin' it. There's no use pokin' over dead ashes."

Hewey rubbed his left hand over a knocked-down knuckle on his right hand, relic of a bad day of bronc stomping that had netted him no more than a dollar at best. "Button, I never said a cross word to you in all your life. I've never raised my voice at you."

"And never lied to me?"

Hewey kept rubbing the hand. It didn't pain him, but somehow he wished it did, as if pain might in some way compensate for whatever hurt he had caused his nephew. "I've never lied to you. Well, never anything serious. Oh, I might've stretched the truth a time or two, tellin' you stories, but never anything to hurt you or lead you wrong. I've never meant you anything but good."

"You made me a promise once, but I expect you turned right around and forgot it. You sure as hell never kept it."

It jarred Hewey a little, hearing Cotton use a word like *hell*. Sure, Hewey used it himself, but he was thirty-eight years old. Times were changing, it looked like. "I reckon I'm guilty, since you say so. But I sure don't remember any promise I never kept."

"You knew how bad I wanted to see a real automobile. You promised me you was goin' to take me someplace where they had them, and you was even goin' to fix it up to get me a ride in one. Then one mornin' I woke up and you had left."

Hewey didn't remember. "Any time I ever made you a promise, button, I intended to keep it. But sometimes things come up . . ."

"Things *always* come up with you."

He didn't see any gain in telling Cotton of the sharp

scolding Eve had given him about his bad influence on the boys. So far as he knew, even Walter had never learned about that. "I didn't go to hurt you."

"You told me you had seen a bunch of automobiles in Midland. After you left and didn't take me yourself, I made up my mind to go anyway. Went over there with Blue Hannigan's wagons. There wasn't an automobile in that town, Uncle Hewey. Not one. Folks said they hardly ever saw one come through."

Hewey frowned. "I don't know why you're so dead set on seein' one of them devil-cars. I've seen a many of them, and there ain't nothin' to them. They smell like a sick skunk. They cause folks so much grief that I don't see how they can hold out much longer. Soon as the last one has run off into a ditch, that'll be the end of the automobile. You ain't really missed very much."

"You're wrong, Uncle Hewey. They ain't hardly gotten started yet. Pretty soon you'll be seein' people drive a hundred or a hundred and fifty miles in a single day. Show me the horse that can do that."

"There ain't any real call for it. I never been in a place I hated so much that I had to get a hundred miles from it in one day."

"You ever ridden in an automobile?"

Hewey hadn't. Another time he might have made up a story, but he sensed that this was a time for being truthful. Anyway, his experience was too limited to feed his imagination much. The noise and the smoke had always discouraged him from getting very close to one when its motor was running. He had always been sure it was going to explode any minute.

He said, "Midland ain't that much of a town anyway. One of these days I'll take you with me and we'll make us a trip to some big place like San Angelo, or maybe even Fort Worth. I'll bet you'll see lots of automobiles there. I might even take you for a ride in one."

Cotton's eyes narrowed again. "Maybe you ought to save back your promises for Tommy. He's still young enough to believe anything."

Hewey frowned, studying his nephew. He had never noticed before how much Cotton looked like his mother.

The windmill appeared almost ready to raise. The tail section lay on the ground, as yet unattached, but the big cypress wheel was mounted to the thirty-foot wooden tower. The top was propped up off of the ground by a rough but strong sawhorse fashioned from heavy mesquite limbs. The wheel and the tail had originally been red, but many pieces had been replaced by new lumber painstakingly sawed and trimmed to fit.

Hewey said, "We ought to paint it before we raise it up."

"It's cypress. It'll stand the weather."

"But it looks bad, some painted, some raw that-away. Looks like a farmer outfit."

"That's what this is."

Hewey would never have admitted it. "A windmill stands way up there, and people can see it from a long ways off. A man ought to want to dress it up, same as he dresses himself up to go to church."

"This is a long ways from church."

"Not from mine." He looked across the horizon and pointed to a distant tower. "Even old C. C. takes pride in the looks of his windmills. You'll notice they're painted, every one."

"C. C. Tarpley's got money in the bank. In fact, he's got the bank. All we have down there is a big note comin' due early in the fall. I reckon the folks'll buy paint when they've burned the note."

Cotton jumped down and began unhitching the team so they could not spook and run off with the loaded wagon. Hewey tried to help him but found Cotton aggressively self-sufficient. He began unloading the tools from the wagon instead. He said, "I'll help you with that tail section, and we'll have this thing fixed up before you know it."

"I can get it," Cotton said. "I had figured on comin' by myself anyway." Perhaps he saw the disappointment Hewey tried not to show. "I reckon you can dig the holes for a pair of brace posts that we'll need to keep the tower from slippin' when we commence to raise it. I've already staked the places."

Digging holes had never been Hewey's favorite part of the cowboy trade, but neither was windmilling in general. He liked windmills for drinking cool water from, not for greasing or repairing. But he guessed digging holes was better than being shut out altogether. He dragged the posthole diggers from the splintered bed of the wagon. He grimaced, gripping the slick handles. It was not his habit to carry gloves. He knew he would work blisters on his hands before the morning was out.

Well, it probably wasn't any worse than forking hay to cows in the Sangre de Cristos snow. At least here he wouldn't take a chill.

The hole had been drilled by a professional windmill man, and the big steel casing extended above the level of the ground. Centered within the casing and standing a little higher was a three-inch pipe through which the strokes of the wheel high above would draw the water. A set of heavy wooden blocks or collars rested on top of the outer casing and tightly gripped the smaller inside pipe to keep it from slipping down to the bottom of the hole. The tower, when raised, would be centered above the pipe. Hewey took it for granted that Cotton hadn't overlooked a thing. It was in his nature to be thorough about mechanical devices.

The well seemed to be in a slight depression. Hewey remarked, "It would've been handier to've had it drilled on higher ground. You could've gotten better gravity flow to your tank without raisin' the pipe so high."

Cotton frowned. "Daddy let Julio Valdez witch the well.

He said this is where the water was. Said it would be sweet water. So this is where Daddy had the hole drilled."

"I take it you don't believe in water witchin'."

"I've read everything I can find about science. I've never seen anything that said a man could walk around with a forked stick in his hand and tell you what's fifty feet under the ground."

"You *did* get water."

"I don't know if it's sweet."

Hewey had never read much about science. He was satisfied that the world by Aught Six had already progressed about as far as it needed to go. People had already invented just about everything that the public could afford to buy. To him, water witching was a science. He had never had the gift himself, but he had watched other people do it, and he had seen the end of a forked peach switch turn downward as surely as if some unseen hand had forced it.

He supposed if Cotton had read it in a book he would believe it.

Hewey kicked one of the stakes aside and vigorously attacked the ground with the diggers. After a few inches the ground seemed to counterattack. Presently he looked at the palms and saw small red spots rising. These would turn to blisters by and by and probably break open. "My hands never was made to fit the handles of these idiot sticks," he said, motioning toward the diggers.

Cotton glanced up from a heavy bolt he was tightening. "I had figured on diggin' the holes myself. Go sit in the shade if you've a mind to."

There was no shade, unless Hewey were to get under the wagon. Once this had been a cattle-watering place for a few years, the tank would probably become surrounded by a growth of mesquite trees, sprouting from the manure. But as of yet the nearby prairie was innocent of plants taller than a broomweed.

"I wasn't complainin', just makin' conversation." He went

back to the digging and didn't stop again until he saw that Cotton needed help lifting the tail section into place. He held it firmly while Cotton bolted it. He welcomed the respite even for a bit of heavy lifting. He studied the intricate combination of wood and machinery that made up the mill's wheel section. It was fourteen feet in diameter. "You must've had to rebuild the bigger part of this. Did you do it all by yourself?"

Cotton nodded. "It got damaged pretty bad when the wind blew the tower over. Old Armbruster didn't have it anchored good. Otherwise Daddy couldn't have bought it in the first place. There's not much to it when you know how. Just a couple of days' work with the forge and the anvil, and a saw."

Hewey couldn't have done it. He would bet Walter couldn't either. Well, everybody to his own way of getting a backache. Hewey's was horses.

By the time he finished the second hole his hands burned from two blisters that had sprouted and broken against the wooden handles. He said nothing because sympathy would not help against the fire, and he reasoned that he would get none from Cotton anyway. He glanced up toward the sun. "Don't you reckon it's time we started thinkin' about fixin' us a bite to eat?"

Several paces beyond the windmill was a shallow fire pit that Cotton had used on other days. Hewey gathered up dry mesquite that Cotton or the well driller had brought here, and some scrap pieces of kindling left over from the windmill-repairing. He placed them in the pit and built a small fire. While the wood was working its way toward a strong red glow, he poured a generous measure of ground coffee into a fire-blackened bucket and then filled the bucket nearly to the top with water out of a wooden keg in the wagon bed.

"Hell of a note," he remarked. "Got us a brand-new well and we haul drinkin' water from the house."

He stirred no response from Cotton. Hewey poked the burning wood into shape, then set the bucket on top of it. He knew a watched pot would never boil, but he watched it anyway to be sure the burning sticks did not collapse and tip the bucket over.

Other than mumbling quietly to himself when something didn't seem to fit or a nut didn't want to take hold of a thread, Cotton had said little all morning. Hewey had started three or four times to tell him of adventures, but Cotton betrayed no interest. Several good stories were stillborn. Hewey would have to save them for Tommy, he supposed, if he could remember them.

When he thought the coffee had boiled long enough he used a forked stick to lift the bucket by its bail and set it back from the fire. From the wagon he fetched a cotton sack Eve had partially filled with cold biscuits and strips of bacon fried at breakfast.

"Chuck!" Hewey called. "It ain't much, but it'll hold till the chicken."

Cotton's hands were hopelessly greasy from handling the working parts of the mill. He rubbed all he could onto an old gunny sack while Hewey poured coffee into two bent and tarnished tin cups. Cotton's hands were still black.

Hewey shrugged. "A little honest dirt ain't goin' to ruin a man's digestion. I reckon I've eaten a ton of it, one time and another."

Cotton broke a biscuit and folded a couple of strips of bacon inside, then closed the biscuit and mashed it down. While he ate, his gaze remained fastened to the mill. Hewey could see pride in his eyes. As Cotton was finishing the first biscuit, Hewey fixed him another with three strips of bacon. "Eat it up. You've done good."

Cotton's enthusiasm got the better of his reserve. "It's goin' to work just fine, Uncle Hewey. It's goin' to be as good as a brand-new one."

"Better, I'll bet. People that work in them factories, they

don't take care like the man who's goin' to use it. They just throw it together and slap it in the crate, and they know that's the last they'll see of it."

"I'd like to work in one of those factories awhile. Not makin' windmills, maybe, but makin' engines, or maybe even automobiles. Somethin' that runs and has a life of its own."

"And be cooped up inside a buildin' with all that smoke and all that noise? I couldn't stay in there for thirty minutes."

"It's what's comin', Uncle Hewey."

"I sure hope not."

"They're even talkin' about buildin' flyin' machines. Speed is what everybody wants today."

"In a horse, yes. A good old cow pony can give a man all the speed he ever needs. I've had some give me a right smart more than I wanted."

"I don't expect Mama and Daddy to understand. They're livin' in the past, and happy enough with it. But you've always been the restless one, Uncle Hewey. You've always been the one who wanted to see somethin' new and try what other people hadn't already done. I'd think you'd be excited over what's happenin' around us today."

Hewey sipped carefully on the hot coffee. "Sure, I always liked to see new country, new people. But everywhere I went I used to feel like I could deal with whatever came up. It was me against a horse, or me against a bunch of cattle, or me against another man. I knew how to take a-hold.

"But now, lots of places, it's different. I been to some big towns. I've seen them automobiles chuggin' up and down, scarin' hell out of the horses, leavin' a trail of smoke that'd choke a bay mule. I've seen a man set down at a telephone in Fort Worth, Texas, and talk to somebody way off at the Kansas City stockyards just like he was in the next room. I've seen streets so strung up with wires that you couldn't see the sky through, hardly. I don't understand it. I can't take a-hold of it. It scares me so bad I can't hardly wait to saddle up and get back into the open country where you've got to look a man in the face to talk to him."

"It ought to excite you, Uncle Hewey."

"It might excite *you,* but it scares *me.*" He nodded toward the reclining Eclipse. "That windmill there, that's as complicated a piece of machinery as ever I want to fool with."

"The world is movin' faster all the time. You either go on with it or you get left behind. You never was one to get left behind."

"Because I always looked forward to the place I was goin' to. But I don't look forward to this world *you're* talkin' about."

"I'm goin' to be a part of it. I want to help build it."

Hewey frowned. "Well, I hope you like it when you get it finished."

He hated to get to his feet. He had finally broken Cotton out of his silence. Maybe from now on things would go a little easier between them. He flung the dregs of his coffee into the greening grass and pitched his cup into the wagon bed.

Cotton stood up and looked toward home. "We'll have it ready for them pretty soon. They can come any time they take the notion."

Hewey rubbed his hands; they hurt a little. The bacon grease would probably help in the long run, but its saltiness brought the fire back. "Don't take a lot of people to raise a windmill."

"The raisin' is just an excuse for everybody to visit and enjoy themselves. First chance we've had since spring came."

Hewey walked to the prone tower and slapped a hand against one of the six-by-six legs. "What say me and you raise this mill ourselves? When they get here they won't have to do anything but party."

Cotton's mouth dropped open. "You don't mean that."

"It'd give them a dandy surprise."

"It might give *us* one. Just us two, and a pair of bronc mules . . . If the least thing went wrong we'd wreck the windmill and have all this work to do over again."

"The odds are with us."

Cotton stared at him with exasperation. There was finality in his voice, the way Hewey had often heard it from Eve. "They're right about you, Uncle Hewey."

"How's that?"

"They say you've got no more responsibility than a one-eyed jack rabbit. You won't ever grow up; you'll just grow old. If you live."

Hewey shrugged. "No harm meant. Just a notion I had, was all."

Cotton said nothing more as he worked his way around the mill, checking the bolts for tightness, fondling it as if it were a pet he had just saved from harm.

That's always the way with me, Hewey thought darkly. *Take one step forward and two backward. Almost had him there for a little bit.* He took out his frustration on the post-hole diggers.

He noticed a lone rider approaching, moving in a sensible slow trot, not pushing his horse. Hewey squinted, trying to identify him. Cotton only glanced, then went back to his work, evidently satisfied that this was the vanguard of the tower-raising crew.

Hewey said, "I believe that's Wes Wheeler. He still sheriff here?"

Cotton took a fresh look. "That's him, and he is. I didn't know he was interested in raisin' windmills."

Hewey had usually been able to recognize law officers about as far as he could see them. They had an intangible manner of standing, of walking, of riding, an official presence that gave them away. Hewey instinctively always classified them as one of two types, usually on first sight: good ones and bad ones. He rarely altered his initial opinion. Wes Wheeler was one he had always put in the *good* category. He didn't go around arbitrarily telling people what to do or trying to run their lives with the excuse that it was for their own good. He recognized that his main function was to keep the peace, and he seldom raised much hell in doing it. He never bothered a man unless he was convinced that a little bothering was going to benefit the community.

Wheeler was a big man who needed a big horse. This one was a stocky dun, still shedding off the coarse winter hair. Wheeler dismounted, keeping his horse between himself and Hewey. That struck Hewey as being a little odd; he decided it was an old habit, a holdover from rougher days when a lawman occasionally needed a shield. Wheeler had cut his eyeteeth in times like that; they had left their mark on him. Wheeler came on afoot, leading the dun horse. Hewey walked out to meet him, and they shook hands firmly.

"Good to see you, Wes."

The sheriff nodded. "Heard at church that you was back."

"Got here last evenin'. Sorry I missed church."

"Guess it won't hurt you to miss it once in a while." The sheriff spoke to Cotton, congratulating him on what appeared to be a dadjimmed good job of rebuilding the windmill. But his eyes kept shifting back to Hewey.

"Hearin' you was back got me to thinkin' about an odd letter I got in yesterday's mail. You have any trouble on the way home, Hewey?"

Hewey shook his head. "Biscuit acted like he was fixin' to come up lame, is all."

"That ain't the kind of trouble I mean. You didn't by any chance have some difficulty with a city marshal back up the way?"

Hewey blinked. "Oh, that! It wasn't no trouble, really. We just had a little difference of opinion. It was over with in a minute."

The sheriff's eyes turned sad. "I got a letter yesterday from the sheriff up there. I imagine he wrote to every sheriff in this part of the country."

Hewey shook his head. "It just happened a few days ago. And you already got a letter about it? The U.S. mails are a wonder to behold."

Wheeler said, "Seems like, by this letter, that they're lookin' for a cowboy by the name of Hugh Holloway."

Hewey mused, "That marshal never did get my name right."

"They got this Holloway charged with attempted murder."

Cotton set down his wrench and stood listening, eyes and mouth wide open.

Hewey said, "That's layin' it on mighty thick. I didn't try to murder him. I didn't even hit him, hardly, just a little tap on the nose to keep him from pistol-whippin' me again. It was a big nose; I couldn't hardly miss." He considered. "Maybe Biscuit stepped on him, too. Things was a little confused there."

The sheriff walked over to the remnants of the fire and looked in the coffee bucket. He was disappointed to find it empty.

Hewey said, "We got the makin's. We'll fix you another pot."

The sheriff shook his head. "I reckon you better tell me all about it, Hewey."

Hewey told him what little there was, about the marshal shouting at him for riding down a residential street, and about him trying to hit Hewey up beside the head with a six-shooter that must have weighed thirty-seven pounds.

Wheeler frowned. "Letter says you taken the gun away from him, and that you ought to be considered armed and dangerous."

Hewey shrugged. "If they ever clean out the water trough down there by the railroad tracks they'll find that pistol.

I throwed it away the first chance I got. I always figured one way to never need a gun was to never carry one around."

The sheriff's eyes were half closed, but he was a long way from being asleep. "You sure you've told me everything, Hewey?"

Hewey nodded. "It didn't amount to nothin', hardly."

Wheeler critically studied the mark on Hewey's jaw. "He done that to you just for ridin' on the wrong street?"

"He seemed like he was a little overwrought."

Wheeler said tightly, "The man was probably descended from a long line of bachelors."

Cotton ventured closer to the two men. Incredulously he demanded, "Uncle Hewey, you mean all he asked you to do was to go over and ride on another street?"

"He didn't ask me to. He told me I *had* to. There's a difference."

"If he'd *asked* you to, would you have done it?"

"Sure. I always try to get along with people."

Cotton shook his head. "I don't understand that at all."

Hewey wasn't sure how to explain it; it seemed so natural that no explanation ought to be necessary. "I'm a free-born American. I even been to war. I'd be a taxpayer, and proud to say it, if I owned anything to pay taxes on. I've got a right to ride down any street anywhere in this country that anybody else can. Somebody tells me I got to get off, and I do it, pretty soon I won't have that right anymore."

Cotton wasn't satisfied. Hewey didn't know how to satisfy him.

Wes Wheeler saw Hewey's chagrin. He looked at Cotton. "Son, I'm a peace officer. It's my job to enforce the law. I'm not allowed to *make* the law; that's for somebody else to do. If I go to makin' it, I can make it anything I want it to be. First thing you know I'll use it to help me and my friends. I'll use it to hurt people I don't like. If that ever happens, I'm dangerous. That marshal up yonder, he was goin' beyond his rightful authority. That makes *him* dangerous. You let people like that get away with it, pretty soon they'll take you over."

Hewey couldn't tell if the message had gotten across to Cotton. But the boy asked, "Mr. Wheeler, you goin' to turn Uncle Hewey over to them?"

The sheriff's mouth twisted. "Letter said they're huntin' for somebody named Hugh Holloway. I don't know any Hugh Holloway. It ain't my fault they got a marshal who can't remember names." He looked at Hewey. "You better hope some other sheriff don't figure out that they want Hewey Calloway, and tell them where to hunt."

"I always tried to get along good with the law."

"If you ever go north again, you might better take a broad roundance on New Prosperity. Not because you *have* to, but because you *want* to."

"I didn't lose nothin' there."

"If they ever come lookin' for you and have the name right, I don't know what I can do to help you."

"You've already helped me, Wes. I appreciate you tellin' me."

Wheeler climbed back into his saddle. Hewey said, "They're fixin' to have a big chicken supper over at the house this evenin'. I know Eve and Walter would consider you mighty welcome."

"Can't stay, Hewey. Might be a good idea if you got your visitin' done and left pretty soon yourself. Just in case."

He waved, and he was gone.

Cotton said, "Just change streets, that's all you'd of had to do. Just ride over one block."

Hewey didn't know how to explain to him that a man could lose a lot of manhood in a single block. He didn't try. "Your mother wouldn't understand about this. I hope you don't feel like you've got to tell her."

"No, she wouldn't. And I won't."

4

Alvin Lawdermilk's buckboard arrived a couple of hundred yards ahead of the others. Alvin stood up to wave before Julio Valdez reined the team to a nervous halt. The mules, young and of Spanish lineage, were as green as the pair Cotton had been breaking. As soon as a Lawdermilk mule team had the "bronc" worn off, they were for sale. Life was too short, Alvin contended, to let it be dull.

Hewey met the vehicle, grinning. "Git down, Alvin. I'm afraid you missed dinner."

Alvin lifted a bottle from under the seat. "I *brought* dinner."

Julio waited dutifully until his boss was through with the greetings, then spoke jovially to Hewey and Cotton. He climbed down with the reins in his hand and began unhitching the team. Cotton hurried to help him with the buckles, snaps, and straps. He shouted back at Lawdermilk, "When you goin' to buy you an automobile, Alvin?"

"When windmills start pumpin' gasoline. You can run a mule on grass and water, but then automobiles have got to be fed." Alvin extended the bottle toward Hewey. Hewey was tempted, but it wouldn't be seemly in front of Cotton. Besides, Tommy was coming yonder with the rest of the horsemen and wagons. "Sun's too high, Alvin. Ask me again when we've raised the mill. Maybe we can bust a bottle against the tower, to christen it, like."

"An *empty* bottle, Hewey." Alvin climbed down from the wagon, and he was rock steady. Whatever little he might have drunk on the way hadn't affected him.

Julio Valdez surveyed the standing pipe with the pride of vested interest. "The water is where I said. It is a strong well, I'll bet."

Cotton frowned. "I don't know if the water is sweet."

"It is sweet."

Alvin Lawdermilk walked around the windmill, silently surveying and approving the work. "Good job. Cotton done it, I suppose."

Hewey nodded. "A wrench and a saw don't fit the shape of my hands."

"Nothin' fits your hands but a rope and a set of reins." Alvin turned. "You interested in a job, Hewey?"

Hewey pondered a moment, looking off in the direction where the sheriff had gone. "I kind of doubt I'll be stayin' long." He saw Cotton glance questioningly at him. Hewey lied, "I'm expectin' word on a job out in the Big Bend country. Not no thirty-a-month cowpunchin' job, but a *foreman's* job."

Alvin seemed to see through him, at least partway. Hewey had never wanted a foreman's job in his life; too much responsibility went with it. "I've always got some broncs that need breakin'. That's a job that fits your hands. You can come over to my place and stay, or you can bring them over here to Walter's. Either way, you've got a job any time you want it."

"Much obliged, Alvin. I'll study on it."

Cotton's brow pinched. "Uncle Hewey, don't you think you're gettin' to an age where you ought to quit ridin' those rough broncs?"

Hewey smiled. "When a man has sittin'-down work, he'd better hang on to it."

Tommy loped up ahead of the rest and slid his pony to a reckless cowboy stop. He wore his working clothes, though he had a church-clean look about him. He also had a boy's eagerness. "Howdy, Uncle Hewey. Bet it didn't take Cotton long to finish up with you to help him."

Hewey didn't look at the posthole diggers. "We each taken the jobs that fitted us best."

Walter Calloway rode up on one of his working mules. His farmer overalls presented a picture Hewey could never quite adjust to. Walter dismounted in a businesslike manner and surveyed the prone mill with a critical eye, looking for flaws. He found none. "You done real good, son," he told Cotton. He turned to Hewey. "Thanks for helpin' him."

Hewey shrugged. "I done my best."

Storekeeper Pierson Phelps climbed carefully down from his wagon and exercised his cramped legs, then moved toward Hewey with both hands outstretched. His grin was broader than a double-tree. He was on the gray side of sixty. His heavy shoulders were bent from a lifetime of heavy lifting and carrying the weight of a mortgage, but his ample belly showed he had always taken home plenty of groceries out of stock. "I declare, Hewey Calloway, it's good to see you again. How come you haven't been to town to visit with us?"

Hewey took several steps to meet the old merchant halfway. "Didn't get in till yesterday. Besides, I didn't bring home much in the way of coin. Didn't figure my welcome would be too good."

"If payin' customers were the only people who ever came, that little town would get awfully lonesome."

For what it was worth, Pierson Phelps was the leading businessman in Upton City, not necessarily a great feat in view of the fact that there were so few. Last time Hewey had been to town he had counted eight, including the Mexican wood and water hauler.

Trailing quietly in Phelps' bulky shadow was a sallow, bacon-thin little man named Schneider. He had materialized a few years ago from some unpronounceable place down in the German-speaking Texas hill country. He was considered something of an oddity, the only person of the Dutch persuasion in Upton City. He was known to read Shakespeare and Goethe and Zola—the last two some kind of foreign radicals—but he was nevertheless generally considered of a bit less than average intelligence because he spoke with an accent and sometimes got his words out of the customary order. He was regarded as beneath the community's established social level, such as it was, because he ran a small saloon for Pierson Phelps. The taint somehow had never attached itself to Phelps, though he owned the place. He conducted it separately from his general store and was rarely seen to enter its door except at closing time, to count the day's receipts. By then all decent women were well inside their own doors so that they never saw him; it was the women who established local social standards. Pierson never poured the whisky. Schneider did that, so it was Schneider who bore the stigma. He had long since resigned himself to the lofty, throat-cutting stares of the womenfolk.

"That horrid little Dutchman," Eve always called him. Hewey doubted she even knew his name.

"Howdy, Dutch," Hewey greeted him. "You bring any samples?"

"It is the Sabbath," Schneider said firmly. He always sat on the back row of the church, alone, keeping his own counsel and making his own treaties with the Lord. It was whispered around town that he was actually a Lutheran, which was probably about as bad as being a Catholic. But perhaps the preacher could yet save him.

It was said of Schneider that no one was ever allowed to get drunk in his saloon if he had a family. Nor could a family man buy more than one bottle at a time if Schneider suspected he might empty them all in one place. Alvin Lawdermilk was a special case. He dealt directly with Pierson Phelps, wholesale.

In another wagon sat a homesteader whose name Hewey vaguely remembered as Neely, or maybe it was Needy. He was always coming over to borrow something. *Needy* was probably right, Hewey reflected. The farmer's son was with him, a boy about Tommy's age. Lester was his name. He *looked* like a Lester, Hewey thought. That rhymed with *nester,* appropriate all around.

A couple of C. C. Tarpley's cowboys from the South Camp rounded out the group. They followed on horseback behind the wagons. C. C. might not take it kindly if he saw them here. He probably wouldn't say anything; he would just cut their wages the next payday and plead hard times. Where possible, he favored a style of punishment that yielded a profit.

It stood to reason that some of these people had brought their womenfolks. They would be at the house with Eve, helping her fix a big supper.

Sure going to be hell on the chicken flock, feeding this bunch, Hewey thought. *There'll be an egg drouth here all summer.*

The boys' black dog trotted behind the last wagon, tongue out. He had probably started following this unaccustomed caravan with enthusiasm, but the enthusiasm was long since gone. He slowed to a painful walk, sought the shade of the nearest wagon and flopped down, panting. A jack rabbit could have walked up and kicked him on the nose for all he cared.

The howdying and shaking didn't take long. Everybody seemed agreed that the sooner they finished the work the sooner they could start the pleasure.

Raising the tower was not difficult. Hewey was still confident that he and Cotton could have done it. In its way it was probably one of the easiest parts of the operation. Walter Calloway didn't trust the bronc mules. He borrowed Pierson Phelps' gentle team for the task. Hewey mounted Tommy's horse. He and the two Tarpley cowboys each tied an anchor rope to the tower and rode off at angles, keeping their ropes taut so the tower could not tip to one side or the other as the team raised it. A cross brace was chained between the two tower legs that rested on the ground, and it was butted against the upright posts that Hewey had placed. This would keep the tower from sliding instead of coming up. As the Phelps team pulled and the mill gained slowly in angle and height, the lift became easier. The anchormen moved with the tower, keeping their ropes tight. In only a minute or so, the two forward legs set themselves on the ground.

Cotton and Walter, using steel crowbars, inched the tower one way and the other until a plumb bob showed it was centered squarely over the well and the pipe. "That's it, Daddy," Cotton said.

The ropes were firmly staked to guard against a sudden strong wind pushing the tower over. Cotton took it upon himself to be sure the tower was level. He prized and shimmed under each leg until the plumb bob and the spirit level showed the mill was in perfect alignment with the hole. The men set in to digging anchor post holes by each of the four legs. That took a while, and Hewey deferred to his blisters so long as there were plenty of other volunteers. When the holes were finished, Cotton tied an anchor post snugly against each tower leg with wire so it would not slip, then began drilling holes with an auger. He drove a heavy bolt through each hole as soon as he finished it. While Cotton went about drilling other holes, Hewey tightened a nut over each bolt, firmly securing the tower legs to the anchor posts.

Walter turned to Tommy. "You can fill in with dry sand now and tamp the holes real good." Dry sand, properly pounded, would grip and hold tighter and longer than cement.

Hewey noticed that the nester boy Lester was adept at making the motions but contributing little muscle to the job. He would move as if to take hold but do it slowly so somebody else was always likely to get on it ahead of him and relieve him of the necessity. He looked eager enough that he got credit for trying without ever actually breaking a sweat. He grunted a lot.

Given any decent start, he probably had a future ahead of him in politics, Hewey thought.

By contrast, Cotton did his work so smoothly that it seemed to involve little stress. People like that seldom received much credit; they never grunted enough. They could not grasp the importance of showmanship.

After a while the anchor posts were well tamped and the tower was considered solid. Hewey helped lower the cylinder and the sucker-rods down the pipe a joint at a time. In a while the top sucker-rod and the red-rod were bolted together. This was the moment of supreme test. Cotton glanced at his father. Walter nodded. Cotton released the lever that held the wheel and the tail locked together. Freed, the tail swung out at a right angle and pulled the wheel into the soft south wind. For a moment the gears groaned as the big wooden fan strained off its lethargy and slowly began to turn. The sucker-rod began to stroke up and down. Hewey took off his hat and knelt with his ear against the pipe. In a minute he could hear the water working its way higher with each stroke. Then it began gushing out the end of the flow pipe.

It was muddy at first, clearing the accumulation which had silted into the bottom since the well had been drilled. In a little while the water cleared. Everybody stood around in silence, watching it gush with each stroke of the rod. They seemed fascinated by the sight. No matter how many times they had seen it, there was always a vague feeling of a miracle beheld in this dry land.

Cotton walked to the end of the pipe, cupped his hand and cautiously took a tentative sip. He blinked, as if only half believing, then took another drink, a larger one. "It's sweet," he said in surprise.

Julio smiled.

One by one, men and boys filed by to take a swallow or two. Presently Julio was the only one who had not. The little man's teeth gleamed. "I do not have to drink the water. The witching rod has told me how it tastes."

Walter signaled for Tommy to shut off the mill. "No use wastin' the water and makin' a loblolly. We've got to take time somehow to get over here with a team and fresno and scoop out a surface tank."

Hewey heard himself volunteering before he had adequately considered the ramifications of the job. "I'll start tomorrow."

Cotton glanced worriedly at him. Hewey said, "It won't take but a few days, button."

He thought about it a little more. If a shovel or a set of posthole diggers didn't fit his hands, the heavy iron handle of a mule-drawn fresno dirt-mover was no better. He already had blisters enough. But he never considered backing out, once the commitment was made.

Greasy, muddy, the men stood around admiring the results of the afternoon's work with all the self-righteousness that comes from knowing a job has been properly attacked and competently mastered. The nester boy looked especially tired, especially self-righteous. Walter told his sons to start loading the tools into the family wagon. Lester Needy trailed along behind, picking up the lighter pieces. His father told him to be careful of his back; a growing boy shouldn't overdo.

Alvin Lawdermilk, gloriously greasy and muddy, brought a bottle from under the seat of his buckboard. Its original contents had already been considerably depleted. "Here's to a good day's work," he said and passed the bottle around. All the men drank except Schneider. Nobody in Upton City could remember ever seeing him drink anything but coffee. When the bottle had made the round, Alvin took a swig from it. A little whisky remained in the bottom. Alvin said, "Every windmill has got to have a name. Walter, name this one and we'll christen it proper."

Walter shook his head. "I hadn't even thought about it."

Alvin turned to Hewey. "Then I'll name it in honor of the prodigal brother, come home to help eat the unfatted calf. From now on, this is Hewey's Mill."

Hewey protested. "Cotton done all the work. It ought by rights to be named after him."

But nobody seemed to hear him, least of all Cotton, who frowned darkly and went on with loading up the tools. Alvin smashed the bottle against a corner post, a remnant of whisky running down the clinging shreds of cedar bark.

Alvin said, "Bet you never had anything named after you before."

Hewey wondered at Alvin's extravagance with good whisky. "Once. A horse. We never did manage to get him broke proper."

"People can see a windmill a long ways farther than they can see a horse. Every time they look at this one they'll think of you."

Hewey looked up at the rejuvenated wheel, a motley mixture of old wood and new. "I wish it was painted, then."

Cotton fetched a shovel back out of the wagon, dug a little hole against the corner post and raked the broken glass into it, then covered it up. It would be like some nosy calf to find that glass before the sun went down. Cotton gave Hewey a quick, exasperated glance as if he counted him responsible for Alvin's exuberance.

The crew trailed out south toward the house. Alvin motioned for Hewey to come up beside him in the buckboard. Julio climbed into Cotton's wagon, which seemed to suit Cotton better than riding with his uncle. The black dog got under Cotton's wagon and trotted along just fast enough to keep himself in the moving shade.

Alvin wanted Hewey to tell him about some of the wonders he had encountered in his travels. Hewey accommodated him, loose-herding the truth a little but not so much that he wouldn't get away with it. Tommy rode alongside, listening eagerly.

Behind their wagon was that of the nester. The boy Lester, rested up from his work, was playing incessantly on a jew's-harp, the only noise Hewey hated more than the clatter of a gasoline engine. The sixth time Lester cut loose on "Hello My Honey," Hewey was ready to go back and finger-thump him over his left ear. But civility ruled, and he stifled his baser nature.

As they neared the house and the tall chinaberry trees, a reddish dog came trotting out toward them, barking a challenge but looking behind him every few seconds to see if help was coming. Tommy's dog took up the challenge and moved out from under Cotton's wagon into the sunshine. Both dogs took care not to carry the contest too close to each other.

The red dog was on the small side, a fact which failed to arouse overconfidence in Tommy's.

Tommy said without enthusiasm, "He belongs to our teacher. I don't know why *she* had to come over here. We see enough of her on other days without havin' to listen to her on Sunday too."

Hewey smiled. "She's not much of a teacher, I suppose."

Tommy shrugged. "She knows a lot. But she ought to, at her age."

"She got a name?"

"Miss Renfro. Miss Spring Renfro."

"Spring? That's an odd name."

"Summer would probably fit her better. *Late* summer."

Hewey smiled. He doubted that Tommy was a dependable judge of a woman's age. If she was over twenty-five though, she probably wasn't much to look at. In this country, where men outnumbered women like the Indians had outnumbered Custer, spinsterhood was a difficult state for a woman to hang on to unless she had a face that would stop a runaway horse in mid-stride. Even the plain schoolteachers tended to get married off with only a modest effort on their part, and the pretty ones seldom made it through the first school year.

Hewey had never had much truck with schoolteachers, plain or pretty. They always made him nervously aware of how much he had never learned, of how slowly he read and how painstakingly he wrote, when occasion demanded that he write anything at all. He never could understand why teachers should seem so superior. He'd never seen a man teacher yet who could ride a bronc more than two good jumps.

Any schoolkid could learn to read a book, but good bronc riders were few and thin on the ground.

It took several minutes for the men to unsaddle the horses, unhitch the teams and turn all the stock into a pen for a bait of oats. Tommy said to Lester, "Let's me and you run to the house and see if we can freeze the ice cream."

Lester displayed no enthusiasm. "Turnin' a freezer always makes my arm tired."

"But the ones who freeze it get to lick the dash. Come on."

Lester followed, but he stayed a couple of steps behind all the way to the house. Walter started toward the house at a slower pace, followed by Pierson Phelps, the Dutchman and the farmer Needy, the two Tarpley cowboys and Julio Valdez. Hewey was about to follow, but Alvin grabbed his arm. "The womenfolks can wait on us a few minutes."

He went to his buckboard, rummaged around and came up with a bottle. He glanced toward the house and evidently decided he could be seen. He stuck it inside his shirt and headed for the little shed out beside the windmill. Safely behind it, he brought the bottle back out from its hiding place. Hewey could see that the cork had never been removed.

Alvin said expansively, "I love the womenfolks, God bless them. But there are times when their talk can drive me to distraction without a little drop of kindness to smooth off the edges." He pulled the cork out and extended the bottle toward Hewey.

Hewey reasoned that he would be standing within smelling distance of Eve in a few minutes. "I believe I'll pass."

Alvin took a long swallow, paused to lick his lips and enjoy the flavor, then tipped the bottle again. "I'll swear, Hewey, that batch must of been blessed by the breath of an angel. You've got to try it." He shoved the bottle into Hewey's hand.

Hewey was sorely tempted, but he had made up his mind. He tried to push the bottle back at Alvin.

A woman's voice cut like rusty barbed wire. "*Mr.* Lawdermilk!"

Hewey knew he was in trouble even before he turned and gazed into the reproachful eyes of Cora Lawdermilk. But she wasn't there alone. Beside her stood Eve Calloway, whose own eyes were like Indian flint. Beyond Eve was a woman Hewey had never seen before, and behind them all stood a man wearing a dust-tinted black suit with frayed cuffs and a top button gone. He was Brother Averill, the Baptist preacher who hammered at the gates of hell every Sunday morning from ten to eleven, and occasionally longer when the spirit was really upon him.

Alvin was the first to get hold of his wits. "Why, howdy, Cora. Hewey was just offerin' me a drink to celebrate his homecomin', and I was tellin' him it wouldn't be proper on the Sabbath afternoon."

Hewey would cheerfully have stomped Alvin with a pair of hobnailed boots, if he had owned any. Cora Lawdermilk swung those narrowed eyes on Hewey and skewered him with them. "*Mr.* Calloway." It was her habit to use the word *Mister* to her husband and other close acquaintances only when she was sorely provoked. Hewey was acutely aware that he still held the guilty bottle in his unguilty hand. He tried to swing it behind him, out of sight, but this was a futile gesture. Right now that bottle seemed bigger than a horse. He would have hurled it across the fence, but that would have called more attention to it.

Eve didn't speak; she only stared at him, her face reddened beneath the cover of her big slat bonnet.

Brother Averill said, "Perhaps Brother Hewey forgot this was the Sabbath."

The third woman's face was impassive, but Hewey thought he saw laughter in her eyes, struggling to escape imprisonment.

She wouldn't think it was so damn funny if Eve was her sister-in-law, Hewey thought, resentment touching him a little. He glanced back at Alvin Lawdermilk. On that face was the innocence of a child picking wild flowers in a field, a soul untainted even by original sin.

"By George, preacher, you're right," Hewey said, "it *is* the Sabbath." He held the bottle out at arm's length and turned it upside down. Alvin's innocence turned to pain as he watched the long stream of golden elixir soak quickly into the sand. But he stood in silence and bore the sacrifice like a soldier.

Cora Lawdermilk said, "In the future, Mr. Calloway, I hope you will remember not only the Sabbath but also my husband's weakness."

"I'll sure try to."

When the bottle was empty, Hewey tossed it into the sand beside the shed.

Cora took her husband's arm and led him away.

Brother Averill said, "You have done the proper thing, Hewey."

Hewey watched the departing Alvin. "I'm sure I did, preacher."

The minister looked a moment at the stiff-shouldered Eve and spoke to the other woman. "Shall we go back to the house, Miss Renfro?"

Miss Renfro still had that laugh in her eyes, though her face never changed expression. After she turned away Hewey couldn't remember what color the eyes had been; all he had seen was the laugh in them.

Eve's hands were on her hips. This was May, but her eyes said October. "You're runnin' true to form, Hewey. Just home one day, and you've already embarrassed me in front of Brother Averill and the boys' teacher, not to mention Cora Lawdermilk."

"I expect Cora has seen a whisky bottle a time or two before."

"Not on *this* place. I trust this will be the last time such a thing ever happens."

"I never had a drop, Eve. You can smell my breath if you've a mind to."

She shook her head. "Not for a ten-dollar gold piece." She set off toward the house, trailing after the others. Hewey slumped, flexing his hands, glancing once at the bottle lying by the shed, wishing he *had* taken a drink out of it since he had endured all the blame for it anyway.

Seemed like sometimes he had two left feet.

Cotton came out of the corral. Hewey hadn't realized the boy was still out there, putting up the windmill tools. He wondered how much Cotton had heard or seen. Cotton said nothing. He walked to the shed, picked up the empty bottle and carried it to a trash barrel behind the yard fence.

There was nothing left to be said except *hell*. Hewey said that and followed after the others.

As was the custom, the men stayed outside, sitting in chairs or on the ground beneath the great rustling chinaberry trees. The women were in the house. Hewey could hear and smell the chicken frying. On the front step sat Tommy, turning the handle of a wooden ice-cream freezer. A wet burlap bag was stuffed around the top to hold in the cold and extend the useful life of the expensive salt-packed ice, thoughtfully brought from town by Pierson Phelps. The boy Lester cranked slowly on a second freezer. Tommy had to remind him two or three times not to stop because the dash would freeze up.

The boys' black dog and the teacher's red one still stalked one another with wary patience, neither allowing the other to get quite close enough for a bona fide acquaintanceship to begin. They traded a certain amount of tentative and shallow growling. They reminded Hewey of his own relationship with Eve.

He wanted to think of something else, so when Pierson Phelps began drawing him out on the details of his recent adventures, Hewey obliged. He told of working his way up through the Indian Territory, and of Homer Ganss' horse race. He told of his attempt to break into the big and easy money of show business by trying to get on as a bronc rider with the 101 Ranch Wild West Show.

"They put me on for a tryout. I'm tellin' you, boys, these broncs we've got down in this country are rockin' horses against them outlaws they gather up for that show. By the third day I had eaten so much dirt that I must of gained fifteen–twenty pounds. One of them throwed me for a belly buster that emptied all the air out of me plumb down to my toes. I drug myself up against a fence post and sat there tryin' to get some wind back into my lungs when old Zack Miller himself walked up. He says, 'If you can't handle them rough ones, then you oughtn't to've hired out.' Says, 'The main trouble with you is that you've done et too many birthday cakes.'

"I says to him, I says, 'Where I've spent most of my birthdays, there wasn't nobody around to bake me a cake.' But I reckon we was both agreed that I wasn't no show-time cowboy. It would've been easy money; I was told they paid some of them boys as much as seventy-eighty dollars a month, and they didn't have to ride but five or six broncs a day.

"I reckon I wasn't cut out for that kind of business anyway. When I do a job of work, I like to know there's somethin' real goin' to come of it. If I break a bronc, it's so somebody can use him in cow work. If I break a mule, it's so somebody can hitch him to a wagon and get some use out of him. But in them shows you just ride for an audience, and when you're through there's nothin' been built, nothin' real been gained. It's sort of like for nothin'." He added as an afterthought, "Except the money, of course."

The farmer Needy said, "You talk as if you don't think money is important." It was a concept he obviously disapproved.

"I've never met anybody, hardly, who thought he had enough of it. Not even old C. C. Tarpley. Since there's no way you can ever get enough of it anyway, I don't see where a man ought to kill himself runnin' after a hopeless cause. There's too many other things in life to pleasure you."

Brother Averill put in, "There are a great many things in this life more important than pleasure."

"If it don't pleasure you, then it ain't worth your time," Hewey demurred.

"Pleasure is for the *next* life. This life was meant to be lived in trial and suffering, to prepare us for the glory of the next."

Hewey said, "I've known a lot of folks who kept puttin' off enjoyin' themselves, figurin' they'd get around to it one of these days. Then one mornin' they woke up and found out they was old. It was too late then."

"Not if they had lived a Christian life. The real joy awaits us all in the next world."

"I don't see no harm in practicin' up for it a little while we're here."

In a little while Eve came out onto the step, where the two boys had finished freezing the ice cream, and announced that supper was ready. "You men can come on in and fill your plates. Then you can come back outside where it's cooler."

Tommy asked her about her promise that he and Lester could clean the dash, but she told him they would have to wait; she didn't want them spoiling their supper.

Eve asked Brother Averill if he would lead them in the blessing. Hewey stood up nervously, forgetting to remove his hat until he saw the other men doing it. It had always seemed to him that the Lord must be awfully busy, and it must be an imposition to Him to have to stop His work three times a day and listen to people all over the world telling Him "Thank you." Surely He knew everybody was grateful without His having to hear them say it so often.

Brother Averill launched into a lengthy blessing in which he named everybody here except Julio Valdez. Hewey didn't know if he had forgotten the Mexican, couldn't say his name or simply considered the poor soul lost on account of his race. Hewey began to feel he was going to get a crick in his neck from holding his head down so long, and he thought the prayer might run on for ten more minutes. The breeze brought a strong whiff of fried chicken which tantalized Hewey almost to the point of sin. It might have reached the preacher, too, for he suddenly brought the long prayer to a snappy conclusion. "And now, Lord, we Thy unworthy servants humbly ask Thy blessings on this food which we are a-fixin' to partake of, amen."

Walter motioned for Brother Averill to lead the way into the house, a courtesy which the minister graciously accepted. His strictures against labor on the Sabbath did not extend to the frying of chicken.

Hewey hung back. So did Julio, accustomed to being last, and Alvin Lawdermilk, who had been casting uneasy glances at Hewey ever since they had seated themselves beneath the trees. At length Alvin seemed to lose an inner battle. He came up to Hewey with his head down. "Hewey, I kind of left you hangin' on the fence out yonder while ago. I hope you won't take it ill of me."

Hewey shrugged. His momentary resentment had evaporated long ago. "Who knows? If I was a married man I might of done the same."

Alvin said, "It ain't I was afraid of her. It's just that I like a peaceful house. You come over and break some horses and mules for me awhile, Hewey. You'll find out that Cora ain't a bad woman atall. It's just that it's a little easier to lie to her than it is to explain some things. You'll learn what I mean if you ever get married."

Hewey shook his head. "I don't reckon I'll ever get married, then, because I've never told a lie in all my life."

Brother Averill returned carrying a plate loaded with chicken, red beans and biscuits. One by one the other men came out. Alvin said, "We better go in, Hewey. The womenfolks won't eat till we're all fed."

Not until Alvin and Hewey went into the house did Julio trust himself to follow, the last of the men to go. Eve was standing at the plain old wooden table forking pieces of chicken onto everybody's plate. Hewey expected her to give him a couple of necks and a back, but she gave him drumsticks. Her eyes weren't warm, exactly, but the frost was gone. Cora was too busy fussing over her husband's welfare to pay any attention to Hewey, which was just as well.

Miss Renfro stood at the bread pan. She said, "You look like a big biscuit-eater to me, Mr. Calloway. How many do you want, five or six?"

They were big biscuits. Hewey said, "Five's enough. I don't want to look like a hog."

She smiled. It was the first time he had really looked at her. She wasn't a pretty woman; he supposed many people would consider her plain, and somewhat skinny at that. But the smile was pleasant. While she wore it, in the dim light of the kitchen, she would almost pass for pretty. And he would bet she wasn't too far over thirty. Well, not forty, anyway.

He poured the coffee for himself. While he was at it he poured one for Julio too. Hewey noticed that Eve had given Julio mostly chicken wings, but he was glad to see that Miss Renfro hadn't shorted him on biscuits. Julio *did* like biscuits, especially when he had plenty of syrup to sop them in. Hewey reached up into a cabinet and brought down a bucket of molasses. "Here's the lick, Hooley. Move them biscuits over and I'll pour some on your plate."

He took one of his drumsticks and exchanged it for one of Julio's wings. "Always *was* a little partial to the wing," he said.

After everyone had eaten, Eve let Tommy and Lester carry the freezers into the house. Soon they were back, each carrying a freezer dash standing in a bowl. They seated themselves on the step and eagerly went to work spooning off the ice cream that clung to the paddles.

Down at the chinaberry grove, two sets of freight wagons had pulled up for the night. Presently the teamsters came up leading their mule teams to water them at the house windmill. Eve shouted at Walter, "You tell Blue Hannigan for them not to go fixin' anything to eat. We've got a-plenty left right here."

Walter walked out and invited the freighters to eat with the rest of the crowd, an invitation they accepted without hesitation or false show of reluctance.

Tommy was chagrined. Hewey heard him tell the nester boy, "That big one's Blue Hannigan. He eats like one of his mules. We better get all the ice cream we want before he starts, because he sure won't leave us any."

About that time Hewey's horse, Biscuit, came up to the corrals from the horse pasture where he was confined. Hewey walked out to look at him, to try to see if the lameness had improved any. Biscuit stood outside the closed gate, shut off from the feed and from the horses and mules that had put in the day at work. Hewey opened the gate and let him in. He found the troughs empty, so he poured some oats for Biscuit, confident that the horse wouldn't let the others steal any of it.

As Hewey turned toward the house, he saw the schoolteacher walking toward him. She was a tall woman and thin, her plain gray dress almost sweeping the ground. In her hand she held a coffee cup with a spoon sticking out of it. "You're about to miss the ice cream, Mr. Calloway. We ran out of bowls. I hope the cup will do."

"You didn't have to bring it all the way out here to me, but I'm much obliged."

"No trouble. I didn't want to see you miss out."

She handed him the cup. Awkwardly he wondered if courtesy didn't indicate that he ought to give her the first bite, but there was only one spoon. Most people were a little squeamish about things like that, and he figured that as a schoolteacher she surely would be.

"I sure thank you, Miss . . ." He stammered, for somehow her name had slipped away from him.

"Renfro. Spring Renfro. I am the boys' teacher."

"Thank you, Miss Renfro." He knew he shouldn't ask, but he did it anyway. "How'd you come to have a name like Spring?"

"I was born in April. My mother said it had been a long winter, and she was glad to see Spring."

He looked at the sparkle in her eyes and decided the name fitted her. He said, "I'm pleased to meet you. I'm Hewey Calloway."

She smiled, and again her plainness disappeared. "I want you to rest assured, Mr. Calloway, that I know where the bottle came from. I have come across many of Alvin Lawdermilk's hiding places."

The country schoolhouse stood at the Lawdermilk ranch headquarters. Other teachers had stayed at the same place in years past. Cora Lawdermilk, who had lost one child in infancy and had never been able to have another, seemed to enjoy the company. It was also good to have someone extra around to help see after her semi-invalid old mother, whose legs were slow but whose sharp tongue was swift.

"Good folks, the Lawdermilks," he said. "Good place they've got." It was an empty statement, but she flustered him a little, like schoolteachers usually did. He didn't want to say much because he knew his grammar bespoke more of the barn than of the schoolhouse.

"I hope the ice cream is good," she said.

He nodded. "Fine. Just fine." He sensed that she was giving him an opportunity to initiate a conversation, and he was doing a damn poor job of it. He asked, "You come from back east, I suppose?"

"Not very far east. Just East Texas."

"We was born in East Texas, too, me and Walter. Been a long time since we left. You was probably no more than a little girl." It struck him too late that he was making a judgment about her age, a judgment one didn't make about strange women, or even those he knew well.

She seemed to take no offense. "It has been a while since I was a little girl."

"Yes'm," he agreed.

He didn't know what else to say, and the sound of a vehicle approaching from beyond the barn saved him from the necessity of saying anything. He stepped out to the side, where he could see better. It was unusual for company to come from that direction, that of the French place, where he had spent the better part of the day helping put up the windmill. Hewey squinted. He made out that this was a buggy, drawn by a pair of grays.

Spring Renfro said, "That will be Mr. C. C. Tarpley." Her voice took on a tinge of distaste. "And I suppose the gentleman with him will be Mr. Frank Gervin."

"We all call him 'Fat,'" Hewey said. He noted her displeasure. "There's some who wouldn't call him a gentleman."

"Including myself." She started in a brisk walk back toward the house, seeming not to want to be outside when the buggy arrived. Hewey walked slower, eating the ice cream and watching her. For an old maid schoolteacher she seemed to have a right smart of judgment. The fact that she didn't like Fat Gervin was proof of that. His smooth manners around the womenfolk were reported to have fooled some of them, awhile.

All the men were standing up by the time C. C. Tarpley brought the buggy to a stop, a testament to the respect—if not liking—which people felt for the rapacious old cowman. They hadn't stood up for Fat Gervin's sake, Hewey reflected.

Walter stepped forward and extended his hand. "Howdy, Mr. Tarpley. Git down; git down."

Back in the days when Walter had been working for him it had always been "C. C." not "Mr. Tarpley." That, Hewey decided, was the difference between simply working for a man and borrowing money from him.

"Just passin', Walter," Tarpley said. "Heard you-all was puttin' up a windmill on the French place. Came by and found you'd already finished."

"Had plenty of help," Walter said, waving his hand toward the other visitors. Hewey noted that the two Tarpley cowboys had somehow melted out of sight, probably behind the house. It wouldn't do them any good. Hewey would bet a dollar to a plugged nickle that the sharp-eyed old man had already spotted their horses in the corral. He wasn't one to miss anything.

Eve Calloway opened the screen door and moved out onto the step. "Mr. Tarpley, we've still got plenty left to eat. You and Mr. Gervin get down and come on in."

Fat Gervin looked hopefully at his father-in-law. Tarpley said, "Eve, we sure do appreciate the invitation, but we ain't hardly got the time." About then he spotted the ice-cream freezers by the step. "You still got some ice cream too?"

Eve assured him they did. Tommy's face fell; he had counted on getting to clean out the last of it.

C. C. said, "Then I reckon we'll just *take* time." His decision was clearly popular with his son-in-law, who could sometimes move with surprising swiftness for a man of his bulk. The buggy seat seemed to rise three inches on its springs when Gervin stepped down.

Hewey frowned as he watched Fat. He had never been able to trust a man who had slick hands and wore a coat in the summertime.

While C. C. and Fat were in the house, the two Tarpley

cowboys quickly said their good-byes and beat a hasty re-treat to the barn. They rode off in a northerly direction where they could not be seen, though the camp where they lived was in the opposite direction. They would get there; it would just take longer this way.

The crowd had fallen silent. It was odd, Hewey thought, how deadening an effect one rich old man could have on a conversation. Fat Gervin, between bites, set up a one-sided dialogue that was more lecture than conversation, all about the state of the nation's economy and the alarming growth of the national debt and such as that. Hewey surmised that he had been spending a lot of time in Tarpley's bank lately and reading banker publications. Five years ago Fat couldn't have counted a herd of cattle, much less figure up the national debt.

Tommy's worst fears materialized. Eve scraped the very last of the ice cream out for C. C. and Fat. The old rancher sat in the chair Walter had vacated for him and ate with gusto while Fat continued a long discourse on the struggle between management and labor.

C. C. said, "In my day I've seen a lot of changes come over this country, and I've been opposed to almost every one of them. But one thing I was never opposed to was ice cream. This is bully stuff, Eve, bully stuff."

"Glad you like it, Mr. Tarpley. We'd freeze some more, but there isn't enough ice. Mr. Phelps was kind enough to bring us what he had."

C. C. looked toward the storekeeper. "I'm told there are people who are actually buyin' ice to put in their drinkin' water, Pierson. Is that true?" He didn't give the storekeeper time to answer. "A dangerous thing, gettin' people accustomed to luxury like that. One luxury leads to another, and pretty soon they'll get to thinkin' they ought to have ice water every Sunday, and maybe even durin' the week. Get people spoiled to luxury and pretty soon it's not a luxury anymore, it's a necessity. It's a terrible waste of this country's resources. There ought to be a law passed right now to stop it." He paused. "But there ought to never be any law against ice cream."

Eve picked up the bowl when Tarpley was through with it, and she waited for Gervin to finish his.

C. C. Tarpley stood up. Fat, always watching him for his cues, did likewise. Old Tarpley looked around a little, taking in the house, the barn, the fences and general improvements. "You've done a right smart with this place, Walter."

"We've done the best we could."

The old man frowned. "That windmill you put up today . . . I looked through the bank records, and I couldn't find where you had borrowed any money from us to pay for it."

"It wasn't a new mill, Mr. Tarpley."

"It still cost money, even for an old one. You got to drill the hole, and I could tell there was some new lumber and fixin's went into the mill. Just about everything you've got is mortgaged to our bank. I was just kind of curious where you got the money, Walter."

Hewey frowned at the implication.

Walter said, "My boy Cotton helped Old Man Maxey drill the well. In return for the old man's time and the use of his machinery, my boy's goin' to give him three weeks' labor when school is out. I haven't mortgaged my boy's labor."

Tarpley grunted, partially satisfied. "But there's still the mill. How'd you pay for the mill?"

"It was a damaged one that had fallen over, south of Midland. It didn't cost me much. Back when it was still too early to plant, I throwed my team and wagon in with Blue's freightin' outfit haulin' lumber from the railroad in Midland. Four loads earned me enough to buy the windmill and the lumber it taken to patch it up."

That seemed to set C. C.'s mind at ease, but it simply launched Fat Gervin on another harangue. As an understudy to the old man he was trying hard to acquire C. C.'s inborn meanness with a dollar. He said, "You know, Walter, our bank has got a mortgage on that wagon and team. What if somethin' had happened to them while you was workin' on that job? And what about the unusual wear and tear? When a man is borrowin' he owes it to the institution to take good care of his collateral and see that it ain't in no way impaired or demeaned."

Tarpley nodded in surprised silence, noting with some pleasure that his hard-taught lessons might be starting to take root.

Fat got started on how great and indispensable an institution the bank had been in the development of the nation, and how everybody owed it to his country as a patriotic duty to stand four-square with the bank at all times.

Occasionally, when Hewey was in a mood of philosophical generosity, he would rationalize Fat's shortcomings and tell himself Fat wasn't altogether to blame. Maybe Hewey and a lot of others like him were at fault too. Cowboys could be merciless in hoorawing the misfit, the inept, the unwilling. He would tell himself that they probably drove Fat inward with their ridicule, making him sullen and mean. But Hewey's spasms of nobility usually dissipated quickly, and he would recover his standing conviction that sons of bitches are born, not made.

He had heard enough about banks in the last ten minutes to satisfy whatever curiosity might arise in him for the next three or four years. He moved away from the crowd, looking toward the barn and thinking he probably ought to go run Biscuit back into the horse pasture.

He noticed the teacher's red dog making his way from one bush, one weed, to another, pausing briefly at certain ones to raise a leg and leave his signature. The boys' black dog followed at a respectful distance, sniffing at each such imprint and endorsing it.

Hewey looked over his shoulder toward Fat. The devil

began to jab sinfully but deliciously at him. Fat's back was turned, and his jaw was still operating at a hearty pace. Hewey looked toward the house to make sure none of the women were outside to witness his surrender to temptation. They wouldn't understand. No properly modest woman knew much about male bodily functions, be they animal or human.

He fished a jackknife from his pocket and walked to a tall green weed upon which the red dog's greeting still clung in amber droplets. Carefully he bent over, holding the top of the weed with his left hand while he gingerly sliced through the base, taking pains not to shake it enough to dislodge the drops. Walking as if he were stepping on eggs, he carried it up behind Fat Gervin.

Most of the men were watching Hewey in quiet fascination, but they did not give him away.

He bent and shook the weed, managing to splatter a goodly amount of the dog's scent on the lower part of Fat's left trouser leg, at about ankle level. Fat was so busy talking that he never noticed. He might have wondered why Alvin Lawdermilk so suddenly turned around and covered his face, or why the dour Dutchman, Schneider, smiled, but he never let it interfere with the point he was making that most of the progress in this country resulted from the selfless generosity of a noble bank.

That had been the extent of the prank insofar as Hewey had envisioned it. In his own quiet way he had made a statement about Fat Gervin without Fat even knowing about it.

Hewey hadn't considered the black dog. That innocent animal, which had followed Hewey's strange motions with curiosity, sniffed at Fat Gervin's trousers, found there an invitation, hoisted his leg and saluted.

First startled, then enraged, Fat let out an oath that would have blistered the ears of the womenfolk if they had been outside to hear. He fetched the black dog a savage kick that sent the bewildered animal flying. As the dog ran off howling in surprise and pain, Fat tried in vain to shake the shame from his trousers.

Alvin Lawdermilk was doubled over, slapping his knee uncontrollably and gasping for breath. Pierson Phelps had choked on his pipe. Teamster Blue Hannigan got up and walked over to the house, leaning against it with his back turned, his shoulders bouncing. The Mexican laughed aloud, which added to Fat Gervin's rage.

Turning, Fat saw Hewey standing behind him, trying for Alvin Lawdermilk's saintly expression of infant innocence. Fat seemed to sense that Hewey might be in some way the author of his embarrassment. The suspicion deepened, and he clenched his fists. His eyes strained from their sockets.

Hewey blinked in bland curiosity as if he had missed the whole thing.

Old C. C. *had* missed it, his back turned. He stared now in consternation. "What's goin' on here, Fat?" He looked down. "Spilled your coffee on you again, hunh? I swear, boy, sometimes you're left-handed on both sides." He noticed then the angry way Fat was staring at Hewey, trying to confirm his suspicions. C. C. seemed to sense that it was time they left.

"Folks," he said, making no attempt to hide his puzzlement, "we enjoyed the supper and the company, but tomorrow's another workin' day. We got to be at the bank on time in the mornin'." He paused, studying his son-in-law but not fathoming the reason for Fat's anger. "Some of you folks might not've heard. I've decided to spend a lot more time with my cattle and a lot less with the bankin' end of the business. I've turned the responsibility of the bank over to Fat"—he corrected himself—"to Frank here. If you folks have business with the bank, he'll be the one you want to go and see. I'll be at the ranch." He started toward the buggy, then stopped to look back for his son-in-law. "You comin', ain't you, boy?"

Fat hadn't been a boy in twenty years, but he mumbled,

"Yes sir." He tore his eyes away from Hewey and followed the old man. He tried to hold his trouser leg away from his boot while he climbed into the buggy. He never looked back as they rode away.

Alvin Lawdermilk couldn't restrain himself. He broke into another fit of hilarity, wilder than the first. Soon he was lying on the ground, beating the packed earth with his fist. His laughter was contagious. It swept the other men and continued until some of them were bent over in pain.

Hewey, laughing with them, noticed that Walter seemed not to be sharing their mirth. He was watching the buggy disappear down the winding trail toward town, his face solemn.

Cora Lawdermilk came out presently and stared at her husband. "You men! There's not an ounce of shame in a carload of you. You've been tellin' those shady stories again, I can tell. And in the presence of the minister. Shame on all of you."

Hewey had noticed that the minister had laughed as hard as any of them, except of course Alvin. If laughter could ever be fatal, there was no hope for Alvin Lawdermilk.

The minister had gained Hewey's respect.

Cora said, "Alvin, dark's comin'. Time we started for home."

The rest decided their holiday was over too. Pierson Phelps pumped Hewey's hand. "Hewey, you come by the store first time you get a chance to go to town. Drummer left me a sample of cigars he wanted me to try. I'd like to see what you think of them."

The Dutchman said, "You come in sometime, Hewey. For you I will save back a bottle of the best we have. No cost. A gift for the thing you did to that Fat Gervin." They pulled away.

Julio Valdez hitched the Lawdermilk team and brought the buckboard around. Alvin climbed into the seat and let Cora struggle up by herself. The schoolteacher called for her dog, which jumped into the back of the vehicle; it was smarter than the boys' dog. She turned to Hewey, glanced around to see that no one else would hear and said quietly, "I was looking out the window a while ago, Mr. Calloway. I saw what happened to Frank Gervin."

Hewey reddened. "You wasn't meant to see that, ma'am." He floundered, trying to think of something to say. "I'm sorry. I didn't go to offend you."

"Offend me? I was tickled to death. In all my life I never saw a more befitting gesture." She gave him her slender hand. "Would you assist me, please?"

He gave her a lift up into the buckboard seat beside Cora and Alvin. Julio took his place on the back, his short legs hanging over. The dog moved up beside him and licked his hand, knowing no prejudice.

Tommy stood beside Hewey, helping him watch the Lawdermilk group disappear into the dusk.

Hewey said, "Button, you boys have got yourselves a real teacher. I'll bet you learn somethin' every day."

Soon the last of the visitors had gone. The teamsters had returned to their camp beneath the chinaberries. Eve called the boys to take the scraps down to the hog pen. Hewey took a seat in a rawhide-bottomed chair and stared at the trail where everybody had gone. He got to chuckling again, remembering Fat Gervin.

Walter seemed to read his thoughts. He pulled up another chair and sat awhile in moody silence. Finally he ventured, "Looks like to me you pleased everybody but Fat."

Hewey nodded. "Looks like. I hope he didn't hurt the boys' dog."

"I don't reckon. But he could sure hurt *us*."

Hewey's grin faded. "How?"

"You heard C. C. say he's all but turned the bank over to him. When we bought the French place we taken out a note, puttin' up this farm for security. Big part of it is due this fall. The way the late rains delayed plantin', we could find ourselves hubbin' up against the due date before we've got the money. I might've been able to reason with old C. C. But now I'll have to talk to Fat Gervin instead."

Hewey frowned. "I didn't know nothin' about that. It was just that he was blowin' so hard . . ."

"You never was one to fret much about consequences. I just hope Fat doesn't find out for sure what happened to him here."

5

The blisters on Hewey's hands had no chance to heal. He had promised to build a surface tank to catch the water pumped by the new mill. This was a brutal, grubbing type of work he would never hire out to do for pay unless he had one foot in the grave from a terminal case of starvation, but he would do it free of charge to fulfill a promise or as a gesture to someone who had provided him bed and board.

There was no dishonor unless a man took money for it.

It was a work that demanded much from the body but little from the brain. His mind was free to soar, to drift away to other times and other places, to people he had known and people he might someday meet, to things he had done and things he intended someday to do. He trudged along behind two half-broken Lawdermilk mules and guided the hungry jaws of a big steel fresno, scooping out ancient layers of deep rich soil and moving them forty or fifty feet to dump them and form the rim of an earthen vessel that would water a growing Calloway cattle herd. The sweat flowed freely and his body sometimes ached, but it was a happy time, for in his mind he relived a thousand cheerful days he had known, unconsciously filtering out and rejecting the unpleasant. He had never allowed himself to dwell on the darker times, for to live them once had been more than enough. While the mules struggled and the sharp blade cut down to the caliche undersurface, Hewey Calloway rode broncs and danced with pretty women and caroused with traveling companions like Snort Yarnell and Grady Welch. He raced horses with Homer Ganss and the Indians. He helped Alvin Lawdermilk find a forgotten hiding place and retrieve a whisky bottle he had all but given up for lost. The reunion had been a joyous thing to see. He followed the schoolteacher's red dog and watched Fat Gervin drown in the wake of a hundred black mongrels with outsized bladders, all the bank examiners in the state of Texas unable to save him.

After the third day he lost count, because time meant little to him. Days, he was by himself because Walter was busy in the fields and the boys were in school. Nights, they would sit outside after supper and talk awhile, but everybody went to bed at dark because to do otherwise meant to burn the kerosene lamps, and kerosene cost money.

"God gave us all the light we need," Eve would say. "When it's gone He means for us to rest."

The stricture was not firmly enforced, because an allowance was made sometimes for Cotton's studying.

Nobody had told Eve about Fat Gervin and the dogs, so she was pleasant to Hewey. Once she even went into her meager reserve of dried fruit and made an apricot cobbler that she knew was a special favorite of his. Watching him come dragging into the house of an evening, sweat-crusted and weary, she would tell him there was still hope of turning him into a Christian.

Tommy kept hanging on to Hewey's words as if they were gospel, prodding him to tell stories. His gullibility was no longer unlimited, however. Sometimes Cotton listened and sometimes he didn't. When he did listen, it was with a mood more of tolerance than of enjoyment. Usually he had schoolbooks to read, or books about mechanics and electricity and things of that sort, subjects in which Hewey saw no future. Nobody ever learned to ride broncs from reading a book, and knowing what made an engine run was no help in judging cattle.

Hewey decided it would do no good for him to counsel his nephew. The boy would have to find out for himself the error of his ways.

Late one evening as Hewey was taking the harness from the mules, preparing to feed them a bait of oats, he saw a horseman approaching on the wagon road. Sheriff Wes Wheeler came quickly to mind, but Hewey soon saw that this was not the sheriff. This was a smaller man, bent-shouldered, riding a worn-out old black horse that could not have carried the sheriff's weight. The rider came by the chinaberry grove, found no freighters and angled on up toward the house.

Hewey was standing at the front step by the time the old man got there. Walter, washing the day's dust off of his face in the outdoor washpan, dried himself on a towel and stepped out a little way to greet the visitor. The old horse eyed the towel suspiciously. Despite his age he acted as if he could pitch or run if the towel made any untoward move. There were some horses that never quite gentled down, just as there were such men.

"Howdy, Mr. Rasmussen," Walter said. "You'd just as well get down. Supper'll be ready directly."

The old man sat hunched. He appeared bone-tired, reluctant to expend even the little energy it would take to get down from the saddle. "Much obliged, Walter. You don't suppose your woman will mind."

She probably would, Hewey thought, *but she wouldn't say anything the old man could hear. She would grit her teeth and be painfully civil.*

He remembered the old man now, though it had been some years since he had last seen him, and Boy Rasmussen had gone downhill a long way. The face was pinched and furrowed, the skin dark and dry as old leather. The blue of his eyes seemed almost faded out, so that the red which rimmed them was dominant. His chin almost touched his nose, for he carried his teeth in a leather pouch hung around his neck, the leather string covered by a once-blue silk bandanna that was faded and dirty and frayed. His hands were shriveled, splotched with liver spots.

He had a smell that made the barking black dog keep its distance.

Hewey could only wonder how many years it had been since this old drifter had been given the name "Boy."

Rasmussen painfully brought his right leg over the high cantle, dragging his foot across the black's thin rump. Hewey heard a popping sound but couldn't tell if it was from the dried leather of the ancient saddle or from the thin and rheumy knees. In a high-pitched, breaky voice the old man said, "Walter, I don't suppose there'd be any whisky about?"

Walter shook his head. "We don't keep any on the place." Hewey saw pity in his brother's eyes.

Rasmussen's disappointment was plain. "It ain't that I'm a slave to it, you understand. It's just that I got the miseries tolerable bad today. There ain't a joint in my body . . ." But there was no use belaboring the point. "I don't suppose you'd have some 'baccy? Chewin' or smokin', I wouldn't be particular."

Hewey had a half-empty sack of the makin's in his shirt pocket. "Keep it, Mr. Rasmussen." It was *Mister* out of deference to age; it made no difference how far down the ladder the old man had descended. On no account would Hewey have addressed him as *Boy*. The old man eagerly took the sack in shaking hands and laboriously rolled a cigarette, spilling tobacco around the edges of the curled brown paper. Not until he lighted it and took a lung-filling drag of the smoke did he pause to thank Hewey. He stared intently through eyes that did not see well anymore except into the past. "You'd be brother Hewey, wouldn't you? Been off roamin' the country, they tell me. It's a big old country.

I seen most of it myself, once. I reckon I'd go again, but this old pony here, I don't believe he could make it anymore. Them poor old feet have carried him too many miles."

Walter spotted Tommy staring curiously at the aging cowboy. "Tommy, I wisht you'd take Mr. Rasmussen's horse down to the barn. Unsaddle him, put him in a pen where the other horses won't bedevil him. And feed him some oats, will you?"

Tommy took the patched leather reins from the old man's arthritis-cramped hands, his gaze roaming over the ragged black saddle that must date back to the trail-driving times after the big war. Hewey could read the thought behind Tommy's eyes: how many wild and glorious scenes had that old saddle been a witness to or even a participant in?

Eve stood in the door, looking in dismay at this wizened old veteran. She would feed him supper; of that there was no question. But if she could help it she would not have him in the house. She said, "It's too hot to eat in the kitchen. Wouldn't you men like to eat outside where it's cool?"

She didn't give them time to argue the point. "Walter, you can fix Mr. Rasmussen a plate and take it to him."

Rasmussen stared at Eve with a shyness that bordered on fear. It was a trait of these old bachelor drifters that they never quite understood women and were always nervous in their presence. The natural urges had been so long suppressed or diverted through the commercialized and mechanical attentions of the sporting women in town that they found it difficult to communicate on any level with the "good" women they encountered along the way. They put these women on a pedestal somewhere beyond the bounds of reality and made it a point to ride a long way around whenever they could.

The old man probably knew perfectly well that Eve didn't want him in the house. But he was happy he didn't have to go in there because it would have been as much an ordeal for him as for her. He took his teeth out of the pouch and put them into his mouth, dust and all. The way he tore into the supper, and ate a second helping when Walter refilled his plate for him, told Hewey it was probably the only thing he had eaten all day. He was a chuckline rider, too old anymore to find any steady work, existing off of the kindness of others, and off of grudging charity when he found no kindness. Almost nobody in this country would turn an old man away hungry, but there were some who would make him pay a price in shame and humility.

Hewey had heard old stories about Boy Rasmussen. He had been a great cowboy in his prime, pushing herds up the trail from South Texas to the railroads in Kansas, and beyond to the Indian reservations in Wyoming and Montana. There had been a time, before the years and the bottle had robbed him of dependability, that he had bossed herds and been a man of substance and repute. But the years had not been benevolent. Whatever might once have been was gone now. All that remained was a shell, a lonely and pathetic remnant, a burned-out relic of another time so far behind him that even he must find it unreal when the ghosts went roaming through his mind, stirring the dead ashes of old campfires, speaking in voices long silent.

After supper he began talking, his narrative wandering aimlessly through some long-ago time, touching on names no one else remembered. Hewey noticed that Tommy listened intently, and even Cotton was drawn to the old man. He spoke of the agonies of that old war, and he spoke of roundups so far behind him that most of the other participants, man and beast, had long since gone back to dust. Somehow he seemed to slip away from reality then, and he was back in an earlier time. He got up from his chair, saying he had best be getting some sleep because he had to be up early in the morning to point the herd for Doan's Crossing on the Red; they had to make it to Dodge ahead of the other outfits, before the buyers could fill their early needs and lower the price.

Hewey watched him shuffle toward the barn. He looked worriedly at Walter. "They let that old man ride around by himself? It ain't safe for him."

Walter shook his head. "He'll remember where he's at when he has to. He drifts through here a couple of times a year. He's got a brother down on the border that he stays with some. He's got a sister up on the plains. He'll get there, whichever way he's goin'."

Eve came outside, holding the screen door open even after she was on the front step, so she could retreat into the house if Boy Rasmussen was still around. "Did he finally go?"

Walter told her he had gone to the barn to sleep.

"Good," she said. She turned her attention to her boys. "You'd have done better to've been studyin' your lessons instead of bein' out here listenin' to the crazy carryin'-on of a senile old man."

Tommy did not agree. "Folks say he was a wheel horse once."

"Maybe so, but he's just a *busted* wheel now. You boys can learn *one* thing from him. You can learn what happens to people who drift through life with no purpose and no direction . . . men wastin' their good years seekin' after the sinful pleasures of whisky and the flesh, playin' cards and consortin' with fallen women."

She looked directly at Hewey.

Hewey said defensively, "Eve, you've never seen me with no fallen women."

"Thank God I have been spared that sight. But I have seen you dally with whisky and cards. The rest is best left to imagination."

Tommy asked, "Mama, what is *consort*?"

She purposely didn't hear him. She kept her eyes on Hewey. "If you don't change your ways you'll wind up an old saddle bum like Boy Rasmussen."

Hewey folded his arms, a gesture of defense. "I've never

been a saddle bum. A bum begs somethin' for nothin'. Sure, I've been on the chuckline now and again, but I've always worked my way. Somebody feeds me or gives me a place to sleep, I always chop some wood or top off a bronc or somethin'. I never leave anybody poorer because he taken me in."

Eve fixed him with a triumphant stare. "At your age I don't suppose Boy Rasmussen did, either." She stood as if daring him to reply. Her point made, she retreated into the house, stopping only to call out, "You boys get ready for bed."

Tommy's question was still unanswered. "Uncle Hewey, what does *consort* mean?"

Hewey studied on that, looking in vain to his brother to step in with a better answer than his own. "I'll tell you some-day, when I'm old enough to know."

Walter got up and left, laughing to himself. Sitting alone, Hewey saw nothing left to do except go to bed too. He walked down to the shed where he had been rolling out his blankets at night. He decided to take them out into the open to get away from the smelly old man, but to his relief he heard the old man's snoring and found that he had spread his thin roll outside the shed, on the ground. That spared Hewey from having to do it.

He awakened in the morning to the first color in the east. Throwing off his blanket, he put on his hat, then his shirt and pants and lastly his boots. He walked to the open door of the shed and called out, "Old-timer, breakfast'll be ready directly."

But the old man was gone. Hewey stepped to the corral and looked for the poor black horse. It too was gone. Boy Rasmussen had arisen earlier than anybody and was on his way to Dodge, or to the Cheyenne reservation, or perhaps to pick up a herd in Mexico . . . whichever fancy might have crossed his fragile mind.

Hewey stared out into the empty land as the sun's first

good light spread across it. Whichever way he had ridden, Boy Rasmussen was a long time gone. Hewey stood a while staring, and an odd chill touched him.

At breakfast Eve remarked that Hewey was unusually quiet. He told her he was thinking about the tank-building job; it was almost finished. But the job had not crossed his mind except at the moment he needed an excuse.

Eve said uneasily, "I wish the old man hadn't left so early."

Hewey blinked. "I didn't think you liked him."

"I don't like to think of anybody, even an old saddle bum, ridin' across this big country hungry. You sure you didn't hear him get up and leave?"

"I never heard a thing."

Walter said, "He's of that old-timey breed, about as much Indian as white. They never did believe in makin' noise about anything they did. He comes quiet and he goes quiet."

Tommy put in, "Like a ghost, sort of."

Cotton ventured, "He *is* a ghost, of a kind. The world has gone off and left him."

Hewey frowned. "He's seen his hard times, but he's seen good ones too. I don't know but what I like *his* times better than the ones you're so hell-bent on takin' us into."

Walter Calloway sat bareback on the gray plow mule atop the fresh new tank dam and smiled as he studied the large basin Hewey had dug and smoothed just below the windmill. He had taken time away from his planting to ride over and look at the job.

Hewey said, "If it don't meet with your approval you're welcome to cut my wages half in two."

"It's a good job of work, big brother. I figured it would take you twice as long."

Hewey shrugged nonchalantly. "I can do anything I put my mind to."

"And your back." Walter nodded. "You've never been

lazy, Hewey. You could do anything, be anything you wanted."

"I *am* what I want to be."

"I'm sayin' you could have a place of your own. Things come easy to you when you want them. You could have a place like mine. Maybe better. All you'd have to do would be to make up your mind that's what you wanted. All you need is the wantin'." He paused hopefully. "I wish you would, while you still can."

Hewey stretched out a long strip of dirty cloth that had been a sleeve. "All I need right now is a shirt. This one is past salvation."

"You can have one of my shirts."

Hewey doubted that Walter had one to spare. "I been wantin' to go to town anyway. I promised Pierson and the Dutchman . . ."

Walter grumped, "You're awful good at changin' the subject. I was tryin' to talk serious to you about gettin' a place of your own."

"I know it, and I'm tryin' to head you off." Hewey looked up at the windmill that bore his name. "I still say it needs a coat of paint."

He hadn't been keeping track of time, but after supper that night he found on inspection of Eve's patent medicine calendar in the kitchen that the next day was Saturday. "I couldn't of timed it better. It'll be interestin' to see how much the town has grown."

Tommy laughed. "One blacksmith shop and three outhouses."

Eve turned quickly, her eyes scolding, "You don't talk thataway."

Hewey said, "Be careful, button, or pretty soon you'll be talkin' like me."

Tommy replied, "That'd be all right. Will you take me to town with you, Uncle Hewey?"

Hewey would have, but Walter said, "I need you boys at

home. There's still a right smart of field work needs doin'. I'll sure be glad when school is out."

Tommy didn't argue. His parents had trained him not to. But Hewey could see the boy's disappointment. He said, "Later on, when things get caught up around here, I'll take both of you boys with me on a trip someplace."

Cotton glanced at him over his book. He said nothing except with his eyes. He went back to his reading.

Tommy's eyes brightened. "You mean that, Uncle Hewey? When? Where we goin' to go?"

"I don't know, exactly. We'll figure somethin'. Maybe we'll go out to the Davis Mountains and down into the Big Bend. Or maybe we'll get us a boat and paddle it down the Pecos River plumb to the Rio Grande."

"I never have learned how to swim."

"Neither have I. But I wasn't figurin' on fallin' out of the boat."

Walter said, "I'd sure like to go on a trip like that myself." He was not joking. Eve cut a sharp, half-fearful glance at her husband.

Hewey said, "Why don't you, then? It'd be like old times."

A warmth came into Walter's face, lighting his eyes, deepening the laugh wrinkles at the corners of his mouth. "It would; it would for a fact. If I could ever see my way clear to get away for a little while . . ." He took a last sip from his coffee cup and found it cold. He got up and pushed his chair back under the pine table. "Long day tomorrow. We better all be gettin' some sleep." He walked out the door, bound for the little house out back.

The boys got up and shuffled around a little, drinking water from the dipper, Tommy wiping his mouth on his sleeve. "Good night, Uncle Hewey. We'll talk some more about that trip."

"You bet we will," Hewey answered, looking at Cotton and finding no belief in that nephew's eyes.

When the boys were gone, Hewey saw that Eve was

studying him with worried eyes. Uneasily he said, "I expect I'll go to bed too."

"No you won't. Not till I say somethin'." She looked away from him, frowning. "Hewey, I made up my mind I was goin' to stay in a good humor with you if it kills both of us. And I'm tryin' to, God knows. But I wish you wouldn't talk to Walter about goin' somewhere with you. It's bad enough talkin' foolishness to the boys that way, but *him* . . . I think it wouldn't take much to get him to go."

"It might be good for him if he did."

Her voice was brittle. "No, it wouldn't. It would just wake up a lot of old notions that it took years to put behind him. He's your brother, Hewey. He's got more of you in him than he has of me." She blinked away a hint of a tear. "He gave up a lot for me and these boys. Nobody but him and me know just how much. So I wish you would leave him alone. Please . . . leave him alone."

Most people who called it Upton City did so out of jest. They said it would have a foot and a half of snow on the Fourth of July before it ever became a city. Hewey couldn't see much change in it since he had left here. He couldn't even see the three new outhouses Tommy had spoken of. The town—what there was of it—was mostly single-story frame structures strung out in a casual line along a street that appeared to owe its original routing to a meandering buffalo trail. The story had been told that a trader had been on his way to set up a small post at Horsehead Crossing on the Pecos, but his heavily laden wagon had broken an axle here. There being no nearby timber big enough to hew a new axle, he had started selling goods out of the tarp-covered wagon. The story was probably a lie, but it made good telling. Hewey had never been one to let dull facts stand in the way of a good yarn.

Almost every house had a windmill of its own. Some

people said that was wasteful, but Hewey disagreed; there was wind enough for everybody.

Dominating the town was a square stone courthouse, two stories plus a tall, domed cupola. It was built in the style of a storybook castle but scaled down to fit the limited assessed valuations of a land-poor ranching county. Beside the courthouse stood the stone jail, built to a similar pattern but smaller, squattier and lacking the cupola. Nobody saw any need in having the jailhouse be as fancy as the courthouse; the society there was nothing to brag about.

The best building in town, apart from the courthouse, was the Tarpley bank. It was built of the same stone as the courthouse, quarried nearby to save as much freighting expense as possible. It was limited to a single story, not one foot wider or longer than it had to be. C. C. Tarpley stressed economy in all things, including space. The fanciest thing about it was the carving of the name and date it had been built: 1898.

Fat Gervin stood in the door, leaning lazily against the jamb. Hewey saw him first and gave him a fleeting wave, smiling as he remembered the black dog. Fat turned without reply and disappeared into the mysterious realm of ledgers and debentures and compound interest.

Hewey looked again at the name over the door's stone arch: TARPLEY BANK AND TRUST.

Damn little trust there on either side of the counter, he reflected.

A man called Hewey's name and came running out from the front gate of the wagonyard, causing Biscuit to shy and step sideways. "Hey, Hewey Calloway! We'd given you up for dead!"

The shout drew the attention of a barber and his customer in a small shop across the street. The barber stepped onto the porch to holler at Hewey. His customer came out with the white barber's cloth still tied around his neck, lifting and falling with the breeze. Biscuit did not like that cloth at all.

Hewey didn't know who to go howdy and shake with first, so he stayed where he was, in the middle of the street. They all came out to him. In a minute others came from other stores and shops, and they clustered there on the street until big Blue Hannigan's freight wagons, two hooked in tandem, came along needing the room.

"Hewey Calloway," Hannigan called, "you're blockin' the wheels of commerce."

But the wheels of commerce stopped right there as Blue got down to join the others in a drink at the Dutchman's to celebrate Hewey Calloway and Fat Gervin and the boys' black dog. The story had gotten around.

Hewey looked back toward the bank. "You reckon Fat Gervin's heard it?"

Blue Hannigan spat a brown stream of tobacco juice at a curious pup ten feet away and made a near miss. "Bound to have by now. There's always some slack-jaw runnin' to tell everything he hears."

It seemed to Hewey for a while that the only commerce in town was probably the Dutchman's, for almost everybody he knew in Upton City seemed to drop into the little saloon to shake hands with Hewey, recall a yarn or two out of old times and demand a new one or two to take along. Many a lie was told there in the space of an hour or so, and one or two stories that Hewey felt were mostly the truth. He made a show of drinking with everybody, but in reality he drank only a little. It was a quirk of the Dutchman's character that although he sold the stuff, he had the greatest respect for his poorest customers. Gradually the well-wishers drifted back to their own business, leaving Schneider and Hewey alone in the long, narrow room. The Dutchman had said little. He said nothing now. Friendship didn't have to be proven in conversation. Hewey leaned his elbows on the dark-stained bar, staring at a row of engravings nailed to the wall beside and above the mirror. In lots of bars the pictures would be of women, sometimes barefoot all the way. In the Dutchman's bar they were of racehorses. Schneider knew what was important in this world. It was said that he had been married once.

The room seemed to darken. A big man had come up to the open door and stood in it. Hewey blinked against the sunlight that haloed the man. He recognized Sheriff Wes Wheeler.

The sheriff said, "Mornin', Hewey."

Hewey sensed that Wheeler was not there to take a drink or to visit with the Dutchman. A little of the glow went out of him. "Mornin', Wes."

The sheriff came up beside Hewey at the bar. "Hewey Calloway, if wealth could be measured in friends, you'd be a richer man than C. C. Tarpley."

Hewey could see that the sheriff's thin smile had no depth. The eyes were coldly serious. He replied, "It is, and I am."

Wheeler turned to Schneider. "Dutch, you reckon you could go outside for a smoke or somethin'? I got a little business to talk to Hewey about."

Schneider gave Hewey a worried glance. Hewey knew the Dutchman was guessing there was trouble over Fat Gervin and the dog. "Hewey," Schneider said, "if you need help I am your witness. I saw it all, and there was nothing."

"There's no trouble," Wheeler assured the Dutchman. "It's a private matter."

Schneider laid down his bar rag and walked outside. The sheriff watched until he was sure he would not be heard. "Hewey, when you make friends you do a real good job of it. But when you make an enemy you do a good job of that too." From his pocket he pulled a sheet of paper, folded many times. "You'll want to take a look at that, then burn it."

Hewey had a good idea what it was before he unfolded it. It was a fugitive notice, printed on a real press and everything. It was the first time he could remember ever seeing his name in print. Well, almost his name. Big block letters read HUGH HOLLOWAY.

A cold feeling settled in his stomach, but he tried to cover it with a surface grin. He doubted he was fooling Wheeler. "Marshal up yonder still hasn't gotten my name right."

"He will, sooner or later." Wheeler's face was deeply furrowed. "I thought you was goin' to visit a day or two and then leave."

"I been buildin' a stock tank out at that new windmill."

"You through with it yet?"

"Finished yesterday."

Wheeler stared at Hewey's glass, the only one left on the bar. It was full, and had been for half an hour. Impulsively he picked it up. "Hewey, do you mind?" The sheriff downed the drink and set the empty glass solidly back down on the bar. He seemed disappointed that the drink didn't make his task any easier.

"I ain't fixin' to tell you what to do, Hewey. You're a grown man, and then some. But if it was me, I'd get my good-byes said and travel on."

"I'd hate to go now. You know, even Eve has been in a good humor most of the time."

"Them folks up at New Prosperity ain't. At least not that marshal. I have a feelin' that if he was to come across you he'd shoot first and then ask you to surrender."

"If he wanted to, he could find me no matter where I went."

"Maybe. But he'll find you for sure if you stay around here. I don't know that there's anything I can do for you if he comes. I'd even have to help him if he had the right papers and asked me to. That would distress me, Hewey."

Hewey stared at the racehorses. He wished Wheeler hadn't drunk up all the whiskey. "I never like to cause distress to my friends. But dammit, Wes, this thing has been blowed up out of all reason. There wasn't nothin' to it, hardly, just a few words and one little punch. Didn't even skin my knuckles to speak of. All I hurt was his pride."

"That's all some people have, is pride. Generally the ones who take on over it most are the ones that have got the least to be proud of. Better you'd broken his head open than to've left him lookin' foolish in his own town."

"I just don't like people tryin' to run my life for me, tellin' me what to do. I don't do that to other people, and I don't want them doin' it to me. When I go someplace it's because I want to, and when I leave it's because I want to."

"I'm not crowdin' you, Hewey. At least I'm tryin' not to."

"It ain't you, it's *them*." He felt somehow trapped. He doubled his fist and beat it against the bar.

Hopefully the sheriff asked, "That mean you're fixin' to leave?"

Hewey had hit the bar too hard. He rubbed the aching hand. "It means I'll think about it."

"All right, Hewey. I just don't want you on my conscience."

"No reason I should be. Whatever I decide, it'll be my own doin', not yours."

The sheriff nodded. "I've had my say." He reached over and touched Hewey's tattered sleeve. A faint smile compromised his solemnity. "Go or stay, if I was you I think I'd get me a new shirt."

Pierson Phelps' general mercantile was the largest store in town. It was a simple frame structure decorated by a liberal application of gingerbread trim along the top of the porch. Canned and boxed goods were stacked high on a shelf inside the window, but Phelps never moved anything out onto the porch for display. It was too much work to move it back in at night. The sign out front was a small one, the letters hardly six inches high: *Phelps General Mercantile and Sundries.* He saw no need in ostentatious advertising; everybody in town knew who he was and what he sold. He also had the post office, and that fact was noted on a separate sign even smaller than the other. Anybody who couldn't find the post office probably couldn't read a letter anyway.

The old merchant stood a little way inside the door, apron around his broad waist, dark sleeve protectors pulled way up on his thick arms. He wore a small black bow tie, which always seemed to bob up and down as he talked. "I heard you were in town an hour ago, Hewey. Thought you had forgotten me."

"Not hardly. Just taken me a little longer than I figured on to get around. I don't suppose you'd have a shirt that'd fit me? Not one of them fancy two-dollar Sunday-meetin' shirts. Somethin' even a broke cowpuncher can afford."

Pierson narrowed one eye and shut the other, studying Hewey's build. He walked behind a counter on the drygoods side, where the bolt cloth was stacked, and pulled out a drawer. He poked around in it a minute and brought out a simple white shirt with gray stripes. "Normally I get a dollar apiece for these, but seein' it's you I'll let you have it for six bits. I'll even throw in a bow tie."

"Any cheaper without the tie?"

"I've already given you my preacher rate, and you're no preacher. But I'll keep the tie and give you a sack of barber-pole candy to take home to the boys."

Hewey took the shirt, felt of the plain cotton material and decided it was too high at the price. Many a time he had worked a full, hard day for a lot less than six bits. But money was getting to where it wasn't worth anything anymore.

"Merchant takes all the best of it," he lamented. "But I reckon I'll settle for what I can get."

"It's the cost of labor that makes everything so high," Pierson sympathized. "You wouldn't believe what some people earn, workin' in factories back east. They're ridin' this country down to ruin."

That was how things had always been as far back as Hewey could remember. Price of cattle was always too low, and price of everything else was always too high. "I'm goin' to find me a corner back yonder and put this new shirt on," he said.

Pierson pointed vaguely with his sharp chin, somewhere toward the rear of the room.

The post office section was along the south wall, a little more than halfway back in the store. Hewey couldn't remember that he had ever received a letter out of it, but it was comforting to know he could if anybody ever wrote to him. He went around the back side of that section, where he wouldn't be seen from the front of the store, and he took off what was left of the ragged shirt that had known hard duty almost continuously all winter and spring. His long-handled underwear wasn't a lot better, but it had one virtue: nobody could see it. He wasn't going to buy himself a new set. Pierson would probably want an extra four bits, at least.

Money didn't mean much to Hewey, but he saw no sense in throwing it away.

He didn't realize how long it could take him to put on a shirt. He hadn't figured on the thing having so many pins. Every time he thought he had found them all, another one stuck him. He was so intent on the pins that he didn't hear the wooden floor squeak under someone's feet.

He heard a woman say, "Woops!"

By reflex he turned, the shirt in his hand. The schoolteacher stood there, eyes wide in surprise. Again by reflex, Hewey brought up the new shirt to try to hide his chest, which the long underwear was doing anyway. "Pardon me, ma'am," he managed, feeling his face burn red.

"Pardon me, Mr. Calloway." She turned her back on him.

He hurriedly pulled the shirt on. A pin he had missed was scratching his neck, but he wouldn't have taken the shirt off again for a box of them, the two-dollar kind. He quickly shoved the shirttail in and buttoned his britches. "I'm decent now," he said uneasily, feeling around the collar but unable to locate the irritating pin. He decided he had rather put up with it than make a show of the thing.

She had moved around to the other side of the post office section and was still turned away from him. "I'm sorry if I embarrassed you, Mr. Calloway. I had no idea you were there. Mr. Phelps must have stepped outside somewhere."

Hewey had wondered why Phelps hadn't headed her off. "My fault," he replied. "I ought to've gone out back to the . . ." He caught himself. One did not speak to a lady about such things as outhouses. Their existence was only privately recognized, never publicly acknowledged. They were, between the sexes, in the nature of an open secret.

She said, "I was just trying to see if I might have a letter. Mr. Phelps always puts them in that box back there."

Hewey could see so many open boxes, letters sticking out of at least half, that he had no idea which one she meant. "Show me where it's at and I'll get it for you."

"Oh no, I wouldn't want to cause you any trouble."

"No trouble atall. I can reach in there easy and get it."

"That's not the kind of trouble I mean. It's against the law for you or me to touch it so long as it's behind the postmaster's counter."

"It's your letter, ain't it?"

"Not until Mr. Phelps hands it to me himself."

With his eye Hewey roughly measured the width of the counter and the reach to the boxes behind it. For the letter it would be a very short trip. "It'll be the same letter then that it is right now. Seems to me like I'd save Pierson Phelps a little work and you a little time."

"I know the rule looks silly, but it is the rule."

"Looks to me like if they want people to pay attention to the rules, the rules ought to make sense."

She smiled. "You have the logic, Mr. Calloway, but Washington has the law. I am afraid I have been put in the position of the devil's advocate."

He didn't know what she meant by that, but it sounded vaguely wicked. And her a schoolteacher . . .

She asked, "Have you always been such a rebel, Mr. Calloway?"

"That war was over a good while before I was born. But my old daddy was in the Confederate Army."

Her eyes seemed to be laughing a little, but he had the feeling that she was not really laughing at him. At least, the laughter did not embarrass or anger him. She said, "I wonder how you ever got along in the Army, with all the regulations you had to obey?"

"There was times when I thought sure I was goin' to wind up in that army jailhouse, but seemed like they always found someplace they needed me worse." He stared at her thoughtfully. "How'd you know I was in the Army?"

"Tommy told me. He has told me a great deal about you, as a matter of fact. He said you were in Cuba, right there beside Teddy Roosevelt."

Hewey squirmed. "Well, I was in Cuba, all right. I wouldn't say I was all that close to the President."

"Tommy told me you were in the charge up San Juan Hill, showing Roosevelt the way."

He felt his face going red again. Where in the world had the boy ever gotten a yarn like that? "You got to watch that button, ma'am. He's inclined now and again to exaggerate."

She smiled. "He's a good boy. They're both good boys. You can be proud to have them for kin." The smile faded, and the laughter gradually went out of her eyes. She seemed to be looking past him a moment, leaving this time and this place for somewhere out of memory or out of imagination, possibly some place lost. She caught herself and looked back at him, but the glow did not return to her eyes. Whatever ghost had crossed her mind, he had taken the glow with him. She said, "I've been interested in Cuba for a long time. I'd like someday to have you tell me about your experiences there."

"They didn't really amount to much."

"They would be interesting to me." She looked away from him again, toward the front windows and the sunlight on the street. She said, "I don't suppose you've seen Alvin Lawder-milk?"

"Not since Sunday, out at the place."

"He has talked about you a great deal. *Everybody* talks about you a great deal."

He grimaced. "I hope you don't listen to everything they say."

"They all speak well of you." She reconsidered. "Mostly well, anyway. One gentleman down at the bank might be an exception."

"I hoped you'd forgot about that."

The smile came again. "I'll never forget it. I'll be eternally grateful to you."

He frowned. "I get the feelin' Fat Gervin done somethin' to you."

"He didn't, but he would have. His intention was clear enough."

Resentment flared in him. She *was* a handsome woman, he decided. He could understand how a man of Fat's character could get to thinking things that should never cross the mind of a married man. Momentarily those thoughts came to Hewey too. But he quickly put them aside, for this was a lady, and a gentleman did not compromise a lady, even in his mind. He had no regret for what he had done to Fat. He was sorry only that Miss Renfro had seen it.

"It was a fool stunt I done."

"Not at all. It fitted him so well." She seemed ready to turn away, but she said, "Alvin Lawdermilk has been talking about how much he would like to have you come over to his place and help him break some horses and mules."

"He told me, but I been needin' to get on down the road."

"He's short-handed. All he has is Julio Valdez, and it's too much for just the two of them. He could really use your help."

Hewey shoved his hands into his pockets. In one he felt

the folded fugitive notice the sheriff had given him. "I wisht I could oblige, but I got a job waitin' for me out west . . ."

"And a job here, if you want it."

Pierson Phelps came in the front door, looking around. He spied Spring Renfro, and his round face lighted up like a barn-dance lantern on a Saturday night. "Miss Renfro! I just saw your paint horse tied outside. I hope you haven't waited long."

"Not at all, I've had a pleasant visit with Mr. Calloway. I came to see if I might have any mail. I've been expecting a letter from my sister."

"Yes, a letter came for you yesterday." Phelps stepped inside the little cubicle that was the post office and reached up into one of the boxes. Hewey grimaced. He could have reached it, and Miss Renfro could have read it by now.

Phelps handed her the letter. She glanced at the handwriting. "It's from her, all right."

Phelps came out from behind the counter and leaned his heavy body against it. "School's about out. I suppose you'll be leavin' us soon for the summer?"

She shook her head. "No. My sister is all the family I have anymore. She has her own home, and her own family. I'd be company for the first few days. After that I'd be a burden. Cora Lawdermilk has asked me to stay and help her see after her old mother."

Phelps smiled. "That's fine. We've gotten used to havin' you around here. We'd miss you if you left."

"And I'd miss this place." She moved to the front door. Phelps and Hewey followed her. She paused and looked out into the street. "Odd, the hold this West Texas country takes on a person. First time I saw what I had come to, I hated it. I was used to trees and tall green grass and running streams. All I saw here was open country and desert. Or so I thought. But it's grown on me. I don't know if I could ever go back to the piney woods again."

"You shouldn't ever have to. If some eligible bachelor here doesn't come along and grab you up, I'll be awful disappointed in the whole bunch of them." He glanced at Hewey.

Hewey felt his face redden once more.

She walked out to her horse, tethered at a rail. She untied him and stood a moment, looking at the sidesaddle, then glancing back at the store.

Pierson Phelps gave Hewey a push. "What're you standin' there for, cowboy? She needs a lift up."

Hewey had been thinking about it, but he had wanted to make up his *own* mind. Stiffly he stepped down from the porch and gave her a boost, careful not to touch her anywhere except the foot. Even being close to her flustered him a little.

Once she had her right leg in place over the horn, and her ankles properly covered by her long riding skirt, she thanked Hewey. "I hope you'll keep in mind what I said about Alvin Lawdermilk. He *does* need your help. And it would be nice to see a new face." She smiled and rode up the street on her paint horse.

Hewey stared after her. He had decided she wasn't really so old as he had judged the first time he saw her. He doubted she was past thirty. Not much past thirty, anyway.

Phelps said, "You could do a lot worse."

"Worse than what?"

"She's a real nice lady."

Hewey could see no argument with that. "Seems like it."

"I'll admit she's not the greatest beauty in the world."

Hewey turned and challenged him. "Show me one in Upton City who looks better."

The way the storekeeper smiled, Hewey suspected he had stepped into a trap. Phelps said, "She's got no gentleman callers, far as I've heard."

"She still ain't got one."

Phelps regarded him with amusement. Hewey was sure now about that trap. The old man said, "I believe you'd better have *two* shirts. Tell you what I'll do—I'll give you the second for just four bits. And I believe you'll be needin' that bow tie after all."

6

Biscuit had never cared particularly for the Lawdermilk ranch. A horse, like a cat, prefers the familiar, and the Lawdermilk headquarters was always unpredictable, always a spooky menagerie. If blue-gray guinea hens were not picking and gossiping their way across the barnyard, a peafowl was spreading its feathers and screeching. A handful of undisciplined Spanish goats always had free run of the place, crawling through corral fences at will, jumping up into the horse troughs and helping themselves to feed that rightfully belonged to their betters. The noise was often distracting. Because Alvin Lawdermilk raised horses and mules to sell, there was always a certain amount of snorting and bawling and shouting, of young broncs threshing and running against ropes and trying to tear down the wooden fences to which they were secured. Worst of all, perhaps, were the numerous burros. As a well-traveled horse, supposedly more sophisticated than most, Biscuit had never conceded much merit in that inferior, intractable breed. His unfortunate encounter with Cotton's burro had only deepened his ingrained prejudice.

The feed was good, but after all other considerations were taken into account, it was a degrading place for a patrician.

Hewey had no such problem. He had always had a happy facility for adaptability into any environment where the chuck was good and the society congenial. Both conditions were met at the Lawdermilk ranch. As a result of his own natural generosity, aided by Cora's insistence, Alvin had built a free-style one-story frame house of mixed architecture that rambled over a considerable plot of ground in the general shape of an L, with a broad and breezy open gallery all the way around it. Cora had intended it for a large flock of children, which she never had. So she alternately babied Alvin and chastised him, much as she would have done to the sons who were never born to her. The two of them had long shared the big house with her aging mother, who sipped copious quantities of Prickly Ash Bitters and spent most of her waking hours talking. She could get around on a cane when she had to, but she usually preferred sitting in a wheel chair of fiendish mobility. Her treatment of Alvin was the same as Cora's only to a point: she never babied him, but she chastised him often. Alvin put up with it with the patience of one of his burros.

In recent years, lacking children but not lacking a love for them, the Lawdermilks had provided a country schoolhouse at their headquarters to accommodate the school-age youngsters who lived on neighboring ranches and farms, too far from Upton City to ride there and back every day. They also provided room and board for whatever person happened to be teaching. Except for the first one, that had always been a woman. The man teacher who had opened the school had made the unfortunate mistake of finding too many of Alvin's secret whisky caches one idle Sunday afternoon. He had done considerable damage to the schoolhouse and had left his opinion of various and sundry local citizens scrawled on the blackboard in correctly spelled but awesome English to greet his pliable young charges in his absence Monday morning. Even students who had never been able to memorize a line of Shakespeare or Keats seemed to have learned that day's lesson by heart on only a few minutes' surprised scrutiny. Now, some years later, it was often repeated verbatim on festive occasions by students and former students who still couldn't remember the opening line to the balcony scene.

Unlike some ranches where Hewey had worked, the hired help always ate in the main house with the owners, at the same table and all. That even included Julio Valdez, who on many places would have been expected to cook for himself, or at best to have filled his plate and to have retired to the gallery to eat alone while everyone else sat at the long plain table in the dining room. Julio made it a point to sit at the far end of the table, well away from Old Lady Faversham, Alvin's sharp-eyed mother-in-law. She could remember back almost to the time of the Alamo.

Hewey always sat by Julio, not so much to demonstrate his liberalism as to keep away from the old lady too. Her opinion of footloose cowboys was roughly the same as her opinion of Mexicans; she lumped both in a general category of undesirables. Some days Hewey and Julio had to move over and share that category with Alvin. The old lady had never forgiven him for proving her wrong thirty years ago when she declared he could never support her daughter.

Nothing the old lady said could offset the fact that Cora Lawdermilk was a splendid cook. Hewey wouldn't have told Eve for all the money in C. C. Tarpley's bank, but Cora's biscuits were better than Eve's, and good biscuits to Hewey were at least half of the meal. Old Lady Faversham could prattle on to her mean old heart's content and say anything she pleased as long as there were plenty of biscuits on a platter within Hewey's easy reach. And there always were. He didn't have to look at her anyway, more than once or twice a meal. Mostly, when he could steal glances without her catching him, he looked at Spring Renfro. She always sat across the table from him, wearing her clean and simple teacher dresses in just the right combination of gentility and poverty to please a country school board. Times, when he looked at her, his mind began involuntarily to stray from a gentlemanly plane, and he would have to force himself to think about horses and mules.

Evenings, Hewey would sit on the gallery with Alvin and swap windies. Sometimes these set-tos took on the nature of a contest, but Hewey had a definite advantage because he had traveled a great deal more. Alvin had been tied down physically, though not in spirit, by the struggle to build a respectable ranch for himself and a comfortable if not excessive standard of living for his wife. He was a man of contrasts, a free soul trapped within a body that was tied to one piece of ground. That soul sought its release in great stacks of books, magazines and newspapers which he devoured with the appetite of a lion. He could at almost any given time name all the crowned heads of Europe, unless the urgency of the horse and mule business had made him miss reading about some overnight revolution. He could describe in some detail all the major cities of the world, though the largest he had ever seen with his own eyes was Kansas City, to which he traveled in the caboose of a cattle train. Now and again, when his soul could not be satisfied by his reading of faraway places, it sought refuge in the bottles he had stashed liberally all over the ranch. Since Hewey had been here Alvin had found little need to drink. His questing spirit found vicarious release through the stories Hewey told him.

Sometimes when Cora felt like it she would sit down in the evening at the upright piano in the parlor and play from the reams of sheet music she had accumulated over the years. Hewey had flipped through the stack and found such titles as "'Tis Not Always Bullets That Kill," or "Do Not Tell Her I Am Bad," or "Please, Sir, Don't Ask Me Again." He could tell that Pierson Phelps always kept her supplied with the latest. Occasionally Spring Renfro would stand beside her and sing with Cora the lyrics to songs like "Is She Only a Friend After All?" and "For the Love of a True Woman's Heart."

Hewey felt himself fortunate to be exposed to so much culture.

At bedtime he would walk down near the barn to a small frame building that served double duty as a cowboy bunkhouse and a shed for storing windmill tools and the like. The walls had cracks he could almost throw a cat through, but that was something of an asset in warm summertime. He didn't intend to be here in the winter.

He shared the room with Julio. To some people this would have appeared an unseemly display of racial equality, but Hewey had a little the best of it. He slept on a steel cot, while Julio's was a less sturdy one of wood and canvas. The proprieties were met.

Sunup never caught Alvin Lawdermilk in bed, or anybody else on the place except Old Lady Faversham. While Cora fixed breakfast, Julio would milk the two Jersey cows and scatter grain for the pampered flock of Barred Plymouth Rock hens. Hewey would saddle the night horse and ride out into the small fenced trap to bring in the mounts the men would be needing for the morning's work. Alvin would be stomping around in the corrals, putting out bundle-feed and oats. He had a field of redtop cane stretching just beyond the barn. In that field he and his help would break and train those horses and mules intended for a lifetime of work to the plow or wagon. In this manner he was able to get some farm work out of Hewey without calling it by its true name. As long as the main object was to break stock, Hewey could tolerate the plow. But if the plow itself became the admitted object, he would ask for his time and move on down the road. So had many another cowboy and horsebreaker before him.

Alvin Lawdermilk was always careful in the way he named his priorities.

A rancher buying "rough-broke" horses might not think to ask, but it would have been to his interest to have done so, whether the bronc buster had been working by the day or was paid by the number of horses he rode. When Hewey was being paid by the bronc, he usually considered one ready to go after being saddled and ridden six or seven times. If he was being paid by the day—as at Alvin's place—he was more likely to put a horse through nine or ten saddlings.

His bronc-riding sessions caused Spring Renfro some difficulty. One morning he had several broncs hackamored and tied to fence posts outside the round corral in which he would ride them. From his rough observation point atop a pitching sorrel gelding he saw eighteen or twenty youngsters spill out of the little white-painted schoolhouse for morning recess. Most of the boys and some of the girls came running toward the corrals to watch the show. Several rushed heedlessly past the tied broncs. This startled the young horses, causing them to thresh against the strong hackamore ropes.

"You kids watch out for them horses," Hewey yelled. "They'll kick the whey out of you!"

He was too busy staying in the saddle to do anything more about the problem. And because the Lord watches out for kids, fools and drunks, nobody got hurt. They perched on the corral fence, watching. Hewey let the pony have his head and gave the kids the exhibition they had wanted to see. When the sorrel had finished pitching and set in to running for all it was worth around and around the corral, lathering itself with sweat, Hewey was able to pick out Tommy sitting on the fence beside the nester boy Lester. Lester was twanging that infernal jew's-harp as if he thought the show needed musical accompaniment. Hewey looked around for Cotton as best he could, considering that he still had a double handful with the sorrel bronc. He could not pick him out of the crowd of kids sitting on the fence like blackbirds.

He'd be here if I was driving an automobile, Hewey thought, feeling a touch of resentment. But any coffeepot polisher and ribbon clerk could learn to drive an automobile. It took somebody special to fork a wiry bronc and keep one leg on each side.

The sorrel finally ran itself down, and Hewey began pulling its head first to one side, then to the other, giving the first lesson in reining. He could hear a bell ringing and in a moment of comparative quiet looked across to the schoolhouse. Spring Renfro stood on its tiny porch with the bell in her hand, calling for the youngsters to come back. A few melted away, mostly girls, but a majority of the boys clung to the fence.

"You buttons better get back over there, or she'll whip you-all and then come after me," Hewey told them.

In a little while all the chicks had returned to the nest. Miss Renfro walked to the corral by herself, having put the youngsters to studying whatever subjects were pertinent to their respective ages and grades. Hewey saw her coming just as he was about to climb aboard a stocking-legged black that had a wicked gleam in its left eye and a wicked kick in its left hind foot. Julio was earing the pony down. "Let him go, Hooley!" Hewey hollered as he jammed his right foot into the stirrup. The bronc bawled and went straight up.

Because the teacher had been so unfortunate as to miss the other show, Hewey was determined to make up by giving her a better one than he had given the kids. The dust was heavy and the action thick for two or three minutes until the black began wearing down. Hewey put on a show that he thought would have impressed Teddy Roosevelt, but it didn't seem to impress Miss Renfro. She stood outside the fence showing more of impatience than amusement. When Hewey finally dismounted she moved up against the fence and peered at him through the dust.

"Mr. Calloway, I think you and I are going to have to come to some accommodation."

"How can I accommodate you, ma'am?"

"I realize you have your job to do, but I also have mine.

For the few days that school is still to be in session, could I prevail on you to find something less spectacular to do during recess?"

After that, Hewey made it a point at that time of day to be out of sight, either in a field pairing a bronc mule to a gentle one and working them to a plow, or in a far corral tying hackamored broncs to Alvin's gentle burros and turning them out to run in the open pastures. There the stubborn little creatures soon taught them the rope was to be obeyed.

At the supper table several days later, Spring Renfro thanked him. "After tomorrow," she said, "I'll not interfere with your schedule anymore. In fact, in honor of the last day of school it might be a nice present to the boys if you *did* put on a little show. I'll let the final recess be a long one."

The black bronc was still unregenerated, still a sure bet for a show even after several saddles. Hewey saved him for recess time. The entire class walked down to the round corral, including Cotton and the teacher. Despite several days of work, Hewey and Julio still had to tie up one of the black's hind feet to be able to get the saddle on him. His back was still humped as if a watermelon had been placed under the blanket. Hewey drew the cinch as tight as he could and untied the rope while Julio took a death grip on the pony's ears.

Tommy yelled from the fence, "That old horse is goin' to throw you."

Hewey said, "Boy, I ain't never been throwed in my life." He looked up at the railbirds as he gripped the saddle horn with his right hand and the heavy rein and a healthy piece of mane with the left. "I'm fixin' to show you buttons somethin' you'll never find in no joggerfy lesson." He swung up, and Julio let go, stepping quickly back out of the way. The youngsters hollered and cheered.

Either the black had saved back a few tricks or he had learned something new. His first jump set Hewey a little off balance, cracking his tailbone painfully against the sharp edge of the snakeskin-covered cantle. He kept his chin down to try to prevent getting his neck popped by the pony's fast twisting and changing of direction, by the hard jarring as all four feet hit the ground at once. It was an old adage in cow country that there never was a bronc that couldn't be rode, and never was a cowboy that couldn't be throwed. Hewey realized after the third jump that he was about to bear personal witness to the latter proposition. It was no longer a question of whether, but only of how.

The *how* was an ignominious belly buster, out over the right shoulder and down to the ground with a dull thud that took most of his breath and much of his pride. He held still, partly because he didn't think the black would step on him except by accident but mostly because he was so numb he couldn't move much anyway. The youngsters' cheering had turned to laughter. Kids, Hewey thought, were bloodthirsty at heart.

Julio's first responsibility was to catch the horse, not to help Hewey to his feet. Hewey pushed up onto his hands and knees and felt around for his hat. It lay just ahead of him, well stomped by one of the black's hoofs. He got to his feet, dusted the hat on his britches leg and pulled it back down over his head.

The first thing he saw was that Cotton was walking back to the schoolhouse by himself.

Hewey's face reddened. *I let him down again.*

The smart-aleck Lester said, "You showed us what not to do. When you goin' to show us the rest?"

Hewey had in mind a little different demonstration, and it involved that jew's-harp. But this was not the time or place. "I'm just lettin' him keep a little confidence in himself. You don't want to plumb kill a horse's spirit."

Julio brought the black back and eared him down. Hewey swung into the saddle again, for it was a cardinal rule of the trade that you never let a horse throw you and get away

with it; that was what created outlaws. This time he rode
the black to a standstill. The pony stood heaving, the sweat
running down his hide and dripping off onto the ground.
Only the flesh had been exhausted; the fighting spirit was
still intact. He reached around and tried to bite a chunk out
of Hewey's leg. Only the heavy leather chaps saved Hewey
from a nasty set of tooth marks.

He said to Julio, "If he can't throw you off he'll pull you
off with his teeth, a mouthful at a time. He'll make somebody a good horse one of these days."

He found the kids still talking more of his fall than of
his final victory. Sourly he remembered something he had
heard one of the Miller brothers say while he had his short-
lived job with the 101 Ranch Wild West Show: "Those
people don't pay to see you ride; they pay in hopes of seein'
you get yourself killed."

He thought it remarkable how young they became corrupted.

Spring Renfro began calling the students down off of the
fence and back to the classroom. "Show is over," she said.
"It's time for a little more learning before I turn you loose
for the summer."

She waited at the fence, and Hewey sensed that she wanted
to speak to him. Acutely aware of his disgrace, he reluctantly
shuffled over there, hat in his hand. "They sure didn't get
much learnin' out here," he conceded.

"Perhaps they did." She smiled. "Humility is a valuable
lesson for anybody."

"Well, I *am* humiliated, that's a natural fact."

"But not too humiliated for some ice cream after a while,
I hope. I'm giving the children a picnic at dinnertime, up
under the trees."

"A bronc-ridin' show and then a picnic? They won't learn
much today."

"If they haven't learned it by now, one last day won't
make any difference. You'll be there, won't you?"

"Sure. I'll fall off a horse any day for a dish of ice cream."

It turned out that the invitation hadn't been necessary. Cora Lawdermilk didn't serve dinner in the house anyway. Everybody ate beneath the trees with the children. Hewey sensed that Miss Renfro had given him the invitation as a special gesture, perhaps to soothe his wounded pride. He didn't know how good she might be at reading, writing and geography, but she knew a lot about human nature that hadn't all come from books. And she had learned it young, for he was convinced by now that she lacked a whole lot being thirty.

After the supper dishes had been washed and put away that night she came out onto the porch where Hewey sat with Alvin Lawdermilk, listening to the night birds setting up a contest out beyond the town road. "May I sit down with you-all?" she asked.

Both Hewey and Alvin got up quickly and offered her their cane-bottomed chairs. She motioned for them to sit back down and dragged up another for herself. She made a few preliminary comments upon the loveliness of the night and the fullness of the moon, observations with which Hewey found no quarrel. Abruptly she said, "I want to thank you, Mr. Calloway."

He tried in vain to remember anything he had done for her, other than offer her his chair.

She said, "I know how badly you felt about being thrown off in front of all those children. But I appreciate the way you got up and went right back to the job at hand. The children don't all realize it, but they learned a valuable lesson."

"What? That a cowboy looks foolish lyin' in the dirt with all the breath knocked out of him?"

"No, that one doesn't just quit when he is faced with a reversal. One gets up and tries again until he has succeeded."

"I don't know if I'll ever succeed with that black bronc. He's pretty strong-minded."

"You'll win. You'll be a better man for having done it, and he'll be a better horse for having fought so hard."

Hewey rubbed his shoulder. He didn't think there was a joint in his body that didn't ache. "I hope I'll be a better man than I feel like right now."

"You're a better man than you know, Mr. Calloway."

Cora Lawdermilk pushed the screen door open a little and poked her head out. "Alvin, you've got some bookkeepin' work to be doin'."

Alvin blinked. "I don't remember any bookkeepin' work."

"Well, you've got some. It's waited long enough."

Alvin stood up, stoked his pipe and seemed confused for a minute while he stared at Hewey and the teacher. His confusion left him. "By George, I do remember." He walked into the house, leaving the two sitting alone.

Hewey found the teacher was studying him. He cut his gaze back to some forlorn-looking and bewildered young broncs staked out on the prairie, obscured by the deepening dusk. "Kind of hard on them. First time they've ever been tied up thataway. They've lost their freedom, and they don't know what to make of it."

"It's something most people go through too. You've never lost *your* freedom, have you, Mr. Calloway?"

"No. I've given up lots of other things at times, but that's one thing I've made it a point to keep."

"I guess you've run on to horses that never would give up, either."

"I've seen some break their necks against a fence. I've seen a few just lay down and die rather than give up to the rope and the saddle."

"You strike me as a man who might do the same thing, in your own way."

"I don't know. I've never had to face up to it."

"You've never been tempted to? Not for a home, a piece of land . . . a woman?"

"Tempted, sure. I've been tempted by a good many

things. I've given in more often than I'd want to admit to a lady. But that's one temptation I've always managed to shed in time."

He saw the same fleeting sadness in her face that he had seen that day in Phelps' store. She said, "I knew somebody once, a lot like you . . ." She looked off into the night. When her gaze came back to him, she had put on the smile again. "I hope you never change."

"I don't intend to. I'm satisfied the way everything is."

"Even though everybody seems to be trying to change you?"

"The way I live doesn't affect anybody but me."

"Eve . . . Walter . . . the boys . . . they all worry about you. What happens to you *does* affect them."

"There ain't nothin' goin' to happen to me."

"It could have today. That horse might've killed you."

"It didn't. Been a many a one tried."

"One may, someday."

"You're startin' to talk like Eve."

"I don't mean to intrude where I have no business. And I'm not trying to change you. I just want to point out that you mean something to a lot of good people, and they worry about you."

Hewey stood up. "If I tried to change, I'd be like one of them colts out yonder, staked to stumps and logs and old wagon wheels. I'd be lost and fightin' my head like them. And sooner or later I'd probably break my neck hittin' a fence. Folks have got to take me like I am or leave me alone."

Hewey was too busy during the week to visit his brother and the rest of the family. On Sundays, right after the women got home from church and served the noon meal, he would hitch a pair of mules to an old wagon and head out across the country. It was partly for pleasure, partly for work, because one of the mules was always a bronc being broken to the harness. The other, for balance, would be relatively gentle and stable. One mule could not run fast or far if the other did not choose to go.

The third Sunday he was there, Hewey had Julio help him hitch up an eye-rolling brown mule that had already seen a couple of training sessions in the cane patch but was a long way from being ready to deliver on Alvin's contract to the Texas & Pacific Railroad for working stock. He intended to match this one to a placid old gray known as Callie, but Callie came up lame. He caught out what was handy, a bay mule with a reputation for kicking when a man's attention was focused elsewhere. The bronc mule put up such a struggle that Hewey was tempted to give up the trip and spend the afternoon gleefully kicking hell out of her. By the time they finally got her harnessed and buckled into place across the tongue from the bay, the older mule was nervous too.

"I think," said Julio, "that maybe you better watch them pretty close, Hooey."

Knowing the answer, Hewey asked, "I don't suppose you'd like to ride over to Walter's with me, Hooley?"

The Mexican smiled. "This is for me a day of holy rest."

As Hewey drove by the big house, Spring Renfro called and waved her bonnet at him from the gallery. "Just a minute, Mr. Calloway. I would like to go with you."

He pulled the team to an uncertain stop, the bronc mule fidgeting in the still-unfamiliar harness, looking around for something to run from. The teacher's red dog barked from a safe distance. Hewey watched with concern as Miss Renfro came down the steps and out into the yard. If the wind should happen to pick up and flare the long skirt of that gray dress, and the mule caught the movement from the corner of her eye . . .

Alvin Lawdermilk followed Miss Renfro into the yard and to the gate in the white picket fence.

Hewey argued, "Miss Renfro, you can see this ain't no

proper team for you to be ridin' behind. I mean, if anything was to go wrong . . ."

"Mr. Calloway, I have promised Eve and the boys a visit. You said the other day that no bronc has ever killed you yet. Well, you may not know it, but I am an old farm girl. I've been around mules all my life, and none of them has ever killed *me* yet. If you would be so kind as to give me a hand up . . ."

Hewey looked to Alvin for help, but Alvin just stood at the yard gate puffing his pipe and wishing them a nice afternoon. He looked around for Cora, hoping she might take up his argument. But Cora was nowhere in sight. There wasn't any use asking Old Lady Faversham. She wouldn't see any danger in the mules, but she would lecture Miss Renfro for an hour on the danger in Hewey Calloway.

Hewey didn't dare get down and relinquish control of these mules for a minute. "Ma'am," he pleaded, "I'd sure a lot rather you'd change your mind." But she wasn't going to, so he leaned down and gave her his hand. She grasped it and stepped up into the wagon. Once seated beside him she proceeded to pull the slat bonnet over her head to protect her face and her long brown hair from the sun and wind. "Ready any time you are, Mr. Calloway."

He made one more weak plea. "This sure ain't no comfortable wagon. The seat hasn't got any spring left in it, hardly."

"I am sure it will suffice. I am not a pampered woman."

He gave up, dropped his chin a little and flipped the reins gently. The older mule started off in a walk, half dragging the younger one until she caught up to the stride and began reluctantly doing her share of the pulling. Hewey felt for a moment that things were going to work out all right after all. But just as they started by Cora's henhouse, one of Old Lady Faversham's pet peafowls strolled out in front of the mules, spread its tail and screeched like a banshee.

The younger mule had been watching for a booger all along, and its terror at the sight and sound of the peafowl was contagious. The older mule caught it too. Hewey felt his neck pop as the mules suddenly broke into a run. "Whoa!" he hollered. "Who-o-o-a!" He half stood up, sawing futilely at the reins. The wagon bounced as the front wheels struck a shallow ditch, and Hewey almost lost his balance. Miss Renfro, holding tight to the seat with her left hand, caught Hewey with her right and pulled him back. Otherwise he might have tumbled out onto the tongue.

"Thank you, ma'am," he said.

"Don't mention it. I didn't think I wanted to be sitting up here by myself."

He managed to exert some control on the older mule, enough to get it running a little to the right and thus pull the wagon into a wide circle. In a minute they were heading straight back toward the ranch house and the corrals.

"Hold on tight!" he shouted needlessly as he saw the ditch coming again. His bronc-riding instincts made him duck his chin to avoid popping his neck, and he saw Miss Renfro do likewise. All of her learning hadn't come out of books. They took the bounce in fair grace, though the ribbon came untied from Spring Renfro's bonnet, and the whole thing went sailing off behind her. Her long brown hair began to string out in the wind.

He thought they were going to run through the front yard, but the mules veered to the left and carried them on a swing around toward the rear. The right front wheel caught the corner of the picket fence and uprooted the corner post, then smashed the next twenty or so white pickets into kindling. Pieces came flying up at Hewey, causing him to throw his arm up defensively over his face.

"Whoa!" he hollered again as he saw they were going to skirt dangerously near the weather-grayed, unpainted outhouse. He tried to pull the mules to the left but didn't quite manage it. The older bay mule, on the right, brushed against the outhouse in passing, and the right front wheel gave it a resounding thump that splintered wood from it and set the little structure to rocking.

Hewey heard a shriek and knew it came from Cora Lawdermilk.

Julio Valdez ran out from the barn, waving his arms. He made a run at the mules and tried to grab at the harness, but the speed wrenched his hands loose and sent him spinning. The left wheels just missed hitting him.

Next came the clothesline, three long pieces of thin cotton rope stretched between tall cedar posts and propped up at strategic points between the posts by long pieces of pine planking, notched in one end.

"Watch it," he shouted. "That line'll cut us to pieces." He grabbed Spring Renfro and forced her down in the seat, then threw himself protectively over her.

The mules swerved and missed the line.

After that they were in open country. He saw nothing to do but let them run off their fear and try not to get bounced out of the clattering wagon. He kept sawing on the lines, giving what little guidance he could to the direction they ran. The wagon bounced and groaned. The right front wheel squealed in protest, needing grease. If the mules would have co-operated, Hewey would gladly have stopped and greased it then and there, in his good shirt and all.

Jack rabbits ran, frightened by the noise and the careening wagon. Cattle scattered, tails hoisted over their rumps. Quail flushed in a flutter of wings.

Hewey had a chance for a good look at Spring Renfro, her brown hair awash in the wind, her face grayed by dust, her dress in disarray. Modesty had taken second place to survival. He expected to see terror in her eyes. Unaccountably, she was laughing.

"Ma'am," he gritted, "I wisht you'd let me in on the joke. I could stand one about now."

"No joke. I just haven't had so much fun in years."

"Fun?" He almost broke into swearing. "I didn't think they let crazy women teach kids in school."

He looked behind but could see little for the dust kicked up by the iron-rimmed wheels. He thought it probable that Alvin and Julio were back there somewhere, spurring to catch up. There had been horses in the pen that they could saddle. Maybe they could throw a rope on the mules and get them stopped.

The team seemed to be slowing. Both mules were shiny with sweat, and saliva dripped in foamy flecks from their mouths. Hewey was about to decide the thing was going to turn out all right.

Then, just ahead of them loomed a washout, a place where runoff water from a steep hillside had cut a deep gash across the sloping prairie. The older mule saw it and turned abruptly, whipping the bronc mule to the right with her. It was too sharp a turn for the wagon to make. Hewey felt a hard bump as the right wheel slammed back against the wagon bed. He felt the wagon lurch upward and heard the loud crash as the coupling pole broke. He realized too late that he had let the leather lines get themselves wrapped around his hands. He felt himself jerked out of the seat just as the wagon bed flipped upward and then over. He heard a shriek from Spring Renfro.

He slammed to the ground belly-first, and much of his breath went out of him. His mouth was full of dirt. His arms felt as if they had been jerked out of the sockets. He felt himself being dragged, the grass and weeds and small brush grabbing at him, ripping at his clothes, scraping the hide off of his arms and his chest. He couldn't see for the dirt that burned his eyes like cigarette ashes blown into his face.

He had no way of telling how far he was dragged before the reins pulled loose from his arms and he stopped sliding. He blinked at the dust and sand and saw, through a painful haze, the two mules still running at full speed, the wagon's front wheels bouncing crazily behind them.

They've took to the tules, he thought, not much giving a damn at the moment. He pushed himself to his hands and knees and started looking back for the schoolteacher. Good God, she was probably lying there somewhere with her neck broken in six places!

He tried to holler, but the sand in his mouth and throat stopped the sound before it rightfully came out. All he managed was a grunt. He spat, trying to work up enough saliva to clear some of the good earth he had plowed up with his chin. He rubbed his eyes, trying to regain enough sight to tell what direction he was moving. He stumbled along, choking for breath, glancing around wildly to try to determine where Spring Renfro was.

He heard her before he saw her. She was laughing. She was sitting on the ground beside the wreckage of the wagon and laughing.

He stopped a moment, trying to get a clearer picture of her. Laughing, dammit!

She sat there with her legs apart, the wind blowing her hair, her face covered with dirt, her dress torn and littered with grass and weeds and chunks of dirt bigger than a banty egg. Her laughing slowed, then started again as Hewey neared. She sat and pointed at him and broke into a fresh seizure.

Hewey's anger rose a little at first, but her laughter was infectious. In a minute he began to smile, then to chuckle, and finally he flopped down beside her, laughing as hard as she was.

He didn't know why. It wasn't all that damn funny. But he couldn't help it. She made him feel heady and drunk, and he couldn't do anything but join her. They laughed until the tears were rolling down their cheeks. He didn't know what prompted them to do it, but they put their arms around each other and laughed some more.

They were still laughing when Alvin and Julio came loping up on horseback. Julio jumped down nimbly and came running. Alvin moved a little slower and more carefully, but he got there only a few steps behind Julio. The two men's eyes were wide with concern until they saw for themselves that nobody was hurt. Gradually the contagion took them, and they laughed with Hewey and the teacher.

They finally managed to quit, only to look at each other and start again.

When Hewey had laughed himself out and his lungs ached as badly as the rest of him, he looked up at Alvin. "I believe I have damaged your wagon."

Alvin gazed at the wagon bed, lying there upside down and sprung out of its proper alignment. God knew how far the mules had gone with the rest of it. "If you improved it any, I'll be glad to pay you the difference."

"You can take it out of my first million."

Alvin shrugged. "It's just an old trainin' wagon. I've busted up better ones. We'll patch it together and use it again." He looked at Miss Renfro. "But we won't let any lady schoolteachers ride in it anymore." He turned to Julio. "Better go see if you can bring home the mules. They'll run themselves down directly."

Julio nodded, still looking first at Hewey, then at Miss Renfro, his face creased from one end to the other by a broad smile that showed two rows of perfect white teeth. He got on his horse and rode off in the direction where Hewey had bade good-bye to the mules.

Neither Hewey nor Miss Renfro had made any move to get up. Hewey said thoughtfully, "Alvin, ain't you had some trouble with coyotes gettin' into your chickenyard?"

Alvin stared critically at him, for the problem at hand had nothing to do with coyotes or chickens. "Happens pretty often. Why?"

"If a man was to slip out there at night and shut them peafowls out of the chickenyard, you reckon a coyote would catch them?"

Alvin grinned. "My mother-in-law would get up out of that wheel chair and throw a stompin' fit."

Hewey nodded. "The exercise would probably do her good." He pushed to his feet. His legs were shaky, but he thought they would hold up all right. He leaned down, stretching out his hands. Miss Renfro took them, and he pulled her up. She swayed. He caught her. She leaned against him a moment, and he was in no hurry for her to get her strength back.

Alvin watched them, his eyes narrowed a little in silent appraisal. "Hewey, you better let her go. I'd hate for us to lose a schoolteacher after she's only been here a year."

"She's all right now. The danger is over with."

"I don't know as I would say that."

Walking was one of the hardest tasks a cowboy ever had to do. A job that could not be done on horseback stood some chance of never being done at all. Hewey figured it was well over a mile back to the house, and he dreaded every foot of it.

If there had to be a washout, why couldn't it be closer to the barn?

Alvin motioned for Hewey to help Spring Renfro up onto his horse. It was a little awkward, for Alvin had not been farsighted enough to bring a sidesaddle. It was an uncommon thing for a woman to ride astride, especially when she wore a long skirt that by necessity slipped up far past the high tops of her buttoned shoes and exposed a limb that had rarely seen sunshine. Hewey tried not to look, but he failed in that effort, as he had failed in many things.

"You comfortable up there, Miss Renfro?" he asked.

"No, but I am probably more comfortable than the two of you."

Hewey glanced ruefully at Alvin. This, when it was over, was sure to send Alvin to one of his secret places. "We ain't goin' to die. We're only goin' to sound like it."

He had been struck more than once by the different view a man got of the range when he was down at ground level, compared to that he saw from the saddle. He had walked to camp many times after having come up second best to a strong-minded bronc. The grass never looked as green or as pretty from down here. His boots' high heels were made for digging into the ground when braced against a rope with a horse at the other end, or for keeping the foot from slipping through a stirrup. They were made to be worn out from the top down, not the sole up. His feet were hurting before he had walked the first two hundred yards. He grimaced and made up his mind not to whimper.

He must have been weaving a little, for the teacher asked with concern, "Are you all right, Mr. Calloway?"

"The Lord has seen fit to keep me alive. Maybe if I'd been a better man in my younger days He would've been merciful and struck me dead before the walk started."

"I hope you're not making light of the Lord, Mr. Calloway."

"No, ma'am. I've never felt closer to Him."

As they neared the barn Cora Lawdermilk walked hurriedly out to meet them. Her mother toddled behind on her cane. It had been Hewey's observation that Old Lady Faversham could move along pretty well when it suited her. It just didn't suit her often.

Cora made a fuss over the teacher's bedraggled look and had to feel twice for herself to be satisfied that there were no broken bones. Old Lady Faversham shook her cane at Hewey. She shrilled, "I could of told you, young lady. Go ridin' with a crazy one like that and there ain't no tellin' what kind of jackpot he'll get you into. They're a wild and uncarin' lot, them cowboys. I ought to know. I've had a daughter married to one for thirty years."

"Now, Mother," Cora said, "Alvin ain't all *that* bad."

Hewey helped Miss Renfro down. He took special care to keep his eyes away from her legs since the other two women were there to seize upon anything he did, and perhaps things he didn't do.

Spring Renfro came immediately to Hewey's defense. "It wasn't Mr. Calloway's fault. He tried to talk me out of going, but I wanted to see Eve and the boys. Under the circumstances, I thought he did a masterful job of handling the team."

Cora was unconvinced. "He could of killed you."

"But he didn't; he saved me."

Hewey nodded agreement with all she said, though he didn't really believe it all. It was luck that saved her, and he knew it. He had had about as much control over that wagon as a matchbox tied behind a freight train. But he took it kindly that she tried to bail him out of trouble with the womenfolks. He cautiously eyed Cora and thought perhaps she was beginning to lean his way. As for the old lady, he didn't even look at her.

Cora dismissed any further pleading. "Land sakes, Spring, you are a sight. We've got to get you into the house and see what we can do about you." She glanced at Hewey. "As for you, Hewey Calloway, you'd better get yourself some needle and thread and do somethin' about your modesty. Haven't you seen the rip in those britches?"

He hadn't. He blushed, thinking how Miss Renfro had seen him that way, all the long walk home. It was not a thing a modest young lady would mention. Nor, for that matter, should an old married woman.

Miss Renfro said, "I'd like to try again, Mr. Calloway, after we've both had a chance to clean up. But I think we'd better ride horses this time."

Alvin said, "I'll catch up Biscuit and the paint."

Hewey had had a bath the day before, it being Saturday, but that was of no help now. He had to do it all over again. He guessed that was all right as long as he didn't make a habit of it. It was his conviction that bathing too frequently was bad for the skin and its natural breathing apparatus. He went to the surface tank behind the barn, out of sight of the house. There he washed away the dirt and the leaves and the miscellaneous and extraneous trash which the dragging had driven beneath his underwear and into his hair. He found numerous hidden bruises and contusions as well as several thorns firmly ensconced beneath a hide that was not as tough as he sometimes liked to think. Some he could remove with the point of his pocketknife. The rest would have to find their own way out in their own good time.

As clean as tank water could make him, he pulled on a clean suit of long cotton underwear and a clean pair of ducking britches. Barefoot, he picked his way carefully through patches of sharp goathead stickers back to the shed which he counted as home. He seated himself on the edge of his steel cot and went to exploring for thorns.

A shadow fell across the open doorway. Alvin stood looking at him. "Find anything broken off?"

Hewey shook his head. "Far as I can tell, everything's here that belongs here."

Hewey's shredded shirt lay on the rough pine floor where he had dropped it. Alvin picked it up and shook his head. "I hope this wasn't your last."

"I got one more." The casualty had been one of the two he had bought from Pierson Phelps' store. It didn't seem any too hardy to have cost six bits. Fortunately, its mate was still intact.

Alvin lifted a saddle rack. That surprised Hewey, for it was the first time he had noticed it was hinged rather than nailed solidly to the rough pine boxing of the wall. Beneath the rack's single leg was a small trap door that had escaped Hewey's notice; Julio had done what little sweeping had been accomplished. From a tin box nailed beneath the door, Alvin drew out a bottle two thirds full of whisky.

"This'll heal your bruises from the inside out."

Hewey took a long drink and handed the bottle to Alvin.

Alvin said, "Never liked to watch a man drink alone. It does injury to his moral fiber." He took a long drink himself. He sat there then, the bottle in one hand and the cork in the other, as if undecided whether to bring the two together. He stared at Hewey.

"For a man with just one good shirt to his name, you're about as rich a man as I know."

Hewey frowned. "I wisht I knew how you figure that."

"You've got one treasure the rest of us can never have— freedom. Any day the notion strikes you, you can saddle old Biscuit and just ride away. You can go anyplace you want to. You don't have to ask anybody, and you don't have to lay awake worryin' that you've shirked your responsibilities, because you don't have any. There's times I envy you."

"You, with this ranch, and that good house yonder, and enough horses and mules to outfit Lee's army? You envy me?"

"Just at times, mind you—times when I'd give my right arm to be you. Just my right arm, nothin' else. I wouldn't give up this ranch, and I wouldn't give up Cora. I just let the thought run through my mind when the pressure gets heavy. I let it pleasure me a little while. Like a man, I guess, who wouldn't really dally with some woman that's not his wife, but he gets pleasure out of thinkin' about it anyway. It sort of eases the load on these old shoulders, knowin' there's somebody with that kind of freedom. I can never be like you because I couldn't bring myself to pay the price. But it makes my load lighter, knowin' you're out there someplace. It's like watchin' an eagle fly high and free. I'll never fly, but at least I can watch the eagle."

Hewey was still frowning. "What's that got to do with a tore-up shirt?"

Alvin took another snort from the bottle. He stared at the floor. "My eyesight ain't as good as it was in my prime; I been thinkin' about gettin' me some eyeglasses. But I can still see when somethin' is shoved up under my nose. I seen the way you and that schoolteacher looked at one another. Now Cora knows without me sayin' a word. I reckon her eyesight ain't too impaired by age. First thing you know, them women'll be workin' up plans for you, Hewey."

"I've always made my own plans."

"That's one thing I've admired about you. But when a bunch of women gets their heads together, you better sleep with one eye open. Pretty soon they're settin' up this thing and that thing and the other for you, and they'll make you think it was your own idea. You're caught like a coyote in a number three trap."

"I've never been trapped in my life."

"Maybe nobody's ever made a brass-plated, double-rectified effort." Alvin's eyes narrowed. "I don't have any notion of tryin' to tell you what to do. But whatever you do, be damn sure it's your own idea and not somethin' some-body has put off on you."

7

Biscuit hadn't worked much since they had been at the Lawdermilk place, a fact which helped offset the indignities to which the menagerie-like atmosphere subjected him. He had established a rapport of sorts with Spring Renfro's paint, though he clearly considered himself the superior. It took some attention on Hewey's part to ride along side by side with the teacher. Biscuit wanted to pull ahead to the position that befitted his rank.

Spring said, "I hope you're making this trip because you want to, and not simply for me. It occurs to me that you may not be feeling well after that dragging you took."

Hewey knew he felt better now than he would feel tomorrow, after the soreness had time to work to the bone. "I been wantin' to see the boys."

"I can understand why. They idolize you."

He shrugged. "I suppose one of them does."

"Tommy has always talked about you in school. He thinks you're without doubt the greatest cowboy who ever lived."

As long as he believed his uncle's stories he would probably continue to think that way. But give him a couple more years and he might turn out like Cotton. "How about Cotton . . . does he ever say much?"

"Cotton's mind is on other things a long way from home. He's looking to far horizons."

"I thought I'd ridden to all there was, but he's lookin' past any I've ever been to. I suppose I'm too old to understand him."

"You should understand him better than anyone. People say you've always had a way of looking at the distant hills."

"But when I got there I always felt like I knew where I was."

"When Cotton reaches *his,* he'll know where he is, too. He's of another generation, Mr. Calloway. More than that, he's of another century. You can't hold him back any more than his parents can. Of all people, you should know that and understand."

"I understand him lookin' away. I wisht I understood what he's lookin' at."

"You don't have to. The main thing is that you understand him, and help him. He needs help."

"He don't act like it."

"He has gone as far as this school can take him. I've taught him all I have to give. He has to be set free now, or he'll be tied to this place or another like it all his life."

"Ain't no use talkin' about it. Eve ain't goin' to let him go."

"She should. Perhaps you can help her see that, if you will. Tommy could stay here all his life and be happy, I think. But Cotton has places to go. I hope you'll find a way to help him."

Hewey stared at her until she looked away self-consciously. "You're somethin' different yourself, Miss Renfro. Not many women around here—or menfolks either—understand how it is with a boy like Cotton, or with an old fiddlefoot like me. Most people are always tryin' to change us into what *they* are instead of lettin' us be what *we* are."

Her eyes softened with a memory. "I knew a man once. He was very much like you. He was always looking to the distant hills. When he heard of gold in the Klondike he made the big run. He didn't find any gold, but it might have ruined things for him if he had. It was the search that always interested him, not the finding. He came back without a dollar to his name. But he was rich with experience, I suppose."

She fell silent. Hewey gave her some time, then asked, "This feller . . . were you-all kin?"

"We were going to be. But he hadn't been home long before the war started in Cuba. He had to go, and I had to let him."

Hewey sensed the rest of it. "He didn't come back."

She shook her head. "A friend sent me a picture of his grave, with a little white cross on it. I carried the picture with me for a long time. I finally decided that was bad for me, so I put it away."

Hewey pondered. "Did he look anything like me?"

She looked at him a moment. "No."

He felt relieved. For a minute he had had an uncomfortable feeling she looked upon him as a substitute for someone else. Never in his life had he wanted to be anyone other than Hewey Calloway.

She said, "I guess you know now why I was interested in your having been in Cuba. Tommy has told me about you at San Juan Hill."

"The boy gets a little enthusiastic, me bein' his uncle and all. He gets his facts mixed up."

"I'd like you to tell me the facts sometime."

"It's not a thing I enjoy talkin' about."

She nodded gravely. "I can understand. But if you ever do feel like telling me, I'll always feel like listening."

The first thing he noticed was the black horse standing where the wire gate was supposed to be, providing an opening in the barbed-wire fence that separated Alvin Lawdermilk's land from Walter Calloway's. He could see that it was an old horse, standing with head down. It was saddled.

"That's Boy Rasmussen's. But where's the old man at?"

Spring's lips were tight. She pointed. "There, on the ground." Her eyes were fearful.

Hewey saw a form stretched out in the green grass. His nerves tingled with alarm. "You better stay back." He touched spurs lightly to Biscuit's sides and moved ahead in a long trot. The breeze tugged at the old man's ragged clothing, fluttering it as if he were a rag doll casually dropped by some careless child's hand. Biscuit made an uneasy rolling sound in his nose.

Even as Hewey stepped down, before he touched the old man, he sensed that Boy Rasmussen was dead.

The drifter lay on his face. Hewey hesitated a moment, then gently turned the body over. Rasmussen had not been dead long.

Against Hewey's advice, Spring rode up close. She looked down with eyes wide and anxious. "Did somebody . . . ?"

Hewey shook his head. "No." His throat was tight. Speaking was painful. "Nobody killed him. He just wore himself out." The wire gate lay twisted on the ground where Rasmussen had dropped it. "Heart seizure, I reckon. He probably got down to open the gate but never lived to go through it."

"It's an awful thing to die all alone."

Hewey swallowed. "He'd lived alone, most of his life. I expect he'd of wanted to die travelin'."

"Where do you think he was going?"

Hewey shrugged. "Dodge City. Cheyenne. Laredo. Who knows? He probably didn't know either." Unbidden, unexpected, a tear rolled down his cheek.

Sympathetically Spring said, "He must have been an old friend of yours."

Hewey stared down at the peaceful face. "I never seen him more than two or three times. But I feel like I knew him all my life."

He knelt awhile, staring. Finally he pushed to his feet, rubbed a hand over his face as if it itched, surreptitiously running a finger across his eyes to wipe them dry, hoping Spring Renfro hadn't seen.

"Miss Renfro, you'd best go on up to Walter's house and tell him. He'll need to fetch a wagon. I'll stay here and watch that nothin' bothers the old man."

"That's the proper thing," she agreed. She rode carefully around the body, the paint horse shying a little, then she went through the gate and struck a long trot down the dim wagon road.

The old black horse stood patiently a dozen steps away, the patched old leather reins dragging on the ground. Hewey walked carefully toward the animal, talking softly to avoid boogering him. Sometimes a horse used to just one man was shy and distrustful of strangers. But the old black seemed to welcome him as a friend. Hewey put his arms around the shaggy neck and patted him and told him of his sympathy for the loss of an old companion. It wasn't the words that counted; it was the tone. The horse nuzzled him a little and thus spoke its own feelings.

Hewey uncinched the saddle and let it slip to the ground, relieving the black of its weight and the binding of the girth. He noted the Meanea, Cheyenne, signature stamped into the leather. The saddle was at least thirty years old, its cantle of the once-popular Cheyenne roll style already old-fashioned when Hewey had been a boy.

"I'd turn you loose over in Walter's pasture, old feller, but you might not find water. You better stay here awhile with me and Boy." He had no fear that the old horse would run away, so he didn't tie him. He went back and sat down cross-legged by the still figure. He studied the sleeping face, wondering where the old man was now. He wondered if he was still an old man, or if in that unseen, mysterious new life to which he had gone he was a young man again. Was he riding the range once more, perhaps taking a herd to Dodge or to the Nations?

Hewey had never spent enough time in churches to know much about conventional preachment. Though he had no doubt whatever of an afterlife—his father and other good people had assured him there was one—he had only the vaguest notion what kind of life it would be. He liked to think heaven was what each person wanted it to be. He could see no future in lying around on a fluffy white cloud and listening to somebody playing on a harp, a picture of heaven he had seen numerous times in one form or another. Even if it *was* that way, his personal preference would have run more to the fiddle.

To him, heaven ideally should have something of the familiar for each person. He would like to think there would be work to do, but only pleasant work, and no more of it at one time than a man felt like doing. There would be sunshine, but only pleasantly warm, never oppressively hot. There would be rain, but only when a man could sit in the comfort of the bunkhouse and watch it through the open door while he sipped his black coffee and smoked his Bull Durham cigarettes. He would never have to be out in it on horseback, miles from house or chuck wagon, soaked to the skin and chilled to the marrow of his bones. All would be familiar in heaven, and all would be friendly, if he could have it made up to order.

"I reckon you know by now what it's like," he said to Boy Rasmussen. "I wisht there was some way you could tell me."

He stared into the quiet, composed old face. It occurred

to him that he saw none of the haunted look, none of the anxiety he had seen that night at Walter's. He saw only peace.

He thought on that awhile, and he decided the old man probably *had* told him.

After a long time he heard the rattle of trace chains. He pushed to his feet and turned to meet the wagon. Walter and Eve sat on the seat. Spring and the two boys followed on horseback. All were solemn as they pulled up. Walter stepped stiffly to the ground, took off his hat and looked at Boy Rasmussen in silence. Following his example, the boys self-consciously did likewise.

Walter looked then at Hewey. "You sure there wasn't no accident? He wasn't dragged or anything?"

"Nothin' like that. The Lord just called him, and he went home."

Eve shuddered. "Knowin' the life he led, I hate to think of the reception he's gettin'."

Hewey lifted the old hat he had used to cover the features. "Eve, just look at that face. They're treatin' him gentle."

Eve said, "He's a merciful Lord." She turned and pointed with her chin at the wagon bed. "I brought a quilt to wrap him with."

Hewey stepped up to fetch it. It was a new quilt, never used. She had spent many a quiet winter's night piecing it together on a quilting frame. Hewey took a quick glance at his sister-in-law, then looked away so she wouldn't see the tears come back into his eyes. She might have spoken harshly about Boy Rasmussen when he was living, but at his death she gave him the best she had.

"This is good of you, Eve."

"He was one of God's children," she responded tightly. "It's for heaven to judge him, not me."

He spread the blanket in the wagon. Carefully he and Walter lifted Boy into the wagon bed, then folded the blanket over him.

Walter said, "We'd best take him into town. You'll need to go with me, Hewey, since you're the one who found him."

Hewey nodded. The sheriff would want to know the circumstances.

Walter turned to Cotton and Tommy. Both boys had watched with solemn eyes and had not intruded upon the occasion with talk. "You buttons see Miss Renfro back to the Lawdermilks', then go on home and take care of the chores. Your mama and me, we'll spend the night in town. We'll probably put up at the wagonyard. We'll see to everything that needs to be done for the old man, and we'll be home by at least tomorrow evenin'."

Tommy had seen little of death. He gave his uncle a cautious glance. "You reckon it hurt him much to die, Uncle Hewey? Do you reckon it scared him?"

Hewey saw that Cotton was waiting to hear the answer, though he had too much reserve to have asked the question. Hewey gave his response a long and careful study. "For a minute, maybe. We're all a little scared at somethin' new. But then, judgin' by his face, the pain was gone, and the scare too. Death comes to all of us sometime. Old Boy done a lot of ridin' the last few years, tryin' to find a place that was really home to him. Well, he's home now."

That satisfied Tommy. Cotton looked once more at the quilt-covered form in the wagon, then turned his horse away. Walter spoke to the team, and the wagon started to move. Hewey was about to fall in behind it when Spring Renfro rode up beside him. Her eyes glistened. She reached out and took his hand, holding it for a moment.

She said, "You're a good man, Hewey Calloway. Don't ever let anyone tell you otherwise."

Because Upton City and its surrounding trade territory were sparsely populated, the nearest thing the town had to an undertaker was barber Orville Mulkey. In his small back room, the shades rolled down, he looked over the body by lamplight with Sheriff Wes Wheeler to certify that there were no marks of violence, bearing friendly witness to Hewey's testimony.

"I'll touch up his hair and his beard," he said, "but it'd be a shame to shave him clean. St. Peter wouldn't recognize him."

"Just make him look as good as you can," Wheeler said. He turned to Hewey and Walter. "You're real sure you don't know the names of his kin?"

Walter said with a sense of guilt, "I don't remember that I ever taken the trouble to ask him. I just know that he's got a brother somewhere down on the Rio Grande and a sister up on the plains. I ought to've taken more interest in him than that. I just never thought about him dyin' at my gate."

The sheriff grimaced. "Nothin' to do, then, but to bury him here. I'll write a letter to officers in that part of the country to see if they can notify any of his relations."

"Seems a shame," Walter said, "for a man to be buried so far away from all kin."

Hewey put in, "It don't matter where they're buried. They'll all find each other by and by."

The barber frowned. "I'm afraid I've got a practical question for the here and now. Who pays for this?"

The sheriff said, "The county will. There's nobody else to do it."

Hewey looked up quickly. "And declare him a pauper? No sir! His friends'll bury him."

Wheeler was dubious. "He didn't have any friends to speak of."

Hewey said firmly, "I'll get up a collection. We'll see how many friends an old cowboy has got."

Wes Wheeler was not the kind of man who smiled much. He came close to smiling with his eyes.

Hewey turned to the barber. "Orville, you just go ahead and fix him up. Put some good clothes on him, too. I'll see to the pay." He glanced at his brother. "You comin' with me, Walter?"

Walter nodded.

Hewey said, "I'm liable to take you to a place that Eve won't approve of."

Walter grunted. "You think I'd let you go into such a place all by yourself?"

They stepped out into the street. Hewey could see a dozen or so horses tied in the vicinity of the Dutchman's saloon. "That'll likely be as far as we need to go. I'll do the talkin'. You just back me up." They walked along the dirt street, found an opening between the tied horses and strode up onto the narrow porch. Hewey paused in the open doorway. Walter had been a step behind him, looking back as if wondering whether Eve would see. She wouldn't. She was visiting with church friends who weren't going to let her sleep in the wagonyard tonight.

Hewey rough-counted a dozen cowboys, most of them Two Cs hands who had delivered a string of Tarpley steers to a trail outfit earlier in the day. Even C. C. Tarpley wasn't insensitive enough to send them home without giving them a chance to partake in a drop or two of kindness. Anyway, the broker they were, the harder they worked. The faces were mostly young, in their low to mid-twenties. Many a young fellow gloried in the cowboy profession a few years but eventually gave it up for something which paid better and involved less physical stress and risk. The man who stayed in it past the age of thirty was likely to remain in the cattle business one way or another the rest of his life, on its fringes if not in the middle.

Hewey stepped up to the bar where the bartender Schneider waited. He ordered a drink for himself and Walter and plunked a silver dollar on the walnut bar. He downed the drink in one long swallow, then turned to survey the cluster of cowboys playing cards and shooting billiards.

"Fellers," he spoke loudly, "I wisht you'd all stop and listen to me for a minute."

The conversations trailed down and finally stopped as the men turned to look at him. Some who knew him spoke to him. Those who didn't know him recognized that the others held him in some regard.

"Fellers," Hewey spoke gravely, "me and Walter here, we just brought an old-timey cowboy to town. He was old Boy Rasmussen. Now, some of you knowed him and some of you didn't. Whether you knowed *him* or not, you all know the breed. He was followin' the mossyhorns up the trail when most of us was still followin' our mothers around the kitchen. It was him and his kind that beat out the trails and shot at the Yankees and fought off the Indians. It was them old fellers that taken the whippin' so me and you could have the easy life we're livin' today.

"Now, I figure we owe an old man like that somethin' better than a pauper's grave. I think I know most of you fellers, and I think you'll agree with me. I got ten dollars in my pocket. It all goes in my hat to help bury old Boy in the style he's rightfully got comin' to him. Walter, how much you got?"

Caught by surprise, Walter said, "Five dollars."

"That's fifteen. We got to start someplace." He took off his hat and put his ten dollars into it. Walter put in his five. Now he couldn't afford to sleep in the wagonyard tonight, even if he wanted to. Hewey held the hat out at arm's length. "Now, how about you fellers?"

The cowboys began drifting up, dropping in whispering money if they were that flush, clinking money if they weren't. Hewey kept shaking the hat so the silver would work to the bottom and only the paper would show on top.

C. C. Tarpley and son-in-law Fat Gervin chose an inopportune time to enter the saloon. Hewey trapped them before they could reach the bar. Hewey ignored the hostility in Fat's eyes and concentrated his first attentions on C. C. He explained the reason for the collection. "Look in that hat, C. C. You don't see nothin' in there but foldin' money. As an old-time trail driver yourself, I know you'd want to contribute as good as your own cowboys have gone and done."

The gaunt old man's gray mustache wiggled as he seemed to say something, though no sound came out. He tried to cover up the fact that he was touched. Reluctantly he extracted ten dollars from a leather wallet that had long been protected from too much sunshine. He said, "Philanthropy will be my undoin'."

"A pleasant giver is a joy to the angels, C. C. When your time comes you can hire a hundred people to cry at your funeral. But old Boy needs our help."

C. C. said, "I'll get my ten dollars back in just a little while on the grub that old chuckline rider won't be eatin' anymore at my line camps." He sounded harsh, but Hewey knew even tight-twisted C. C. Tarpley had never turned a rider away unfed. There was a practical as well as a humanitarian reason for it. These drifters were occasionally a source of cheap short-term labor. Sometimes, moving casually across a country, they would come upon something amiss and report it if they were friendly. On the other side of the coin, a drifter who had been accepted and fed wouldn't sct a range afire out of spite.

Hewey swung the hat over to Fat Gervin, challenging him with his eyes. With all the men watching, Fat could do no less than equal the contribution his father-in-law had made. Hewey saw how much it pained him. "You can make that up in a few days, Fat. Just raise the interest."

He carried the hat to the bar and dumped the money carefully, grabbing at a couple of coins that tried to roll away.

C. C.'s eyes narrowed. "All foldin' money, you said."

"Foldin' money is all you saw."

The collection lacked only seven dollars and some cents of being an even hundred. The Dutchman dug into his cash drawer and made up the difference.

The gesture brought thanks from Hewey. "A hundred dollars ought to send Boy off in style."

Schneider nodded. "You did well, Hewey. I think it is due you another drink."

"I'm broke."

"I am not. For you and Walter, one on the house." To Hewey's surprise, Schneider poured one for himself. It was a thing he rarely did. He raised his glass. "To Boy Rasmussen."

Hewey looked around the room. Some of these were men he had never seen before, men he probably would never see again. But not one of them was a stranger. He lifted his glass. His voice almost cracked. "To *him,* and to all other good old boys!"

The bank stayed open, but most of the few other business houses closed for a couple of hours out of respect for Boy Rasmussen's funeral. Though nobody in town had known him well, a goodly crowd followed the casket out to the burying grounds. Brother Averill, the preacher, didn't say a word about Boy's shortcomings, his failings in the sight of the Lord. He spoke only of his contributions to the civilizing of the West, of the hardships he had endured, of the new home he had found where the grass was always green and the water everlastingly sweet. When he was done, everybody filed by the open box for a last look at a link to another time that was rapidly becoming a faded memory, only occasionally revived in pale colors through meandering tales told by old men awaiting their time to go.

Finally Eve's quilt was folded over the old man's face. The lid was nailed down, and Boy Rasmussen was lowered into his final resting place, a long way from Doan's Crossing on the Red.

Eve wept.

Hewey tied Biscuit behind the wagon and rode away from the cemetery on the wagon seat beside Eve and Walter. They held their silence a long time, Eve clutching her old family Bible. At length Hewey told her, "I'm glad you was here. I'm glad there was a woman or two here to weep for him."

"I wasn't weepin' just for him. I wept a little for you, too."

"For me?"

"You'll end up just like him someday, buried by strangers in some strange place. I only hope there's somebody around who will do for you what you did for Boy Rasmussen."

"And maybe some good lady who will donate me a new quilt."

"I'm serious, Hewey. I've never told you before, but I've prayed for you sometimes. The answer to those prayers is at hand, if you'll just open your eyes and see."

"See what?"

"There's a certain fine lady who thinks a lot of you, Hewey. She sees possibilities in you, the same way I saw possibilities in Walter."

Hewey was suddenly appalled. "You tryin' to marry me off?"

"For your own good. I've been tryin' to marry you off for fifteen years. I don't want you to be lowered into your grave by strangers. I want to see family and loved ones mourn over you. That is the Christian way."

A one-eyed mule could have seen that some type of conspiracy was afoot between Eve Calloway and Cora Lawdermilk.

Hewey had two eyes.

Though the two women had been friends for years, they had done most of their visiting in church. Only occasionally had they spent time in each other's homes. Now Eve was over to the Lawdermilk place every few days. The two women were everlastingly using a hot curling iron on Spring Renfro's long hair, putting more waves in it than Hewey had seen on the troopship bound for Cuba. Afraid Hewey

wouldn't notice for himself, Eve or Cora were always pointing out to him how pretty Spring looked. It was embarrass-
ing to agree out loud, but it would have been more so to have
denied it. The two women were continually whipping up
something new in the way of clothes for Spring to wear.
Hewey wondered where the material came from, for Eve
had been making her own housedresses from the same bolt
of plain cloth for years. There was a great deal of talk about
filling Spring's "hope chest." Hewey had a strong notion the
hope was higher on the other women's part than on Spring's
or on his. He sensed an uneasiness, even an embarrassment,
in Spring. It was much like his own.

Times he walked in unexpectedly and caught fragments
of their conversations. Once he heard Eve assuring Spring
that Hewey was not lazy, that he did not shrink from
honest labor when there was a need for it to be done and
that all he really needed was the gentle but firm hand of
a good woman to set him on the path of righteousness and
industry.

"A good woman's love will make a man out of him," she
said.

The old Mrs. Faversham was the only one who kept faith
with the truth, as she saw that truth. "He's just another cowboy with the itch in both feet. A woman would be a lot
better off with a good dog and a hot-water bottle, Spring.
You've already got the dog." When Cora and Eve protested
that she was wrong, she declared, "I have never understood why we women always seem to settle for less than we
should have."

One Sunday afternoon, pursuant to custom, Hewey and
Spring rode over to Eve's and Walter's. After the amenities
had been met at the front door, Eve looked around for
Tommy. She said, "Spring, the sorrel mare had a colt a
couple of nights ago. I'm sure you'd like to see it. Tommy,
take Miss Renfro out and show her the colt."

Spring Renfro had seen a lot of colts and wasn't all that curious, but Eve made it plain that she intended for her to see this one, too. As soon as the teacher was halfway to the barn, Eve turned to her husband. "Walter, tell him."

Walter gave his wife a sidelong glance of impatience. "Don't rush things, Eve. Hewey'll think we're puttin' pressure on him."

"We *are* puttin' pressure on him. When the iron is hot, strike it."

Walter gave her that glance again.

Hewey said, "I don't see no hot iron."

Eve demanded, "How much money have you got?"

It wasn't a subject he ever let concern him much; he hadn't added it up lately. "If it cost a hundred dollars to go to heaven, I might make it to Fort Worth."

She said, "House Barcroft has proved up his place. He'll sell it to you real cheap."

Hewey immediately began looking for boogers that he could point out. "How come he wants to get rid of it?"

"It's a good place," she said. "A person could make a good livin' there."

"House never did. He's been haulin' freight for Blue Hannigan. If the place would make him a livin', he wouldn't be skinnin' mules."

"But he's a bachelor."

"If a man can't make a livin' as a bachelor, he sure can't make one yoked in double harness."

"A man with a woman to help and encourage him could do a lot with a place like Barcroft's. He could make a garden out of the desert."

"If he was like me he'd probably make a desert out of a garden. Anyway, I don't have a woman, Eve. I was born a bachelor, and I've stayed one for these thirty-odd years."

She angered. "Sometimes I think you're stone deaf to what people are tryin' to tell you."

"Sometimes I wish I could be. But it's hard when I've got

two women like you and Cora, both tryin' to make me jump over the broomstick."

"You like her, don't you?"

"Cora? Sure, she's all right."

"I'm talkin' about Spring Renfro, and you damn well know it!" When she let herself use a word of that intensity she was at the point that a man had better agree with everything she said or find some other place to pass his time.

He said, "I like lots of people. That don't mean I want to get married. Anyway, how do you know *she* does?"

"That's for you to find out. All you have to do is ask her."

"If she wanted to get married to me, she'd of let me know."

"A woman can't do that."

"Why not? She speaks English, and a damn sight better than I do."

"It just isn't done that way, at least not by decent, God-fearin' women. They let the man do all the askin'."

Hewey remembered that Eve had made it clear enough to Walter when she wanted to get married. If she hadn't exactly asked the question, she had hazed him into a corner and shut all the getaway gates. But he wouldn't point that out to her in her present state of agitation.

"Even if I was inclined to ask her, it'd be embarrassin' to ask and have her say *no*."

"I bet you she won't."

"She should. I sure ain't no prize catch."

"Why not? You're Walter's brother, and look what I managed to make out of him."

Walter turned and walked off toward the barn, saying he was going to help Spring and Tommy look at the colt.

Hewey made an excuse about going into the house and getting himself a cup of coffee. Cotton sat there reading. He only half hid a grin which showed he had been listening to all of it.

Hewey asked, "You readin' about automobiles again?"

"I think you could make good use of one yourself, Uncle Hewey. It could take you a long way from here between now and dark."

Riding home after an early supper, Hewey noticed that Spring Renfro was having nothing to say. Whatever thoughts were working behind those studious eyes, she was keeping them to herself.

He said, "I hope Eve hasn't embarrassed you as much as she's embarrassed me."

She gave him a faint smile. "She and Cora both. They're about as subtle as a sledgehammer."

He didn't know what *subtle* meant, but if it had been bad she wouldn't have said it. He observed, "Looks like we've got a problem, me and you."

"I suppose we have."

"You're a nice lady, Miss Renfro. It's pleasured me considerable, bein' around you, ridin' over here with you and all. But I don't reckon you'd want to get married, would you?"

She was suddenly flustered, caught unprepared. "Well, I don't know . . ."

"I didn't think you would. That's what I kept tellin' Eve, but she don't listen to anything she don't want to hear."

Spring turned her head away. He decided she was embarrassed by the whole uncomfortable situation; he knew *he* was. "If I was a marryin' kind of feller, you're sure the one I'd ask, Miss Renfro. If I was thataway inclined . . ." He let it go.

She was looking straight ahead, not at him. In a minute she said in a strained voice, "Thank you, Mr. Calloway. There's not anyone I'd rather have ask me, if *I* were so inclined."

His face warmed. "The last thing I'd want to do on this earth would be to cause you any more embarrassment.

I figure the only way to put a stop to it is for me to leave. Alvin's got a string of horses ready to deliver over into the Concho country. I'll take them, and after I get to San Angelo—for the good of both of us—I'll just keep on ridin'."

She looked at him then. Tears glistened. "You'd leave?"

"Seems to me like it's the only way out for either one of us."

She did not reply. He took that as an indication she agreed. He stole a long look at her, riding along with her head turned away a little. He felt a sudden strong desire to put his arms around her. He knew that as a decent woman she was sure to resent it. He was glad he had self-control. A man who would give in to such a base impulse with a good woman would deserve the horsewhipping some strong and righteous citizen was likely to give him.

He said wistfully, "I almost wisht we *was* thataway inclined. We'd make a handsome-lookin' couple, me and you."

For the next two days Cora Lawdermilk saw to it that Hewey received biscuits with the bottoms thoroughly burned, and steaks with plenty of fat and gristle. Her eyes were cold as a witch's breath. She had little to say, and that little was in clipped words, punctuated by a look that would kill cotton at twenty paces.

Old Lady Faversham, on the contrary, managed a civil word for Hewey now and again. Her behavior had shown a definite improvement.

Hewey saw little of Spring except at mealtime. She always seemed to have things to do elsewhere when he was around. It was just as well, he thought. It had been a narrow escape for both of them.

He couldn't drive the horses to San Angelo by himself, and Alvin needed Julio too much to spare him for six or seven days. Hewey remembered a promise he had made to

Cotton and Tommy. He asked Alvin, "If Walter can spare the boys a few days, would you pay them cowboy wages?"

Alvin didn't wheedle. "A dollar a day." Some ranchers would hire a kid for fifty to seventy-five cents and expect as much work out of him as out of a man.

Alvin had always been inclined to smile a lot, but he was smiling even more than usual the last couple of days. He put his big hand on Hewey's shoulder, then went to his secret cache beneath the saddle rack. He held up the bottle in toast. "To wise decisions. May that be the only kind we ever make!"

Hewey accepted the bottle in the spirit in which it was offered. "I hope I made the right one, Alvin. She *is* a good woman. Sometimes when I'm with her I get feelin's . . ." He could hardly bring himself to the admission. "I get feelin's I'm downright ashamed of. I get to thinkin' things a man don't think about with her kind of woman."

"You've always lived a free man, Hewey. For the sake of us who got ourselves caged, don't let anybody ever shut the gate on you."

Eve hadn't been to Cora's, nor Cora to Eve's house, so Eve hadn't found out yet that her wedding plans had gone for nought. He rode up to the Calloway house late in the evening and said he needed the two boys for a few days' wrangler service.

"I don't know," Eve said dubiously. "Walter put his plow on Blue Hannigan's freight wagon day before yesterday and went into Midland to get some smithin' done. He won't be back till at least tomorrow."

"I came by the field. I didn't see no weeds in there that'd take over the cane patch in the week or so these boys'd be gone."

"I don't know that I can spare them. There's so many chores . . ."

"Alvin'll pay both of them full wages, a dollar a day

apiece. Six days, six dollars. Two boys, twelve dollars. You could buy a whole wagonload of groceries with that kind of money."

He had found Eve's weak spot, if she had one. There were never enough dollars around here to stretch over everything that needed covering. It had always been Eve's job to do the stretching, for Walter had never been a much greater money manager than Hewey. Hewey could see her counting the money in her mind. But she was still hesitant. He didn't give her a chance to turn him down. He stepped outside and hollered for the boys. He had seen both of them working by the barn.

"Cotton, Tommy," he half shouted as they approached the house, "you-all hurry up and get your chores done so your mama won't have to worry about them. Me and you are drivin' Alvin's horses to San Angelo."

Tommy gave a whoop and turned back toward the barn in a dead run. Cotton moved up a little closer to Hewey, his hands in his pockets. He stared at his uncle with a measure of lingering doubt. "You really mean to take us this time? You ain't just loadin' us again?"

"You'll see pretty quick if I'm loadin' you or not. We go back to Alvin's tonight and leave with the horses at daylight. Now, you go do up your chores like I told you. I'll pitch in and chop some wood to be sure your mama has enough to last till your daddy gets home."

Eve stood on the front step, her right hand shading her eyes. "Hewey Calloway, I never told you those boys could go."

Hewey was not a very good poker player, but he knew when he had a royal flush. "Then I reckon it's up to you to tell them they can't."

She could see Cotton working feverishly to feed the stock while Tommy was milking the cow. "If a horse doesn't kill you someday, Hewey, I may just do it myself. I'd best get a little supper started so those boys don't ride on an empty stomach." She turned back into the house. Hewey flexed his reluctant hands as he walked to the woodpile, looking for the ax.

At the supper table Cotton queried cautiously, trying not to show too much interest, "You reckon we're liable to see an automobile in San Angelo?"

"Things are mighty up to date in San Angelo. I'll bet you they've got half a dozen automobiles around there by now."

Eve frowned. "San Angelo's a big place. I've heard it's even wickeder than Midland. That's a long way for two little boys to go away from home."

Hewey argued, "They're not little boys. Anyway, I went up the trail when I was younger than either one of them."

"And look at you now."

It was something akin to rites of manhood for a boy to go off away from home on his first paying job. Cotton had done so before, but Tommy hadn't. His mother hugged him. "You take care now, son, and come home safe."

The boys didn't need long to get their horses saddled, tie their small bedrolls behind the cantles and wave at their mother as they started up the wagon road. Tears on her cheeks, she yelled after them to turn their eyes away from the evils they might encounter in a godless city like San Angelo, Texas.

They had ridden perhaps fifty yards at Hewey's side when he drew rein. "You boys just keep on ridin'. There's one thing I neglected to tell your mother." He turned around and rode back.

Eve was watching from the front steps. She moved out into the yard. Hewey rode up just close enough for her to hear him as he hollered. "They're good boys, Eve, so don't you worry none. They're plenty big enough to find their way back by theirselves."

"By theirselves?"

"After I deliver the horses, I'm ridin' on."

"But what about the Barcroft claim? What about Spring Renfro?"

"Me and her, we talked it over. We decided neither one of us has got a marryin' urge. So long, Eve. See you one of these days."

He turned and spurred Biscuit into a stiff trot to catch up with the boys.

Eve cried, "Hewey Calloway, you come back here!"

She tried to run after him, but she was no match for Biscuit. Hewey didn't look back, and in a little bit the wind whipped her words away. It was just as well, because she was saying some things she would regret Sunday when she went to church.

Cotton looked around as Hewey came up to him and Tommy. "What was she hollerin' back there?"

"Just tellin' you boys to behave yourselves and earn your dollar!"

8

The weather was warm but beautiful. Rains had come at decent intervals all spring so that the grass was good. Tommy's excitement was contagious. It was a bad thing, Hewey thought, that most boys weren't turned loose on their own anymore like they used to be. Some boys these days didn't leave home until they were fifteen or sixteen. They should not be so deprived of the many wonders the world held for them.

It was always less monotonous moving a band of horses than driving a cow herd. Horses moved faster. Of all the broncs Hewey had broken in this string, he had given the most cussing to a long-tailed bay that showed by looks and temperament a goodly drop of mustang in its veins. But now that bay had established itself as the leader. Its sharp teeth and ready hoofs defended the front position when another horse moved up as if to challenge its lead. The bay seemed to know where it was going and to look forward to being the first to get there.

When Tommy wasn't singing, he was asking questions.

"How big is San Angelo?"

"Last time I heard it was five or six thousand people."

"That many? That must be near as big as Chicago. I'll bet it's a mile and a half across."

"I wouldn't be surprised."

"You reckon they got an ice-cream parlor? A real ice-cream parlor?"

"I believe I remember seein' one, but I never was in it. It was a few doors up from the Arc Light Saloon."

"You've been in the saloon though, I suppose?"

"Had to go in there to see a feller."

Cotton hadn't said much, but he had done a lot of quiet thinking. "I hope you're right about them havin' some automobiles."

"I wisht I knew what gets you buttons all so muzzy over automobiles."

Cotton smiled. "You keep sayin' they're just a passin' fad. I'd like to see one before they're all gone."

"They ain't much to see. When the new wears off and everybody goes back to sensible transportation, I'll bet the price of good horses and mules will go up by fifty or seventy-five dollars a head."

They cut across country until they struck the head of the Middle Concho. Once they made the river, all they had to do was follow, because it would ultimately lead them to town. The three Conchos—Middle, North and South—all converged at San Angelo and formed one Main Concho River. It flowed on east to contribute its clear waters to the red-muddy run of the Colorado a little way beyond the Indians' painted rocks.

It seemed to Hewey there wasn't a foot of this region that

he hadn't ridden over at some time or other. Seeing it again was like meeting an old friend after a long separation. He had ridden from the Mexican border to Canada, and he was hard put to say which was his favorite part of the country. Usually it was the place where he was now, or the place he was on his way to.

He found himself singing along with Tommy, though he couldn't carry a tune in an oaken bucket. It was nice to go home, but it was good also to be out moving again, not knowing, really, where he was going once he got the horses delivered, free to make up his mind at any time and to change it just as suddenly in the middle of the road without pausing for consultation with anybody.

The horses suddenly stopped and bunched up along an unexpected fence. The barbed wire was shiny and new. The horses tentatively moved down it a little way, then up, uncertain which way they were expected to go. Tommy rode out to one side, Cotton to the other, to keep them from taking any wrong notions. When the horses had quieted and seemed disposed to graze the good grass awhile, Hewey rode down closer to the river. He found no gate, but he found a drop-gap where the barbed wire was tied to the posts with slick wire rather than fastened down securely with steeples. This was a substitute for a gate. He untied the wires from several posts and signaled to Cotton to help him push them down to ground level. This opened a pathway for the broncs to pass over. When they were all on the other side, Hewey tied the wires back in their proper places.

"Seems like it ain't been more than a year or two since I was along this very same way. There wasn't no fence here then."

"It's sure here now." Cotton looked at the big cedar posts, more permanent than the mesquite posts he was used to at home. "Looks like they mean for it to stay."

Hewey grumbled, "Every time you turn around anymore

you run into a new fence. Seems like somebody is bound and determined to turn this whole world into one big barbed-wire jail."

"We came a long ways before we ran into this one."

"Used to not run into *any*. Used to ride a thousand miles and never open a gate unless it was to somebody's yard or his tater and turnip patch."

Not far ahead somewhere lay a set of old wooden corrals he remembered from years past. They were near the river and would be a good place to hold the horses while they camped for the night. Dusk was closing as he saw a pinpoint of firelight ahead. Disappointment touched him. If someone was already there and using the pens, he and the boys would have to go on a few miles farther to a ranch house he knew about. He hadn't brought hobbles or bridles and picket line because for him this was to be a one-way trip, and there was no handy way of getting them home. They would be too bulky for Cotton and Tommy to carry. Yet they were worth too much to leave or give away. Even Alvin Lawdermilk wasn't that generous.

Nearing the pens, he saw to his relief that they stood empty. The campfire was down by the river, where a man had a horse staked on a long rope to graze beneath a towering stand of big native pecan trees.

"We'll water them first," he told the boys, "then we'll pen them."

They hazed the horses down to the river and let them spread out to drink. Hewey gave them all the time they wanted. He saw the man at the fire saddle his blue roan horse and ride up to the pens to throw the gate open. It was less than a hundred yards, and it took him longer to saddle up than it would have taken to walk the distance. That told Hewey he was a cowboy, not some town dweller casually passing through.

He saw something familiar in the way the man sat on his

roan as Hewey and Cotton and Tommy pushed the freshly broken broncs up to the pens. When the rider moved in to help them, Hewey knew.

"Well, I'll swun!" he exclaimed. "Snort Yarnell, you gotch-eared old mule!" Snort did have a little wilt in the upper edge of his left ear. Depending upon when he told the story, and to whom, it had been acquired either from a horse or from a saloon fight.

"Howdy, Hewey Calloway. What you doin' in God's country?"

"Tryin' to get across before God sees me."

Snort Yarnell was a legend over Texas and half of New Mexico. When people talked of great cowmen they spoke of Charles Goodnight and Shanghai Pierce. When they talked of cow-country bankers they might bring up the names of George W. Littlefield or Charles Schreiner. But when the conversation turned to bronc stompers and wild, reckless cowboys who knew not fear nor hesitation, they were likely to speak of men like Booger Red Privett and Snort Yarnell. Snort, it was often said, could ride more broncs, heel more calves and drink more whisky—separately or intermixed—than anybody who had ever trailed Longhorn cattle out of the South Texas brush. He was always the envy of other cowboys, and occasionally the dread of county sheriffs, city constables and lone bartenders who had big breakable mirrors.

Snort sported a full gold tooth in the middle of his broad grin, installed by some show-off dentist during one of Snort's rare moments of temporary prosperity. Standing next to it like a kid brother was a gold cap filling out a tooth that had been only half broken off. Snort's nose was nearly flat and a little askew, a mark of the bad moments that inevitably arose to one in the bronc-stomper trade.

He said, "Hewey, I know you don't own them horses legal, so where'd you steal them at?"

Hewey explained that he was delivering them to San Angelo for Alvin Lawdermilk.

"Now, ain't that a stroke of good luck for you? I'm headin' for Angelo myself. Goin' to slip up on the boys' blind side and win the money at the big steer ropin'."

Hewey's pulse quickened. "I never heard about no ropin'."

"Day after tomorrow. You ought to get in on it. I'm fig-urin' on takin' first place, naturally, but you're welcome to second prize."

Hewey shut one eye and narrowed the other. "The day I couldn't beat you with a rope was the day I was laid up with my right arm broke."

Snort turned to Cotton and Tommy. "You're Walter's boys, ain't you?" He didn't wait for the answer. "Your Uncle Hewey is a notorious liar, but in spite of all that he's the second-best cowboy in this whole neck of the woods, me bein' number one. Your old daddy was no slouch in his own time. I'd of ranked him number three before he taken him-self to the plow."

The boys stood slack-jawed. They had seen Snort Yarnell before, but he was ever a wonder to them.

Hewey shut the gate on the broncs and tied it securely. He wouldn't have trusted that mustang bay not to open it. He would have liked to have brought some corn or oats for the broncs, but he had let them graze enough through the day to carry them through. "Let's stake our horses and let them at the grass," he told the boys. "Snort, what you got down yon-der that we can graze?"

"Three cold biscuits and a can full of coffee. I was hopin' some pilgrim like you would happen along and take pity. Don't tell me you ain't got nothin'."

Hewey let his disappointment show. "Some jerked beef, which is the next thing to nothin'. Half a slab of bacon. We'll have to cook that."

"I can wait. If you need more firewood, there's aplenty down yonder. All you have to do is go fetch it."

The best that could be said for the supper was that it was filling. Hewey didn't eat much; he left most of his for the boys, because he could remember how painful hunger had been to him when he was that age. Nowadays it was no stranger to him; he took it in stride. He made up the difference with black coffee, boiled strong enough and thick enough to pass for blackstrap molasses.

Snort did the major part of the talking. Tommy hung on every word, his eyes wide and credulous. Snort didn't have to embellish much. In his case even the truth strained belief. After telling about having his leg crushed in a horse fall, he pulled up his pants leg for proof. The scarred and crooked leg was an awesome thing to behold. "Them San Antonio doctors said it had taken an infection and there wasn't nothin' I could do but let them saw it off if I wanted to live. But I told them the Good Lord had sent me into this world on two good legs and I wasn't goin' to shortchange Him when I turned them back in. I had some friends take me out to a little adobe house on Salado Creek. I packed this old leg in horse manure and wrapped it up tight with gunny sacks. I smelt like I was three weeks dead, and I lost most of my friends for a while. But when I left that place I left there walkin'."

Cotton said, "They've made a lot of progress. I'll bet nowadays they could do you a lot better job."

"A wore-out one-eyed horse drops better medicine on the ground behind him than most of them quack doctors have got up their sleeves." Snort slapped the leg smartly. "You couldn't ask for nothin' sounder than that."

After Hewey sent the boys to their blankets, he sat up awhile with Snort. Mostly they hunched in thoughtful silence, smoking, thinking. Spring Renfro kept coming to Hewey's mind, unbidden. He tried to shut her out by dwelling on other times, other people. At length he said, "I heard you was with old Grady Welch when he got killed."

Snort's face saddened as he stared into the remnant of the fire. "I was there when he taken his last breath on this earth. I cried like a baby."

Hewey nodded, for he could understand that.

Snort said, "Every time we lose one like him, a little flavor goes out of life. There ain't many of us left."

"Horse stepped on him, Walter said."

"Big black horse, it was. Sixteen hands high, four stockin' feet. I never did trust a horse with four stockin' feet."

"Tough way to die."

Snort shrugged. "Maybe. I don't know but what it's the way old Grady would've wanted to go, though. Beats hell out of livin' till you get so old you can't ride anymore. Or gettin' bad hurt. Most ranches don't feel responsible for you if you get crippled for life, workin' for them. They'll thank you for your help, give you a little foldin' money and send you to town to fend for yourself. If you're damn lucky you might get a job cookin' for a wagon. If you're lucky but not *that* lucky you might get a job washin' out spittoons in some saloon. If you're not lucky atall you'll wind up beggin' for handouts on a street corner and tellin' everybody how great a cowpuncher you was before you fell on hard times. I've seen all three. I'd druther it'd happen to me like it happened to Grady, when my time comes."

Hewey frowned deeply, staring into the fire, remembering grand old times with Grady and Snort, and with others who had gone on. "When we get to town we'll have a drink to old Grady."

Snort looked up, struck by the appropriateness of the idea. It was, in its own way, almost a form of prayer. "We'll do that, Hewey. We'll sure as hell do that."

They delivered the horses to Nasworthy's stables across from the huge courthouse. There buyer Norton Bates waited with a couple of Mexican cowboys to pick them up. Bates rode with Hewey to the First National Bank, a block east. It was a brand-new structure with four magnificent white columns and a stone eagle perched on top.

"You wouldn't believe it," Bates said, "but they spent twenty-five thousand dollars puttin' up that buildin'."

Hewey whistled. A man could buy a good-sized ranch for that kind of money. They could have lost C. C.'s Upton City bank in a corner of this one and not found it for a week.

Bates drew a draft and arranged for the bank to mail it directly to the Upton City bank for Alvin's account. Hewey knew nothing about the handling of such big financial transactions. His twenty or twenty-five or thirty dollars a month had always been paid in cold cash.

"I owe you boys a drink," Bates said when the business was done. "The Arc Light Saloon is down yonder a ways." He pointed south.

Hewey knew full well where the Arc Light was. "These younguns here are a mite underage. They been wantin' to visit a real ice-cream parlor. Reckon you could point the way to one of those?"

Bates opined that ice cream was dangerous because it froze the stomach. But if the boys were bound and determined to risk their lives, he would pay for a spread. Afterward he took Hewey and Snort to the saloon, where the goods had the opposite effect, warming all the way to the toes. There Hewey found a lot of cowboys in town either to watch or to participate in the roping. By the time all the howdying and shaking was done, his arm was almost too tired to lift a rope.

The boys were waiting outside, both excited. "Uncle Hewey," Cotton exclaimed, "we've seen us an automobile."

Tommy pointed. "It's just around that corner yonder."

Hewey wasn't all that interested. He was itching to go and get his name into the pot for the roping. But he decided to smile over an automobile and act as if he liked it, though telling a lie was a mortal sin.

To him it looked like every other automobile he had ever seen in his travels, mostly just a glorified buggy with rubber tires, and without a horse. Down beneath the bed was an ugly-looking engine, leaking oil. Over the dashboard was a long shaft with a wheel on it that he knew was the mechanism for guiding the brainless contraption. All in all, he didn't see much there to detain a man for more than a minute or two.

Cotton walked around the automobile, learnedly pointing out all its features, telling what each was for and what part it played in making the monster lumber down the road and scare good horses half to death. Cotton seemed to know a lot, never to have laid eyes on one of these before.

Snort Yarnell seemed impressed by Cotton's knowledge, though he understood no more of it than Hewey did.

Cotton was leaning over the seat, pointing to some doodad and thingamajig on the dash when a tall man with a derby hat, a new suit and a waxed mustache stepped out of a nearby barber shop. He reeked of bay rum. "Boy," he shouted, "you get your grimy hands away from that automobile!" He came striding purposefully down the plank sidewalk.

Cotton drew back as if he had been shot.

The man pointed a finger at him. "Don't you know the meaning of private property, kid? Don't you know that's an expensive piece of machinery? Be damned if I'll let some ignorant farm boy hoodoo it."

Cotton reddened.

Hewey moved between his nephew and the angry-eyed dude. "The button didn't mean no harm. And he may be a farm boy, but he's noways ignorant."

The well-dressed gent gave Hewey a hard stare that silently put him in a class no more than one notch above a yellow mongrel dog. There were a lot of people who didn't realize what a good cowboy was worth. "Every generation ought to make a *little* improvement over the one before it."

This time Cotton stepped between Hewey and the man. "Uncle Hewey, I've seen the automobile now. Let's get away from here."

Hewey had never been a fist fighter and had customarily gone well out of his way to avoid a fight when he could. In this case he was disposed toward making an exception.

Cotton caught him by the arm. "Let's go, Uncle Hewey."

Snort had put a fresh chew of tobacco in his mouth after the drink. Now he needed to spit. He deposited a brown blob on the rear tire. It began to stretch and run and drip. The dude made a strong comment about Snort's ancestry and stepped quickly to wipe away what he could with his white handkerchief. Snort said, "Hewey, we better go see about that ropin'."

Hewey nodded but looked back as he walked away. "I hope he's forced to trade that thing for a mean Missouri mule. And I hope that mule kicks him so hard it melts the wax out of his *mus*tache."

Snort tried none too subtly to change the subject. "I had a *mus*tache one time. Kept it two or three years. You remember it, Hewey? Finally got rid of it. Kept burnin' it off smokin' my cigarettes short."

After he had put up his five dollars, Hewey ran a finger down the handwritten list of entrants and glanced quickly at Snort. "They got Clay McGonagill and Joe Gardner here, the champions of the whole world. And Fred Baker and Jim Barron and Bob Mims. All the good ones, just about, except Ellison Carroll. You ever rope against these fellers before?"

"Nope. But that gives us the advantage, don't you see? They don't know what they're up against."

Hewey and Snort and the boys went to the Trimble Grocery and splurged a dollar and a half on luxuries such as cheese and crackers, sardines and canned peaches. These they carried down to the bank of the Concho River. They squatted in the dense shade of the big native pecan trees, where Hewey opened the cans by slashing a big X in the tops with his Barlow knife. They fed sumptuously. Done, Hewey rubbed his stomach. "Them bankers in Kansas City don't have it a tittle or a jot better than this."

Tommy enthusiastically agreed. "If I ever get rich, I'll do this every day."

The fairgrounds lay in a big open flat east of town. The arena was almost the size of a horse trap; Hewey guessed it at ten acres, its far end reaching all the way to the steep bank of the Main Concho on the south. At the north end was a small grandstand and the holding pens where sixty or seventy long-legged, long-horned Mexico steers pulled hay out of wooden racks as if it were free, trampling half of it underfoot. Wagons and buggies lined up along the arena fence on either side. The roping was supposed to begin at two o'clock.

Snort strayed off to visit with old friends and to bask in the glory of his reputation. Hewey rode Biscuit leisurely through the crowd, looking for people he knew, studying the ropers and their mounts. He gave special but quiet attention to big Clay McGonagill, freshly back from a triumphant tour of South America with some other noted ropers like Joe Gardner. Hewey sort of liked McGonagill's big bay horse, which had an apple branded on the shoulder, but not enough to propose a trade for Biscuit.

Once his breath came short as he saw a woman in the crowd. She looked for all the world like Spring Renfro. He couldn't imagine what Spring would be doing here. He eased Biscuit up closer and saw that he was mistaken. She didn't look like Spring at all. The woman stared at him, disturbed by his uninvited attention. Hewey turned away, perplexed by his error. He had no idea why Spring should remain so strong on his mind.

Cotton shouted, "Uncle Hewey, yonder comes that automobile."

Hewey reined Biscuit around and saw the same red vehicle, driven by the slicked-up dude. Sitting with him in the front were two young and handsome women dressed like Christmas packages. Hewey doubted that they were his sisters. The driver tooted his horn and almost caused a runaway. A man with a woman and three kids in a hack had to saw desperately on the reins to keep his team from taking the bits in their teeth and leaving there. Horses snorted and scattered as the dude pushed the automobile through the crowd to seek a place beside the arena fence.

Someone shouted, "Be slow with that noise. You'll hurt somebody."

For answer the dude tooted the horn again. One of the girls laughed.

If some husky fellow would go over there and take the curl out of that mustache, he would be the most popular man at the fairgrounds, Hewey thought. He was not seeking honors, however.

Presently Snort was back. "Hewey, how much money you got?"

As little stock as Hewey placed in money, Snort cared even less. Hewey had most of the pay from Alvin, but caution made him reply in the most general terms. "Some."

"Let me have it. I'll double or triple it for you. There's a damn fool over yonder got more money than sense. He's givin' odds."

Hewey kept his hands in his pockets. "The competition is fierce."

"Competition is like sugar sprinkled on cobbler pie. Where's your faith?"

"Faith is one thing. Charity is somethin' else."

"It's that fool yonder who's bein' charitable. Come on, let me have what you've got."

Snort Yarnell was a hard man to refuse. Against his judgment Hewey dug out most of what he had. He was careful to retain a little wad of paper in his pocket, hoping it didn't show. He had no idea how much it was, or how much he handed over. Snort disappeared again.

Cotton stared at Hewey in exasperation. "Uncle Hewey, you've ridden broncs, doctored wormy cattle, done God knows what all to earn that money."

He had that much of his mother in him and couldn't help it, Hewey thought charitably. "Easy come, easy go."

Cotton shook his head over lost causes and turned to watch Tommy, who was making a tentative and cautious acquaintanceship with some town boys of about his own age. Hewey kept an eye on the youngsters for a minute. Sometimes town boys were prone to hooraw country boys shamelessly. But there seemed no harm in these.

Hewey turned his attention to the roping. His name was two thirds of the way down the list, which gave him time to see how most of the others performed before he had to go out and give his due.

The roper who was "up" held his horse in readiness beside a narrow wooden chute into which cowboys had put a single spotted steer. Fifty feet out from the chute gate was the score line, drawn with white powdered chalk. As the gate opened, another rider chased the steer out toward the line. When the steer crossed the chalk mark, a judge dropped a red flag and gave the roper his signal to start. By this time the steer was gaining speed and distance. The roper might require sixty to a hundred yards of running room to catch up with him and make his throw.

Snort was up just before Hewey. He spurred out, swinging a loop big enough to catch a boxcar. As the loop sailed, its size diminished. When it fitted over the steer's horns there weren't more than a couple of inches to spare. But success was what counted. He spurred past the steer, flipped the rope over the animal's rump and rode off hard at an angle. The steer was jerked into a sudden hundred and eighty-degree turn that lifted it off its feet and thumped it down soundly on its side. Instantly Snort was on the ground with tie rope in his hand. He gathered and wrapped three feet while the steer was still too stunned to kick much. He threw up his hands to stop the timekeepers' watches. Snort swaggered to his roan horse and remounted, waiting to hear the time and get his rope back. The crowd cheered.

The time: thirty-eight and three fifths seconds. That put him in the lead for the first go-round.

Snort rode toward Hewey, those gold teeth shining. "You better whip up if you want to take second."

It had been a long time since Biscuit had been in a steer-roping contest. He remembered enough to be nervous. So did Hewey. The flagman stood poised at the end of the chalk score line, the flag up. The gate was opened. A paint steer with a horn span of more than three feet entered the arena in a long trot. The whip-up man put it into a good run across the line. The red flag dropped. Hewey touched spurs to Biscuit, but he didn't really need to. Biscuit remembered. He leaped out and after the steer in a dead run. Hewey had his loop built and ready. It was a big Blocker, after the style of the trail-driving Ab Blocker, but not as big as Snort's. He gave it a few swings, judged he was positioned right and flung it over the steer's horns. He jerked up the slack, sent it across the thin rump and rode away. He felt a jarring impact at the end of the rope. He caught a glimpse of four legs in the air, then a small cloud of dust. He was on the ground and running as Biscuit kept charging ahead, dragging the steer to keep it from gaining its feet. Hewey made a quick tie, threw up his hands and lost his balance. He fell backward, landing hard. He heard the dude honk his horn two or three times. Hewey got up and dusted himself off, his face warming. His embarrassment was more than offset by the far-off announcement of his time: thirty-eight seconds flat.

Grinning, he sought out Snort with his eyes. *Second, hell. That's the best time yet.*

He rode out of the arena expecting to accept the congratulations of the two boys with becoming modesty. But they hadn't seen his performance. Tommy was out past the crowd with several boys, testing his prowess with a slingshot. Another automobile had arrived, this one green. Cotton was down there on the arena fence inspecting it.

Hewey remembered the applause and reflected glumly

over the fact that it always seemed easier to impress strangers than one's own family.

Snort said, "I hope you appreciate me lettin' you get your confidence."

Hewey would have more confidence if he still held his lead after McGonagill and Gardner had performed. As each man roped, he held his breath. They were good, but they came in just shy of his and Snort's times. McGonagill scored thirty-nine seconds, Gardner thirty-nine and two.

The second go-round started immediately. Warmed up now, many of the ropers bettered their original times. Snort went out and finished in thirty-eight one. He came back laughing. "You better draw her down fine, Hewey."

Hewey drew down fine and came back with thirty-eight flat.

The girls who sat in the red automobile cheered and clapped their hands for him as he rode by, to the annoyance of the dude. Hewey made a little show of tipping his hat to the ladies.

Again he looked around to see if the boys had witnessed his moment of triumph. Tommy was out of sight. Cotton was on his knees, studying the running gear beneath the green automobile.

Thank God for pretty women, Hewey thought wryly.

He felt the tension building in him as McGonagill roped, then Gardner. Gardner trimmed Hewey's time a little and came out fastest for the second go-round. Hewey scratched the figures in the dirt with his finger, did a little arithmetic and found to his satisfaction that he still led for the average. If he could do that well on three more steers, he might still carry away the silver watch he had seen down at the saloon.

He didn't know what he would do with it if he won it. He wasn't in the habit of carrying a pocket watch because if it ever stopped he might be three months getting the correct time to reset it. He lived by the sun.

Hewey and Snort seesawed through the next two go-rounds, not taking the best time in either but staying close enough to be in strong contention. Snort did his third steer up a little faster than Hewey, which brought him back laughing loudly enough to hurt Hewey's ears a little. Hewey topped him by almost a full second on the fourth.

The last go-round was usually the wildest in any roping. Those men who trailed would bust a buckle trying to catch up. All they had to lose was their necks, so they took long chances and fast loops. Some missed altogether, some caught just one horn. One let his horse get off stride just as he hit the end of the rope. The horse went down and rolled over him. The crowd jumped to its feet. But the cowboy got up with nothing worse than a slight limp and a shredded shirt.

Hewey was beginning to feel the pressure building on him when he saw a familiar figure striding through the crowd, and heard a familiar voice call his name. It was Walter. Hewey's chin dropped in surprise. He put the shock behind him and rode over to shake hands.

Walter said, "You're a hard man to catch up with once you hit the trail. But I heard there was a ropin', and I figured I'd find you. How you standin'?"

"Pretty good, up to now. What you doin' here? Ain't the weeds growin' up out at the place?"

"Eve didn't trust the boys to get home by theirselves, and not to get in trouble. She sent me to fetch them, and to maybe talk you into comin' back too."

"Mad, wasn't she?"

Walter rubbed his jaw. "I'm not sure *mad* is the word. But it'll do till I think of a stronger one."

"You ain't goin' to try to talk me into goin' back, are you?"

Walter thought about it. "You're of age, Hewey. You've got a right to make up your own mind and live by your own lights."

"Damn few people seem to think so."

Snort Yarnell's time came. He took a fresh chew of tobacco and rode up into place. He was the picture of supreme confidence, sitting straight and proud, shoulders reared back, gold teeth agleam.

He spurred after the steer, swung his loop and completely missed.

It was a big surprise to both Snort and his blue roan horse. The horse slowed, confident Snort had made a catch; he almost always did. By the time Snort built a second loop and finally caught his steer, he was way out of the money. But defeat rolled off of his shoulders like water from a duck. He came back grinning as broadly as if he had won. "Did you notice the shape of that loop, Hewey? I do believe it was as pretty a one as I ever throwed."

"But kind of empty, don't you think?"

Hewey sensed when he spurred out after his own steer that everything was perfect. The steer was just right. Biscuit was just right. The loop felt like prize money when it left his hand. It fitted over the horns as if it had been measured and trimmed. He laid the rope over those red and white hindquarters and rode off. The steer flipped over and flopped down as if it were trained and on his payroll. Hewey jumped down to finalize his victory . . .

. . . and tripped over his spurs.

He went down hard on his face and belly. He pushed up just in time to see the steer before Biscuit dragged it right over him. His face was pressed down into the arena, and he came up spitting dirt. His eyes burned from the sting of sand, and his ears burned from the laughter of the crowd. He got to his feet, looking around desperately for Biscuit and the steer. He saw them far down the arena, still going. Hewey spat some more dirt, hollered at Biscuit to "Haww!" and went chasing ignominiously after them. He heard the honking of an automobile horn over and over and over again. The dude was taking his revenge.

He managed to make his tie, just to keep the record

straight. But he didn't hear his time and didn't much give a damn.

The dude and one of the girls laughed at him as he rode by. The other girl looked guardedly sympathetic.

Snort and Walter were waiting for him. Snort said, "You'll never get anywhere, Hewey, tryin' to put both feet into one boot."

Walter didn't say anything.

The two boys were there. They had finally watched Hewey, one time. Cotton took a cue from his father, but Tommy said, "Uncle Hewey, that was awful."

When all the times were tallied up, McGonagill finished first in the average, Gardner second.

Hewey shrugged. "Well, I reckon I got a little coffee-drinkin' money comin' to me for the first go-round, anyway. Aside from that, I'm purt near broke."

Snort said, "You-all wait for me," and disappeared into the departing crowd. In a little he was back. He counted out a considerable handful of bills to Hewey and shoved the rest of the roll into his own pocket.

Hewey's mouth dropped open. "What's that for? We lost the ropin'."

"But not the bet. You didn't think I'd bet our hard-earned money on *us,* did you? I put it on Clay McGonagill and Joe Gardner against the field." He swung back onto his roan horse. "Let's go to town. We'll get them boys a ice cream and us somethin' stronger."

The traffic strung out in a long, dusty line of wagons, buggies, hacks and horsemen, as well as numerous bicycles and a goodly number of people afoot. From behind came the insistent honking of a horn. Hewey looked over his shoulder and saw the dude impatiently making his way through the crowd in that ugly red automobile. He wasn't having any trouble clearing the horses; they were snorting and faunching to get out of the monster's path. As the auto-

mobile came up close behind Cotton and Tommy, the dude
tooted that horn again.

Tommy's horse squealed and broke into pitching. Surprised, Tommy grabbed too late for the horn, sailed up into
the air and came down on his belly. Walter jumped to the
ground to see about him.

The dude honked again and went around without stopping. The crowd was shouting ugly threats but doing nothing about it.

Snort and Hewey looked each other in the eyes. Hewey
saw the intention in Snort's face and concurred with a nod.
Both unfastened their horn strings and shook loops into
their ropes. Snort shouted, "I'll rope the head of the goddamn thing, Hewey. You come in there and heel it!"

Spurring the roan horse, swinging the loop, Snort gave
chase. One of the girls glanced back, saw him and gasped.
The dude looked over his shoulder, recognized Snort's intention and began trying for more speed. But the wagon
road was rough and bouncy.

"Damn you, cowboy, don't you dare!" he shouted as
Snort came up abreast of the vehicle. The roan was rolling
its eyes and snorting in fear, but Snort kept spurring. In the
final analysis, the horse feared Snort more than it feared the
automobile.

Snort threw that great boxcar loop and landed a catch
around the dashboard, one carbide lamp and a front wheel.
He jerked up the slack and took a dally around his saddle
horn. "Now heel it, Hewey!"

Hewey spurred Biscuit in, cast a quick loop over one of
the rear wheels and rode south. Snort rode north.

The dude shouted and shook his fist. The girls grabbed
hold of the seat and screamed.

As the two cowboys hit the ends of their ropes, they
jerked the automobile half around and ran it into the ditch.
The dude was thrown out over the dashboard.

Snort shouted, "We got it roped, but how do we hog-tie an automobile?"

The dude was stunned only for a moment. He got to his feet, eyes blazing and looking for somebody to fight. Hewey was closest. He came running, his fists knotted. Hewey dismounted and stepped away from Biscuit. As the dude swung on him, Hewey ducked under and took a solid hold. He wrestled the man to the ground. Snort, still on horseback, pitched Hewey his tie rope. "Since we can't tie up an automobile, maybe we can tie up an automobile jockey."

Hewey got the little loop over both of the man's hands and then over one foot. He trussed him the way he had been tying steers.

In a sudden flush of showmanship he stepped back and threw up his hands in the manner the ropers used to stop the timekeepers. A goodly crowd had gathered around. Most of them clapped their hands and cheered.

Clay McGonagill rode forward and leaned down to shake Hewey's hand. "Friend, if you'd done that in the arena, *you'd* be carryin' that silver watch."

One of the girls sat big-eyed in the car, saying over and over, "My goodness." The other climbed down and untied the dude. Snort rode the blue roan over to her. "Pretty miss, I'd be much obliged if you'd throw me my strang."

Some of the crowd rescued Hewey's and Snort's ropes from the automobile. The driver rubbed his hands where the rope had burned him, and the fight was still in him. But the crowd was laughing him down. He climbed back into the automobile and sat there baking in the heat of his anger. He looked at nobody and spoke to no one.

Snort showed those gold teeth. "I do believe he's sulled on us."

Hewey looked back to be sure Tommy was all right. He was. The laughing, cheering crowd then swept him and Snort along toward town, rejoicing.

Snort declared, "I'll bet you we made history here today,

Hewey, old pardner. I'll bet me and you are the first cow-boys to ever head and heel an automobile!"

All the way to town they were congratulated and back-slapped by well-wishing strangers who now considered them friends. Snort looked behind him to see if the auto-mobile was coming. It still sat in the ditch.

"I read in a paper a while back where some damn fools are a-fixin' to try to drive an automobile all the way from New York to California."

"Hope they ain't in a hurry," Hewey said.

"Hope they don't run into no ropers along the way."

Cotton and Tommy found new friends among the town boys, who wanted to show them how good the night fish-ing was in the Concho River. Coming out of a dry country where it was hard to find even a water dog, Walter's boys were receptive to the notion. It was just as well, because Hewey knew he would have been a poor chaperon. Boys that age needed a lot of leaving-alone, anyway.

As they started to leave with the other boys, Tommy ad-monished, "You watch out now, Uncle Hewey, and don't you get drunk."

"Button," Hewey assured him, "I ain't ever been drunk in my whole life."

He could have gotten roaring drunk without spending a dime, had he wanted to. Snort was well on the way. Friends and strangers kept crowding around them in the Arc Light, trying to buy drinks for the men who had roped and thrown the wild devil-car.

Walter sat at the table with Hewey and Snort, but he drank very little. He grimaced each time he lifted the glass to his lips. "Whisky must've come a long way downhill. Seems to me like it used to taste better than this."

Hewey thought perhaps a residue of something had been left in Walter's glass. He took a sip from it. "Nothin' wrong with the whisky."

"It's me, then. I've lost my taste for it. One drink is fine. The second drink ain't worth a bucket of cold pee."

"I'm sorry, little brother."

"It's just as well. If I didn't have anything in life that I liked better than whisky, then I'd really have somethin' to worry about." Restlessly he looked around him at the growing crowd, noisily bustling about the tables, clustering at the bar. He listened to the clink of glasses, the jingling of silver coin, the roaring of boisterous laughter as someone told a joke that would not have stood the daylight. His frown deepened.

Hewey asked, "What's the matter?"

"Nothin'. Just kickin' myself for the time I've wasted the last few years, worryin' about missin' all *this*."

Hewey looked at the people. "Everybody seems to be havin' a good time."

"Maybe they got nothin' better at home."

"You tryin' to lecture me? This is a poor place to be holdin' church."

"I promised I wouldn't argue with you, and I won't. But I'll have to admit that I don't understand. There was a feelin' between you and Spring Renfro. Anybody could see it. Wasn't it strong enough?"

Hewey poured himself a fresh shot of whisky, but he didn't drink it. He stared into it. This wasn't a thing he wanted to talk about, especially not here. But he supposed everybody was making so much noise that no one except Walter would hear him. "It was strong." He remembered a feeling of guilt because of its strength. "It scared me, I reckon."

"Scared you? That's not the way it's supposed to be. It's supposed to lift you up and make you happy."

Hewey turned the glass in his fingers. He looked around to see if anyone was listening. Nobody could have heard him. Walter would be lucky to. "I had feelin's about her that wasn't right and proper. She's a lady, Walter. She's got a right to decency and respect. But when I was around her I'd sometimes get to thinkin' things . . ." He turned up his hands. "I know about women; I ain't no schoolboy. I been upstairs with a many of them wheeligo girls, and no blush ever touched my cheek. Spring ain't that kind of a woman, but sometimes she gave me the same feelin' I'd get from them wheeligo girls. She deserves a lot better than that."

"It's a natural feelin'. Everybody gets it. It's nothin' to be ashamed of."

"Well, I am. And if I was to marry her I'd have to face up to it. Sure, I know everybody does it. If they didn't, this old earth would get short of people in a hurry. But, Walter, I couldn't see *me* doin' it, not with *her.* How could I, the first time? How could I look her in the eye afterward and not want to crawl off under a rock and hide?"

Walter's eyes softened. A smile seemed about to break, but he restrained it. "Hewey, you're worryin' about a ladder when there ain't even a wall. Believe me, when the time comes it'll be the most natural thing in the world. There won't be any guilt. It'll be the opposite, if anything. It'll be like you went to church."

Hewey couldn't visualize any resemblance.

Walter said, "There won't be any shame in it for her, and there won't be for you either. You think there was any shame in it for me and Eve? No sir, it's a natural thing, a part of life. It's part of bein' human, for the woman as well as for the man."

He finished what was left of his drink and showed no pleasure in it. "You'll never know what I'm talkin' about till it happens to you. Then you'll wonder why you waited for thirty-eight years."

"Thirty-six," Hewey said. It *was* thirty-eight.

Walter shrugged. "Whichever, you've wasted too much time already." He pushed to his feet. "I'm goin' down by the river where me and the boys made camp. I've had about all of this wild pleasure that I can stand." He gripped Hewey's shoulder, then nodded at Snort.

Snort acknowledged the benediction with a salute of his glass, which he promptly emptied. When Walter was gone, Snort said, "You know what he's tryin' to do to you, Hewey? He's tryin' to get you to fit into the same tight little mold as everybody else. But me and you, we broke the mold that made *us*. We're free men. There ain't many of our kind left in this world."

"Walter was free once. Givin' it up don't seem to've killed him."

"Because they've changed him. They've cut him. A steer don't realize what he's missed, but he's missed it just the same. You ain't no steer, Hewey. Don't be lettin' all them people make a steer of you. Show them you're a bull, and damn proud of it."

Hewey poured a drink and downed it all at once. "We showed them today. We showed them we was bull enough to head and heel an automobile."

Snort poured Hewey another drink. "Damn betcha we did." He lifted his glass in toast. "Here's to the best automobile ropers that ever straddled leather."

Hewey drank to that.

Snort leaned across the table, anticipation bright in his eyes. "What do you need with a skinny old-maid school-teacher, anyway? Somebody to tie you down and put a ring in your nose, and what do you get out of it? A life sentence to hard labor is all." He pointed his thumb back over his shoulder. "I know where we can find us a couple of the prettiest gals a man ever slid under a sheet with. Not skinny, either. Plump. Somethin' you can really get ahold of. Not coldblooded like some schoolteacher, but hot like Mexican peppers. They don't ask you where you been or where you're goin'. They don't tie no strings on you or cry when you leave. But they'll be somethin' to remember on them long nights you're layin' out alone in some cold camp. What you say we go over yonder and get us a couple of them gals? We got it comin' to us for the work we done here today."

Hewey shook his head. "I don't know, Snort. I ain't sure I'm ready."

"You got that schoolteacher on your mind. You ever see a schoolteacher erase a blackboard? One good sweep of her hand and it's all gone. Well, erase *her*. We'll find you a pretty gal down yonder, and that's the last you'll ever worry about that schoolteacher."

Hewey still didn't move.

Snort said, "You don't have to really do nothin' if you ain't got the notion. Let's just go down there and look. Won't hurt nothin' to just look."

The whisky burned Hewey's stomach, and his eyes were blurry. He was not yet so drunk that he didn't realize he wouldn't stop at just looking. They always looked good, those wheeligo girls, and they smelled good. When a man got close enough, they *felt* good. Once he ever went that far he wouldn't stop. He never had.

Snort was up on wobbly feet, trying to talk a couple more cowboys into taking a walk with them down West Concho Avenue. Before he could help himself, Hewey was out in the street with them. They were hustling him along in the cool night, singing an outrageous song in three keys. Hewey hoped to hell those two boys of Walter's had gone to bed by now and weren't still up prowling around where they might see him.

It was a two-story house a block or two down from the Landon Hotel. Hewey's vision was none too clear; he couldn't tell much about the place. The electric lights hurt his eyes. He had never been around the damn things enough to get used to them. San Angelo had set up a power plant in the nineties. Some people nowadays even had a light bulb hanging in their cowsheds.

A player piano was twanging away unattended over on one flower-papered wall. Hewey thought it was badly in need of a tuner's services, but maybe it was just his ears. Some couples were dancing. Among them was the dude.

They saw each other at about the same time. Snort saw him too. He made loud and public mention of the fact that this was the jelly bean whose automobile he and Hewey had brought to its knees. The dude's face reddened, and he showed some momentary disposition to fight. The girl he danced with told him the house had strict rules against violence, and they had a bouncer as big as one of the Twin Mountains to enforce the regulation. He would keep things peaceful around here if he had to kill half the cowboys in San Angelo.

Hewey saw the bouncer standing in a corner. He was tall enough that he had to duck to come through the door, and he stood two ax handles broad. Hewey could understand why the dude quickly quieted down.

It occurred to him that the girl the dude danced with was one of the two who had been with him in the automobile. She was doing a lot of whispering in the man's ear. Presently the two of them disappeared down a hallway. Hewey felt confident that when the dude came back he would be in a better humor.

A hand gently touched his shoulder, and he tried to turn his head. That proved difficult. He finally brought his eyes into focus on a pretty face he remembered seeing before. "How's the great car roper?" she asked, grinning. He thought she had the brightest-looking teeth he had ever seen. Maybe that was from the electric lights.

His tongue was thick. He thought he had a good answer, but he couldn't bring it out. He mumbled something which even he didn't understand. This was the second girl who had been with the dude, the one who had had gumption enough to get out of the automobile and untie him. The fact that the dude now had gone down the hall with the one who just sat and whimpered told him something, he thought, about the man.

"Old Foxy has had that comin' to him," she said.

"Foxy?"

"Fox is his name. Us ladies just call him Foxy. He's got a right smart of money but damn little else." She smiled again. "I don't want to talk about him. I want to talk about *you*. What's your name?"

For a minute he thought he had forgotten it. He had to try twice before he got it said.

She tried it slowly. "Hewey. My, that's a sweet name."

He never had thought of it in that light before. It occurred to him that, yes, it *was* a sweet name.

Her hand kept moving slowly along his back until her arm was around his shoulder. "I don't believe I ever knew but one other man named Hewey. That one liked to dance. I'll bet you like to dance too."

"Sure do," he said, though in reality he had always had two left feet. Shortly he was with her in the center of the parlor floor. The player piano was still off key but trying hard, as was Hewey. His feet weighed fifty pounds apiece.

She said, "What you need, cowboy, is a drink."

He vaguely remembered already having one or two, but her arms and her soft, warm body rubbing tantalizingly against him persuaded him that whatever she thought he needed, he needed. He took that drink, and soon another. She was whispering things in his ear that sounded very nice, though he never quite understood the words. That damn piano.

First thing he knew, she had her arm around his waist, and his around hers. They were stumbling up the stairs together. They were both laughing, and he was pinching her where it seemed nature had intended for her to be pinched by making it so irresistible. She led him to a door, opened it and helped him into a small room. He saw a brass bed and a bureau, and a washstand with a china bowl and a pink-flowered pitcher. The place had a strong aroma of perfume. Over the bed was an embroidered and framed motto: "God Bless Our Home." He thought the sentiment was nice.

She sat him down on the edge of the bed and put her arms

around him. He turned his head to kiss her but made the mistake of looking up toward that bare, glowing light bulb. He realized he shouldn't have tilted his head so far, but he was somehow hypnotized by the blazing filament. The light seemed to start circling around and around over him like some fiery bird of prey about to swoop down and grab him. His head became heavy. He sank back onto the bed. All of a sudden the light seemed to go out, and he was falling backward, falling, falling . . .

He awoke slowly, dreaming that twelve spans of Missouri mules were running over his head, and when they finished the freight wagon behind them got him too. He became conscious of daylight through the drawn paper shade that covered a window. He found his hand, which weighed seventy-five pounds, and then his hand found his head. It came to him gradually that he was lying in a bed. He blinked. Slowly his vision began to clear. He saw dimly the outline of a woman sitting in a straight chair, slowly brushing her long hair. His first thought was that she was Spring Renfro, and he tried to understand what she was would be doing in his bedroom. It came to him in a minute that he *had* no bedroom. He managed to clear his eyes a little more and see for certain that this was not Spring.

The girl continued brushing her long brown hair and watching him dispassionately. She said, "I do believe, old boy, that you'll live after all."

Hewey rubbed his head. "Damn, I hope not."

He blinked again, trying to remember where he was and how he got here. The smell of the perfume helped bring it all back. The memory slowly seeped through his brain. With the memory came shame, drawing over him like a shroud. What would Walter's boys think? What would Spring Renfro think?

They ought to pass a law to keep anybody under forty from drinking.

He hadn't intended for anything like this to happen. Only

three or four days gone from Spring Renfro, and now he lay in an upstairs bedroom of a Concho Avenue parlor house.

Eve had been right in everything she had called him.

As he studied the girl with clearer eyes, he decided she looked ten years older. He rubbed his hand down his side and found that he was barefoot from heel to forelock. "What happened to my clothes?"

"You took them off," she said evenly. "You did pretty good, up to that point."

"I don't remember a thing that happened."

"There ain't nothin' to remember." She seemed to be laughing at him a little. "Quick as you laid down, you was gone to China, or someplace. You sure wasn't here."

He blinked, hope beginning to flare. "You mean I didn't . . ."

"I mean you *couldn't*. You went out faster than an electric light." Her brow knitted into a frown. "I hope you ain't figurin' to ask me for your money back. I was here all night, even if you wasn't."

Never in his life had Hewey been so glad not to get his money's worth. "Honey, you keep it. In fact, I'll be glad to give you five dollars more."

Her frown was gone. She suggested, "It's still early. I got nothin' particular to do right now."

"But *I* have. If you'll get me my underwear and my britches . . ."

He swung his feet over the side of the bed and almost fell off. She caught him and cradled his aching head against her breasts. "Honey, you're in too much of a hurry."

Reluctantly he pulled himself away. He knew if he stayed any longer he would become attached to the place and not leave until bankruptcy strained his welcome. He got his underwear on, then his hat, his britches, his shirt and finally his boots. He said, "I reckon my pardner, old Snort Yarnell, is in the house somewhere."

She nodded. "He taken a shine to Flo."

"Well, when you see him, tell him Hewey Calloway has decided to go back to school."

She didn't know what he was talking about, but Snort would understand.

She kissed him one more time and patted his cheek. "You come back, honey, anytime you take the notion."

He fumbled his way down the stairs, the girl following a few steps behind him, showing a concern that wasn't all bought and paid for. The early morning sunlight hit him like a sledgehammer when he stepped through the door. He had to cover his eyes with his hands for a minute.

She asked, "You goin' to make it, hon?"

"If I can live through the next ten minutes." He hitched up his pants, pulled down his hat, straightened his shoulders and staggered out into the street. It took him a minute to get his bearings. He looked up toward the big Landon Hotel and remembered the red-light district had always been to the west of it. The hotel itself was impeccably clean and moral, a place where preachers could stay and feel at home. But if they took a constitutional, they were usually advised to walk east, not west.

Walter and the boys should be more or less south, somewhere down on the riverbank. He headed in that direction, trying to get his feet under better control. Presently he spotted the camp. Rather, he spotted Biscuit tethered on a long stake rope, and with him Walter's and the boys' horses. A lot of other horses and other camps lay beyond. Many people had come to watch the roping but could not afford or did not choose to spend the price of a hotel room or even a little space at a wagonyard.

He heard voices and looked back. Far behind him he saw four men. At the distance and in the condition of his eyes he could not make out who they were. He knew no reason it should make a difference. Trudging down toward camp, he smelled coffee on the fire or on some other. At the moment coffee seemed vastly superior to whisky.

Tommy shouted, "Yonder comes Uncle Hewey." Walter, hunched over the fire, turned and glanced at his brother but made no move. Tommy came running. "Where you been, Uncle Hewey? We thought you'd come down here last night and camp with us."

Hewey avoided meeting his nephew's gaze. "I ran into a friend."

"You must have friends everywhere."

"I try to."

Walter beckoned. "We found a woman who had some eggs to sell. You look like you could find a place for a few."

Hewey's stomach roiled. He wasn't sure eggs would find hospitality in there, but they stood as good a chance as anything. He was about to reply in the affirmative when a rough voice shouted:

"Yonder he is. Now get the son of a bitch!"

He turned. Three of the biggest men he had ever seen advanced down the riverbank toward him. Their eyes were purposeful and cold. Behind them, hands on his hips, stood the dude who owned the red automobile. He was disheveled, unshaven, a far cry from the handsome picture of yesterday. He, like Hewey, evidently had put in a bad night.

Hewey backed away a few steps, holding up both hands. "Fellers, I don't know what he's been tellin' you about me, but it's all lies."

He knew immediately that truth was of little interest to them. One he recognized now as the bouncer from the parlor house. He looked as if he could wrestle a bull to the ground.

"Fellers," Hewey argued, still backing, "there ain't no use in us goin' through all this. I'll gladly give up before we start."

The bouncer said, "It ain't nothin' personal, cowboy. Mr. Fox yonder, he paid us to stomp hell out of you, is all."

Hewey was almost to the edge of the river. If he backed

any farther he would take a bath he had not planned on. "Tell him I've already repented of my willful ways."

"Talkin' won't fix things. He wants to see some blood spilt. You can just stand there and take it, or you can fight. To us it don't much matter one way or the other."

Fox stood well behind the three advancing men, waiting to get his money's worth. Hewey saw that argument was useless, and apology never crossed his mind. It had always been his contention that when you faced a snake you didn't waste time stomping on its rattles; you tried to smash the head. He attempted to dart around the three and get to Fox, but his heavy feet didn't dart well. The bouncer grabbed him, hauled him off of the ground and swung a fist the size and consistency of an oak stump. Hewey thought his head had exploded. He thumped down solidly on his back.

He heard Walter shout, "Boys, go for the law!" With an angry roar Walter came running, swinging a chunk of firewood. The bouncer went down with a grunt. The other two quickly turned their attention to wresting the firewood from Walter. One of them bear-hugged the wooden chunk to keep it from causing harm while the other furiously pummeled at Walter. Cotton jumped up on that man's back and tried to take a strangle hold around a thick neck that would have been counted an asset to a Durham bull.

"Boy," Walter shouted, "I told you to go for the law!"

"Tommy went," Cotton gritted, still struggling for a hold that would have any effect. The big man pitched like an outlaw horse. In a minute Cotton went sprawling. The man kicked at him but missed. Anger boiled up in Hewey and brought him to his feet. They didn't seem so heavy anymore. He made for the man who had tried to kick Cotton. The man turned to meet him and they went down rolling, wrestling. Hewey didn't have much chance to see what else was going on, but he caught a glimpse of the bouncer trying to push to his feet and dropping back on his knees. He heard Fox shouting at him to get up and get back in there.

Hewey had only a vague idea what to do; he had never been much inclined toward this type of endeavor. During most of his life he had been able to talk his way out of scrapes, or to have a horse that would outrun anybody else's. He twisted and punched and gouged where and when he could. Sometimes he was on top, sometimes on bottom. His head was reeling so much he didn't always know. But he had the drive to keep struggling.

He sensed that Walter was making a better show of himself, helped along by Cotton until finally the bouncer made it to his feet and punched Cotton in the stomach so hard that Cotton went down choking, gasping for breath. Then the bouncer and the other man together gave their full attention to Walter. In a minute they had him down. The bouncer, his head bleeding because of the lick he had taken from the firewood, angrily began stomping on Walter. Hewey bawled in rage but couldn't work loose from the fellow holding him. He heard something snap, and Walter cried out in pain.

Someone shouted from on top of the riverbank. Fox started running away. Men spilled down toward the fighters. In a minute the three hired toughs stood hunched together while a big man with a shining badge addressed them in terms that would blister a mule skinner's ears. They stood and took it like whipped pups.

Somebody lifted Hewey to his feet. When they tried to lift his brother, Walter screamed.

"His leg is broke," somebody said. "Send for a doctor."

Hewey wiped the back of his bruised and torn hand across his face, and it came away bloody. He knelt beside his brother. "Walter, do you hurt bad?"

Walter couldn't answer. He gritted his teeth and tried to keep from crying out again. Hewey almost touched Walter's leg but caught himself in time. He turned and looked back over his shoulder. "It was that biggest one done it. That bawdy-house bouncer."

The big man's anger was gone, and fear had taken its place. "You takin' us off to jail, Sheriff?"

The lawman's reply left no possible doubt of his intentions. "Plumb to the third floor. What did you do it for, Jayce?"

"For money. We come after that feller"—he nodded his chin toward Hewey—"but there wasn't no hard feelin's on our part. We was paid to teach him a lesson, is all."

"I hope everybody has learned one," the sheriff declared. "Who paid you?"

"That fancy gent, that Fox."

"If there wasn't anything personal, how come you to break this feller's leg?"

"It got personal when he hit me up beside the head with a tree stump."

The sheriff had a deputy with him. He detailed him to go hunt up the dude and deliver him to the courthouse. "I'll take these three fine gentlemen up to the jail and entertain them at county expense." He turned to Hewey. "You'll want to stay with your brother, I expect. A doctor's on the way. When you can, I wish you'd come on up to my office in the courthouse. We've got some talkin' to do."

Hewey nodded. He looked back at Walter. The two boys were with him, one kneeling on either side. Tommy cried at the sight of his father lying hurt. Cotton's nose had been bleeding, but that had stopped. A big splotch was turning blue on his left cheek. He lifted his gaze to his uncle. Hewey couldn't decide whether he saw rebuke in the boy's eyes or not. Cotton said, "This all come about because of you ropin' that automobile."

Hewey had nothing constructive to say. He only grunted.

Cotton said, "I reckon it seemed like a good idea at the time. But I remember somethin' my daddy told you. He said you never was one to think about cost, or about consequences. What do you think about *this*?"

"I wouldn't have had it happen for the world."

"But it did, and Daddy has got to live with it." Cotton grimaced, close to tears. "You're a good old boy, Uncle Hewey. But sometimes you're a danger to everybody around you."

Hewey bowed his head. He could see no argument with that. He heard Walter rasp to Cotton, "Leave your Uncle Hewey alone, son. He didn't mean nobody any harm."

"He never does."

The doctor drove up in a buggy. He examined Walter's leg and found what everybody already knew. He made up a temporary splint and directed some of the crowd in loading Walter into the bed of a wagon. They hauled him to the doctor's office. There he completed his examination, set the leg with help from somebody steadier than Hewey, and he put it into a cast.

"How long's he got to stay in that thing?" Hewey asked.

"Six weeks at the least. Eight, more likely."

Cotton protested, "Doctor, my daddy's a farmer. We've got crops to finish up, stock to be worked."

The doctor sternly shook his head. "I don't care what he is. If he tries to walk on that leg in less than two months he'll be a cripple the rest of his life."

Cotton turned to Hewey, his eyes stricken. "What're we goin' to do, Uncle Hewey?"

Hewey had no answer. At times like this it seemed he never did. The best he could muster was a weak and meaningless, "We'll get by."

"How? You just tell me how!"

"Someway."

The courthouse was a huge Gothic stone structure like something out of a book on the terrors of the olden times when young princes were smothered to death and queens had their heads chopped off. Its cupola stood a full two stories above the three-story building itself. It made Hewey's head hurt all over again to look up at the big clock near the top. He didn't know why he looked. It made no difference what time it was.

He found the sheriff's office without trouble. He could hear the sheriff's stern voice as he entered the hallway. He walked in reluctantly, hat in his hand. The sheriff had Fox and the other three men sitting on a bench along one wall, thoroughly cowed before the majesty of the law. He looked up at Hewey. "How's your brother?"

"In a bad fix. He won't walk for a long time."

The lawman frowned. "I suppose you know you're partly responsible?"

Hewey hung his head.

The sheriff asked, "How you figurin' on gettin' him home?"

"I don't know. I reckon I'll have to borrow or hire a wagon."

"A banker in town is fixin' to leave early in the mornin' to inspect a loan out in that part of the country. He's takin' an automobile. I believe I could talk him into carryin' your brother."

Hewey considered. "You reckon that'd be faster than a wagon?"

"Anything is."

Hewey gave his consent. "If there's any expenses . . ."

The sheriff pointed his chin at Fox, who looked very little like the dude he had been yesterday. "Mr. Fox here is in a generous mood. He has already agreed that he will foot any and all expenses havin' to do with your brother's . . . accident. Otherwise he'll roost in the jailhouse till the snow flies." He looked at the other three. "Unless you have some objection, I've decided to let these men go. They all seem to have remembered that they were about to leave town anyway."

Hewey nodded. "As long as it ain't west."

The bouncer looked at his huge hands. "Don't worry, I ain't goin' west. They got some rough old boys out there."

The automobile had a broad seat in the back. With some effort they were able to prop Walter up so that he could be reasonably comfortable. Cotton was to go along and help take care of him on the trip. Hewey and Tommy would follow, bringing home the four horses.

Hewey said, "Cotton, I always promised I'd get you a ride in an automobile. I didn't mean for it to be like this."

"You can't help bein' the way you are, Uncle Hewey."

"I'm goin' to change, boy. Believe me, I'll change."

Cotton gave him a quiet gaze that told all of his doubts, then he climbed into the green automobile.

Hewey watched the machine pull away, leaving a trail of smoke that smelled to him as if it would chase the devil out of hell. Cotton never did look back. Shoulders slumped, Hewey turned to Tommy.

"Boy, we'd just as well be on our way too. We've seen about all there is of this place."

They went first by the Alvin Lawdermilk headquarters, getting there at dinnertime the second day. Hewey had talked little to Tommy on the way; his mind had dwelled much on what he would say here, and later at home. He burst through the front screen and faced a surprised group at the table. Spring Renfro looked at him in astonishment, holding her fork motionless halfway to her open mouth. As he had expected, she looked a lot better than that wheeligo girl.

"Miss Renfro," he blurted, "I've changed my mind. I'm thataway inclined. But before I ask if you are too, there's somethin' I want you to know. While I was in San Angelo I tried to consort with a lewd woman. I couldn't do it, but you got to know that I tried."

She pushed her chair back and slowly came around the table. Her initial surprise gave way to the beginnings of a smile. "It's all right, Mr. Calloway."

He held up his hands. "There's somethin' else. I wasn't at San Juan Hill. I never even *seen* Teddy Roosevelt except from a long ways off. The day they went up that hill I was flat on my back with the drizzlin' dysentery."

She walked up until her thin body was against his. Smiling, she laid her fingers across his mouth and brought her left arm around him. She momentarily forgot all her school-teacher training and lapsed into the vernacular as she leaned her head against his chest. "Hewey Calloway, I wisht you'd just hush."

9

Hewey had rather have taken a whipping with a wet rope than face the reception he knew he would get from Eve. It would be colder than a witch's kiss. He put it off as long as he could, taking the horses to the barn, unsaddling, pouring out oats. Cotton came from the house to see his brother and his uncle. Hewey found no cheer in his nephew's face. The bruise was almost black.

"How's your daddy?"

Cotton shrugged, eyes downcast.

"How's your mother takin' it?"

Cotton took a long breath and slowly expelled it. "You'll just have to go see for yourself."

"You-all make it all the way with that stinkin' automobile, or did you have to swap for a wagon?"

"We got in before dark. Fixed three flat tires. Only had motor trouble once, and I got that cured in about half an hour."

"*You* did? How about that banker?"

"He don't know much about engines." Cotton looked up. "Uncle Hewey, he offered me a job. Said I could work for him, drivin' and takin' care of his machine."

Hewey pondered that. He couldn't think of any job he would personally like less. But Cotton had a right to his own view. "You take him up on it?"

"I can't, with all that's facin' us here now. But I wisht I

could. In San Angelo I could take some more schoolin'
while I worked. He told me I could."

"Maybe things'll work out, son."

Cotton looked at the ground again, a catch in his voice.
"There ain't nothin' to work out around here. Not anymore."
Cotton walked on down toward the barn. Tommy turned
and followed him in silent understanding. They quarreled
on occasion, but at a time like this they were brothers.

Hewey took a long look at the house, then started toward
it. He glanced back once, wishing the boys would follow
him. But they were at the barn, and there they intended to
stay. He took that for a bad omen.

He thought he had prepared himself for anything, but the
look in Eve's face was worse than the wildest stretch of his
imagination. She met him at the front screen, blocking his
entrance. In her eyes was a cold fury, almost hatred.

"Hewey Calloway, you'll not set foot in this house!"

Stung, he moved back down from the step and stared
at her from the ground. He felt as if he might choke. "Eve,
I'm sorry."

"Sorry! You're always sorry. But sorry doesn't fix anything. You blunder around like a bull in a china shop, you
ruin other people's lives, and then you think all you have to
do is say you're sorry? Well, it's not good enough.

"You hurt other people and don't even know it. You have
no idea how that good woman cried after you when you left.
And Walter! For years you've tried to lure him away from
this place to wander around with you willy-nilly over the
country. You've tried to tell him this farm wasn't good
enough for him, that he ought to leave it. Well, you've finally succeeded in takin' care of that, Hewey Calloway.
You've just lost us this place!"

"Eve, I didn't mean . . ."

"He's laid up here now, helpless as a child. You think
those two boys and me can make enough money to pay off
Fat Gervin and C. C. Tarpley? They'll come and take us this

fall, lock, stock and barrel. Everything we've worked so hard for, suffered for . . . it'll be gone. And it's all your doin', Hewey. But of course you won't be here to see it. You'll be off to Timbuktu or some such of a place."

She came down the step, pointing her finger into his face. He backed away some more. She declared, "I ought to shoot you, Hewey. No jury would convict me, and I don't think even God would care. If you don't get on your horse and leave here now, I swear I'll do it!"

Words had left him. Shame brought fire to his cheeks. He couldn't even bring himself to look into those furious eyes. She had every right to take a whip to him, and maybe even a gun.

"Eve, I . . ." Hell, there wasn't any use. He backed off a few more steps, then walked toward the barn with his head down. He stopped once and turned, but she towered in front of the door like some avenging angel, her eyes ablaze.

Biscuit hadn't finished his feed, but Hewey pulled him off and left the rest of it for that burro which had no name. He bridled and saddled the horse, his lips pinched hard against his teeth.

Tommy stared with wide eyes. "What did she say?"

Cotton touched his brother's arm and shook his head. As Hewey swung into the saddle, Cotton broke his silence. "We're goin' to lose this place, Uncle Hewey."

Hewey's throat was tight. He knew if he tried to say anything he would break down like a child. He didn't want to do that here, not in front of the boys. He might later, but it would be where nobody could see him. He gave the boys a tentative wave of his hand and touched spurs to Biscuit. Reluctantly, for he was leaving good feed, Biscuit moved into a trot. Hewey headed him in the general direction of the Lawdermilk place. But he drew off a little to one side, skirting around the lower end of the field. There, green leaves rustling in the wind, was the crop of redtop cane which was Walter's hole card toward paying off what he owed the bank this year. Standing outside the fence, trying to reach across to the feed but unable to stretch their necks that far, were three of the yearling cattle also intended to pay part of the obligation.

That much, he knew, the boys and Eve could somehow handle. But it wouldn't be enough. Walter had counted on breaking horses and mules for pay to finish out the balance. Laid up the rest of the summer, he had no chance to do that. Eve was right. All Fat and C. C. had to do now was wait. A nice juicy plum was about to fall into their laps.

And Hewey Calloway was the one who had shaken the tree.

He reined up and turned in the saddle, looking back down toward the house. It wasn't much, just a box-and-strip, hot in the summer and cold in the winter. But dammit, it was home. He remembered the work he had done, helping Walter nail the thing together out of fresh green lumber. He looked at the shed and the corrals and remembered his part in building those. He regarded the chinaberry trees and let his mind go back to the day he had dug the holes to transplant them.

A lot of his own life would go when the place fell to the bank.

When! Not *if,* but *when.* It struck him that he was taking it as a foregone conclusion. And by God it wasn't! There was still time, and there was still a chance.

"Biscuit," he declared, "before C. C. adds this place to his ranch he's goin' to know he's seen him a horse race!"

He reined the brown around and touched him none too gently with the spurs. He put him into a lope that ate up the ground in a hurry. Biscuit started to turn in at the gate where the feed was, but Hewey held firm to the rein and took him right up to the front of the house. He saw the two boys at the barn look at him in surprise and climb up onto the fence to watch.

He slid Biscuit to a stop and stepped down as if he were

back in the San Angelo arena. He strode up to the step and pushed through the screen door. Eve, standing at the stove, turned to look at him, first in astonishment, then in rekindling anger.

"Eve," Hewey declared, "everything you said was right. The worst of it wasn't half bad enough. But this place ain't lost yet, and by God it ain't goin' to be. You can go ahead and cuss me all you want to, but I'm stayin'. I put Walter where he is, so now I'm here to take his place. We're goin' to make that crop. We're goin' to raise the money, and we're goin' to pay the bank!"

Her face was flushed with anger, and her eyes crackled. But this time it was Eve who couldn't bring up the words to say.

Hewey pointed to the rifle on the wall. "If you're goin' to shoot me, go ahead and do it now or forget about it."

The words came to her then, mostly a repetition of what she had been saying before, though this time her voice was on the verge of breaking.

From a bedroom came Walter's voice. "Eve . . ."

She heard, but she went on with the invectives. Walter's voice was stronger this time, and commanding. "Eve, goddammit, shut up!"

That shocked her into silence.

Hewey said, "I'll sleep out in the shed. If you don't want to feed me, that's all right; I'll cook for myself, out yonder. If you don't want to look at me, that's all right too. I'll stay out of your sight as much as I can. But I'm here, Eve. And right here I'll stay!"

Tears trailed one another down her cheeks. She looked at him awhile, gazed at the floor, then raised her chin and looked at him again. She squared her shoulders, cleared her throat and wiped her eyes on her long, faded sleeve. In a quiet, half-breaking voice she said, "You'd better go unsaddle your horse and then wash up. Tell the boys, too. Supper'll be ready directly."

He slept little that night. He rolled out his blankets in the shed and lay on the floor, his eyes wide open in the darkness. In his frustration and anger he lashed out at various people in his mind: at Snort Yarnell for starting the escapade that had led to trouble; at Fox and his three hired toughs for breaking Walter's leg; at Walter himself for mixing into a fight that was not his own. He made these rounds a dozen times, but each time at the end of it he had to come back to himself and accept, for a little while, the blame upon his own shoulders. He could have said *no* to Snort and ended the whole fiasco before it started. But he had joined into it with whole heart and empty head. No matter how he rationalized it—and he tried—the ultimate fault was his own.

So was the ultimate responsibility for salvaging whatever was possible out of a deplorable situation.

He might have dozed a little, or he might not. He was smoking cigarettes and staring at the ceiling of the shed when the first light came. His stomach hurt as if a cold lump of pure lead lay in the bottom of it. His eyes were as blurry as if he had been on a three-day drunk. He got up and rolled another cigarette, which seemed only to burn his tongue. He rolled his blankets and trudged toward the house when he saw smoke rising from the chimney. Eve was in the kitchen. They exchanged a quick glance apiece, but neither had any words. It was just as well, he thought. If she had any they wouldn't be pleasant to listen to. They would be a repetition of the ones he had used against himself all night.

He poured a cup of coffee and started out the door with it.

She said in a rough voice that told him she hadn't slept either, "I'll have breakfast ready directly."

"Ain't hungry. I need to go and look things over."

He saddled Biscuit and set out on a round, surveying his problem. He found it worse than he had anticipated. The frequent rains had been good for the growth of the feed Walter and the boys had planted, but they had also been healthy for the weeds that were always trying to take over. Normally, in this region where rainfall was usually light, a farmer could raise a crop of feed without the weeds getting bad enough to cultivate, provided he planted on good clean ground. Walter had no cultivator; those cost money, and he owned nothing he could do without.

He did own some good strong hoes, and he had a couple of boys who knew how to swing them, whether they enjoyed the work or not. It was going to be a mean job to get ahead of the weeds and stay ahead. It might take a mean man to push the boys and keep their noses to the grindstone. Hewey could have been a straw boss or even a foreman on several ranch jobs if he had been willing to take it upon himself to supervise other men and get the maximum work out of them. That kind of drive had never been part of his make-up. He had always preferred to stick to cowboy wages and keep his friends.

He grimaced, surveying the start the weeds had made. The boys were likely to be calling him something stronger than *Uncle Hewey* by the time this crop was made. The thought made his stomach hurt worse.

His relationship with Eve was not true peace, not by a long way. At best it was a cold and silent truce. But at least it *was* silent, except for her accusing eyes. For the next two or three days Hewey made it a point not to look into them more than he had to. He never went into the house except to eat, and he wasn't eating much.

Alvin Lawdermilk always had horses and mules that needed breaking. Hewey set the boys to hoeing the feed, then rode over to Alvin's and made a deal on price to bring a string of animals to the place and break them here rather than at Alvin's. The facilities were not nearly so good, but the convenience of having them here counted for a lot.

In the first days he needed someone to help him catch and hackamore and tie and saddle them. He alternated between

Cotton and Tommy until he decided Tommy was somewhat better at it. Cotton's inclinations ran to the mechanical. When he was through with Tommy each morning he sent him on out to join Cotton at the field. Twice a day Hewey put the broncs through their paces. At other times he went out to help the boys or he rode among Walter's cattle looking for cases of screwworms that needed treatment.

He had a raw mule snubbed to a post and was bringing up a wagon with a tame mule hitched to it when he saw a buggy coming at a brisk pace on the road from town. The boys' black dog always barked at Hewey every time he rode up, but he didn't bark at the buggy. He trotted out to meet it, tail wagging.

Hewey knew the occupants by the way the vehicle listed badly to one side from the poorly balanced weight. They were C. C. Tarpley, whippoorwill-poor, and Fat Gervin, packing fifty extra pounds of pure hog lard. C. C. was driving; he never trusted that to Fat. He almost hubbed Hewey's wagon as he came up alongside it and stopped.

C. C. stared at Hewey in surprise. Fat didn't look at him at all.

"Howdy, Hewey," the old rancher said, his voice pleasant enough. "Thought you'd be in Mexico by now, or Canada, or some other damn place."

Hewey shook his head. "None of them, C. C. This is home."

"Maybe you're takin' a step toward reformation after all. Or maybe it's just age. Always seemed to me like age has reformed more people than religion."

"Speakin' from personal experience, C. C.?"

"I ain't reformed. I've just turned some of my romantic responsibilities over to a younger generation." He glanced at his silent, simmering son-in-law. Hewey read between the lines that the old man knew things Fat had as soon he hadn't found out.

C. C.'s gaze shifted toward the house. "Mighty sorry to hear about Walter's hard luck. How's he comin' along?"

"He ain't chasin' any rabbits."

The old man frowned. "I come out to see about that. You know I—the bank, that is—has got a lien on this here property. I was countin' on the obligation bein' met this fall. Now I can see that it won't be. I thought I better—*we* better—be gettin' a man over here to see after our interests. There's a crop out yonder we can't let ruin, and there's cattle that need carin' for, and . . ."

"It ain't your interests yet, C. C. That obligation is goin' to be met."

The old man didn't seem to hear him. He went on talking about the things that needed doing.

Hewey said again, "We'll meet that obligation."

The rancher blinked. "We? You said *we*?"

"Me. Eve. Them two boys. *Us*."

C. C. had to suppress a smile. "Now, Hewey, me and you have known each other longer than either one of us wants to talk about. You may think right this minute that you're goin' to stick, but I know better. One mornin' you'll see a rainbow and go ridin' off after it. You can't anymore stay here than you can flap your arms and fly."

Hewey squared his shoulders. "I'm stayin', C. C."

Fat Gervin had been staring at the black dog, skewering him with an evil gaze. The black dog looked back and cheerfully wagged its tail, assuming friendship where none was offered. Fat turned to Hewey and put in an unsought opinion. "You won't stay here three weeks."

Hewey glared at him. C. C. turned and cut his son-in-law short with a hard glance that made him shrivel, if a fat man can. When men were talking, boys didn't stick their bill in. C. C. said, "You won't stay here three weeks. You'll never see a bundle of cane cut or a yearlin' delivered."

"I'll be here."

C. C.'s smile turned hard. "If you're still here this fall, I'll kiss your ass."

Hewey said, "I'd rather have Fat do it, if it's all the same to you."

Fat showed a flash of anger, then his eyes turned little and gloating. Hewey shoved his hands into his pockets to keep from doubling his fists. Tarpley was a greedy old man with narrow ways, but at least he was open and basically honest about it, after his fashion. Something about Fat Gervin reminded Hewey of a coyote, sneaking around looking for a way in when a man wasn't watching.

The old man started to flip the reins, then thought of something. "Almost forgot, Hewey. We get the San Angelo *Standard* at the bank every week. Thought you'd get a kick out of the article about you and Snort." He pitched Hewey the newspaper. The buggy rolled. C. C. called back, "You won't stay three weeks."

The dog trotted after the buggy, wagging its tail as if imploring them to stay. *Dumb dog,* Hewey thought, *doesn't know who his friends are.*

Resentment glowed as he watched the buggy retreat. But resentment presently took a back seat to curiosity. He unfolded the newspaper, searching. He found the story on an inside page, circled by a pencil mark.

Disappointment touched him. It was the first time he had ever read his name in a newspaper. Seeing it misspelled shook his faith.

The festive spirit engendered by the big steer-roping contest here extended a bit further than many of its jovial participants expected, with the net result that one man took home a broken leg as his prize, and a local sport spent a night as a guest in the county hotel, later enriching the public coffers at the kindly suggestion of the judge.

The set-to was initiated when two lads of the limber loop took affront at the automobile-herding activities of one J. Fox, a member of this city's sporting community. Having done none too well in the afternoon's hemp-twirling contests, these daring cowboys headed and heeled the automobile belonging to said Fox. When that gentleman complained vigorously about their prowess with the lasso, one of these knights of the range proceeded to hog-tie him in the fashion normally restricted to the beeves.

This fun-loving cowboy was, according to public record, one Hugh Colloway of Upton City, that fledgling metropolis to our west. The other was the redoubtable Snort Yarnell, late of San Antonio and any other point you might choose to name.

This was by all accounts a crowd-pleasing affair, roundly cheered, and the two lads acquired many admiring new friends by their feat. However, it did not please the said Mr. Fox, who according to officials sought redress in the form of blood. He hired three husky and fearless fellows of our nocturnal society to exact the payment.

In the course of their attentions to Mr. Colloway they bestirred the wrath of his brother, whose name we were unable to discover, with the result that he attempted the rescue of his kinsman. In the ensuing unpleasantness his leg was broken.

The authorities were sent for and calm restored. The three hired revengers have remembered urgent business in other climes. Mr. Fox spent a restful night as a guest of Sheriff J. S. McConnell and paid his compliments next morning, along with fifty dollars and costs to the court on a charge of malicious mischief. He also is said to be considering a removal of his business ventures, whatever they may be, in the very near future.

The cowboys have retired back to the range to consider adding one more event to the next steer-roping contest here, namely car-roping.

Eve came out of the house and worked her way down to the
front of the barn, where Hewey had resumed his activity
with the wagon and the bronc mule. She stood back out of
the way, for she knew the havoc a raw mule could create.
When Hewey volunteered no information she asked, "What
did C. C. want?"

Hewey didn't look her in the eye. "He came to take
over."

"He's a little premature, isn't he?"

Hewey thought *premature* was something having to do
with babies. Eve rephrased the question.

He said, "That's the view I taken of the matter. I told him
this place still belongs to the Calloway family."

"The *Walter* Calloway family," she stressed firmly.

"And it'll stay that way. I gave you my word, Eve."

She turned and walked back toward the house, her shoulders drooped. Hewey watched her, his face furrowed. She
had all but given up already. If her loss of hope became contagious, he was going to have a hard time pushing the boys
enough to get the job done.

But he would do it. By God, he would do it!

He turned back to the mule, which was fighting as he attempted to bring it into the traces. Gentleness had always
been his way with horses and mules. But he slapped the mule
alongside the head with the flat of his hand. "Settle down,
damn you! You'll work whether it pleases you or not!"

West Texas was never an easy, benevolent land. For whatever it yielded up, it exacted a price. The most common
price was drouth, which put to severe test the endurance of
those settlers who dared accept its challenge. In the uncommon years when rain was plentiful—as it had been this

year of Aught Six—the tariff was imposed in other ways. There were the weeds which sprang up and thrived, robbing the crops upon which the homesteaders' toenail hold was based. And there were the insects, which seemed to explode by the millions after a rain. In particular there was the screwworm, which brought death of a slow and agonizing kind to animals wild and domestic.

The screwworm fly thrived in warm and humid weather. It was attracted to any scrape or cut that brought warm blood to the surface. This could be a man-made wound such as a castration cut or a peeling brand. It could be accidental, from running against a rough tree or a barbed-wire fence, or horn gouges incurred in fighting. It could be natural. In newly born calves the flies attacked the bleeding navel and set death's time clock to work in the very same place where the umbilical cord had given life. The flies laid their eggs, which soon expanded into a wriggling white mass of flesh-eating screw-shaped worms that gorged themselves and drew more flies and grew in numbers until death put an end to the animal's torment.

Every cowboy carried worm medicine, usually in an old cut-off boot top tied to his saddle. In this stained and odoriferous makeshift case would be two bottles or cans, one of chloroform for killing the worms in the wound, the other of cresylic ointment to smear on afterward as a healer and fly repellent. It was a bloody, smelly, unpleasant chore and a constant one, for every day that an animal went untreated made crippling or death a greater probability.

Each morning early, Hewey went through a self-imposed quota of work with bronc mules and horses. That done, he set out a-horseback to ride over the Calloways' eight sections—eight square miles—watching for screwworm cases. If he saw a cow lying down while the others were grazing, he took that as suspicious. If he saw one retreat into the occasional mottes of heavy brush, he rode in after her, for an afflicted animal usually seeks solitude and shade. He made it a point to ride up close for a thorough look at every small calf, for these were the most vulnerable, the quickest to die in bewilderment and pain. Much more often than he would have liked, he found screwworm cases that needed doctoring. It was one of the heaviest infestation years in his experience. Every time he found one, he knew the graveling feeling that he was probably overlooking another, somewhere nearby. Moreover, when he doctored a case today that was no assurance he was through with the animal. A raw wound could reinfect swiftly despite the cresylic ointment.

It was hot, sweaty, exhausting work, for usually he had the boys assigned to the fields, and he had to do this job alone, roping the infected animals and doctoring them where he found them. It gave him an opportunity to ride some of the Lawdermilk broncs that had advanced to the point of some cow-work schooling. On the other hand, roping was difficult on a bronc because it always took time for the animal to get over its fear of the lariat. Caught in any bind, it was likely to pitch, or at least to run away, perhaps dragging a caught calf at the end of the rope. It was a dangerous job, but Hewey knew it was necessary. He would need every dollar he could earn, from Alvin or from anyone else.

Often this search for worms gave him no chance to come in at noon and eat. He had missed many a meal in his time, and he did not mourn. But some days he seemed not to have the stamina he had always taken for granted. Times he came in from a screwworm hunt and faced another working-out of broncs in the late afternoon with little energy or enthusiasm.

The fields were a critical problem. Hewey rode a sorrel bronc by the field one morning and saw the boys working close together, evidently talking, moving somewhat slowly through the cane. Hewey swung down, tied the hackamore rein to a fence post and strode purposefully through the open gate. It seemed the weeds were growing faster than the boys could get around to them.

He walked up to Tommy and grabbed the hoe out of his

hands. Curtly he said, "Damn weeds are goin' to grow right up your pants leg if you don't work faster than that!" He chopped fifteen or twenty with a flare of anger he couldn't rightly explain, and he did it rapidly. "There! That's the way you chop weeds. You don't love them to death, you whack them down. And you don't take all day about it!"

Tommy stared at him in surprise and dismay. A few feet away, Cotton was chopping, but his eyes were on Hewey. "Another thing," Hewey said, "you, boys been talkin' instead of workin'. Cotton, you get yourself on down yonder, *way* down yonder. I want you where you can't even holler at each other, much less talk." He pointed, and Cotton quickly moved to comply. Hewey thrust the hoe at Tommy. "Take it now, and see if you can earn your keep instead of leanin' on the hoe."

He got on the bronc, using the spurs when it seemed a little reluctant to go north the way he wanted it to. He looked back once and saw the boys bent over, working in earnest.

That night was another of his sleepless ones. Lying on his back, he listened to the night birds out in the mesquites and up in the chinaberries. He heard a coyote, or maybe it was half a dozen, setting up music somewhere toward the field. He listened to horses nosing around in empty feed troughs they had cleaned up hours earlier.

Over and over in his mind he went back through the way he had jumped on the boys. He kept seeing their surprise, their hurt faces.

That's not me, he thought miserably. *That's not the way I am.*

But he knew that if a similar situation and similar stress were to come up again, he would probably act the same.

Eventually he dropped off into fitful sleep, only to be confronted by C. C. Tarpley and Fat Gervin. He opened his eyes and found himself in a cold sweat, the faces still clear in his mind. Fully awake, he began picturing Walter and Eve and the boys leaving this place, Walter lying in the back of a wagon, helpless, the family's few belongings piled on either side of him, Eve and the boys crying. Over to one side, in that buggy, would sit Fat and C. C., watching in smug satisfaction as the plum fell off of the tree and into their laps. Walter, if lucky, would wind up working for C. C. again on patched-britches pay, and Eve would again be cooking for Two Cs cowboys and getting no pay at all.

He hammered his fist on the floor. *It's not goin' to happen! I ain't goin' to let it happen!*

But the nightmare played itself over and over in his mind. He made the rest of the night on Bull Durham cigarettes. The nightmare was still playing when he pushed to his feet and walked to the shed door to stare out into the cool, damp dawn.

That morning he rode by the mill which bore his name and heard it squeaking when he was still a hundred yards away. He growled, remembering that he had told the boys to be sure they greased it. Eclipse mills needed a greasing at least once a week. Twice was better.

He found and doctored several cases of screwworms, reluctantly turning the cattle loose because there was nothing else he could do with them, knowing half would probably have to be doctored again. By the sun, and by the gnawing of his belly, he knew it was well into afternoon when he rode by the field to see what kind of job the boys were doing against the weeds. He did not find them there.

He looked up at the sun and took another guess as to the time. Knowing boys and their hunger, he doubted they had just now gone to eat. They should have had dinner an hour or two ago and been back out here hoeing down the weeds that kept springing up anew, threatening to outgrow the feed.

His shoulders ached from the work and the loss of sleep on that hard shed floor. He was hungry yet felt no particular pleasure at the thought of stopping to eat. There just weren't enough hours in a day, and those two boys were wasting the ones they had. Resentment smoldered in him.

He knew it was a childish feeling, but it persisted in spite of his efforts to put it down.

Dammit, he thought, *I can't do it all by myself.*

Approaching the barn, he heard hammering and reined the bronc toward the sound. Under the shade of the lean-to he found Cotton hammering some lumber and pieces of steel together. Tommy stood behind him, looking on.

Hewey's anger slipped out of his grasp. "Boys, them weeds out yonder are gettin' ahead of you again. You better quit this shade and go back to work."

Cotton said, "The hoes are too slow, Uncle Hewey. We're fallin' behind. What we need is a go-devil or some other kind of a cultivator."

"There ain't money for such as that."

"I'm experimentin', Uncle Hewey. I think I can take some scrap and make us somethin' that'll do the job without costin' us a dollar."

Hewey's eyes narrowed. "When you say *experiment,* what you mean is that you don't know if it'll work or not."

Cotton looked at him, catching the implied criticism. "I think it might."

"And again, it might not. But I know what *will* work, and that's elbow grease and a good sharp hoe. If you feel like you've got to experiment, do it at night when you can't see to use that hoe. Right now, you two drag your butts back out to that field and get busy!"

Reluctantly Cotton laid down the tools and the lumber and the steel sweeps he had been handling. He didn't look Hewey in the eye but started toward his horse. Tommy quickly followed his brother's action.

The pet burro tagged along after Tommy. The boy turned and walked back into the shed. He came out in a minute with a bucket partly full of oats.

Hewey demanded, "What you doin' with that feed?"

"The burro is hungry."

"Those oats are worth money. That burro ain't been workin' for his keep, so he doesn't get any oats. Save those for the *workin'* stock. Turn him out in the grass; let him hunt for his feed."

He turned away, but he heard Tommy softly calling the burro, trying to get it to come to the gate. "Here, Hewey. Come on, Hewey."

Hewey stopped and looked back. "I didn't think that burro had a name."

"He's *always* had a name," Tommy replied resentfully. "But I didn't used to think it fitted him."

Eve, tired and harried, turned from the stove as Hewey entered the house. She wiped her hands on her apron, more out of nervousness than of need. "I put some dinner on the back of the stove for you, but I don't know what it'll taste like; it's been there too long."

"It don't matter. I ain't hungry anyway."

"Hungry or not, you've got to take nourishment, or I'll have you laid out in there with Walter."

"I'll just take a biscuit and a piece of meat. I got to be gettin' after them broncs."

Eve slipped the apron from around her waist and slapped it smartly across the corner of the table. "I said you'll eat, and by God you'll eat!"

Surprised, Hewey pulled out a chair and sat down at the table. "First time I can remember you ever bein' so concerned about my welfare."

"First time I ever had to be," she replied curtly.

After he had eaten he walked into the bedroom where Walter lay with his leg propped. "How you doin', little brother?"

"Terrible. I wisht I was up takin' care of things."

"Well, you ain't, and you won't be for a while. So you just lay back and let me take care of the work and the worry." Hewey started to leave. Walter called him back. "Hewey, the boys have been a little downcast lately. You sure you're not ridin' them too hard?"

"No harder than I have to."

"They're just boys. I wisht you'd go easy on them."

"Fat and C. C. won't go easy on them. They'll throw them off of this place the same way they'll throw you and Eve off. I'll go easy on them boys when we've finished our job."

Hewey rode broncs the rest of the afternoon. After supper he went back to ride one more before dark. He took it on a good circle, tiring it mercilessly to work out any inclination toward pitching. As he returned at dusk he heard hammering again at the shed. He unsaddled the bronc and staked him where he had been before. Then he walked to the lean-to.

Cotton was again working on his contraption. Tommy was again watching interestedly from just out of his brother's way.

Hewey could feel the boys' uneasiness. He studied Cotton's design, trying to figure out how the boy intended it to work. "You really think that contraption will cut weeds?"

"I think it will."

Hewey watched a little longer, then walked into the shed and got a kerosene lantern he had been using. He lighted it, carried it outside and hung it from a nail up under the lean-to roof.

"Then you'd better have some light. You boys'll put your eyes out tryin' to work in the dark."

Spring always rode straight-backed and proud, with the ease of a woman who has spent much of her life on a sidesaddle. Her paint horse was gentle enough, but it was no lazy pet. She demanded a standard of performance from him and got it. Riding along, Hewey was looking at her rather than at the landscape. He had seen this part of the country a hundred times. The wide flats, the low hills didn't change. But Spring seemed fresher and younger and prettier every time he saw her. Perhaps, in part, it was the contrast between her and Eve which made it so. This summer was being extremely hard on Eve.

Spring pointed. Excitement crept into her voice. "Yonder it is, the Barcroft place."

Hewey pulled his gaze away from her and turned to face forward. Somehow, what he saw did not bring a rush of excitement to him. He saw a three-strand barbed-wire fence, reasonably tight, with a wire gate where the wagon road went through. He had always suspected these treacherous wire gates were designed to keep the womenfolks at home; a lot of women couldn't open one without tearing a dress or half breaking a jaw on the discarded wooden hames invariably used as a boomer to pull the wire tight.

Two or three hundred yards beyond the gate stood—or sat, or maybe crouched—the small box-and-strip house the settler named Barcroft had built to live up to the requirements of the Texas homestead law. He had not expected it to last forever, but it had had to last at least three years to satisfy the state. From here Hewey would casually guess that it might still have another three years left, if the wind didn't get too strong.

In front of the house stood two small and lonely looking chinaberry trees. "I always liked trees," Spring said, pleased.

"I'm partial to them myself," Hewey agreed. He wished he saw some.

He got down and opened the gate, pulling it back and letting it lie loosely on the ground because there were no cattle here to get out. If any got in, they were probably welcome to the grass.

Spring said, "To begin with, it has a good stout outside fence."

Hewey swung back onto Biscuit and looked behind him. He had never decided when he went through a fence if he had the feeling of going in or going out. Something about a fence seemed always to choke him a little, to cut off the flow

of air like shutting a door into a room. "At least I won't have
to build one," he said.

Riding to the house, Spring spotted the small bachelor
garden and talked about how easy it would be to expand it to
family size. She pointed farther west. "There's a nice little
field over yonder. You could expand it a little every year
until it was a good-sized farm. You'd hardly even miss the
grass."

Hewey nodded, making a show of agreement. From here
he could almost see across the whole claim. C. C. Tarpley
had horse traps bigger than this.

Spring said, "Since he's moved out already, I don't think
Mr. Barcroft would mind us going inside." That was her way
of inviting him to help her down from the saddle. As he did,
she touched her lips softly to his cheek, catching him by
surprise. "There." She smiled. "I did it to you before you
could do it to me."

"I'm keepin' track. I always like to square up my accounts
sooner or later."

"Anytime you want to."

The wanting boiled up in him, and he knew a wicked impulse to rush her into the house and then see just how much
she was willing to abide. But as they walked through the
door together and he looked at the place, the wanting ebbed
out of him. It was all in one room, and not much of it, kitchen,
bedroom, the whole thing. The walls had been covered with
old newspapers instead of wallpaper, mainly to keep the cold
air from blowing through the siding and the blowing dust
from filtering in quite so badly. A small stove was the only
piece of furniture; it had been left only because one leg was
broken off. Ashes lay black and cold on the floor.

"It would need some brightening up," Spring admitted.
The house had dampened her spirit a little too, but only for
a few minutes. Soon they were back outside again, and she
was stepping off rough plans for a yard fence, a flower bed.

Hewey stood slump-shouldered and tried not to let his feelings show in his face. He looked around in silence and thought of a time he had once spent in jail.

They rode back to Walter's place together because Hewey had promised Eve he would bring Spring home for Sunday supper. The women went into the house together, talking about the Barcroft place. Hewey walked to the barn, looking around at all the improvements Walter and Eve and the boys had wrought here. He tried in his mind to transplant them to the Barcroft place to see if it could be bettered.

Before long he was back at what he enjoyed most, looking over the broncs staked out to teach them respect for the rope. He picked a sorrel which had developed considerable tolerance for the saddle. Talking softly, he walked up to the doubting bronc, holding his hand out in front of him. The horse pulled to the end of the rope, then leaned back on its haunches. Relentlessly Hewey moved his hand up the rope to the hackamore, then up the side of the horse's head and back out onto his neck. He talked gently all the while. The pony trembled a little but gradually relaxed and let up on the tension of the rope.

The tenderness Hewey had never felt free to express to a woman, he had always felt free and easy in expressing to animals, especially horses. He spoke to the bronc as if it were a child, an advanced child. "Whoa, son, see there, I ain't fixin' to hurt you. Just wantin' to love on you a little. You're a pretty one. Goin' to make somebody a damn good cow horse, if I'm any judge. Like to have you myself, only I got all I can afford."

He rubbed on the pony's neck, gradually letting his hand move down to the shoulder. The skin would ripple a little, a showing of fear. Hewey would back off, but then he would return, and when the ripple didn't show he would go farther. It occurred to him finally that in a way he was substituting the horse for Spring Renfro. He didn't know whether to laugh at himself or be ashamed.

He had been so wrapped up in the pony that he had not noticed the approach of a horseman. The man swung down from a blue roan and peered at Hewey through the corral fence.

"Well, Hewey, I see you ain't lost your touch. I don't know which you're the best at, handlin' horses or ropin' automobiles."

Hewey saw the gold tooth shine in a grin that stretched as wide as a singletree. The heaviness lifted from his shoulders. He trotted eagerly toward the fence with his right hand shoved way out. "Snort Yarnell, I wouldn't of thought about you for a dollar and a half."

"I ain't offerin'. I ain't got a dollar and a half."

They shook hands through the fence. About that time Eve came out onto the front step and hollered, "Supper!"

She saw the blue roan horse, and she saw Snort. Even at the distance, Hewey could tell that she sagged a little. She said something, and Spring Renfro came out. The women stood together, watching the two men walk up from the barn, slapping each other on the back.

Snort removed his old greasy hat and bowed slightly to the women. "Howdy, Eve. You're always a sight to my sore old eyes." He shifted his attention to Spring Renfro. "Well, I'll swun. I'll just bet you're the pretty schoolteacher that's turned Hewey's head."

Spring was too embarrassed to know what to say. She stammered something to the effect that Hewey hadn't turned his head very much.

Eve asked, "You'll have supper with us, won't you, Snort?" Her eyes were saying she hoped he wouldn't.

Snort didn't seem to read eyes very well. "I'd be much obliged."

Eve would be hospitable if it killed everybody. A little stiffly she pointed to the washstand. "You-all can wash up over there." The words were directed at both men, but they were meant especially for Snort.

Snort visited a little with Walter in the bedroom, then came out to the table. He visited very little with anybody for a while then; he was too busy eating woman's cooking. For a man who had no interest in permanent alliances, he always made top hand at the table any time he was privileged to eat in a woman's house.

When Snort seemed to be tapering off on his third helping of everything on the table, Hewey said, "You headin' anyplace special?"

Snort nodded, going after the cobbler pie. "On my way out to the KC outfit in the Davis Mountains. Goin' to pick up some horses and take them back to Old Man Dotson on the Middle Concho. Thought if you didn't have anything to do you'd like to go with me."

Eve spilled half a cup of coffee.

Hewey rubbed his tired shoulders. He thought of unbroken broncs and wormy cattle and weedy fields. And of the Barcroft place. Travel seemed a grand idea.

He happened to look across the table at Spring and catch the sudden concern in her eyes.

Snort said, "I'll bet you never been out to that place, have you, Hewey?"

"Not right there, no."

"You *ought* to see it. It's all mountains and canyons and wide pretty valleys with clear blue creeks runnin' down through them. If the Lord was to ever get heaven overstocked and start lookin' for a place to branch out, He couldn't do no better than them Davis Mountains. They're a feast to the eyes and the soul. I wisht you'd come and go with me."

Hewey remembered the times he had seen the fear in Eve's eyes when he was telling Walter about some place he had been, urging him to get away from here awhile and go somewhere with him.

Spring's eyes had that look now.

He took a long, silent sip of the coffee and tried to keep his growing disappointment from showing. "No, Snort, I got more work here than I can see around. I reckon I'll have to let you go on without me."

10

Hewey had made a round looking for screwworms and, as usual, came by the fields to see how the boys were doing in their constant battle against the weeds. The black dog came running out to bark a challenge at him. Hewey spoke back to him in kind.

To his surprise he saw a mule working in the feed, Cotton following close behind him. Hewey rode up to the turn-row, hooked a leg over the saddle horn to show the bronc he wasn't afraid of him, and waited. To pass the time he lectured the dog on fidelity and true friendship. The dog gave him a haughty look which told him to mind his own business.

In a few minutes Cotton came out to the end of the row, following the mule-drawn contraption he had designed and built. Tommy trailed behind him with a hoe, giving the *coup de grâce* to any weeds Cotton had missed or left wounded.

Hewey's mouth hung open. "Boy, does that thing really work?"

Cotton made a cautious, tentative smile. "It's no go-devil, but it cuts weeds." The evidence lay behind him, in the row he had just finished.

Hewey marveled at his nephew's ingenuity. "It ain't much for pretty. Any honest-to-God farmer was to come by here, he'd die laughin'."

Cotton said defensively, "While he's laughin', we'll be cuttin' a good clean crop of feed."

Hewey looked across the field. The cane was soon going to be ready to harvest. He dismounted and stood there a little, studying Cotton until the boy self-consciously turned away. Hewey put a heavy hand on his shoulder. "Cotton, I been hard on you boys. I ain't real bright, so the chances are that I'll do it again. But if I ever fuss at you about takin' time for an invention, I want you to hit me over the head with that contraption there."

Cotton's cautious smile came back. "I hope you'll remember that."

"I probably won't. But you remind me."

"Uncle Hewey, you reckon when we get this job done and the crop all in, you might talk to Mama about me?"

"You still thinkin' about that job in San Angelo?"

"I lay awake nights, thinkin' about it."

"Your mama doesn't take much stock in what I say. You'll need to ask her yourself."

"I have."

"What did she say?"

"You can guess what she said."

The dog looked up, lifting its ears, then went trotting out on the trail that led up from the house. Hewey saw a familiar buggy, this time with a lone occupant. "Damn!" he grunted.

Cotton looked. "Fat Gervin."

"In the flesh, and there's a hell of a lot of it. You boys get on back to your weedin'."

The black dog had reached the buggy and now came trotting back alongside it, tail wagging vigorously.

"Damn dumb dog," Hewey grumbled. He remounted the bronc, holding the rein up tight. He had no intention of putting on a free show of riding skill for Fat Gervin, a man who did not know how to appreciate true ability.

Fat reined the gray buggy horses to a stop and sat looking across the waving green feed. He pointed his round little chin toward Cotton. "What kind of a rig do you call that?"

"That," Hewey said evenly, "is a bank beater. That little contraption is one of the things that's goin' to beat you, Fat. We've got that feed crop as good as made, unless you can stir up a hail-storm or somethin' pretty soon."

Fat nodded. "You've got some yearlin's to sell, too, ain't you?"

"They're as good as sold already. Walter says him and Old Man Thomas made an agreement back in the spring."

"Did he get anything written down on paper?"

Hewey began to feel a touch of doubt. "You don't need anything on paper in this country. They shook hands."

"That's not enough anymore. Old Man Thomas can't help you. He can't even help himself. He's overdue on some notes he owes us. We've got him tied up to where he can't buy smokin' tobacco, much less some nester yearlin's."

Hewey swallowed, then caught hold, trying to keep Fat from seeing his misgivings. "Too bad about the old man. But we'll sell them to somebody else."

"Who?"

"I don't know. Somebody."

"There ain't anybody this side of Midland'll buy your cattle, and there ain't anybody there who'll come this far and buy them from you. You'll have to drive them all the way to town." Fat began to smile, but the smile carried a touch of frost. "That feed you're so puffed up about . . . who you goin' to sell it to?"

"No problem there. Walter's been sellin' it to ranchers around here for years."

"You talked to any of them lately?"

A chill touched Hewey somewhere down below his belt buckle. "No."

Fat said, "Then I wouldn't count my chickens till you see them pop out of the shell." He flipped the reins and brought the buggy team around in a long circle, then set them into a trot on the way back toward town. The black dog followed him a long way before giving up and limping back, its affections unrequited.

Worry gnawed at Hewey's belly all the way to the house. He drank a quick cup of coffee and left his dinner untouched on the back of the wood stove while Eve complained about cooking for nothing. He staked the bronc, saddled Biscuit and rode out in a hurry.

Late in the afternoon he came to a ranch house not far back up from the Pecos River. He found the rancher milking a Jersey cow to feed a growing flock of youngsters. Hewey waved, tied Biscuit to a fence and entered the cowpen, watching his feet. He shook hands, getting his right hand wet with milk.

"Howdy, Willis. I noticed comin' in that your feed stack's almost fed up."

The rancher nodded, glancing unnecessarily in that direction. "About time for the new crop to start comin' off."

"That's what I come to talk to you about. We'll be cuttin' Walter's pretty soon. You'll be needin' about the same as last year, won't you?"

The rancher shook his head and looked away. "Matter of fact, Hewey, I won't. I already got my feed bought. Contracted, anyway."

Somehow Hewey had known it all the way over here, but it hit him in the stomach anyway. "Mind if I ask who sold it to you?"

"It was Fat Gervin. He come by and contracted to furnish me all I need, and to do it at a little under the Midland market."

"Under the market? But him and old C. C., they don't raise any feed; they're always buyin'. How can he sell cheaper than the market?"

"I don't know, but he done it. Times like these, Hewey, a man takes his savin's where he can find them. There ain't no loose money floatin' around, you know."

"I'm *beginnin'* to know." Hewey reached up for Biscuit's

mane and the saddle horn. "You know anybody else upriver who might want some feed?"

"I understand that Fat pretty well made the rounds. I think he's sold just about everybody."

Hewey gritted his teeth. "Nice to see you, Willis. You take care of them kids now."

"Doin' the best I can. Seems like I been takin' too good a care of my wife."

Hewey rode away with his shoulders drawn in. He would visit some more ranches tomorrow, but he already sensed what the outcome would be. A dark and ugly suspicion came to him. Fat Gervin was doing this to box him in. Worse, he was probably figuring on the Calloway feed to meet some of his contract obligations, after he took over the place.

I'll burn it first, Hewey thought bitterly. He spurred Biscuit a lot harder than he intended to.

He didn't get in until after dark. He nibbled a little at the cold leftovers and filled up on black coffee. Eve asked what was eating at him, but he gave her no answer.

Next day, keeping his mission from Eve, he visited a couple more ranches. As he had expected, Fat Gervin had been there a few days ahead of him. Hewey knew of a certainty now: they had a crop of feed almost made, and there wasn't a soul in the Upton City country to sell it to.

On Sunday morning while Eve sought salvation in church, and in taking the boys with her allowed the weeds a day of grace, Hewey was out on his daily rounds seeking after screwworms to kill. In the afternoon he pursued romance in his own uncertain fashion. He tied some work into it, however. He rode to the Lawdermilk place on one of the broncs he was breaking for Alvin. This served the double purpose of training and transportation. It was an efficiency of which Eve could approve.

The Lawdermilk menagerie was out in force, blissfully unaware of the sacredness of the Sabbath. The peafowl momentarily put Hewey in some jeopardy of a hard fall from the skittish bronc. But Hewey was prepared for the sight, if the bronc wasn't, and he held the little sorrel down to a couple of short crowhops. He had no intention of ruining the last dress-up shirt he owned.

Julio watched from the shed door, waving. He seldom got to town. He had to appreciate whatever small amusements chanced to pass his way.

Alvin stepped out onto the porch to investigate the commotion, then walked down the steps to meet Hewey. Coming out the yard gate and shutting it behind him, a precaution to protect Cora's flowers from four-footed invasions, he looked the bronc over with a discerning eye before turning his attention to Hewey. "The bronc looks better than you do."

Hewey's good white shirt only accentuated the sun-browned face, the wind-chapped lips. "Maybe he ain't been workin' as hard."

Alvin grunted. "You ought to take better care of yourself." He reached out to try to touch the bronc on the shoulder. It pulled back, eyes wide enough to show the whites. "I expect you're about through with a bunch of broncs."

"I'll be bringin' them home in a few days to swap you for some more."

Alvin frowned and tried again to touch the bronc. He managed it this time, though the sorrel was not wholly in favor. "It'd be a lot easier on you if you'd come over here and ride them. Be easier on Walter's grass, too."

"I got to be there and watch after things. Got to hunt screwworms every day. Got to keep them boys a-workin'."

"You sound more like a daddy than an uncle. They probably liked you better when you was just Uncle Hewey."

"They'll like me a lot less if they lose the roof from over their heads."

Alvin's frown sank deeper. He studied Hewey as carefully as he had studied the bronc. "It don't fit on you, Hewey. You're tryin' to make yourself into somebody you're not."

Hewey's voice was pained. "You got any better ideas?"

Alvin had no answer for that.

Hewey said, "I don't reckon you need to buy any feed, do you, Alvin?"

"No. Matter of fact, my crop's comin' along so good I'm liable to have a little more than I need." He brightened. "Would you believe Fat Gervin came by here a few days ago and offered to buy any extra that I find I've got?"

"I'd believe it," Hewey said darkly.

Spring Renfro appeared on the porch. Her eyes met Hewey's and came alive with joy. Hewey's tired back straightened. A smile flirted with his leathery face, but it didn't quite come alive.

Alvin looked from one to the other, his brow still twisted. "I believe I'll go down to the barn and see what Julio is up to. Come down later if you've a mind to, Hewey." He waited for a response but received none. He shrugged and walked toward the corrals.

Hewey stepped up onto the porch, glanced over his shoulder to be sure Alvin wasn't watching, then opened his arms for Spring. She came to him smiling, saying nothing, needing to say nothing. They held each other in a long, warm silence. She brought him a measure of comfort he had badly needed.

"I've missed you," she said finally. "A week can be a long time."

"There's been a lot of work to do."

She stepped back to arm's length and looked him over carefully, critically. "You don't feel well, Hewey."

"How can you tell the way I feel?"

"It shows in your eyes, your face. You're drawn, Hewey. You're not eating enough. I don't think you're sleeping."

"I'm all right. Just got a lot on my mind right now, is all."

She ran her fingers gently through his hair. She said, "The gray seems to be showing a little more. Taking responsibility is one thing. But you're letting responsibility take *you,* and that is something else."

"I've worked hard a lot in my life. It's never hurt me."

"It's not the work; it's what goes on up there." She gently tapped his forehead with her finger. "I'm not sure you know how to handle it."

Defensively he said, "I've never had a job of work yet that I couldn't handle."

Holding hands, they walked to the porch swing and sat down close together. The touch of her body against his was both bliss and pain, bliss in that it felt so good, pain in that he wanted to do so much more and couldn't, or wouldn't.

Hewey heard the squeak of the wheel chair making its way slowly across the parlor floor, and the bump as it was stopped by the screen door. From the doorway came Old Lady Faversham's voice, raw-edged and cold. "It's just that Hewey Calloway again, botherin' our Spring. If I was her I'd tie a dead cat to him and run him off."

Spring looked at Hewey, her eyes sparkling with laughter.

Cora's voice came from within the house. "Come here, Mother. I want you to hold this yarn for me."

"Somebody ought to be out there watchin' him. That kind'll take advantage of a woman every time."

"Mother . . ."

"It's an awful thing to be a woman. We yield up so much and receive so little in return."

Cora's voice turned strident. "Mother, you come here!"

The chair squeaked again as the old lady reluctantly retreated deeper into the house.

"If they ever hang me," Hewey said ruefully, "I hope they send that old lady an invitation. It'll be a high point of her life."

"She's just worried about my welfare."

"That's for me to do."

"I'm not your responsibility yet. Right now I'm afraid you have more worries than you know what to do with."

He stared morosely toward the low blue mountains, the flat-topped desert mountains of the Trans-Pecos. "I've never had it like this before," he admitted. "I've worked hard on a-plenty of jobs, but I always knew I could walk off and leave it any time I taken the notion. That made it easy. This time I can't ride off. It's like I was chained to a post."

"Most men are chained to some kind of post. Women too."

"I've just started kind of late. I'm like an old dog tryin' to learn a new trick and fallin' back on my tail. I growl an awful lot and learn damn little."

"Have faith in yourself, Hewey." She picked up his rough hand and pressed it against her lips. She looked at him so directly and without reservation that he felt his face warming. He tried to think of something to say, but nothing came. Romance had been sadly neglected on his part.

She said, "With all you've had to do, I don't suppose you've had a chance to see about making a deal on the Barcroft place?"

He stared at his hands, his eyes troubled. "Spring, I been wonderin' how to tell you. We'd better not figure on that place for a while. It'll take everything I've got—everything I can get—to keep C. C. and Fat from takin' that place."

"I can help. It's hard to save much out of a schoolteacher's salary, but I've managed. I have a little money set aside. We could put it down on the Barcroft claim, just to hold it."

He looked at her in surprise. "Use your money? If we get married it's *my* place to do the payin', not yours. A man don't take a woman's money."

"That's old-fashioned. In a lot of the world a bride brings a dowry into the marriage."

"We're livin' in *this* part of the world. And here it's up to me."

He went home a little earlier than usual from his Sunday courting, for a dark mood had settled over him, and he feared it might be contagious. To his surprise he saw Walter sitting up in front of the house, his leg stretched out straight in front of him in the cast, a pair of crutches resting against his hip. They were homemade, Cotton's doing. Hewey went on to the barn and unsaddled, then came back to stand and gaze upon his brother.

Walter's face was pale from the long confinement. He had never been one to carry any excess flesh, and he was even thinner than usual now. But Hewey saw pleasure in his brother's eyes at being able to get outside and see the world without a ceiling over it.

Hewey tried to pretend a cheerfulness he could not feel. "I got some broncs that need ridin', if you feel up to it."

Walter smiled thinly. "Ask me again tomorrow."

"You sure it's safe for you to be gettin' out?"

"I been goin' crazy lyin' in there where I can't see anything. I never knew how pretty an old barn could be, or even a milkhouse, or several broncs staked out on a flat." He turned his head in the direction of the fields, though he could not see them from here. "How's the feed lookin', Hewey?"

Hewey hesitated. "Fine. It'll be ready to cut pretty soon now."

"You'll need to be goin' around to the ranchers and tellin' them. We've got to start pullin' the money together."

Hewey couldn't tell him the truth. "I'll do it, Walter, first chance I get."

Eve called them to supper. Hewey helped Walter get the crutches under his arms and pull to his good foot. Walter moved awkwardly. It would be some time yet before he could do much for himself. Hewey hung back, brooding, until Eve called him a second time. He sat down at the table but found the food tasteless.

Eve watched him worriedly. "Hewey, are things all right between you and Spring?"

"Sure. Sure, everything's fine." He pushed to his feet and slid his chair back. "If you-all will pardon me, I think I'll go outside and have me a smoke."

He sat down in the chair Walter had vacated. Down by the grove he saw several freight wagons, the teamsters un-hitching. One of them, he could tell, was Blue Hannigan. Somehow Hewey welcomed the company. He couldn't talk to anyone in the family about his problem. Maybe he could talk about it to Hannigan. Sharing it with somebody might make it easier.

Presently Hannigan and a couple of other men started walking toward the windmill, leading their horses and mules. Hewey moved out to the mill and stood with his shoulder against the tower. Blue greeted him and stopped to study him a minute.

He said, "You look like you been run over by a gut wagon."

Hewey found a touch of dark humor in that and almost smiled. "You could say that, in a way. I been run over by Fat Gervin."

Hannigan watered his teams; that came ahead of pleas-ant conversation or food or anything else when a man's livelihood depended upon his animals. He said, "Come on down to the camp, Hewey, if you've a mind to. We got a pot of coffee started. I expect you've already had your supper."

Hewey gladly walked down to the grove with the mus-cular, begrimed teamster. He helped him to take the rest of the harness off and tie the mules in their places alongside the wagons, then tie the morrals of feed over their heads.

That done, Hannigan fetched a pair of cups, poured cof-fee, then sat down for a few minutes of comfort on the heavy wagon tongue. "Now then, Hewey, what's that fat son of a bitch done to you?"

Hewey squatted on his heels and gritted his teeth. In a way he hated to tell. He felt somehow belittled that he could ever be in the position where another man could take such an advantage of him. But he told Hannigan the whole thing.

Morosely he said, "I don't know whichaway to turn, Blue. We can do somethin' or other with the yearlin's. Midland's a long ways to have to drive a little bunch of cattle, but we can do it. We can ship them to the Fort Worth stockyards if we have to. But that feed, that's what's got into my craw. If we can't sell the feed we just won't have the money to pay off that note. We can't go haulin' feed all over the country to try to sell it. The freight would eat it up."

Blue Hannigan scowled. When he did that, his face somehow reminded Hewey of a storm boiling up, about to let loose thunder and fire. Hannigan seemed to withdraw into himself a little while, thinking. At last he said, "It finally makes sense, Hewey. I hadn't been able to figure out what he was up to, but now I see."

"See what?"

"Fat hired him an agent in Midland to go out visitin' farmers and try to tie up all the feed they're raisin'. I didn't understand it because him and C. C. never bought that much feed before, not for their own use. Fat's doin' it just to nail you up in a box, Hewey."

"He's done it."

"Not yet. Maybe you can crawl out before the lid is hammered shut." Hannigan got some coffee grounds in his mouth and spat them violently. "He's a crafty devil, but you *could* out-craft him."

"I don't see how."

"That agent is buyin' from anybody who'll sell to him. He'll buy from *me* if I tell him I can line him up some feed. He don't have to know where I got it. You and the boys, you get that feed cut soon as it's ready. I'll get a bunch of the mule skinners together, and their wagons, and we'll haul that stuff to Midland for you."

"That's a long haul, Blue. Time we pay the freight . . ."

"There ain't goin' to be no freight. Half the time we're empty on the trip to Midland anyway. Most of our haulin' is *out* from there, not *in*."

"I wouldn't ask it of you. Neither would Walter."

"You ain't askin'. I'm tellin'. All of us boys, we like Walter, and we owe him. You think everybody in the country lets us water our teams without payin' for it? Hell no, they don't. And if Fat Gervin gets control of this place, you can damn well bet he'll charge for water and grass both."

Hewey could see some logic in that, enough to ease his conscience.

Blue added, "This country ain't got so many good people in it that it can afford to lose a family like the Calloways. You're damn right we'll do it for you, and be tickled to get the chance." His eyes narrowed. "But we got to keep it quiet. We got to slip up on their blind side or they'll fly the nest."

"There won't nobody know but me and you and whoever you tell."

For a long time now a stifling, heavy weight had been building on Hewey's shoulders. Part of it fell away. The evening had just turned dark, but he could see daylight. "Blue Hannigan, if you was a woman I'd kiss you."

"If I was a woman, be damned if I'd let you."

Hewey couldn't afford to tell the family yet for fear the plan might somehow leak out. Besides, none of them knew of the block Fat had thrown in their way; Hewey had kept that to himself. In the days ahead he worked at tying up all the loose ends. In the course of riding, looking for screw-worm cases, he started picking up the yearlings that were due for sale and hazing them to the milk-cow pasture.

He began trying to put the finishing touches on the current set of Lawdermilk broncs. Tommy was getting to be a problem there. He was too eager and too reckless.

"Stay out from behind that horse," Hewey yelled at him. "He'll kick you plumb into next Saturday."

Tommy *had* been too close, but he didn't recognize it. "Why don't you let me ride this one, Uncle Hewey? He's not so tough."

"You're too young to be ridin' broncs like this."

"I'm older than you was when *you* started. You've told

me many a time. Spinner James is ridin' broncs already, and he's a year younger than I am."

"One broken leg in this family is enough."

But Hewey could tell by Tommy's actions that he had all the makings of a good cowboy. There wouldn't be any holding him back much longer. The boys were growing up and getting away from him while he stood there and watched them.

The day came when Hewey knew the feed was ready to cut. He took his string of broncs to Alvin Lawdermilk and pronounced them broken. He gladly accepted the pay which Alvin counted out for him, including a few dollars in extra bonus which Alvin said he felt was due for the speed and thoroughness of the job.

"And now, Alvin," Hewey said, "could I ask you for the borry of your row binder?"

Alvin's own feed was probably about ready to cut, but he didn't have a big note falling due at the bank. "You can have it on one condition. I've got a couple of green-broke work horses that sure do need the practice. Take them and you can take the binder."

"I won't charge you a red cent for the trainin'."

Cutting and bundling the feed was hot, dry, dusty work. The chaff got into Hewey's shirt despite his buttoned collar and sleeves, and it itched like a rough-wool coat on a sunburn. It was a type of work he would normally have ridden a hundred miles on a lame horse to avoid. But he gloried in this because it marked the end of his captivity, the payment of his debt. An added pleasure, like a side bet, was that he would be able to kick Fat Gervin in the butt with his own boot.

Hewey sang as he worked, a manifestation to the boys that their uncle had been kicked in the head by a bronc without their knowledge.

The black dog, lying at the turnrow and watching for rabbits to flush ahead of the binder, raised his head and turned to stare at something. He got to his feet and went trotting off, wagging his tail. Hewey's curious gaze moved past the dog and picked up an approaching buggy. He broke off singing "Bringing in the Sheaves" and groaned, "God Almighty damn!"

The gray horses and the buggy belonged to C. C. Tarpley and Fat Gervin. Fat was driving. Easing the binder team on up to the turnrow, Hewey assumed the second man would be C. C. But as he stepped down from the binder and wiped the gritty sweat from his face onto his sleeve and then onto a handkerchief, he noticed a dun horse tied behind the buggy. Hewey blinked his chaff-burned eyes and stared at the second man. He combed his memory, and suddenly his breath went short.

The marshal from New Prosperity!

Fat Gervin reined up and looked a moment at Hewey. He turned to his passenger. "Marshal, is that your man?"

The marshal held a pistol in his hand. It was pointed at Hewey. "That, sir, is sure as hell him." To Hewey he said stiffly, "Hugh Holloway, I arrest you in the name of the law."

The breeze was light, but it worked through Hewey's sweaty shirt. He felt a chill. "The name is Calloway." He stared into the muzzle of the pistol. It looked as big as a cannon in a courthouse yard.

The marshal said curtly, "You raise those hands, Holloway."

"If I turn a-loose of these lines, this green team is apt to take fright and run over all of us."

Cotton and Tommy watched wide-eyed. Hewey motioned for Cotton to come up and take the reins.

Fat said, "I'd watch that man closely, Marshal. He is a slippery character."

Hewey frowned. "Fat Gervin, I hope when you get home that your old mother comes runnin' up to you on all fours and bites you on the leg."

Tommy trembled. "Uncle Hewey, what's this about? What does that man want with you?"

Hewey looked at Cotton, but he spoke to Tommy. "Your brother can tell you."

The marshal smiled coldly. "I had just about given up on you, Holloway. I wrote letters to sheriffs all over the country, and not a one of them answered me. But your kind always floats to the surface like a dead fish. You want to know how I caught up with you?"

Staring at that pistol and feeling that chill, Hewey didn't much give a damn. But the marshal told him anyway. "Last week our paper picked up an old item that had been printed in San Angelo. The name wasn't quite the same, but a little bird lit on my shoulder and whispered in my ear. So I came to Upton City. The sheriff here wasn't no help. He swore he'd never heard of no Holloway. Left me feelin' kind of low. But I went to the bank to get me some travelin' funds and happened to mention my trouble to Mr. Gervin. Now, he's a good law-abidin' citizen, Mr. Gervin is. He knew right away who I was after. So here I am, Hugh Holloway, and justice is fixin' to be done."

Hewey and the boys all glared at Fat Gervin. Fat said, "I've always tried to do my civic duty."

Hewey argued, "I never done anything to you, Marshal, at least nothin' to justify you takin' all this trouble."

"You ignored an order from an officer of the law, and you attacked that officer in the carryin'-out of his legal duties. Let one man get away with such as that and you open the doors for all kinds of dangerous elements to come in and take over the country."

"I ain't no dangerous element."

"Any man who disrespects the power of the law is a dangerous element."

Hewey turned his head and surveyed the field. It wouldn't take long to finish the cutting. "I got a job of work to finish here. If you'll let me do that, I'll go along with you real peaceable."

As he expected, the marshal vigorously shook his head. "I been lookin' for you ever since last spring. I've finally got you, and you're goin' back with me right now."

Hewey looked at first one of the boys, then the other. "It's up to you two, then, to finish here. You know what you've got to do."

Cotton protested, "I don't know if we can do it without you, Uncle Hewey."

"You can, and you've got to, for your mama and daddy."

Cotton's lips were tight. Tears came to Tommy's eyes.

Hewey couldn't look at the boys anymore. His eyes burned, and not just from the chaff. He turned back to the marshal. "I need to go down to the house first and speak to my folks."

"And have them help you escape? No sir, you're comin' with me. We're leavin' from right here."

"My horse is down at the house too."

"You can take one of those out of harness."

"These don't belong to me; they belong to Alvin Lawdermilk."

The marshal clearly didn't believe him. "They'll do."

"I'll still need my saddle."

"You can ride bareback. By the time this trip is over with, you'll be more impressed with the majesty of the law." He fished a set of handcuffs out of his pocket. "Will you please put these on him, Mr. Gervin? I'll keep him covered so he won't try anything."

Gervin said, "The pleasure will all be mine."

Hewey agreed, "It damn sure will."

He had had a few minor run-ins with the authorities in his time, but never had steel cuffs been snapped shut around his wrists before. Their embrace was cold. He felt that chill again.

He was sorry the boys had to be here to watch this. He

felt humiliated, demeaned. But he brought himself to look back at them. "It's up to you boys to keep on. Finish the job just like I was here."

Cotton said, "We'll do our best." But his doubt was painfully clear. Hewey wanted to hug the boys, but he couldn't, not with these cuffs on. His throat went tight again, and he turned away from them. He chose the horse he thought might be the easiest to ride, and he started unhitching him from the binder. The handcuffs made it difficult.

Cotton moved to help him. The marshal swung the pistol toward the youngster. "Boy, you stand back from him."

Cold fear struck Hewey. "Marshal, don't you point that gun at the kid." He stepped back away from the horse, away from Cotton. "If you got to point it at somebody, point it at me."

The marshal seemed to realize what he had done. He let the muzzle dip a moment, then brought it back to bear on Hewey.

Cotton swallowed hard. His face had paled. He said finally, "If it's any comfort to you, Uncle Hewey, I know now that you and Wes Wheeler were right."

"It is a comfort."

When Hewey had mounted the plow horse bareback, and Fat Gervin was satisfied that everything was proceeding according to his pleasure, he bid his goodbyes to the marshal and turned the buggy around. He set the team of grays into a good trot and departed whistling. The black dog followed after him a way, wagging its tail, hating to see him go.

Hewey watched him, wondering if Fat knew anything about Blue Hannigan's wagons. He was glad they hadn't been here yet, for if Fat had seen them he might have been able to figure things out for himself.

The dog came back in time to bark at Hewey as he rode off in a northeasterly direction with the marshal, leaving the boys standing desolately to watch.

They rode across country awhile, Hewey's head down as

he darkly pondered the misfortunes he had brought upon himself and others. The marshal talked incessantly, mostly about other desperate criminals he had managed to bring to justice. Try as they might, they had never been able to escape the long arm and longer memory of the law at New Prosperity. Listening to him, Hewey wondered why the state hadn't disbanded the Texas Rangers and saved itself a lot of money. The marshal of New Prosperity could have handled the whole job by himself.

They came eventually to a barbed-wire fence. Nowhere up or down as far as they could see along the length of it was there a gate. Hewey said, "This is Alvin Lawdermilk's. If we follow along a ways we'll find a drop-gap tied with wires instead of fastened with steeples."

The marshal contemplated him in dark suspicion. "We'll cross right here."

"Alvin's kind of narrow-minded about people messin' with his fences. We'd better find where he's made a place to cross."

Suddenly the pistol was back in the marshal's hand. "I am the law, and I can do what I goddamn please!"

Hewey swallowed. He shuddered, fearing the man might get overwrought and accidentally squeeze the trigger. There were no witnesses. He could tell any story he wanted to. "I sure wisht you'd point that thing off to the side a little."

"You pull the steeples out of that post."

"I've got no pliers."

"You've got a pocketknife, haven't you? Use that."

Hewey poked around and broke a blade out of his good Barlow that he had bought one time in Miles City, Montana. But he managed to worry the steeples out. The wires were fairly tight, but the posts were far enough apart that he was able to put his weight on the barbed wires and push them down to ground level with his foot. He led the plow horse across, then looked up expectantly at the marshal.

The marshal's dun must have had some bad experience

with wire at one time or other. It rolled its eyes and made worried noises in its nose as the marshal tried to make it approach the fence. He made two tries, both unsuccessful. Each time he circled the horse out a little way and came back, never taking his eyes or the pistol off of Hewey.

The third time the horse shied a little, then nervously picked one forefoot up high and stepped across the wires that Hewey held stretched. He picked up the other forefoot and brought it over, trembling. For a moment he stood that way, half on one side, half on the other, fearful about bringing his hind feet across. The marshal cursed and spurred him, and for a moment he let the pistol point upward.

On impulse Hewey let go of the wires. They sprang up, the top one catching the dun horse just a little past mid-paunch. The horse squealed in fright and went straight up. The surprised marshal let the pistol fly and grabbed at the saddle horn with both hands. He bawled louder than the horse. The second jump brought the dun clear of the fence, and also clear of the marshal.

There was only one small clump of prickly pear within fifty feet, and the marshal slammed down on his back squarely in the center of it. He lay there rigid, the breath knocked out of him, his startled eyes staring straight up into the sun.

Hewey saw a badger hole dug beside a fence post. He picked up the fallen pistol, dropped it in and caved off the edge of the hole with his boot. The marshal lay groaning and rolling his eyes, seeing little or nothing, struggling for breath, impaled on the mushy green but hostile round pads of the prickly pear.

The dun had stopped pitching and stood looking back, trembling in the aftermath of panic. The saddle was half turned, resting on the horse's right side. Hewey mounted the plow horse and rode to the dun, talking softly. "Whoa, son. Ain't nothin' goin' to hurt you now. Whoa there." He caught the trailing reins, got down and lifted the saddle back into its proper position, then led the horse to the marshal.

By now the man had partially recovered his breath. He lay staring at Hewey in terror, sure Hewey was going to murder him in cold blood.

Hewey looked the dun horse over carefully for cuts. He found none of any account. To the stricken marshal he said, "You're awful lucky. This horse ain't hurt a bit, hardly."

Not daring to move, the marshal groaned. "I think my back is broken. I've got pain in a thousand places."

The prickly pear had cushioned his fall. Hewey knew the pain was not caused by broken bones. But a broken back was much more dignified than a butt full of thorns. If the marshal preferred the importance of a catastrophic injury, who was Hewey to deprive him?

"You *do* look like you're in a bad way," he agreed. "If I was you I wouldn't move a muscle. I'll ride over to Lawdermilk's and send help."

For the first time the marshal realized Hewey wouldn't kill him. "You wouldn't leave me here?" he protested hoarsely.

"You might die if I don't get somebody here who knows what to do. Don't you worry; there's some good ladies over at that house who'll take care of you. And don't you worry about *me,* either. I'm goin' to finish up that job I was workin' on, and then I'll come back and turn myself over to you. That's a promise."

Losing his prisoner seemed a mild concern to the marshal at the moment. He groaned piteously.

Hewey said, "Till Alvin comes with a wagon, you'd better lay real still. Try to be comfortable."

He fished in the marshal's pocket for the handcuff key. It took some doing to fit the key with his teeth, and he had to hook it into a steeple in a fence post to turn it. But in a few minutes he had freed himself from the cold embrace of the cuffs and hooked them over the horn of the marshal's saddle. He tied the dun horse, pushed the wire down, led the plow horse back over it, then set out in an easy, swinging lope toward Alvin Lawdermilk's.

When he finally got back to the field he saw that the boys had finished the cutting. Blue Hannigan's freight wagons were there, the men starting to load the bundle-feed. The boys came running. Both threw their arms around him.

Cotton demanded, "Uncle Hewey, how did you get away?"

"I didn't. The marshal just decided to take himself a rest before we start all the way back to New Prosperity."

11

Hewey and the boys worked with the freighters until dusk, loading the itchy, dusty feed until they were exhausted, and until they knew it was time to get home and do up the chores before dark. The teamsters camped where they were so they could resume loading the rest of the feed at daylight. By the time the sun was up, Hewey and the boys gathered the sale yearlings he had been putting into the milk-cow pasture. They tried to push them through the wire gate nearest the field. The cattle warily eyed the opening and rushed past it, refusing to go through.

Tommy suggested, "Maybe they realize they're leavin' home."

"They don't realize nothin'," Hewey replied. "They're just actin' like cattle." He rode up to the gate and pulled it shut, then casually dropped it to leave only a narrow opening. He rode Biscuit back to where the boys waited, holding the cattle in check. "Let's ride off a little, boys, and give them air."

They retreated fifty yards and watched. Presently a couple of the more curious yearlings worked their way cautiously to the gate, sniffing at it, looking around in suspicion. One of them lifted its tail and half ran, half pitched through the opening. The second did the same, and the others followed suit.

Hewey said, "All it takes to be a good cowboy is to be a little smarter than the cow-brute. Let them think they're sneakin' out and you can put them anyplace."

By the time the yearlings reached the field, the teamsters were finished loading the wagons. The cattle hungrily scattered through the fresh stubble, enjoying a luxury to which they would never be able to become accustomed in this part of the country. Tommy looked toward Hewey with concern about the cattle scattering. Hewey said, "Let them fill up. It's a long ways to Midland."

The feed was stacked high on the wagons. Hewey entertained some fears that it might be top heavy enough to tip over in a little visitation of bad luck, but he had to trust Hannigan's judgment. The big man had probably followed mules far enough to make five or six trips around the world if all his traveling could have been put together in one straight line. Hewey rode up to Blue and shook his hand.

"Blue, I wisht I could tell you how I appreciate this."

"And I wisht you'd learn when to shut up." Blue looked across the newly cut field at the scattered yearlings. "You're goin' to *follow* us with them cattle, ain't you? It's bad enough lookin' a set of mules in the rear."

"Every man to his own brand of whisky. We'll follow you."

Hannigan climbed up onto his wooden seat and uncoiled a long blacksnake whip. He circled it once over his head, then popped it behind him and again in front of him. The mules leaned into the collars and started Hannigan's pair of wagons into a slow, protesting movement. He hadn't touched any of them with the whip, but they knew from past experience that he could. He could not only lift the hair from any mule of his choice but could pick the spot where the snake would strike.

Not all the mules took up their fair share of the load immediately. Blue had all the vocabulary considered vital to a

Texas mule skinner, augmented by extra verbiage learned along the Mexican border. That language, and a little judicious application of the whip, soon had every mule toting fair. In a few minutes the wagons were lined out in tandem pairs, Blue Hannigan in the lead.

Hewey and his nephews slowly and patiently coaxed the yearlings out of the stubble and back onto the kind of pastureland they were used to. They followed in the wake of the wagons, Hewey riding point awhile to set the pace.

More than once he turned in the saddle to look behind him. He half expected to see that marshal trailing him. But in all probability the lawman was not going to feel like sitting in a saddle—or anything else—for three or four days.

He dropped back with the boys. "When you've got grandchildren, you can tell them you made one of the last great trail drives north. You don't have to tell them you was followin' a shirttail set of spotted yearlin's and a string of freight wagons loaded with bundle-feed."

Tommy squared himself in the saddle, pleased by the concept. Cotton didn't seem overly impressed.

They watered the cattle at the windmill which bore Hewey's name. He climbed most of the way to the top, surveying their back trail and looking across country toward Alvin Lawdermilk's. He saw no one.

Even if the officer *did* show up and carry Hewey away now, it wouldn't ruin things for Walter and Eve. Blue Hannigan would handle the sale of the feed, and he would take it upon himself to look over the boys' shoulders to be sure they weren't cheated in selling the yearlings. From here on, if Cotton and Tommy had to, they could handle the situation without Hewey. He had met his responsibilities.

The thought started him humming to himself. He climbed down the wooden ladder and dropped the last long step to the ground, resolving to waste no more of his energy worrying about the marshal and the New Prosperity jail. Those were problems for another day. He glanced up once more at the mill tower. "Damn," he muttered, "but I wisht that thing was painted."

The trip took three days . . . three days in which Hewey knew once more the joy of being on the move, of riding free, of good camaraderie, of being without a heavy burden of worry and guilt. His old humor came back to him. For three days he regaled Tommy with outrageous stories of places he had been, great jackpots he had gotten into and out of, stories of the wide-open country of blessed memory when there were no barbed-wire fences and improved roads, no poverty farms checkerboarding the broad seas of prairie grass like smallpox scars on the face of a beautiful woman.

Tommy listened with enthusiasm if not with total belief. Sometimes Hewey wished the boy had been born earlier so he could have seen all these things for himself rather than have to share them vicariously with an uncle whose selective memory helped him recall the smiling times and pass over the dark as if they had never been.

Cotton listened with easy tolerance but without Tommy's occasional open awe.

Slowly, as Hewey watched these two boys, it came to him how different they truly were. Cotton talked of the future as a time of automobiles and great machines and fantastic inventions waiting to burst forth upon the world. Hewey shuddered. He tried, but he could picture no place in such a world for him. The wonders that made the future look golden to Cotton made it bleak and terrifying to Hewey.

Tommy showed no anxiety about those mysterious times which lay ahead; yet, he still had a lively interest in the times already gone. Hewey suspected that Tommy would probably make his life right here in this country of his youth. If Walter and Eve could weather the rough years and save what they had acquired, Tommy would be the one to carry it forward, to build on it and keep the Calloway name alive on this land. He had the adaptability, Hewey thought, to accommodate to the changes the Cottons would bring upon him, but he would always have roots deeply implanted in the traditions of the past. He would be one of those men blessed with the ability to save what was good of his heritage without slipping hopelessly behind the pace of his own times. In his way, Tommy would never grow so old that he would not somehow need his Uncle Hewey, even when Hewey was no more than a distant memory.

But Cotton had already outgrown him. Cotton needed and wanted little from what had gone by. His gaze was fixed on the future. To him the past was a ladder already climbed, to be left behind without regret, without nostalgia.

Sadness came over Hewey along with this gradual realization. Cotton already had all he would ever need from Hewey—a searching mind, a lively interest in things unseen. This, and the Calloway name, was all they really shared anymore. Hewey had his memories of a closeness that once had been; he would have to settle for that. He would have to let go of Cotton as Cotton had already let go of him. He felt a strong need to pull up beside Cotton and hug him once before he was gone forever.

But he did not do it, for Cotton would not understand. It was too late to say good-bye, for the boy was already gone. In his place was a man—a man for whom time started—not ended—with the year Aught Six.

Hewey swung the little herd away from the wagons as they approached Midland from the south. No one needed to know—until the feed was sold and the money in hand—that any connection existed between Hewey Calloway and Blue Hannigan. Blue waved as he started his wagons up the grade that led across the Texas & Pacific Railroad tracks, and into the town that looked like a forest of wooden-towered windmills.

Hewey hunted around for a likely looking patch of good green grass on which no other cattle seemed to have any immediate claim. He found one a little way east up the tracks and back far enough that a passing train would not throw the yearlings into a panic. They had never seen anything bigger than a freight wagon or heard anything, man or machine, with a voice louder than Blue Hannigan's. Hewey told the boys to stay and loose-herd the cattle, letting them graze while he went into town and scouted the market.

Midland was a moderately bustling railroad and cow town, a supply center not only for the outlying ranches but for a dozen or more small and speculative towns which lay back off of the railroad and which had only a tenuous claim on existence. Many of their names had been penciled onto maps for easy erasure in case they lost that claim. Some already had; more still would. This was a time of quick land promotions, quick disappointments, of boom today and bust tomorrow.

Hewey spotted a black automobile parked among a dozen farm wagons and knew Cotton would enjoy his stay here. Damn contraptions, seemed like a man ran into one of them everywhere he turned anymore. Next thing, people would want to ride to the outhouse in an automobile to save walking from the back door.

He visited two saloons and invested in two shots of whisky while he plied the denizens about the cattle market. For about a dollar's expenditure on liquor of uncertain quality he learned what he could logically expect to get for the yearlings. He then visited two local butcher shops and set up a time for the butchers to ride out and bid him for what they needed—not both at the same time, of course. He knew they would want only the fleshier of the cattle, usually heifers. For the rest he visited a cattle trader whose occupation it was to ride around the country picking up small numbers of cattle from farmers and little ranch operators, putting them together until he had a boxcar load or two. Then he shipped them to the Fort Worth market and hoped he could sell the whole lot for more money than he had invested in them. Usually he managed to do so, or he would long since have gone back to working for wages. Hewey set it up for him to come out to the herd after the butchers had finished and gone.

Thus it was that before the day was done he had split the little herd three ways and had the money in hand for all of it. As the trader and a kid helper started drifting the yearlings toward holding pens on the tracks, Hewey made sure the roll of greenbacks was safely stowed in the bottom of his deepest pocket.

"Boys," he said expansively to his nephews, "I'll set you both up to an ice cream."

As he expected, the sight of the automobile meant more to Cotton than all the ice cream in town. Hewey watched him, reading the wanting in his nephew's face. It was all Cotton could do to keep from lifting the hood and getting in where the motor was. It would be futile to try to make a farmer or a cowboy of Cotton. He knew how, but his heart was not in it; it never would be.

Tommy saw all he needed in two minutes, and he was ready for the ice cream. "If he doesn't come on, Uncle Hewey, we ought to go without him."

Hewey shook his head. "Let him be. Your brother knows what's important to him."

When Cotton finally did come along, he told them more than Hewey really cared to know about the automobile, who had built it, how it operated and what service could be expected of it.

Cotton said wistfully, "It'd be fun if that feller had a breakdown right here in the street. I'll bet I could fix it."

Hewey smiled. "I'm glad you don't have ambitions to be a doctor. You'd be wantin' me to fall down sick so you could poke at me with a pocketknife."

He found an ice-cream parlor and left the nephews there for safekeeping. He mounted Biscuit and rode to the Springer wagon yard, which Blue Hannigan customarily frequented when he put in at Midland. Blue was turning his mules loose in a pen which Springer had assigned to him or which, more likely, Blue had simply claimed by being there first. Blue's wagons were empty. So were the wagons of the other freighters. Hewey grinned. It was a relief to see the wagons shed of their loads.

Blue forked hay into wooden racks while a swamper spread oats into the long open troughs beneath. He finally laid down the fork and walked to where Hewey leaned patiently against the fence.

"Any trouble?" Hewey asked.

Hannigan laughed. "They asked me where the feed come from. I just said, 'South of town.' They didn't ask how far south, and I didn't say. They acted real glad to get it." He reached into his pocket and brought forth a leather wallet. Inside was a sheaf of bills greener than a barnful of alfalfa hay. "They offered to pay with a bank draft, but I told them they was dealin' with a man who couldn't read nothin' but the numbers on a greenback."

Hewey riffled the bills and tried to add them in his head. He feared the first time that he had made an error. A recount showed he had more money than he could rightfully have expected from the ranchers who normally bought from Walter. "Blue, you sure you didn't get some of your own money mixed up in this?"

Blue shook his head emphatically. "I been known to make a mistake or two with a mule, but I never make a mistake with my money."

Fat Gervin was paying more for feed here at Midland than he had contracted to sell it for to the ranchers down south. *Damn,* Hewey thought, *but he's God-awful anxious to freeze us out.*

The other teamsters finished their feeding and began to gather round. Hewey's spirits soared as he stuck the roll into his pocket to keep company with that which he had received for the cattle. He said to the teamsters, "I—me and Walter, that is—we owe you-all somethin' for makin' that haul. I'd sure like to pay you."

Blue made an exaggerated gesture of putting one hand behind his ear, as if deaf. "I don't hear a word you say, Hewey."

Hewey's throat seemed to swell shut. None of these men had any intention of taking money. They had done it for friendship, a commodity beyond price. He cleared his throat but couldn't speak. He tried again. "I reckon I've eaten too much dust. A drink of good whisky might be just the cure. I'd be tickled to set you fellers up to a round."

Blue Hannigan grinned. "Funny how my hearin' has all of a sudden come back to me."

With all that new wealth in his pockets Hewey felt able to give the boys a dollar apiece to spend any way they saw fit. He turned them loose to seek their own entertainment. He figured if two boys couldn't have a night's fun on a dollar per head, they weren't trying very hard. The only requirement he made was that they show up at the wagonyard by sunup, because that was when he planned to start south. Eve would probably raise hell when she found out, but she couldn't keep the boys under her thumb forever.

As it turned out, both were in their bedrolls asleep long before Hewey got through drinking a pint or two with Blue and the other freighters at the wagonyard.

The last thing Blue said before Hewey left him was, "I've got a load of freight to take north off of the railroad. You wouldn't guess in a month what it is."

Hewey didn't try.

Blue said, "It's gasoline, to power them horseless carriages. Seems like just about every little town has got at least one or two of them stinkin' things anymore." He laughed. "Funny, ain't it? People say them glorified spit-cans is goin' to replace the horse, but without the horse or mule to haul gasoline to them, they can't run a lick. The more of them things they get, the more horses and mules this country is goin' to need. You ought to take up freightin', Hewey, while you can still get in on the ground floor. There ain't nothin' goin' to take the place of a good stout freight wagon."

Hewey and Cotton and Tommy set out south before good daylight. A trip that had taken three days with the wagons and the cattle could be done in one day by men a-horseback, moving in a good steady trot. Biscuit was by instinct a pacesetter, not a follower. The boys' horses had no choice but to keep up.

Hewey intended to reach Upton City while the bank was open because he itched to get this money out of his pockets and the note paid. He pushed hard. He sent the boys home when he was close enough and took out across country to short-cut the wagon road's meanderings. By midafternoon he rode into the lower end of Upton City's dirt street.

He didn't think much of it when barber Orville Mulkey waved at him and then set out following him up the street. But in a minute he looked back and saw half a dozen or more men walking along beside the barber. Somebody saw him coming and shouted into the Dutchman's saloon. Hewey saw five men come out, one of them Schneider. They stood watching as he rode by, then fell in with the procession. Pierson Phelps left his store and joined the parade.

Hewey looked back uncertainly, suddenly nervous.

Ahead of him, at the courthouse, big Sheriff Wes Wheeler walked down the steps and strode casually out to meet him, nodding a silent greeting. Hewey reined up, glanced back, then looked at the sheriff. "Wes, if I'm in trouble . . ."

Wheeler was not much given to smiling. He said, "If you are, Hewey, looks like you'll have a flock of reliable witnesses."

These men were friends, or at least acquaintances. He saw no hostility anywhere and knew no reason there should be, unless that New Prosperity marshal had been spreading lies about him. Nervously he wiped a sleeve across his mouth, waiting for somebody to say something. Nobody did. He tugged the reins gently and set Biscuit into a walk, crossing the street to the front of the little stone bank. The front door, set crossways on a blunted corner, was still open. He was in time. Hewey looked once more at the crowd who had followed him afoot. There had to be sixteen or eighteen of them now, not counting Wes Wheeler. Wes was big enough for two men, all by himself. Hewey licked dry lips and said uncertainly, "Howdy, fellers." All he got was grins and silence. He swung out of the saddle, wrapped the reins around a hitching post and stepped up into the bank.

His gaze fastened immediately upon Fat Gervin, sitting at a rolltop desk behind the stockade-like fence through which the sheep and the goats were customarily separated before they ever reached him for an audience.

The look in Fat's florid face was of sullen dismay.

"I come to see you, Fat," Hewey announced.

Fat said nothing. He only stared.

Hewey said, "You got a note here against my brother Walter. I come to settle up with you."

Fat still said nothing. A young man who had been hired out of a Fort Worth mercantile company as a bank clerk pulled a file drawer from a heavy oak cabinet and rummaged through the papers. He withdrew one and laid it in front of Fat. "This is the one, Mr. Gervin."

Fat flared, resenting his mixing in, then stared down at the paper. Hewey pulled the rolls of greenbacks out of his pocket and laid them on Fat's desk, flaunting them a little. He picked them up one at a time and counted out the bills. He knew to the penny what Walter owed. He had lain awake nights adding it up in his mind. When he finished counting the feed and cattle money, and that which he had earned from Alvin Lawdermilk, he said, "I got authority to draw on Walter's account for what else is due. You tally it up and write the draft, Fat."

Face a deep red, Gervin dipped a pen into an inkwell and wrote out a check. He turned it slowly and shoved it roughly toward Hewey. Hewey took the pen from Fat's stubby fingers, made a long flourish and signed his name.

"Now, I'll thank you for a receipt. In handwritin'."

A delighted clamor arose among the crowd, and several clapped their hands. Fat Gervin seemed to shrink, to draw inward, shutting all of them out.

A thin, bent-shouldered old man pushed through the festive onlookers with some anxiety and a little profanity. C. C. Tarpley demanded, "What's goin' on here? We had a bank robbery?"

Hewey blew on the receipt, trying to rush the drying of the ink. "Same thing, C. C., only just the opposite. I've headed off a robbery *by* a bank. I paid off Walter's note."

C. C. stared at him in momentary disbelief until a look at Fat's sullen face disabused him of doubt. C. C.'s disappointment was keen and painful, but he made a gallant effort at covering it up. Nobody could accuse C. C. Tarpley of being a sore loser; well, not a *very* sore loser.

"That's fine, Hewey. To tell the truth, I never thought you could do it."

"I know. In fact, I remember a little pledge you made." He shifted his gaze to Fat, who remembered it very well also. Hewey said, "I intended to hold you to it, Fat, but I'm a generous feller at heart. I'll let you off because I don't want to take my britches down in front of a crowd like this."

The bystanders laughed. Somehow they all seemed to know about C. C.'s pledge.

C. C. regarded his son-in-law without any fondness. In his face was a look that said he wouldn't care if Hewey demanded full payment. He said, "I know what Fat done to you about your yearlin's and your feed. I would have to figure you found a buyer anyway for the cattle. But what in the hell did you do with all that feed?"

"I found buyers for that too."

"Who?"

Hewey let his grin break wide open, warm and bright. "You and Fat."

The old man's face reddened as realization soaked in. "For how much?"

Hewey told him.

C. C. Tarpley's anger built slowly, like water coming to boil in a chuck-wagon coffeepot. Finally it would hold no longer. Making angry noises deep in his throat, he ripped off his dusty old felt hat. He began to beat Fat about the head and shoulders with it, while Fat cringed and tried to cover his face with his arms.

Hewey lost interest in banking affairs. He sought out Schneider. "Dutch, I'm goin' to set up one round of drinks for this bunch. After that, I'm savin' my money."

Hewey had ambivalent feelings about the Lawdermilk place. Spring Renfro had been much on his mind, and he itched to see her. But she wouldn't be the only person waiting for him there. He dreaded facing that marshal from New Prosperity, whose prickly-pear wounds, if not yet healed, should at least have reached a point of toleration.

Somebody must have seen him coming, for when he rode up to the ranch house, Spring, the Lawdermilks, Old Lady Faversham and Julio all stood on the porch waiting for him. The old lady was on her cane. Spring ran down the steps to meet him at the gate. She was no longer shy about showing her feelings in front of people. She threw her arms around him. Hewey hadn't realized a small-built woman could be so strong. She kissed him and didn't seem to care whether Old Lady Faversham watched or not.

"Did everything go all right, Hewey?"

"Like a brand-new Ingersoll watch. You ought to've seen Fat Gervin's face when I paid him off."

"I wish I could have been there. Have you told Eve and Walter?"

"No." The joy left him. "I'll have to let you go tell them for me. I came to give myself up to that marshal. You-all get all the stickers out of him?"

She smiled. "That was a private matter between him and Alvin and Julio. I think they left a few where they thought they would do the most good."

"They won't do *me* any good. Where's he at?"

Alvin came down from the porch. His voice held a promise of laughter. "He's halfway back to New Prosperity, I imagine. He decided they needed him at home more than he needed you."

Hewey turned, not quite believing. "What did you do to him?"

Alvin held up his hands. He was the personification of purity and innocence. "Not a thing. Never laid a hand on him except to pull pear thorns. But I had Wes Wheeler come out and explain a few things to him about law in *our* part of the country. Like when he made you pull the steeples out of my fence. That was willful destruction of private property. Then there was the matter of my plow horse that he made you ride. Horse theft, pure and simple. I had Wes explain to him how narrow-minded we are about such as that.

"Then I just happened to mention to him that if he would drop his charges against you, I'd try my best to talk Wes into tearin' up the charges I had sworn out against *him*. He got to actin' kind of homesick, all of a sudden."

If Preacher Averill had been there, Hewey would gladly have made a contribution to the church. He squeezed Alvin's hand so hard that the old horseman flinched. "Alvin, I'll owe you as long as I live."

Alvin shook his head. Wistfully he studied Hewey's face. "You done proud for yourself." He looked at Spring, then back to Hewey. "I liked the old Hewey an awful lot, and I hate to lose him. But I reckon I'll get used to the new Hewey by and by. He's a pretty good old boy himself."

Julio saddled Spring's paint horse for her so she could ride to Walter's and Eve's with Hewey. Hewey turned and waved at the family as he rode away. Alvin and Old Lady Faversham looked sad. But Cora was smiling, and so was Julio, a romantic to the end.

Spring suggested, "I don't suppose you'd want to make a little circle by the Barcroft place on the way?"

Hewey hunched a little, finding no joy in the thought.

"Tomorrow, maybe. Right now I'm anxious to turn this receipt over to Walter and Eve."

She gave him a worried glance but said nothing.

The sun was going down as they approached the Calloway house. Hewey could feel how tired Biscuit was; the steps were labored and slow, for it had been a long, long day. It was seldom that he ever pushed a horse so hard.

As at the Lawdermilk place, they had evidently been seen. Everyone stood in front of the house, waiting for them. Walter leaned on his crutches, his face expectant. Eve was trying to smile confidently, but Hewey had disappointed her many times before; the anxiety showed in her eyes.

Hewey stepped down from a grateful horse which was almost trembling from fatigue. He turned to help Spring to the ground. He stood with his left arm around her while he fished in his shirt pocket for the signed receipt. He brought it out, extended it toward Eve and grinned broadly.

Hands shaking, she unfolded it, glanced at it, handed it to Walter and threw her arms around Hewey's neck. She hugged him as tightly as Spring had done at the Lawdermilks', but for much different reason. She stood back, her eyes brimming with tears. Her voice broke when she tried to speak. She got it under control.

"Hewey Calloway, there've been times I've said hard things to you in anger, and most of them were justified. But right now I take back every word. Every word."

Then the four of them were standing with their arms around each other. The two boys stood off to the side, watching, smiling, Tommy turning sheepishly to wipe his sleeve across his eyes.

Walter's voice cracked. "Hewey, I wisht I knew how . . ."

Hewey said, "You got a lot to thank them boys for. Without them, it wouldn't of got done."

Walter nodded. "The boys know how I feel . . . how me and Eve both feel." He crumpled the receipt. "We still got a hard row ahead of us, but we've taken the roughest of it. We're goin' to make it from here on."

"Damn right you'll make it."

Eve wiped her eyes and turned toward the door. "Let's get into the house. We'll have supper directly."

Hewey started toward the horses, but Eve caught his arm. "The boys can turn the horses loose. You come on in this house."

Hewey poured coffee for Spring and himself. Spring put sugar in hers, but Hewey liked his coffee the way he liked his whisky, straight. He stood at the window, looking out toward the barn.

Eve couldn't get through thanking him. She put her arms around him again. "Hewey Calloway, you just don't know . . ." She leaned her forehead against his shoulder. "If there's ever anything me and Walter can do for you, anything you ever need . . ."

Hewey shook his head. "You don't owe me a thing. I owed *you,* and I done what I could to pay. I don't want a thing." His gaze fell upon Cotton, pulling the saddle off of Biscuit. He watched thoughtfully. "I take it back, Eve. There *is* somethin'."

"Anything we've got, it's yours."

He looked at her. "You may not like the price."

"We'll pay it."

He pointed his chin at the window and looked back at the boy by the barn. "Let Cotton go."

Eve drew a sharp breath. "Hewey, I couldn't do that."

"You'll have to, sooner or later. Do it now, while he knows what he wants and has a real chance to go and get it. Eve, it's been six years since we came into the new century. We still belong to the old one, me and you and Walter. We always will. But there's a different road in front of Cotton. One day he'll pick up and follow it whether you let him go or not. Let him go now, with no hard feelin's to pain him when he looks back."

Eve turned to Walter. She began to sob. Hewey couldn't look at her; he kept gazing out the window.

He heard Walter say, "Hewey's right. Cotton's come to his time."

Eve fished in her apron pocket but didn't find what she was looking for. Spring gave her a handkerchief. Eve used it, then wadded it in her hands. "It's a scary world out yonder that you're askin' me to send him off into. I don't understand half of what I hear or read about it."

"Us three, we never will. We was born too soon. But Cotton'll make himself a place in it. We don't have to understand it; all we have to know is that he'll be all right."

Eve didn't answer. She hadn't made up her mind to it yet, but she would. Tomorrow . . . the next day . . . one day soon, she would. She turned to the stove, to busy her hands and perhaps thereby busy her mind on something else.

From behind, Spring put her arms around Hewey and laid her head against his back. She said softly, "Thank you, Hewey, for Cotton."

Eve said the blessing at the supper table, and it was such a long one Hewey was afraid the food would get cold; she had a lot to thank the Lord for, and he couldn't think of a thing she overlooked. The last little while the realization had begun to come upon him with some force that he hadn't eaten anything all day. It was an experience not unknown to a drifting man, but one to be avoided whenever possible. He was into his second helping of red *frijole* beans and cornbread when he heard a commotion outside. It sounded like a bunch of horses, running.

He pushed his chair back and went to the window.

"I'll be damned!" he exclaimed.

"You probably will be," Eve scolded, "usin' language like that. What's the matter out there?"

Hewey pointed his chin, smiling. "Look who's comin'." He walked quickly out into the yard and hurried toward the corral.

From the west, like phantoms out of the dusk, came a remuda of horses in a hard trot, heading for a gate someone had loped ahead and opened for them. Snort Yarnell swung back into the saddle and pulled off to one side to give them room. The horses raised a gray cloud of dust as they rushed through the opening. Hewey climbed over the fence and grasped the wooden gate, pushing it shut as Snort rode his blue roan in behind the string of young horses.

"I'll swun, Snort," Hewey exclaimed, "you're like a bad penny. Where'd you come from this time?"

"From the KCs. Like I told you, I went out there to pick up a string of horses to take back over onto the Concho. I wonder if Walter would mind me keepin' them in the corral here tonight?" He knew very well that Walter would let him; few people would turn away a stranger, much less an old friend.

"Unsaddle and come up to the house," Hewey said. "We're in the middle of supper. There's a-plenty."

Snort's gold teeth gleamed. "I been countin' on that."

The rewards of the day had been so great that even Eve had a nice welcome for Snort. Spring stood back away from him a little, eying him with reserve, even a touch of fear. Tommy kept wanting to bring things from the stove for Snort, and when Snort had more spread in front of him than he was likely to be able to eat, Tommy said, "I'll go out and feed your horses, Snort."

"Not too much, boy," Snort cautioned, pointing a fork at him. "These is wild ranch horses, and they're like wild ranchmen, used to doin' for theirselves. We don't want to be spoilin' them none."

The kitchen fell silent except for the clinking of Snort's

utensils on his plate, and the loud slurping noise he made over his coffee. He could put away a fearsome amount of food when he set himself to it. But finally he pushed his chair away from the table and rocked back on its two hind legs. He belched. He glanced from Hewey to Spring. "This good lady got the knot tied on you yet, Hewey?"

Spring looked at the floor. Hewey said, "Not yet."

"Well, when are you-all goin' to commit the deed?"

Hewey rubbed his hands together, suddenly self-conscious. "I don't know. We ain't really talked about that."

"You in any great rush, Hewey?"

"Rush?"

"I was thinkin' if you-all wasn't in any real big hurry, you might like to go off on a little trip with me. Last bachelor trip, you might say."

Hewey's interest began to pick up. "Trip? Where to?"

"To Mexico. *Old* Mexico. I got a job lined up down there with an American outfit, soon's I get these horses delivered. They said if I found any more good cowboys that wanted a job, just to bring them along. Got a winter's work, at least. Maybe on into next year too."

Hewey's pulse began to pound at the thought of it. Mexico.

Snort leaned over the table, his voice eager. "It ain't just on that penny-ante border, Hewey. It's way down yonder, way down deep. Beautiful country. Not spoiled like this country's gettin' to be, but big and wild and wide open. It's like Texas was before they commenced puttin' fences across it and cuttin' it up for farmin'. It's like goin' back to when we was young. I think me and you ought to see that just one more time, while there's a little of it left."

Hewey was still rubbing his hands together. He felt a hand gently touch his arm. He saw Spring staring at him, her eyes pinched with pain.

Eve cleared her throat. "Mr. Yarnell, I believe Tommy is havin' some trouble down at the pens. I believe some of your horses are tryin' to get out."

Snort jumped to his feet and hurried out the door.

Eve said severely, "Hewey, don't you listen to him. It's the devil that's brought him here."

Defensively Hewey said, "I wasn't listenin'. I mean, I *was* listenin', but I wasn't really studyin' on goin'."

Spring reached up and put her fingers under his chin, turning him to face her. He saw tears in her eyes. Quietly she said, "You *would* like to go, wouldn't you?"

"You oughtn't to pay any attention to Snort Yarnell," Hewey said. "It's always a beautiful country if he's never been there. He's fiddlefooted, just like I used to be."

"Used to be?" She tried hard to smile, but she couldn't bring it out. "Hewey, I can see it in your eyes. I saw it at the Barcroft place. I saw it when Snort was by here the last time, but I tried to tell myself I was wrong. I tried to tell myself you'd changed. You *haven't* changed. You never will."

He wanted to say something to convince her she was wrong, but no words presented themselves. Nothing came, because he knew she was right. "Spring . . ."

She touched her fingers against his lips to stop him from trying to speak, to argue. "There was never anything false about you, Hewey. I loved you for being just what you were. You were happy, and I felt happy just being around you. But lately I've watched you trying very hard to be something else, some*body* else. You've been miserable, and I've hurt for you. If I marry you, you can't stay the same as you've always been. You'll have to change, for me. And when you change, you won't be Hewey anymore.

"Some things we just can't have, because if we try to hold them they die. There's no way I can have you without changing you. So go ahead, Hewey, go with Snort. I know it's what you really want to do, deep in your heart. Go on then . . . go on to Mexico."

Hewey took her hand and gripped it tightly in both of his own. "I do love you, Spring. You know that."

Nodding, she whispered, "I know. But I know that you love freedom even more."

"Spring, are you sure you won't regret this?"

"Certainly I'll regret it. I'll regret it a thousand times. But I'll always know I was right."

Eve protested, "Spring, you don't know what you're sayin'. Let him go down there and you'll never see him again. We may none of us ever see him again. Like as not he'll wind up dead someplace under an outlawed horse."

Tears welled up in Spring's eyes and spilled down her cheeks. "Alvin knew all along. He said Hewey is a free spirit, like an eagle. I can't bring myself to put an eagle in a cage."

At daylight Snort Yarnell opened the gate and strung the horses out eastward, into the pink glow that came just ahead of the sun. He shouted and slapped his coiled rope against his leg and put them into a long mile-eating trot. He looked back once for Hewey, then went ahead.

Hewey stood halfway between the house and the barn, leather reins in his hand, Biscuit waiting saddled and patient behind him. The family stood lined up to see him away. Spring Renfro waited alone, a little to one side.

Hewey extended his hand, and Walter leaned forward on his crutches to take it. "Walter, you're goin' to make it. You and Tommy, you'll build yourselves a place here better'n anything old C. C. ever had."

"It's always part yours, Hewey."

Hewey shook his head. "A piece of land is for those who'll root down on it. You know *me*." He moved to Eve. She couldn't talk. She put her arms around him and said, that way, all there was to say.

He moved down to Cotton. "Boy, you really think them automobiles are goin' to put us old cowboys out of business?"

Cotton swallowed, his voice thin. "In time, Uncle Hewey. In time."

Hewey gripped his nephew's shoulder. "Well, you go out there and give them all you've got. But just remember—me and old Biscuit, we ain't goin' to lay down easy."

Tears had cut a trail down Tommy's face. He put his arms around Hewey's neck and hugged hard. "You'll be back, won't you, Uncle Hewey? You ain't goin' to let some old bronc kill you?"

"Button, I ain't never been killed in my life."

He turned finally to Spring. He saw her through a haze, because his eyes were burning. He tried to speak to her, but his throat had swollen suddenly. He put his arms around her and pulled her against him, and he felt the warm strength of her arms against his shoulders. She said nothing either.

From the distance he heard Snort Yarnell holler at him. Reluctantly he let Spring go and stepped back. She lowered her head, trying to hide her eyes. Gently he put his fingers under her chin and raised her head a little. He winked at her, though doing so squeezed out a tear that tickled as it ran down his cheek. He gave her a half-smile and got one from her in return.

He turned quickly. The gal-leg spur tinkled as he shoved his boot into the stirrup and swung up into the snakeskin-covered saddle. Biscuit was rested and rearing to go. Hewey touched him very lightly with the spurs, and Biscuit set out in a trot to catch the horses.

Hewey turned once, reined up and waved his hat. Then he rode on.

The sun broke over the prairie in a sudden red blaze. The family all pulled together, arms around each other, Spring standing to one side, still alone. They watched as Hewey seemed to ride into the fire, sitting straight-shouldered and proud on Biscuit's back. And finally he was gone, melted into the relentless glow of a new day.

AFTERWORD

In 1978 Elmer Kelton brought out the third of his novels to be published in hardback. *The Good Old Boys* was different from its predecessors, though. *The Day the Cowboys Quit* (1971) marked Kelton's emergence from the constraints of the formula, though on the surface it looked like a paperback shoot-'em-up. *The Time It Never Rained* (1973) represented a still further departure from the formula as Kelton brought his stubborn, archaic, and endearing figure of the frontiersman into the present, into drought-ridden West Texas of the mid-1950s. Today *The Time It Never Rained* has the highest standing among critics of Kelton's work. Some go so far as to rank it among the best works produced by a Texas writer. Some go so far as to rank it among the best American novels of this century.

I have no argument with the accolades won by *The Time It Never Rained.* But I would lay equally strong claim for the merits of *The Good Old Boys,* a novel that in the long run may stand as high in achievement as *The Time It Never Rained,* maybe even higher. If *The Good Old Boys* is not yet taken seriously, perhaps that is because it is a comic novel. But as Flannery O'Connor has observed, comedy is the most serious form of all. Kelton's own remarks on the circumstances under which the book was conceived are pertinent. He began the novel in the hospital room where his father lay gravely ill. Out of such personal grief, the writer forged a comic novel. Serious? Absolutely.

Like all fiction about the frontier except the sentimental, phony, and therefore untrue, *The Good Old Boys* takes place

during a period of transition. From James Fenimore Cooper
to Sam Shepard, the frontier has always been on the verge
of disappearing. So it is in Kelton's novel. The time is 1906,
and the automobile has penetrated West Texas. Kelton has
wry comic fun with his hero's dismissal of the automobile
as a transient folly. At the same time, though, Hewey Calloway, the perpetual cowboy, sees that the future belongs to
the machine. He himself belongs to the vanishing past,
which is always just over the next rise. At novel's end, the
past, the old frontier, still exists south of the border, down
Mexico way.

Kelton's theme of the vanishing frontier may remind
some readers of another genre that often deals with the
passing of the American West: the Western movie. Three
especially come to mind: *Lonely Are the Brave* (1962), *Ride
the High Country* (1962), and *The Misfits* (1961). Each of
these films laments the passing of the cowboy, the end of
an era, and each employs symbols like those in *The Good
Old Boys:* barbed wire, automobiles (in one, a helicopter),
shrunken or bloated capitalists (the two most common
shapes capitalism takes in human flesh), and cowboys as an
endangered species.

Kelton places his principal characters in a thin social
world of small farms and ranches in the arid country near
Midland. The basic opposition between cowboy and settler,
drifter and home-owner, freedom and family, is fully
worked out. It is an opposition one finds throughout the
literature of the West. *Shane* is one version of the pattern,
a kind of fable about a divine drifter who helps a hard-
pressed yeoman farmer struggling to carve out a living in a
hostile land presided over by forces both natural and, worse,
man-made.

There is nothing of the divine or transcendent about
Kelton's drifter, however. Hewey Calloway is a typical
Kelton hero, "five feet eight and nervous," as Kelton has
hilariously defined his hero in comparison with Louis

L'Amour's giants. Bronc buster, fiddle-footed cowboy, good old boy par excellence, Hewey likes the open range and fears farms, mortgages, and all the ties that bind. In his preference for the cowboy's amiable lack of attachments, Hewey replays a theme familiar in Texas literature. J. Frank Dobie, our most celebrated celebrant of cowboy lore, wrote of his own brief, painful enslavement to the plow and hoe: "All ranch work was congenial to me as I grew up, even doctoring wormy calves by day and skinning dead ones by lantern light, but the year we boys tried raising a bale of cotton remains a dark blot" (*Some Part of Myself,* 1967). And George Sessions Perry, who wrote one of the best books about the agrarian life of tenant-farmers, a kind of hymn to nature and cotton farming in *Hold Autumn in Your Hand* (1941), in another book extolled the life of the cowboy over that of the farmer: "But to us Texans there is a quality of go and glamor about cowmen that farmers never attain" (*Texas, A World in Itself,* 1942).

But Kelton is fair; he gives both sides their due. Hewey's brother Walter is a good man, too, a good father and ex-good old boy beset with economic woes. Besides, there is something irresponsible about Hewey's carefree disregard for the claims others make upon his time and freedom. The women in the novel—his sister-in-law Eve and his fiancee, Spring—define the human cost of Hewey's commitment to rambling. Eve especially fears his ending up like Boy Rasmussen, the ghostly old drifter whose death sounds the saddest, most darkly prophetic note of Hewey's rootless future.

So far I have said nothing directly about the artistry of *The Good Old Boys.* It possesses artistry aplenty. Kelton builds his plot carefully. Realistic fiction depends upon the successful integration of character and incident, and *The Good Old Boys* is seamless. From one action to the next, from Hewey's insistence upon his own freedom and dignity in the incident with the sheriff in the strange town, to his adolescent indulgence in pranks such as roping the dude's automobile, Hewey is masterfully ensnared in a web of moral consequence. Wildly comic incidents, such as the memorable dog-wetting scene with Fat Gervin, move the story to a logical and satisfying climax. Kelton's long apprenticeship in the pulps, where plotting is sometimes crudely handled, pays off richly in this comic novel in which plotting is crucial. It is a beautifully constructed book in which all the parts mesh, in a metaphor Hewey wouldn't approve of, like a fine-tooled machine, like a graceful, well-made roadster.

DON GRAHAM
University of Texas at Austin

THE
SMILING
COUNTRY

To Kindra, Kelby, Tyler, Kourtney, and Kyle

1

Hewey Calloway did not know how old he was without stopping to figure, and that distracted his attention from matters of real importance. In his opinion anyone who wasted time worrying about his age had more leisure than was good for him. He had not acknowledged a birthday since he had turned thirty a dozen years ago—or was it fifteen?

In horse years, Biscuit was older than his rider, but the brown gelding was equally indifferent to the passage of time. Any minor concessions to his age were offset by steadiness and a light-reined response to any task Hewey called upon him to perform. He could outguess a cow in nine of ten confrontations and outrun her the other time.

Hewey could not say nearly so much about the green-broke pony on which Skip Harkness picked his way along the rocky mountainside above Limpia Creek. Since Hewey and the freckle-faced kid had left the corrals and chuck wagon camp down on the yucca flat, the colt had stepped high and kept its ears working nervously while it watched for a booger. Any booger would do. It had already pitched twice, once spooking at a jackrabbit skittering through the underbrush, then taking fright at the cry of a disturbed hawk that sought to scare the horsemen away from its nest high in a tree. The two outbursts had been little challenge, for Skip was young and wiry and laughed at every jump.

Hewey respected anyone efficient at his trade, but he worried about this button's long-range prospects. A kid from a blackland farm back in East Texas, Skip had cowboyed a couple of years and learned just enough to be dangerous to himself and everybody around him. Small triumphs tempted him to kick trouble in the ribs when it could just as well have been left asleep. Instead of pulling up on the hackamore rein to stop the pony from pitching on treacherous sloping ground, Skip had encouraged it to buck harder by spurring high in its shoulders and back in the flank. The colt pitched until its sorrel hide glistened with sweat.

Hewey could not bring himself to criticize, for he used to show off too, not all that long ago. He still gloried in a challenge, but he saw no future in suicide. He said, "I've seen broncs that'd throw you so high the hawks'd have to look up to see you."

"Ain't been a bronc throwed me since I was sixteen."

Hewey guessed Skip to be eighteen, no more than nineteen at the outside, with his heart in the right place but his head on backward. "Biscuit would've busted you good when he was a colt. He flattened me several times."

"Was that before or after the War between the States?"

The kid was thumbing Hewey in the ribs about his age and Biscuit's. This was 1910.

"Wasn't nothin' I could do then that I can't still do. I can ride more miles, find more cows and rope more calves . . ."

He quit talking, for Skip's satisfied grin said he had thrown out the bait and Hewey had swallowed it, hook and all. Hewey never understood why some buttons barely weaned from mother's milk took such pleasure in warting their betters. His nephews would never do such a thing, not Cotton or Tommy. They showed respect, even when he knew they disagreed with him. He wished he had one of them here now instead of this reckless kid with more brass than good sense. They could teach Skip something about manners.

If he put his mind to it he could almost feel sorry for the youngster, born too late to see Texas before the grasping hand of civilization reached out and spoiled it. Hewey had ridden across more country than Skip was likely ever to see.

He had driven cattle to the Kansas railroad and had broken broncs from the Rio Grande to the Canadian line. He had shipped out to Cuba under Teddy Roosevelt. He had traveled horseback across much of the West before it was parceled out by barbed-wire fences and ribboned with roads for the automobile. Skip would never have that opportunity or even realize what he had missed. Hewey Calloway had done it all, yet here he was, still in the prime of life.

He would admit, when he looked into a mirror, that his hair and his whiskers showed about as much gray as brown, but that was a sign of maturity and reliability. If his joints sometimes ached when he threw the blankets aside of a morning, most of the pain faded once he got the muscles working and the blood flowing freely. He was sure he was a better hand now than he had ever been. He would never ask, but he was probably drawing down five or ten dollars a month more than Skip or the other weanlings on this outfit. At least he should be. He could ride anything they could and rope rings around them.

If a genie were to pop out of a whiskey bottle and offer him three wishes, Hewey would give one or two of them back. There wasn't much he would change, beyond tearing down the fences and ditching all the automobiles. Anybody who couldn't get where he was going on horseback or in a wagon was in too much of a hurry.

The kid offered, "You want to ride my bronc a little while, just to keep your hand in?"

"There's no fight left in him now. You've already spurred it out of him." A real hand didn't let some button sweat the rough edges from a bronc and then turn it over to him as if he were too old to do it himself. Hewey *could* still do it himself, any time he wanted to. And he often wanted to, for he still enjoyed a good contest between man and horse.

The J Bar crew was rounding up two-year-old steers to ship to Kansas for summering on Flint Hills grass, but the wagon boss had sent Hewey and Skip to look for a bunch-quitting bull that had fled from yesterday's drive. It had evaded three years' worth of roundups, the branding iron and knife, and had left a long scar across the chest of one unlucky cow pony that had not moved out of its way. The bull had a reputation for being easy to find but hard to catch. The few pursuers it had not outrun, it had outfought, so most local cowboys accorded it an averted gaze. It ranged in one of the narrow, brushy canyons that time and rainfall had carved through the Davis Mountains. Grazing mostly in the dark of the night, it drank from the small and hidden *tinajas,* depressions that eons of runoff water had scoured from flat rock.

The solitary maverick responded to its mother's wily Longhorn blood, which overpowered the gentler influence of its Hereford sire. Old Man Morgan Jenkins was trying to breed the Longhorn blood out of his herd, and this bull was putting its outlaw stamp on too many calves to suit him. Such brush-popping fugitives furnished entertainment to cowboys who loved the chase, like Hewey and Skip, but they were a financial albatross to ranchers and their bankers.

Hewey was bothered a little when Skip was the first to spot their quarry. He knew his own eyes were still sharp enough; he figured Skip just happened to be looking in the right direction at the right time.

Hewey stepped to the ground and tightened Biscuit's cinch so the bull's strength and weight would not pull his saddle down on one side. Skip took no such precaution, and Hewey was not given to offering advice that had not been asked for. If the kid was half as smart as he thought he was, he shouldn't have to be told.

Skip had a way of turning routine into a contest. "Reckon that old horse of yours can catch him?"

"Biscuit'll kick gravel in your eyes."

Skip did not give him the chance. He spurred the bronc and took the lead. Hewey was tempted to overtake and pass him, just to demonstrate that he could, but he decided the trail the bull followed in its hasty retreat was too narrow and treacherous to accommodate two fools. One was enough.

Hewey took his time, loosing the horn string that held his rope. His sun-browned hands were leather-tough, scarred by rope bums and mesquite thorns, the knuckles large except for one knocked down years ago in an encounter much like this one.

The fugitive bull outran Skip into a heavy brush thicket. Skip followed him partway, then stopped in confusion. As Hewey caught up, Skip said, "Can't see him anyplace. Looks like he sprouted wings and flew."

"Outsmarted you is what he did." Hewey listened intently for the sound of popping branches but heard none. "He's laid down in some thick brush where you can't see him. Let's go root him out." He motioned for Skip to take the left side of the draw. Hewey moved up the right, weaving around the mesquite and catclaw.

Though he was watching closely, the bull almost took him unawares. He heard a snort; then a black apparition exploded out of a tangle of mesquite, head down and sharp horns coming straight at Biscuit. The horse whirled so quickly that Hewey had to grab the saddle horn to keep his seat. The bull made a thrust at Biscuit's haunches as it passed, but the horse was an old hand at avoiding such calamities.

Skip shouted, "I've got him." He spurred by while Hewey was trying to collect his wits and get his breath back. The bronc crow-hopped as Skip shook out the coils. Its only experience with a rope had been on the receiving end, frightening and painful.

Dread burned in Hewey as he saw that Skip had the near end of the rope secured to his saddle horn instead of taking a couple of dallies that he could turn loose in a hurry. There were many places more pleasant to be than sitting on a nine-hundred-pound bronc tied to an ill-tempered bull that weighed sixteen hundred pounds and was looking for something to kill.

Boy, Hewey thought, *you're fixing to learn not to suck eggs.*

The chase was fast and rough, the bull shattering brush, its cloven hooves scattering small rocks in their wake. It probably would have gotten away had it not lost its footing on a bare, slanting slab of rock and slid on its belly. It arose quickly, but its speed was hindered by a limp. Foamy saliva streamed from its mouth. When it became weary enough and provoked enough, it would turn to fight. Then it could be roped, though retrieving that rope might cost bull, horses and men some blood, hide and hair.

Hewey had once seen a tiger in a circus. The sound welling from deep in the Longhorn's throat reminded him of the great cat's roar. The bull wheeled and lowered its head.

Skip shouted, "You stay back out of the way. I can handle him."

Like Richmond handled Grant, Hewey thought.

Skip's rope hissed like a snake as he sailed his loop over the horns. The bronc tried to buck just as the bull hit the end of the line. The impact jerked both animals off their feet. Skip gave a surprised shout and hit the ground on his back. The bronc regained its feet and ran in panic. As the rope again stretched taut, it snapped at the saddle horn, popping like a whip. The horse galloped away, holding its head high and wringing its tail.

The loop was still around the bull's horns, the frazzled end of the rope lying on the ground. Skip jumped to his feet, instinctively grabbed it, then dropped it as the bull lowered its head again and charged. The boy sprinted toward a catclaw bush not much taller than he was. "Hewey! Do somethin'!"

It was high time this scatterbrained kid learned that the way of the braggart was strewn with shame and regret. "You told me to stay out of the way."

"Hewey!"

The bull stepped on the trailing rope and broke its stride long enough for Skip to reach the other side of the catclaw. He looked desperately for his bronc, but it was still running. It might as well be ten miles away for all the good it could do him. The bull made a run around the bush after the boy, hooves clattering on the hard ground. Skip managed to stay two paces ahead, circling.

Hewey suggested dryly, "Why don't you climb the tree?"

The catclaw was well named, for its branches were armed with needle-pointed thorns shaped like claws. Perhaps a cat might climb that bush, but Skip never could, not even with a sharp-horned bull providing incentive.

The bull stopped and began to paw dirt back over its shoulder, a sign it had barely begun to fight. Skip crouched on the opposite side of the tree, ready to run to the left or the right as circumstances might require. "You just goin' to sit there and laugh?"

Hewey leaned on his saddle horn. "Been a long time since I saw a circus. You might be able to run faster if you took your boots off."

The bull feinted to the left, then the right, but Skip kept the bush between them. Stymied, the animal stopped and pawed dirt again.

Hewey said, "I wish the boys at the wagon could watch you handle this bull. I've got half a mind to go back and get them."

Sweat cut trails through the dust on Skip's flushed young face. It was hard to see which was strongest, anger or fear. "Time you got back there wouldn't be nothin' left to see, just a puddle of blood and a little bit of hair."

Hewey decided the lesson had gone on long enough. He eased Biscuit toward the bull, which shifted its attention from Skip and charged at the horse. Hewey kept Biscuit far enough ahead to avoid the horns. At a safe distance from Skip he cut around and brought Biscuit up behind the bull.

His loop sailed down around the long horns. He left enough slack that the bull stepped into the loop with its right foot. Hewey quickly drew the rope tight, pulling the foot up against the head. The animal faltered, lost its balance and fell heavily, raising a puff of dust. It lay struggling, unable to rise with its leg immobilized against its muzzle.

Skip complained, "You took long enough." His voice cracked, perhaps from outrage, perhaps from a remnant of fright, most likely from both. The red in his face exaggerated the freckles.

"Wanted him to wear himself down a little." Hewey untied a short length of rawhide rope coiled on the back of his saddle and pitched it to Skip. "Tie him."

Skip struggled to bring the other three legs together, accidentally backing into the catclaw bush in his efforts to stay clear of the threshing head and dangerous horns. The clutching thorns ripped the back of his shirt.

Hewey dismounted and untied a short dehorning saw he had brought for good purpose. "First thing we'd better do is to tip his horns so he won't gore any more horses."

Skip knelt on the bull's head to keep the animal still while Hewey sawed off the outer several inches of horn. He gripped the muzzle and raised the head to let Hewey work on the other side. The bull snorted mucus in Skip's face.

Hewey ran a finger over the rough edge after the sharp tip was gone. "He could still bust your ribs with that. But he wouldn't poke a hole in you that the Lord never intended."

Skip's emotions began to subside. "I thought you were fixin' to let him put a new hole in my butt."

"I just wanted him to educate you a little. I'll bet you're a lot smarter than you were twenty minutes ago."

If Skip felt any appreciation, he kept it well concealed.

Hewey said, "I'll let you and that bull sulk together while I go catch your horse."

Skip's bronc gave up running after catching a forefoot in the looped hackamore rein. At first it resisted Hewey's efforts to free it from entanglement, and it stepped on Hewey's toes before it calmed down. "Broncs and farm-raised buttons," Hewey muttered. "You deserve one another."

Skip's face had lost its angry color by the time Hewey led the bronc back. The boy said, "At least Old Man Jenkins ought to be tickled. We got him his bull."

Hewey watched the animal fight against the restraint of the rawhide that bound its feet. "Mr. Jenkins didn't send us out here to *not* get him."

A ranch owner paid little attention when cowboys did the work he expected of them. He paid close attention when they didn't. That you could and would do the job was taken for granted when you went on the payroll. Excuses were worth only about a nickel a carload, and good reasons about a dime. Hewey rarely offered either.

Skip asked, "Now that we've caught him, what're they fixin' to do with him?"

"Take away his bullhood and send him to Kansas with the steers. He's a throwback to the old days."

"Like you?"

Putting the spurs to me again. He learns awful slow. "Them old Longhorns had a lot of good qualities."

"They were mostly leg and horn, and the meat was so tough you couldn't cut it with a cleaver."

"Nature bred them to survive in a tough country. They could grub out a livin' where nothin' else but a horned toad could stay, and you couldn't hardly kill one with an ax."

"Looks to me like you're kin to them, a little. All you old cowpunchers are."

"Maybe that's why I hate to see the last Longhorns go. It's like buryin' old friends."

Skip studied the helpless form lying on the ground, straining against the rawhide that bound its feet. "If that's the way you feel about it, we could turn him loose and tell the wagon boss we never did find him."

Hewey suddenly appreciated the kid a little better. "I hate

to tell a lie." He pondered the ramifications, then knelt to untie the knot in the *peal*. "Better hit the saddle. He's liable to be on the prod when he gets up."

The bull realized its feet were no longer secured. It kicked free of the loosened rawhide and rose shakily, hind end first. It pawed dirt, bellowing its anger to the world. Then it turned and trotted off, tossing its head.

Hewey said, "Looks like he's gettin' away." He followed the fugitive but did not let his horse out of a walk, so that the bull quickly outdistanced him. "Biscuit's tired. We'll never overtake that outlaw like this." He turned back to pick up the fallen rawhide. "No need in tellin' a lie, exactly. We'll just say we had him but he got loose. The horses were too give out to catch him again."

Skip grinned.

Hewey said, "You ought to never deceive the man you work for. Except when you need to."

They watched the bull disappear into a thicket three hundred yards away, crackling brush and bellowing its indignation. Other cowboys might eventually catch him, or he might live out his life in these hidden canyons, his wild spirit undiminished. In either case he would be less of a hazard to men and horses because his horns had been blunted.

Hewey said with satisfaction, "There'll be at least one more calf crop carryin' that Longhorn blood."

"It'll take real hands to run them down."

"Wild cattle and wild horses are the makin' of a good cowboy. You don't learn much handlin' gentle milk stock."

"I just wish we could've throwed him into a bunch and seen him challenge some of them other bulls. Ain't nothin' I'd rather watch than two big stout bulls fightin' one another."

"You've got a streak of mean in you."

Hewey and Skip turned away, heading back toward the chuck wagon camp. His scare past and anger drained, Skip reverted to his more typical high spirits. "Gave us some fun for a while, didn't he?"

"Me and you would call it fun. Some people call it work."

"My old daddy throwed a fit when I left home for a ridin' job. Said I'd never amount to a damn, takin' up the saddle instead of the plow. But I wouldn't want to be anything except a cowboy."

Hewey said, "My brother Walter got him a homestead and took up farmin', but them lace-up shoes never fit my feet."

"Only thing is, there's always a boss like Old Man Jenkins or Bige Saunders watchin' what you do."

"They don't own you. You're free to saddle up and go any time you want to. It's easier to take a few orders when you know you've got an out."

"Ever been tempted to do somethin' besides cowboy?"

"Not much. You've got to make choices. You choose one thing, you give up another. You can't have it all."

The cowboy occupation offered many pleasures, though there were days when Hewey wondered if they were worth the bruises, lacerations and general soreness that often supplemented his meager wages. He believed being a cowboy was a privilege reserved to a chosen few. He did not know how the Lord had come to pick him, for his willful nature caused him to stray from the gospel path now and again. But he was not one to question his maker's judgment. He was grateful to be among the chosen.

He looked off to the distant blue mountains and fell quiet, withdrawing into the bitter and the sweet of old memories. There were times when he felt like talking and no one could shut him up. Other times he had nothing to say.

Skip kept his jaw working, making profound observations based on the accumulated wisdom of his eighteen or nineteen years and trying to prod Hewey out of his silence. But Hewey barely heard. In his mind he was at home in

Upton County with Walter and Eve and their two boys. And he was remembering a teacher whose name conjured up images of wildflower fields. They called her Spring.

The chuck wagon and its accompanying "hoodlum" wagon were camped beside an old set of rugged corrals constructed of heavy tree branches stacked between double posts and tied in place with rawhide. The corrals were a remnant of the 1880s, as Hewey knew himself to be when he bothered to give the matter any thought. Approaching camp, he saw horses circling in a run, raising a cloud of dust inside the largest pen.

Several cowboys, a mix of Mexican and Anglo, stood outside the rough fence, watching as Aparicio Rodriguez swung a rawhide reata and dropped its loop around a long-maned neck. The bite of leather made the caught horse pitch and squeal in protest. Aparicio began speaking in a soft Spanish and slowly working his way up the rope. Soon the bronc quieted down, its ears pointed toward the wiry vaquero.

Hewey would acknowledge that Aparicio was the best hand on the ranch, except for himself. He smiled much but talked little except to horses.

Skip said eagerly, "Looks like they brought in that new set of broncs."

Hewey grunted. Cow work in this rough mountain country was challenging enough just on its own account. The challenge was compounded by having to do it while breaking a set of raw ponies that knew nothing except bite, kick and pitch. But that was what the ranch paid him thirty dollars a month for.

Old Man Jenkins was reputed to be worth a million dollars. Hewey was taking it away from him at the rate of a dollar a day. A million days, a million dollars.

Skip said, "It's a wonder the old man don't dock us for the entertainment we get out of ridin' them broncs."

"I saw how much entertainment you were gettin', runnin' around that bush ahead of them horns."

Skip's face became troubled. "You don't have to tell the boys about it, do you? They'll hooraw me for a month."

Cowboys could be merciless to a braggart. They would do whatever it took to bring him down, then laugh at him until he ate crow or quit the outfit.

"Just promise me I won't have to listen to any more chin music about what all you can do."

"You sayin' I'm boastful?"

"If brag was whiskey, you could open a saloon."

Skip took it in fair grace. "I'll try to remember."

He might try, but Hewey knew he would backslide. It was not in Skip's nature to hide his light beneath a bushel.

Hewey recognized Old Man Jenkins sitting on a tarp-covered bedroll near the chuck wagon. Morgan Jenkins was a rancher of the 1880s school, as much a relic now as the Longhorn. More than six feet tall, he had probably weighed two hundred pounds of pure muscle and bone in his prime. Now, well into his seventies, he weighed a bit more, and his shoulders were bent a little. But in moments of stress Hewey had seen him straighten his back and become once again the formidable figure he had been. It was said of him that once he had single-handedly trailed and confronted four horse thieves, shooting one and escorting the other three to jail.

In contrast to his physical size, he was given to economy in his gestures as well as in his expenditures. Where others might holler and wave both arms, Jenkins beckoned with the index finger of an arthritis-knotted hand. Hewey sensed that the come-along was meant for him.

"Think you can unsaddle that bronc by yourself?" he asked Skip.

The youngster already seemed to have forgotten Hewey's cautionary words about boastfulness. "I could do it with one hand tied behind my back."

I ought to have let that bull chase him a little longer,
Hewey thought.

He tied Biscuit to a corral post and spent a minute surveying the new broncs that still milled around nervously,
looking for a booger strong enough to make them break out
of the pen and run. He was fixing to have his work cut out
for him the next couple of weeks, but nobody ever said life
had to be dull. As a matter of fact, he looked forward to pitting his skill as a bronc stomper against the wild rebellion
of the young horses.

He turned and walked toward the wagon so Jenkins
wouldn't have to tire himself out crooking that finger again.
He stopped at Blas Villegas's chuck box and dug a tin cup
out of a drawer, filling it from a coffeepot suspended over a
pit of glowing coals. Blas raked the coals with a pothook.
"Don' burn yourself, Hooey. She's plenty hot."

"Fine. I'd sooner drink dishwater than cold coffee."

Blas had been a vaquero much of his life, but one bronc
too many had left him with a shattered knee and a crooked
leg that would never straighten again. He had turned to that
refuge of many a crippled cowboy, cooking at a wagon.

Jenkins did not get up from his seat on the bedroll or
waste a lot of breath in his greeting. "Hewey."

"Mr. Jenkins." The *mister* was more in deference to age
than to the old man's money. Hewey stood in awe of no one's
bankroll. In fact, he felt sympathy for Jenkins because the
rancher's age and infirmities prevented him from making a
hand on horseback anymore. In Hewey's eyes nothing was
sadder-looking than an old cowboy too stove-up to ride.

Jenkins gestured for Hewey to sit on a nearby bedroll.
Hewey waited for him to initiate the conversation. When the
old man did not, Hewey asked, "You bring them broncs with
you?"

He knew better, for he could see Jenkins's open touring
car parked a respectful distance from the wagon. But the

idle question broke the silence. The driver had the hood up, messing around with something on the engine. Hewey had no idea what; he had never had any truck with automobiles. To him they were the ruination of the country. For a long time he had hoped they were a passing fancy and everyone would get back to the horse as God intended. Now it appeared they would bankrupt the nation first; then maybe the fad would die the death it deserved.

As for that driver in his duster and goggles, he seemed as out of place in a cow camp as a monkey in church. Hewey thought anybody who went around holding his nose that high was in danger of drowning if he ever got caught in a rain. The man seemed to have an exalted opinion of himself because he knew how to drive a car, but he probably couldn't drive a Jersey cow down a sheep-fenced lane. Hewey had to feel a little sorry for him.

Jenkins said, "Them broncs ain't none of your concern. I got a proposition for you."

The rancher had red-rimmed eyes that indicated he liked whiskey more than he should. It probably gave him comfort from his arthritis and other miseries that went with having celebrated so many birthdays. Hewey had heard he could put away a prodigious amount under the right provocation, though he could not remember that Jenkins had ever offered him a drink.

Jenkins had made his start in the freewheeling maverick-catching times after the Civil War, when an ambitious young man with a fast horse and a quick loop could build toward a fortune by burning his own brand on unclaimed cattle. The period had been relatively short, for those who made theirs first declared further mavericking illegal, kicking down the ladder by which they had climbed so Johnny-come-latelies could not follow.

Hewey had arrived too late to take advantage of the opportunity, though accumulation of worldly goods had never been of much concern to him anyway. Property he could not tie to his saddle and carry with him to the next job was a burden, not an asset.

"Hewey, I just bought the Circle W outfit, a hundred sections down yonder under the rimrock."

Hewey was not surprised, for Jenkins was never comfortable knowing he didn't own everything within a day's trip from his headquarters. Since he had acquired that car, the miles he could travel in a day had stretched a right smart.

Jenkins said, "I want you to run it for me."

Now Hewey was surprised. "Me, run an outfit? I've never done nothin' like that."

"It's time you did. Look at you, six years older than God and still workin' for cowboy wages. It's time you taken a grip on yourself and tried to amount to somethin'."

"I ain't that old, and I've always made you a hand."

"True enough, but I can hire more *young* hands than I need. All I have to do is honk that horn in Alpine, and a dozen come runnin' down the street draggin' a saddle and a bedroll. But somebody who's had experience enough to run an outfit . . . that's a horse of a different complexion."

Hewey struggled for words he thought Jenkins might understand. "It's a lot of responsibility. I've never liked bein' responsible for anything or anybody except myself."

"I never could understand a man that didn't want to better his lot in life."

"I'm satisfied with myself the way I am. Ain't much I'd want to change."

"Nature's changin' you whether you like it or not. Them creases in your face keep gettin' deeper, and your gitalong don't get along like it used to."

"I can still move fast enough to get out of the way."

"From all them years of work, have you saved up any money?"

"A hundred dollars, maybe. But I've had ten thousand dollars' worth of fun."

"A hundred dollars! That ain't even enough to bury you in any style."

"I wasn't figurin' on that happenin' for a long time yet."

Jenkins's frown furrowed his face like a prune. "Ain't often I give a man a chance to go from forty dollars a month to seventy-five."

"You're only payin' me thirty."

"Sixty-five, then. All the more reason you ought to consider the opportunity."

Never had Hewey felt comfortable giving orders, so he had given very few in his life. He had always liked best just being one of the boys, doing whatever the job called for with easy competence and without pressure. If the work became tiresome or the boss got under his skin he would draw his time, saddle up and ride away without regrets. For a good hand, there was always another job down the road.

That was what he would do now if Jenkins tried to twist his arm too much. Lately he had been looking off toward the north a lot anyhow. He had already worked two years for the J Bar, longer than he was used to spending in one place. It had been a long time since he had cowboyed in the Guadalupes, and he had studied on going back. It was a smiling country, like Upton County, where Walter and Eve and the boys had their homestead. For that matter, just about everywhere Hewey had worked had been a smiling country.

Jenkins knew cowboys, for he was still one at heart. He knew when to stop pushing. "I won't try to make you do somethin' that's against your religion. I'll just have to find me somebody that's got ambition. I'd do better with a family man anyway." His eyes narrowed. "You ain't never found a woman that gave you a marryin' urge?"

Hewey stared into his half-empty cup. "I did once."

"What happened?"

Remembered pain softened Hewey's voice. "We both smartened up before it was too late, and I left."

Jenkins thought about it. "You ever wonder if you did the right thing?"

"Doesn't everybody?"

Jenkins shifted his gaze to the touring car and its driver, who was clamping the hood shut. "Looks like he's finished monkeyin' around with that engine. Wish sometimes I still used a horse and buggy. Didn't need to hire no fifty-dollar driver for that."

Fifty dollars! Hewey was just drawing thirty, and he was a top hand. But he wouldn't trade places, not for a hundred.

He said, "I wouldn't swap one bronc in that pen yonder for a dozen of them stink wagons."

Jenkins frowned. "Them broncs are for the young hands to break. I don't want you ridin' any of them."

Hewey almost spilled the coffee that remained in his cup. "I've already broke twenty-five or thirty broncs for you, and I ain't ruined one yet."

"I ain't worried about you ruinin' them, I'm afraid one of them is liable to ruin *you*. I know your age, Hewey, even if you don't. I don't want you on my conscience." Jenkins dropped his coffee cup in Blas's washtub and walked toward his car. He hollered at the driver, "You got that contraption fixed?"

The driver wiped his greasy hands on a cloth. "She'll run like a young filly on a spring day, Mr. Jenkins."

Hewey snorted. He would bet that driver wouldn't know a young filly from an old stud. And he was being paid fifty dollars a month!

The car started with a backfire that set all the broncs to circling again in the corral. Jenkins shouted back, "You stay off of them green ponies, Hewey."

Hewey did not respond, for he did not want to make a promise he would not keep. He watched the automobile kick up a trail of dust across the pasture until he was satisfied that Jenkins would not think of something he had forgotten and come back.

What the old man did not know would not hurt him.

Hewey walked to Biscuit and untied the rope from his saddle. He said, "Skip, let's take a close look at them broncs."

2

Blas Villegas took the chuck wagon ahead to the railroad pens while Hewey and the other hands followed with the herd. Hewey rode point, ahead of the dominant steers that had taken it upon themselves to move into the lead. Afar, Hewey could see the smoking locomotive, and he wondered how Biscuit was going to take to it. Biscuit was a ranch horse, not used to the commotion that went with being in a big town like Alpine.

Hewey had been riding a couple of the new broncs, but he thought it advisable to use Biscuit for the last stage of the drive because Old Man Jenkins would almost certainly be waiting at the pens. He would remember, even if Hewey had chosen to forget, his admonition that the broncs be left to the younger hands. Hewey did not want to risk raising the rancher's blood pressure; that could be dangerous for a man of his age.

He noticed a truck bumping its dusty way toward the herd, following the ruts of a rough wagon road that led from town. To him, a truck in cow country still looked badly out of place.

The driver honked his horn and spooked Biscuit. Skip Harkness's bronc began to pitch. One stirrup flopped free, and the surprised kid saved himself only by grabbing the saddle horn. Hewey thought the truck driver was probably Old Man Jenkins's high-toned car jockey, badly in need of a stern lesson in cow-camp etiquette. As the truck pulled to a stop, Hewey reined toward it, rehearsing the lecture in his mind until he saw that the man behind the steering wheel was a stranger.

A passenger stepped out on the right-hand side. Hewey blinked in surprise, for he recognized the tall, thin figure of his brother, wearing denim overalls, a farmer's brogan shoes and a floppy felt hat that offered only limited protection to a face used hard by the elements.

"Walter," Hewey shouted. Biscuit sidestepped, wary of the clanking motor until the driver cut it off. When the noise stopped, the horse moved closer but remained like a coiled spring, ready to jump away at the least provocation. Walter turned to offer a big, rough hand to the woman who had been sitting in the middle. She stepped to the ground and dusted herself the best she could. She wore a slat bonnet that almost covered her face, but Hewey knew she was his sister-in-law.

He had been about to dismount, but he decided to remain in the saddle until he determined which direction the wind blew. With Eve Calloway, he never could be sure whether it would be a warm, pleasant one from the south or a cold one from the north. She could change quicker than West Texas weather. Their last parting had been amicable, but he remembered others that were frosty as a February morning.

Walter walked slowly toward Hewey, careful lest he cause the nervous Biscuit further fright. "Big brother," he said, "when're you goin' to give up tryin' to be twenty years old? You need to quit ridin' these skittish broncs."

"When I'm a hundred and six."

"You'll never get that old. Some fool horse'll kill you first."

"Many a good one has tried. But anyway, it's been years since Biscuit was a bronc." Hewey gripped his brother's calloused hand, which felt like dry rawhide. He tipped his hat to Eve. She said only, "Hewey."

At least she did not seem angry. Hewey decided to step

down from the saddle. He ventured, "You're lookin' good, Eve."

She wasn't, really. She had always tended to be on the skinny side, but her long, plain gray cotton dress hung loose as if she hadn't been eating lately. She was moving along toward forty and showed every year of it. The lines in her face indicated deep worry as she stepped close to give Hewey a perfunctory peck on the cheek. He held his hands up awkwardly, never knowing for sure if he should hug her or not. He decided against it.

"Hewey," she asked quickly, "where's Tommy?"

He blinked in confusion. "Tommy? Where's he supposed to be?"

"At home, but he's not. We figured he'd be here with you."

Hewey looked in surprise at Eve, then Walter, then Eve again. "I ain't seen him. Or heard from him either." He had not seen his two nephews since the last time he had been to Upton County. That had been three . . . no, four years ago, or pretty near. It was hard to keep track of time, busy as he had been.

Anxiety pinched Walter's eyes. "He left home. Took a little dun horse Alvin Lawdermilk gave him, and he rode off without sayin' anything. We thought it was likely he came up this way lookin' for you."

"If he did, he hasn't found me." Hewey began to share their concern. "I understood why Cotton wanted to leave home when he came of age. He had his sights set on other things besides the hoe and the plow. But Tommy was a farm boy at heart. I thought he'd be content to stay there all of his life."

Walter shoved his hands into his pockets and stared at the ground. "We thought so too, but lately he's taken an itch to see other places, do other things. Eve says he's a lot like you."

Hewey gave his sister-in-law a sideward glance, knowing she would not have meant it to be complimentary. When anything threatened the stability of home and family, Eve found it easy to blame Hewey's wayward influence. Much of the blame was justified.

He detected a hint of that blame as Eve said, "I don't reckon you intentionally enticed him, but Tommy's always looked up to you. I just hoped he wouldn't pick up your roamin' ways."

Hewey replied, "You've made it plain many a time that you'd be a sight happier if I gave up ridin' and taken to the plow."

"We'd all be glad if you did, but we decided a long time ago to quit tryin' to change you. You'll be Hewey Calloway as long as you live."

"I've tried bein' somebody else, and it never worked." He had taken Walter's place one summer when Walter's leg was broken. For a while he had forced himself to become a farmer and bring in Walter's crops, but he had hated every day of it.

He saw disappointment in Eve's blue eyes before she turned and touched a handkerchief to them. He wished Tommy *had* shown up here so Walter and Eve could take him home and stop worrying. Now Hewey had something to worry about, too.

He wanted to change the subject. "How about the farm? You-all makin' it all right?"

Walter said, "We stay ahead of Old C. C. Tarpley and his bank, if that's what you mean. Fact is, CC.'s softened up considerable. His health has been failin'."

Eve said, "He may be startin' to worry about whether they'll let him into heaven or not."

"I'd say he's got a right smart to worry about." Hewey looked toward the steers. The herd had moved past him while he was talking to Walter and Eve. "Chuck wagon's camped on the far side of the shippin' pens. We'll be havin' dinner after we've penned the cattle."

Walter said, "Can't stay. One of Blue Hannigan's truck

drivers had a load of freight to deliver to Alpine, and we caught a ride with him. He's got to be back in Upton City tonight."

Hewey was surprised again. "That's Blue Hannigan's truck? He's always done his freightin' with mules and wagons."

"He's bought two trucks since you saw him last. Says a man has got to keep up with the times or they'll roll over him and leave him layin' in the road."

"They've rolled over me, all right. Just about flattened me out. But I can't feature Blue Hannigan drivin' a truck. I always figured he was half mule."

He had never had a better friend in the world than Blue Hannigan unless it was Snort Yarnell and the late Grady Welch. They were kindred spirits, cowboys to the core, even though Blue had eventually married and turned to freighting to make a better living. Grady had died beneath the hooves of a two-bit bronc.

He said, "If Tommy shows up, I'll send him home."

The lines deepened in Walter's face as he put his arm around his wife's shoulder. He seemed to read something in her sad eyes that Hewey could not see. "No, let him stay if he's set on it. Maybe he'll work it out of his system. But let us know, and watch out for him, won't you? Don't let him get himself hurt or into any trouble."

"I'll do what I can." Hewey tried to hide his reluctance. He had turned down Old Man Jenkins's offer of a good-paying job because it would give him responsibility he did not want. Now, like it or not, he would be considered responsible for his nephew.

Walter gripped his hand. "Obliged, Hewey. Come see us when you can."

Eve gave Hewey a silent hug. The tears in her eyes told him why she did not trust herself to try to speak. She turned away, letting Walter give her a boost up into the truck.

Hewey called, "Walter, just a minute." He had to work up nerve to ask the question. "How's Miss Spring Renfro?"

"She's still teachin' school over at the Lawdermilks'."

"Has she . . . has she gotten herself married yet?"

"She's been waitin' for the right man to come along, I guess. We all thought you were him, once."

"So did I, once." Hewey looked away, clearing his throat. "Tell Cotton hello for me, next time he's home."

"And if we see Spring Renfro?"

Hewey could only shake his head. He did not know what to tell her.

The locomotive backed the empty cattle cars along the spur track to the shipping pens as Hewey and the rest of the crew brought up the J Bar steer herd. Old Man Jenkins's touring car was parked to one side, out of the path of the cattle. The driver leaned against the automobile, goggles pulled up over the broad-billed cap he wore. Jenkins was opening the gate to the largest pen. He could have delegated that job to his driver, but Hewey guessed the old man wanted to see it done right, as if there were any *wrong* way to open a gate.

Hewey rode up a little ahead of the herd and stationed himself just past the opening so the steers would not pass it by. He hazed the leaders in, then backed away so those that followed would not shy aside. Most of these cattle did not often see men on horseback, and those few occasions were usually associated with unpleasantness of one kind or another.

The pens were dry and dusty, for the hooves of earlier herds had already stirred the bare ground after a long winter of relative inactivity. Skip Harkness rode up on the bronc that had come near throwing him off when the truck's horn sounded.

Hewey said, "Caught you asleep, didn't he? You've got to learn to stay awake every minute when you're sittin' on a bronc."

Defensively Skip declared, "He never even come close."

Hewey wondered why he felt duty-bound to nursemaid every green farm kid who wandered onto the J Bar. They should be the foreman's responsibility, not his, but somehow most of them seemed to gravitate toward Hewey. The gringo kids anyway. The young Mexicans drew toward Aparacio Rodriguez, who, at thirty, give or take a little, was sort of a big-brother figure to them.

Watching Skip, wishing the boy were a little smarter and a lot less sure of his invincibility, Hewey thought of his nephew Tommy. *Where the hell has that kid got off to? He could be anyplace from here to El Paso.*

A trainman signaled the engineer to back the wooden cattle cars slowly until the one nearest the coal car was evenly aligned with the slanted loading chute. The foreman, Bige Saunders, rode to where Old Man Jenkins waited on an elevated walkway beside the chute. There they could look down upon the steers and count them as they ascended into the cars.

Hewey tied Biscuit to an outside fence and beckoned with a jerk of his head for Skip to follow him. The boy dismounted carefully, for the hissing of the steam locomotive made his bronc step sideways, its ears nervously pointed forward and its eyes rolling.

Climbing over fences to reach the loading chute, Hewey and Skip pried the car door open and slid a platform forward to bridge between the end of the chute and the sand-covered floor of the car. Hewey jumped on it to be sure it was set solidly. A collapse under the weight of the steers would be a small calamity. He motioned for Skip to help him swing the side gates forward and complete a closed corridor that would prevent cattle from jumping to freedom between the chute and the car.

Jenkins shouted for the cowboys to bring the steers on. Hewey picked up a long pole propped against the fence and took a place on the elevated walkway where he could lean over and prod any animals reluctant to pass through the door into the darkness of the car. *This is why they call us cowpunchers,* he thought.

Jenkins and Saunders both counted the cattle as they ascended, Jenkins calling a halt when the proper number had passed to fill the car without overcrowding it. Hewey turned back the extra animals and put his shoulder against the car door, sliding it into place and closing the latch.

The trainmen had not helped with the loading. Hewey could not blame them for standing back, for the railroad did not count that among their duties. But he wished he could see Jenkins's car driver lending a hand. For a man paid fifty dollars a month, he didn't seem to be doing much. Remaining well out of the dust, he stood by the automobile as if afraid it might decide to run off like a horse left untied.

Following signals made by one of the trainmen, the engineer moved the train forward to spot the next empty car into place, aligning the door with the chute.

Skip asked, "Is the grass really greener where these steers are goin'?"

"They'll think they've died and gone to heaven. Them Kansas Flint Hills look like a wheat field when it rains."

"You've seen that country?"

"Spent a season up there once, takin' care of summer cattle for a feller who lived down at Uvalde."

"Is there anyplace you *ain't* been?"

"Never been to California yet, or Nevada or Utah, but me and Biscuit'll visit all of them before we're done."

"Think the two of you have still got time enough?"

"Time don't mean much to Biscuit. He wouldn't know a calendar from the United States Constitution."

As the loading progressed, Hewey counted the empty cars and realized there were a couple more than were needed to carry all the Jenkins steers. The trainmen called a halt, claiming some sort of difficulty with the locomotive that had to be fixed before work could continue. Sitting on the fence, rolling a cigarette, Hewey noticed a string of horses pushed by four cowboys approaching the loading pens. He recognized one of the riders and walked down to open the gate to a pen that had been emptied of cattle.

"Howdy, Hewey," a lean and lanky puncher shouted jovially as the horses rushed past him into the corral. The sun caught a glint of gold where a front tooth should have been.

"Snort Yarnell!" Hewey shouted back. "Somebody told me you was dead. Guess you just smelled like it."

Snort reined up and looked at the Jenkins outfit's horses, tied along the outside fence. His gold tooth gleamed in a broad grin. "When did you J Bar punchers start ridin' burros?"

"About the same time you Slash R waddies commenced ridin' camels." Hewey shut the gate as the last of the loose horses passed through. "Or are those goats you just brought in?"

Snort dismounted and thrust his big hand forward. Hewey took it. Each man tried to squeeze hard enough to make the other holler, but it came out a draw. Hewey slapped Snort on the shoulder, raising a puff of dust from the cowboy's blue work shirt. "I didn't think you could get any uglier, but damned if you ain't managed."

"Ain't much a man can't do if he makes up his mind to it."

Snort was accompanied by three eager young cowhands, none of whom looked to be out of their teens. His loud talk and boisterous manner attracted a youthful following wherever he went. Most of the kids would eventually outgrow him and pull away as maturity overtook their playful spirits and they realized Snort would remain an adolescent forever except in years.

He knew how to have a good time, though. Hewey could hardly remember when he had not known Snort and welcomed his company, for a little while at a time.

Snort peered through the fence at the remnant of steers

in the next pen. "I'm surprised you're still workin' for Old Man Jenkins. He's tighter than the bark on a tree."

"Old Blas cooks good, that's the main thing. If I had more money, I'd just spend it. What you doin' with the horses?"

"Fixin' to load them on that train and ship them to Fort Worth for the horse and mule auction."

"Scrubby-lookin' bunch. Looks to me like they got burro blood in them."

"You think so? I wisht you'd look at that black yonder, the one with the white stockin' foot. Throwed every cowboy on the Slash R payroll. Even me, and I'm the best bronc rider this country ever seen."

Hewey was not impressed. The black horse stood hipshot, its head down as if asleep. "He's got feet the size of a number two washtub. The Slash R must have a bunch of sheepherders workin' out there."

Hewey should have been warned by the calculating gleam that came into Snort's eyes. Snort licked a tongue across that gold tooth and spat a brown stream of tobacco. "I guess you think some J Bar hand can ride him."

"I'll bet any hand on the place can ride him except maybe Old Blas. He could too if he wasn't crippled up."

"You got some money to go where your mouth is at?"

"I will have when we get the cattle loaded. Mr. Jenkins is due to pay us."

"I'll take credit. Bet you thirty dollars, but I'll pick the J Bar hand to do the ridin'."

By this time the two men were surrounded by cowboys, including the three who had come with Snort and most of the J Bar hands. Skip Harkness declared, "Let me ride him, Hewey. I'll turn his hide inside out."

Hewey shook his head. Skip was not half as good as he thought he was. "That'll be up to Snort. It's his choice who makes the ride."

Snort's youthful companions offered side bets, and some of the J Bar cowboys took them up, betting five, ten, fifteen dollars apiece. Old man Jenkins and Bige Saunders noticed the commotion and came down to see what was causing it. Jenkins frowned at the hands' eagerness to bet. "I never did approve of gamblin' unless it's on cattle." He took a long look at the black horse in question. "But it don't appear to me like there's any gamblin' to this. If these Slash R boys want to contribute to you-all's fortunes, I don't see any harm in it."

He did not put up any of his own money, nor did Saunders. Hewey figured they were too old to have any sporting blood left. He said, "All right, Snort. Pick your man."

Snort let his gaze drift over the J Bar hands, quickly dismissing Aparicio Rodriguez because the good-natured vaquero had a reputation all over the Davis Mountains country as being *puro jiñete*, a bronc rider of exceptional ability. He lingered a little longer on Skip than the others, and Hewey feared he was about to choose the kid.

Snort took his time, coming back finally to Hewey. Hewey smiled, knowing he was by all odds the best rider in the outfit, by his own estimation better even than Aparicio. He could ride that black and darn his socks at the same time. But Snort turned and walked to the fence. He pointed at Jenkins's driver, who stood on the outside looking in, his goggles turned up over the top of his cap. "I pick *him*," he said.

Hewey sputtered. "But he's not a hand. He just jockeys that automobile."

"He works for Jenkins, don't he? He's on the J Bar payroll, ain't he?"

Hewey looked to Jenkins for support, but the old rancher offered him no help. Hewey protested, "That don't count. He ain't paid to ride."

"You're the one agreed to the deal. Either he rides or you forfeit the bet." The gold tooth gleamed. Hewey thought Snort looked like a fox eating watermelon.

Hewey, for his part, felt like a coyote with both forefeet

in a trap, being rinkydooed by a sly old sport like Snort Yarnell. It wasn't that he would mind seeing the driver get thrown halfway to the moon, but Jenkins might fire the whole outfit if he was left without the services of his chauffeur. The old man probably couldn't even crank the motor, much less handle the wheel.

Disgusted with himself, Hewey said, "Looks to me like we've got no choice but to forfeit."

The driver took off his duster and laid it across the fence. "You ain't lost yet."

Hewey gaped. "You would try to ride that bronc?"

"Why not?"

"You couldn't ride a kid's stick horse. You'd be about as much use as teats on a boar hog."

"What've you got to lose?"

"Mr. Jenkins stands to lose a driver."

"Then maybe you'd have to learn to operate an automobile yourself." He climbed into the corral and began unlacing his high-topped boots. "Your feet look to be about the same size as mine. Lend me your boots and spurs."

"What for? You won't make it past the first jump." But Hewey could see that the man was serious. He sat in the sand and removed his boots, leaving the spurs on them. He pulled off his socks to keep from getting them full of dirt. Not for a hundred dollars would he put on the dude's lace-up boots. He would look almost as ridiculous as the driver did with that combination of jodhpur britches and cowboy boots.

The chauffeur had to pull hard to get his feet into Hewey's boots, and his pained expression indicated that they pinched his toes. "All right, who's goin' to catch that horse?"

Hewey looked at Jenkins, hoping the old man would put a stop to this, but the rancher only muttered something about fools and their money and stomped off to see if the trainmen were making any progress fixing their locomotive.

Bige Saunders warned, "If you-all get Mr. Jenkins's

driver killed, the old man won't be fit to live with." He
trailed after Jenkins.

Doesn't want to watch the massacre, Hewey thought
glumly. He had rather be somewhere else himself.

Snort's companions seemed only too happy to catch up
the black horse. The animal appeared unperturbed. It stood
calmly while the hackamore was slipped over its head
and the saddle girted down tightly. Snort turned to the
driver, his voice condescending. "Ready any time you are,
Marmaduke."

"The name's not Marmaduke. Friends call me Peeler."

"Peeler?"

"Like in *bronc peeler.*" The driver handed his cap and
goggles to Skip Harkness. "Try not to let these get dirty."

One of Snort's friends held the black's ears, though the
horse looked as if it might be asleep. Peeler gripped the
hackamore rein, a handful of mane and the saddle horn
as he swung up. It occurred to Hewey that Peeler was doing
this properly. He had probably watched somebody sometime.

The cowboy released the ears and stepped back out of
the way. For a moment the horse seemed not to notice.
Then with a loud bawl and a breaking of wind, it made a
violent leap forward and came down solidly on all four
feet. Hewey imagined he could feel the ground tremble
under the impact. It should have been enough to bust the
rider's teeth, but Peeler was still in the saddle as the horse
made its second jump.

Hewey stared in amazement. The rider seemed to anticipate the bronc's moves and meet them halfway. Very little
daylight appeared between him and the saddle, and never
for long. Pitching, twisting, spinning half around, the horse
failed to shake him. Its long jumps dwindled into crow hops
as it tired, and finally it ran in slowing circles around the
corral. Peeler drew on the hackamore rein and brought the
bronc to a stop, stepping off to the ground.

He handed the rein to Snort Yarnell. "Thought you said this pony could buck."

Snort made a resigned smile. "Thought they said you was just an auto jockey."

"I am, but I wasn't always." Peeler sat in the sand and began struggling with Hewey's boots.

Snort turned to Hewey. "Looks like you-all ran a ringer in on us."

"Like you done with that sleepy-lookin' black? Anyway, you chose him. I tried to get you to pick somebody else."

Snort laughed. "That's when I ought to've known you had somethin' up your sleeve. You're a licensed and certified liar, Hewey Calloway, the only one I know that can hold a candle to me. So we'll pay up like men and try to get you the next time."

The locomotive's whistle blew. Old Man Jenkins waved his hat over his head, meaning they had all better get back to work if they wanted to have a job tomorrow.

Hewey put on his socks, then his boots. He shook hands with Peeler. "I've never been mistaken but two or three times in my life. Reckon this was one of them. You're entitled to share my winnin's."

"Forget it. This helped remind me why I learned to drive an automobile."

Hewey sat at a table in a corner of the saloon, staring down at a blank sheet of paper. The J Bar cowboys and the Slash R hands were spread out along the bar, Anglo and Mexican all mixed together. Racial lines were easily blurred by a little whiskey. Snort Yarnell motioned. "Come on, Hewey, you're fallin' behind."

"I'll catch up. Got to write this letter first."

He was momentarily distracted by an elderly swamper, dragging a stiff leg as he swept up glass from a bottle that had rolled off a table and broken on the floor. He was another old cowboy too broken up to ride anymore and reduced to a demeaning job to earn his grub and sleep in the dry. *Hell of a way for a good man to end up,* Hewey thought.

He touched the sharp end of the stub pencil to his tongue and began a slow and halting effort.

> Alpine, Texas
> May 21 1910
>
> *Dear Walter & Eve—*
> *I take pencil in hand to tell you I have not seen Tommy.*
> *I have just come into a little extra mony and am sendin*
> *it to you to put against your dett on the farm, like I have*
> *done before. Dont worry, I dont need it. If Tommy*
> *shows up I will let you no.*
>
> > *Yours very truly,*
> > *Hewey Calloway*
>
> *P. S.—If you see Miss Spring Renfro*

He could not think how to end the last sentence and tried to erase it, but it would not all come off the paper. He addressed an envelope to Walter and Eve Calloway, Upton City, Texas, and tucked the letter into it with fifty dollars in paper money. He licked the envelope, sealed it and handed it to the bald-headed bartender along with a quarter. "I don't have a penny stamp, but I'd be obliged if you'd put one on this and see that it gets to the post office. Keep the change."

"You're a generous man, Hewey Calloway. It'll be the starvin' of you someday. You ready for another drink?"

"Ready and rarin'."

He had had several already, but not enough to make him overlook the risk of falling over the edge, splurging the wages Old Man Jenkins had paid him and the bet he had won from Snort, most of which he was sending to Walter and Eve.

Jenkins had been in the saloon earlier and had enjoyed a drink at cowboy expense. After he left, Snort had demanded, "Don't he ever buy any himself?"

Hewey replied, "How do you think he got rich?"

Now Snort had his arm around Peeler's shoulder. "Where in the hell did a car jockey ever learn that kind of ridin'?"

Almost everybody in the room had bought Peeler a drink. His cap and goggles lay on the floor where he had dropped them without realizing it. Hewey picked them up and placed them on the bar so nobody would step on them. Peeler said thickly, "I was raised in Callahan County, helpin' my old daddy break horses and mules. Rode awhile with Booger Red Privett's bronc show 'til I got tired of them outlaws bustin' my back. Figured herdin' an automobile ought to be easier than stompin' broncs."

"Pays better, too," Hewey put in. He had never been apt at figures, but he knew the difference between thirty dollars a month and fifty.

An out-of-tune piano stood in a back corner. A kid from the Slash R was playing it in a heavy-handed and discordant way. Nobody seemed disposed to criticize his musicianship.

Hewey did not know where the girls came from, but three appeared, dancing with the cowboys. One of them took Hewey in her arms and did a reel with him, though the kid at the piano was playing a waltz. Hewey's head was spinning by the time they finished. He collapsed into a chair, leaned back too far and fell heavily. He struggled to free himself from the overturned chair but hung a spur in one of its braces. He floundered like a turtle on its back.

He saw someone hovering over him and heard a youthful voice. "Need a little help, Uncle Hewey?"

Hewey blinked, trying to bring the face into focus as it swayed back and forth like a pendulum. It was somehow familiar, yet he could not see clearly enough to identify the features.

"It's me, Uncle Hewey. Tommy."

"Tommy?" The voice was his nephew's, though it sounded deeper and more mature than he remembered. Hewey said, "Don't you know a saloon ain't no place for a self-respectin' Calloway?"

He did not expect the strength his nephew showed as Tommy took his hand and helped him to his feet. Hewey kicked his spur loose from the chair, which fell back with a clatter, almost tripping Skip Harkness and the young woman he was dancing with. They did not seem to notice.

Hewey leaned against the table for balance and scolded, "Your mama'd be awful disappointed to find a boy like you in a place like this."

Tommy said, "She'd be disappointed in both of us. And I ain't a boy anymore. You just ain't seen me in a long time."

Tommy still seemed to sway from side to side. "Hold still," Hewey told him, "so I can get a good look at you."

Tommy righted the chair and held it steady. Hewey seated himself, careful not to knock the chair over again. Funny, he thought, how much a kid could change when you weren't watching. Tommy appeared broader in the shoulders and a foot taller than Hewey remembered. He looked much like his older brother, Cotton. Hewey could see a lot of his father in Tommy's features and some of his mother in the eyes. "You're not a man yet, though, not quite. Why ain't you at home, in school?"

"I finished all the schoolin' there was two years ago. I decided to come lookin' for you."

"How'd you find me?"

"Just asked around. Anywhere you've been, they remember Hewey Calloway."

Hewey tried to sound severe. "You ought to be helpin' your daddy right now. Plantin' time, ain't it?"

"Me and Daddy ain't gee-hawed too good lately. I want to learn to be a cowboy like you."

"You're too late. They ain't makin' no more cowboys like me, hardly. The times have gone off and left us."

"You always said I was a natural hand. I've been breakin' horses and mules for Alvin Lawdermilk the last couple of years when Daddy could spare me."

"Then why don't you stay home and work for Alvin?"

"I've learned all there is to learn around Upton City. I want to see different country, different people."

"People are pretty much the same wherever you find them, most of them good, a few not worth hangin' with an old rope."

"I thought maybe you could get me a job where you're workin'."

"Old Man Jenkins runs a pretty tough outfit."

"I can make him a hand if he's got any openin's."

Hewey knew that a couple of the J Bar cowboys had ridden the caboose when the train pulled out, committed to seeing after the steers when they reached the Flint Hills. They would not be back until fall, and maybe not then if they stumbled onto some good-looking Kansas girls bent on getting married. Hewey had known it to happen.

He said, "We'll talk about it in the mornin'. Maybe you'll see things a little plainer in the light of day."

Tommy smiled. "I'll bet *you* will."

The bartender came over, eyeing Tommy with suspicion. "Hewey, this boy don't look like he's shavin' regular yet. They got a town ordinance . . ." He had been nervous all evening because many of the hands from both ranches looked under age.

"We was fixin' to leave." Hewey pointed his chin toward Snort Yarnell. "You-all let too much riffraff in here anyhow."

Snort took that as a compliment and saluted Hewey with a whiskey toast.

> *"Here's to the boys that labor and sweat,*
>   *And thirty a month is all they get."*

The Jenkins driver had a death grip on the edge of the bar, his eyes wide and glassy. Hewey hoped the old man didn't need to go anywhere tomorrow.

Hewey beckoned to Tommy and walked outside, where a dun horse was tied to a post. A couple of rolled blankets were tied behind the cantle, and a war bag of miscellaneous belongings hung from the saddle horn on the left side, opposite a coiled rope. Tommy asked, "Where we goin'?"

"Biscuit's in the wagon yard. Chuck wagon's camped at the shippin' pens. You had any supper?" It was an idle question, for Blas would have crawled into his blankets hours ago, and his cookfire would be down to a few lingering coals at best.

"Ain't hungry. I shared supper with a sheepherder out east of town."

"Mutton, I'll bet." Hewey could eat almost anything if he had to, but he could stay happy for months on end without eating any mutton.

"It ain't bad atall. Daddy's bought him a little bunch of sheep. Looks like they're goin' to be moneymakers."

"Don't you let them J Bar cowboys hear you say that. Or worse, Snort and that bunch from the Slash R. It'd be a chaps offense." That was a form of punishment in which a cowboy had to bend over and let somebody lash his backside with a pair of leather chaps. It was performed more in the spirit of fun than in seriousness, but it did nothing to enhance dignity.

Tommy led his dun horse to the wagon yard and waited while Hewey retrieved Biscuit. He had a little trouble getting the saddle on the brown and afterward stirred a couple of dogs into a barking fit. Hewey wondered why he always seemed to have that effect on dogs. He had never harmed one in his life, but they never quite trusted him. Horses, on the other hand, usually came around to his way of thinking after he had ridden them awhile.

He saw the flickering light from a lantern Blas had set atop the chuck box to guide the cowboys back to camp when their night of celebration was over. He said, "Stake your horse out here and be right quiet. Last thing you want to do is wake up the cook. He'd burn the breakfast biscuits sure as hell."

Hewey found his own bed. Knowing he was likely to be somewhat impaired on his return, he had had the foresight to roll it out before he left camp for the night's entertainment.

Tommy spread his blankets. Hewey noted that he had no tarp to repel rain. It did not rain often in these mountains, but on those rare occasions the downpours could be heavy. If Tommy stayed, Hewey would have to see about getting him a tarp to cover his bedroll.

Tommy was likely to come up short in other ways too. Breaking horses and mules for Alvin Lawdermilk at home was a far cry from working on a big outfit like the J Bar in the Davis Mountains. Without even trying, he could think of twenty easy ways a green kid could get himself skinned and bloodied. Hewey would have to watch over him like a mother hen. Best thing was to try to talk him into going home. That would take the responsibility from Hewey's shoulders, and he avoided responsibility like he avoided measles and chicken pox.

He drifted off to sleep rehearsing the speech he would lay on Tommy to hasten his return to the farm.

Next morning he could not remember a word of it.

3

Hewey was not ready to quit his blankets when Blas clanged his pothook against an iron rod and hollered the hands up for breakfast. He had been half asleep, half awake, his nose assaulted by sharp smoke from the cook's fire and his ears by Blas's reckless banging of lids against the pots and Dutch ovens. Hewey did not know why his head hurt so badly and his stomach was so sour. He remembered eating a couple of boiled eggs from a bowl on top of the bar last night. One of them must have been bad.

He had not bothered to remove his clothes before going to bed. He put on his hat, then his boots with their pair of sporty gal-leg spurs that had a shank shaped like a woman's leg, complete with garter and high-heeled shoe. Loud talk told him Snort Yarnell and the other Slash R cowboys were coming into camp. As a neighborly gesture Bige Saunders had invited them to share breakfast because they had brought no chuck wagon to town.

Hewey hurried to his feet, not wanting Snort to catch him in his blankets this late in the morning. The sun was almost ready to come up. Snort was always looking for something to hooraw a man about. The better he liked someone, the louder the hoorawing.

Snort shouted, "Hey, Hewey, you up?"

"Been up for an hour. Already had my coffee."

Snort seemed in much too good a humor for the night to have been so short. He could drain a barrel of whiskey and still wake up at daylight, ready to go. Hewey wondered sometimes if Snort was all human.

Snort recognized Tommy and made a big fuss over him. "I heard you say you're lookin' for a cowpunchin' job. If old Bige don't hire you, come over to the Slash R. I'll take you under my wing and show you things you never heard of."

Hewey said dryly, "His mama'd be tickled to hear that." He felt a bit guilty, realizing that as an old family friend Snort had visited the Calloway homestead periodically and had seen Tommy since Hewey had.

Cold sober now, Hewey felt the weight of responsibility even heavier than last night as he introduced Tommy to Bige Saunders. Because Bige was foreman, it was his place to hire and fire, though Old Man Jenkins was likely to whisper in his ear on occasion. Bige was a man of fifty years and a solid hundred and seventy-five pounds, his shoulders broader than Hewey's, broad enough to carry the weight of a boss's responsibilities.

"So you're Hewey's nephew," he said, contemplating Tommy in the first light of dawn. "Can't say you favor him, though I'd mark that as an asset. Had any experience workin' stock?"

Tommy explained that the Calloways raised cattle in a modest way as well as crops. He did not mention the sheep.

Hewey hoped Bige would decide Tommy was too young and inexperienced. There was a lot of difference between growing up on a stock farm and being an honest-to-God cowboy. He put in, "Up against a big outfit like the J Bar, that little old place of my brother's ain't big enough to make a decent horse trap."

Hopefully Tommy described his experience in breaking horses and mules for Alvin Lawdermilk.

Bige said, "I knew Alvin way back yonder. He still favor the whiskey like he used to?"

"Not anymore. He's taken the pledge."

That didn't sound like Alvin, Hewey thought. He had probably just said so to satisfy the preacher, Brother Averill.

Bige favored a little toddy himself once in a while, but Hewey had never seen him take one when there was a job to see after. Old Man Jenkins could not have found a more responsible foreman and wagon boss if he had hunted all over hell and half of Texas. Hewey thought it ought to be clear to Bige that Tommy was not ready for a job like this, but the favorable gleam in Bige's eyes indicated that Hewey was going to be saddled with the worry of looking after Tommy whether he liked it or not.

Bige said, "Goin' wage around here for a green hand is twenty-five a month, chuck and all the ground you need to roll out your beddin'."

Tommy had never earned twenty-five dollars a month.

Alvin Lawdermilk would likely have paid him thirty or thirty-five had he been able to work full-time, but Tommy's responsibilities on the family stock farm had prevented that. His father probably needed him at home a lot more than Bige or Old Man Jenkins needed him here. Still, Hewey could understand the boy's need for independence. He had been a lot younger than Tommy when he had set out on his own.

Bige shook Tommy's hand. "Well, son, with your uncle Hewey's help I expect you'll be makin' us a top hand in no time. Two men went to Kansas with the cattle, so I'll pick you a string of horses out of theirs."

Tommy pumped Bige's hand and grinned with delight.

Hewey's stomach went a little more sour. Damn those boiled eggs!

Before they left town, Hewey insisted that Tommy write his parents a letter and let them know where he was. He watched Tommy to be sure the job was done and the letter posted.

Hewey said, "Any time you get to feelin' homesick, just let me know."

Tommy did not take the hint. He inhaled a long breath of fresh mountain air, his blue eyes shining with pleasure. "I think I'm really goin' to like it here."

Hewey could see that he would have the boy on his hands for a while if Walter and Eve didn't come and take him home.

Snort and the Slash R cowboys drifted away, back to the ranch they worked for. Hewey had half expected Snort to draw his time and set off for someplace new. He had already stayed at the Slash R longer than anywhere Hewey could remember. Perhaps Snort was getting old and looking for a place to light. For that matter, Hewey's tenure at the J Bar had stretched well beyond his usual limit. But in his case he was not getting old; he was just getting easier to suit.

Tommy watched Blas lift up and latch the chuck box lid, preparing the wagon to move. The boy asked eagerly, "Where do you reckon we're goin'?"

"Back to the ranch. We've got calves to brand and a new bunch of broncs to break."

"Broncs? That sounds like fun."

Hewey glanced toward Skip Harkness. That was what Skip would say, too. *I'll have to watch this boy pretty close,* he thought.

Hewey was still riding Biscuit so Mr. Jenkins would not worry about him forking broncs. The first gate they reached, he would turn Biscuit into the remuda and catch out one of the broncs he had been breaking.

As was typical of ranches so near the Rio Grande, the J Bar crew had more Mexican vaqueros than Anglo cowboys. Border conflicts were not altogether a thing of the past— they still happened on occasion—so the tendency was for members of the two groups to draw toward their own kind when the work did not push them all together. Last night's celebration in the saloon had let the fences down for a little while.

Part of the problem was a language barrier. Hewey had worked along the border and picked up just enough Spanish to get by on, though Mexican children who heard him often covered their mouths to hide their amusement. Most of the vaqueros spoke little English and frequently called upon Blas or Aparicio to interpret. Hewey doubted that Tommy knew much Spanish, if any at all. He would probably starve in Mexico; he would not know how to ask for food or water.

Before the outfit was two miles from Alpine and the remuda strung out toward the broken country, Tommy and Skip Harkness had struck up a friendship. They rode side by side. Hewey was too far back to hear more than fragments of their conversation, but he could see that they laughed a lot and gestured with their hands, exchanging shady jokes they probably thought were new. Hewey had heard them years ago.

He understood why the two would hit it off. They were within a year or so of the same age, and they had in common that both had been brought up to be farmers but had left home to taste the cowboy life. Hewey wished Tommy would pair up with someone who exhibited more judgment—like him, for instance. Hanging around with Skip, Tommy might be exposed to all kinds of foolish notions. It was not Hewey's business to tell Tommy who his friends ought to be, though he might give the boy a subtle hint, like telling him that Skip had the brains God gave a ground squirrel.

He thought of his own long friendship with Snort Yarnell. Snort had never appeared to worry about consequences; he simply did what he wanted when he wanted and to whomever he wanted. He had gotten Hewey into many a ticklish jackpot, but so far none had been fatal. Most had seemed funny later, looked back on from the safe vantage point of time, funny and totally foolish.

Loose horses tended to move faster than the wagons, so Hewey had to ride out in front and slow them down after a while to prevent them from overtaking Blas. The driver of the hoodlum wagon laid back the first wire gate they came to because Blas's crippled leg made it inconvenient for him to climb up and down. The gate was left open for the horses to follow. Hewey signaled for Tommy to close it after the remuda had passed. Skip and Tommy both held back, giving chase to a jackrabbit and trying unsuccessfully to rope it. Hewey could hear their laughter a hundred yards away.

They returned in a long trot. Hewey demanded, "Did it take both of you?"

"Tight gate." Tommy grinned.

"I don't know what you'd've done with that rabbit if you'd caught it. Try a badger sometime."

He had done that himself once and had found the badger

coming up the rope to meet him and in no mood for compromise. Catching a badger was not terribly difficult. Getting the rope back could be hazardous.

Next time he saw a badger he would point it out to the boys. The experience would broaden their education.

No one had bothered to put up signposts along the way, for the wagon road to the J Bar was not a public thoroughfare. Anyone who did not know his way had no business following it anyhow. Blas needed no signposts, or even a road. There was probably not a wagon rut or cow trail in these mountains which the old vaquero had not traveled at some time or other, and few ranches on which he had not worked.

Folks claimed he had helped the army track holdout Apaches thirty or forty years ago, though he never made claims or even answered questions about those times beyond a nod or a negative shaking of his gray head. Perhaps he was ashamed of something there, for both sides had done terrible things to one another. Or perhaps it was simply so far in the past that it no longer held interest for him.

Hewey had a keen eye for horses. In a short while he had surveyed the penful of new broncs, deciding which would be likely to make dependable working horses and which would never be even decent bait for the Mexican panthers that prowled their way up from the Big Bend of the Rio Grande. Horses were much like men in that most found a level at which they functioned comfortably, a few like Biscuit would prove outstanding, and a few never would be worth the price of the cartridge needed to put them out of everybody's misery.

It was customary that the foreman assign a "mount" of broncs as each hand's individual responsibility. Bige Saunders preferred that each man take turns, picking one at a time to avoid any appearance of favoritism. He did not make the Mexican hands take second best after the Anglos; he treated everyone the same.

Aparicio was roping out the broncs one by one. Hewey had his eye on a likely-looking sorrel. He pointed to it and said, "Catch me that one, *por favor.*"

Saunders waved Aparicio off. "Hewey, seems like you neglected to tell me that Mr. Jenkins said you wasn't to ride any more broncs."

Hewey tried to look innocent. "He said that? I must've forgot."

"Forgetfulness overtakes us all when we get older. You've celebrated too many birthdays, Hewey. You've got to quit ridin' these broncs before one of them cleans your plow for once and for all."

"I'm just now comin' into my prime."

It occurred to Hewey that he would probably have to quit the J Bar one day soon and find a job on some ranch where they didn't discriminate against a man simply because he had had more experience than most. But he couldn't leave just yet because Tommy would want to go with him, and he hadn't been on the payroll long enough to earn his first paycheck.

Saunders looked at Tommy. "Which one do you want?"

Tommy said, "That sorrel."

Hewey said, "You've got good judgment. Alvin Lawdermilk must've taught you a right smart."

"I picked him because you did."

"Then you *do* have good judgment."

Skip Harkness made his first choice on the basis of the wildest-looking, the most likely to offer him a rousing fight. By that measure, he selected well. He picked a long-tailed bay whose conformation indicated a strain of mustang and whose rolling eyes suggested war.

Skip said, "I believe he'll give me plenty of fun."

Hewey responded, "I believe he'll kill you."

Most of the broncs bore rope burns across their noses, indicating they had already fought through a session or two with the hackamore, being staked to a heavy log or wagon wheel until they learned the hard way that the rope was boss. The marks would heal, but the lesson would remain with all except a few unreachables. Supposedly the broncs had been saddled and ridden—or ridden at—a time or two by the outfit that raised them, but horse dealers could be notoriously cavalier with the facts. Hewey contended that most had missed a calling in politics.

Ideally, breaking broncs was a task best done in winter when cowboys had more free time on their hands, but Jenkins believed the best training for a cow horse was working with cattle, and Hewey could not argue the point. When the broncs were well broken and had learned something about following a cow, Jenkins would resell them at a profit and bring in a new batch of raw ponies. A believer in the adage that idle hands are the devil's workshop, he had a strong commitment to protecting his employees' moral fiber.

Hewey advised Skip, "If I was you, I'd work up to that bay sort of gradual. I'd ride them other two first and get myself in shape."

"I'd rather start with the roughest one while I'm fresh. After him, the others'll be like pets."

Warmed-over advice was as stale as warmed-over coffee, so Hewey seldom made the same suggestion twice. "If I was you, then, I'd take time to write a letter home. It might be the last one your poor old mother ever gets."

Tommy eyed the boy with misgivings. "I think Uncle Hewey's right, Skip. That pony looks like a bad one."

"That's the way I like them."

From the moment the loop circled its neck, the bay bronc went into a stomping, squealing fury. It plunged against the rope, dragging Skip and Tommy halfway across the corral, their boot heels firmly dug into the dirt, raising dust like a dry fog behind them. When it reached the fence, it whirled and quartered back the other way. The impact when it hit the end of the line sent Skip sprawling on his face, but Tommy braced the rope around his hip and hung on. The bronc reared and pawed.

Hewey hollered, "Watch him, Tommy. He'll stomp you." He started out to help, then decided to hold back. The boys had to learn.

Skip pushed to his feet, picking up his fallen hat and dusting himself with it. A hint of fear insinuated itself into his eyes, or perhaps it was an awakening wisdom. "He may be a little tougher than I figured."

Tommy said, "It'd do him a world of good to drag a log around for two or three days before you try to get on him."

"If you say so. I guess he'll keep."

You're getting smarter all the time, Hewey thought. Perhaps Tommy was a good influence on Skip instead of Skip being a bad influence on Tommy.

They had to put a loop around the bay's forefeet and throw him down to put a hackamore on him. Hewey tried to leave it to the boys but finally could hold back no longer and pitched in to help. He tied a length of heavy rope to the hackamore as a rein, dallied it to his saddle horn and led the bronc out onto the flat, where several long logs lay scattered over a beaten-out stretch of ground covered only by a thin stand of short burro grass. Tommy started to tie the rope to a log that had once been part of a cottonwood trunk.

Hewey said, "It's Skip's horse. Let him tie the rope."

The log was heavy enough that the bay would have difficulty in dragging it, yet it would yield enough to minimize the risk of injury. The colt made a running start and was jerked up short at the end of the rope. It fell backward onto its rump, kicking, then scrambling to its feet. The log had moved six inches.

Tommy said, "Time he's drug that thing around for a few days he'll be a heap better educated."

Hewey said, "Time Skip's tried to ride that knothead a couple of times, *he'll* be a heap better educated, too."

Skip said, "I'll have him eatin' out of my hand."

Hewey grunted. "Or maybe just eatin' your hand."

Tommy's sorrel fought the rope, but he put up less fight than Skip's long-tailed bay. Tommy handled him with quiet ease. Hewey warmed with pride.

The hands rode their new broncs in the evenings after they finished the day's rounding up and branding. The location was central enough to a large part of the ranch that camp did not have to be moved for several days while the nearby pastures were being worked. The fresh colts were left staked through the day while the cowboys rode out on their regular business. By the time the wagon had to shift to another camp, most of the broncs would be more tractable. They might progress far enough to be ridden on roundup, earning their keep.

Though Tommy's sorrel and most of the others quickly adapted to their new situation, Skip's bay seemed no gentler after spending two days tied to the log, led away only for feed and water. When approached, it rolled its eyes and challenged the end of the rope. The impact jerked it around unceremoniously but did not alter its behavior.

Hewey warned, "That horse is plumb mean, and maybe half idiot to boot."

He saw dread in Skip's eyes. Sooner or later the boy had to either climb into the saddle or back down in front of everybody. He would not back down. Hewey doubted that any man in the crew would. None of the Mexican hands would want to retreat in front of the gringos, and none of the gringos would want to look diminished in the eyes of the Mexicans. The rivalry was friendly enough, but it was real. The battle of the Alamo had not been laid entirely to rest.

The third evening Skip could no longer put off the confrontation. He looked out across the flat where some of the young broncs were still tied. All had been ridden except his. He said, "I reckon it's time he learns who's boss."

Hewey thought Skip's voice sounded hollow. "I don't know that he's ready to get religion yet."

"I can handle him."

What Skip couldn't handle, Hewey thought, was the feeling that the rest of the crew might consider him afraid. "If you're bound and determined . . . Come on, Tommy, let's give him a hand."

Hewey wrapped the end of the hackamore rein around his saddle horn and led the bronc into the corral. It resisted all the way, setting its legs, hopping, twisting, tugging back on the rope as Biscuit stubbornly dragged it forward.

Hewey secured the bronc to a snubbing post in the center of the pen and backed Biscuit away to avoid being kicked by the flailing hooves. Bige Saunders stood near the fence, frowning. Hewey rode back to him.

"Bige, I don't believe that boy can handle this one."

"He seems to think so." Skip was carrying his blanket toward the thrashing bronc. Tommy followed with the saddle.

"He's too game to quit on his own, but you could tell him to. You could say that pony needs to be staked out some more."

"He's already had three days. I don't think three *weeks* would make much difference."

"Then tell Skip you've decided to let somebody with more experience ride him first. Me maybe, or Aparicio. That'd give the kid a respectable way out."

"It'd shame him. Skip picked that pony. He'll have to ride him, or try to."

The bay fought so frantically that Skip was unable to keep the blanket on long enough for Tommy to follow it with the saddle. Hewey got a rope on one foot and tied it up so the bronc could not paw or kick without falling. After several tries, he and Skip and Tommy, all working together, got the saddle on and cinched down. The pony humped its back so much that it reminded Hewey of a camel.

Hewey threw his right arm around the bronc's neck and grabbed both ears. "All right, get on him." He would bite down on an ear if necessary, but he had rather not get all that hair in his teeth. It always left a gritty taste that kept him spitting until he could wash it down with coffee.

Skip swung into the saddle. The pony tried to jump but went down on its rump. Tommy untied the rope that bound a foot.

Skip's voice was shaky. "All right, turn him loose."

Hewey relinquished his hold on the ears and jumped back. The bronc lashed a hind foot at him as it went by. The hoof just missed Hewey's ear. Out by the fence, Aparicio Rodriguez laughed. Cowboys almost always laughed at a near thing, especially when it happened to someone else. The trait was common to Anglo and Mexican alike.

Hewey had not seen many range broncs pitch harder than this one. He thought it could hold its own against professional buckers in the 101 Ranch Wild West Show. Skip's hat sailed off and was pounded into a shapeless lump beneath the hooves. He grunted each time the pony hit the ground. Every jump lifted Skip a little higher from his seat. He gave up trying to make a show of it and gripped the saddle horn. Pride gave way to the instinct for survival.

Though Skip was making a good fight, he was wearing down while the bronc seemed only to gain strength and determination. Daylight between the kid and the saddle grew broader with every jump. One stirrup flopped free, then the other. As Skip left the saddle, Hewey rushed forward, waving his hat and shouting, trying to spook the horse out of kicking range. But the bay managed to strike the kid with one hind foot while Skip was still in the air. Free of the rider, it pitched on across the corral, squealing its rage, the stirrups bouncing. The back of the kid's head hit the ground.

Hewey rushed to Skip's side, Tommy and Saunders and Aparicio close behind. The young cowboy lay limp and unresponsive. No one was laughing now.

Saunders said, "He's knocked out cold." He motioned for a couple of the young hands to lift Skip and carry him out of the corral so the still-excited bronc could not run over him.

Hewey and Aparicio trapped the horse in a corner, and Tommy grabbed the hackamore rein.

Hewey yelled, "Boy, what you fixin' to do?"

Tommy said, "Ride him. Worst thing we can do is let him get away with it. He needs to be rode, and right now."

Hewey argued, "If your mother could see you she'd kill both of us."

Aparicio offered to take over the ride, but Tommy said, "You take ahold of his ears." The boy gripped the horn with his right hand, the rein and a handful of dark mane in his left. He swung into the saddle and pulled his hat down tight. "Ready," he said.

The first long jump lifted him several inches from the saddle. He regained his balance and gripped firmly with his knees. Watching, Hewey could almost feel the jarring impact of each landing. But Tommy rode the bronc until it quit pitching and began circling the corral in a run, its hide dripping sweat. It drew its breath in great sobbing drafts.

At length the pony quit running and stood still, trembling in confusion and fatigue. Tommy swung down quickly and stepped away so it could not kick him if it took a notion to. It was too weary to try.

Hewey felt weary too from witnessing his nephew's performance.

Bige Saunders walked up to Tommy. "Good ride, but you look kind of gray around the gills."

"Just winded, is all. Is Skip still out?"

"He's tryin' to rally, but he doesn't know whether he's in Cape Cod or Hickory Bend."

"He made a game try. Let's don't tell him I finished his ride."

Saunders grunted. "I don't imagine that bay'll buck as hard the next time Skip tries. You took the starch out of him."

Hewey said, "It took the starch out of me, watchin' him. I told you, Bige, us Calloways know how to ride."

Bige frowned. "I hope you know how to quit, and when."

As Bige walked away, Hewey put his arm around Tommy's shoulder. "Young'un, I never taught you to ride like that."

"I learned by ridin' broncs for Alvin Lawdermilk. I wanted to be just like you, Uncle Hewey."

"Like me?" He thought of Eve and what she would say. "God help us all!"

When the branding was finished, Tommy asked Hewey what they were likely to do next. Hewey said, "First thing you need to learn is that you don't ask questions. You watch the boss. If he saddles his best drive horse, you catch your best drive horse. If he saddles his best cuttin' horse, you're fixin' to work the herd, so you catch up the one that's quickest and quietest around the cattle."

"But Bige didn't saddle a horse at all. He left a while ago on the chuck wagon, headin' for town."

"In a case like that, you just keep workin' on your broncs and wait for them to tell you what to do."

Bige returned with a big load of flour, coffee and other camp necessities, which caused Hewey to wonder some, but pride still would not let him ask questions. With the branding finished, he saw no need to restock the chuck wagon. When Bige was ready, he would tell them what he wanted them to know.

That happened in the bunkhouse dining room at supper. Bige said, "Mr. Jenkins'll be here after a while in his automobile. First thing in the mornin', him and me are goin' down under the rimrock to the Circle W outfit that he just bought. Hewey, I'd appreciate it if you and the boys would bring the horses and follow the wagons. We'll be countin' the Circle W cattle."

Bige was the kind of boss who issued orders as if he were asking a favor, not giving a command.

Hewey replied as if he were consenting to the favor out of the goodness of his heart and not as a condition of employment. "We'll be tickled to do that. You reckon Blas knows the way?"

"Blas knows every cow trail from the Guadalupes to the Rio Grande. All you need to do is follow him. I'd be obliged if you'd keep an eye on everything, Hewey."

There they were again, giving him a sort of straw-boss responsibility he had not asked for. But how could he refuse a favor so politely requested? "Why, sure."

He had never been to the Circle W and had only a general notion how far it was from J Bar headquarters. It made no real difference whether the trip was short or long; making it was simply part of the job he was being paid for, and trailing horses was always pleasurable. He relied on Blas to set the pace and the route.

As they went along, the going became rougher, the trail steeper and rockier, so the chuck wagon and hoodlum wagon could not make good time. It was a challenge to keep the remuda from overtaking and passing them. Blas camped the first night beside a clear-running narrow creek where an old set of brush corrals would hold the horses. The grass was green, so Hewey suggested that the hands loose-herd them and let them graze awhile, though the traveling had been slow enough to allow considerable grazing through the day.

He was glad for the stop. He wondered why he felt tired. The shipping, then the branding, had kept him going at a steady clip for weeks, but that had never seemed to bother him much in the past. He speculated that it was the responsibility of watching out for Tommy, seeing to it that he did

not let Skip Harkness lead him off into some kind of foolishness that might get him hurt or fired. In some ways, Skip
reminded him of a young Snort Yarnell.

Hard work had never bothered Hewey, but responsibility
had always been a smothering burden.

While the horses were grazing, he found a pair of markings on a boulder twice the size of Blas's wagon. One was
a name and a date and the words "10th CAV" scratched into
the rock, like a tombstone without a grave. The other was a
faded black painting of a strange oblong figure with a square
head and stick arms, a spear in one hand.

Tommy and Skip rode up to look at the markings with
him. Tommy pointed to the painted one. "What you reckon
that's supposed to represent, Uncle Hewey?"

"Some kind of medicine man maybe, or some kind of a
god. There used to be Apaches here, and before them I expect there was others."

"There's probably a story behind it, and behind that other
one, too. Tenth Cavalry. Those were buffalo soldiers, weren't
they?"

"I think so. That was before my time. There was all kinds
of people passed through here in the years gone by—
Indians, Mexicans, white men . . . all of them gone."

Many stories went untold in these mountains, secrets hidden beyond the haze of uncountable years, old victories
now forgotten, old crimes long buried. Sometimes Hewey's
skin prickled as he imagined he could hear ancient spirits
whispering to him in languages he could not understand,
trying to tell him something no one but God knew anymore.

It was a grand country, on its face at least, but through
those stories he *had* heard, he was aware that it had known
darkness, too. Some of the people who had passed this way
had been victors, some of them victims, some seeking peace
and some on their way to war. They had left little trace of
themselves beyond random markings on the stones. Men
probably lay buried where he now rode, but he had no way

of knowing. Whoever they had been, however long or short their stay, whatever triumphs and tragedies they had experienced here, the stones were silent and the wind had long since taken their tracks away.

One day Hewey would also be gone, and he had not even carved his name on a mountainside so that someone in the future would know he had once been here. It was a disturbing thought, one he did not allow to burden him for long. Tomorrow could take care of itself. This was today. Today had always been more important to Hewey than either yesterday, which could not be changed, or tomorrow, which he could only guess at.

Skip said, "I'm goin' to scratch my name on there, too."

Hewey said, "You oughtn't to. It'd be like markin' up somebody's tombstone."

"A hundred years from now that may be the only trace left of me."

Tommy shook his head. "I'm figurin' on still bein' around a hundred years from now."

Hewey said, "And me with you."

Skip argued, "A hundred years from now you'd be a hundred and fifty years old . . . maybe a hundred and seventy-five."

"That," said Hewey, "is when I may decide to give up ridin'."

He was gratified when Skip rode away without adding his name to the inscriptions on the rock.

Hewey inspected the old corrals and shored up a couple of weak places where horses might slip through and escape in the night. After the remuda was safely penned, he staked Biscuit outside on grass at the end of a long rope so the brown could graze freely. He patted the horse's neck and talked as if the animal could understand whatever he said. Working alone much of his life, he had picked up the habit of talking to his horse when he had no fellow humans to talk to.

He heard Skip Harkness's voice behind him. "I'd like to be around the day he answers you back. I'll bet you jump two feet high."

Hewey felt a twinge of embarrassment along with faint resentment. This had been a private conversation. He sensed that Skip was trying to impress Tommy with his wit, for he still could not resist showing off a little. Reformation came slowly to some. "At least he doesn't talk a lot of nonsense, like some cowpuncher kids I've known."

"Too bad he *can't* talk. I'll bet he could tell some funny stories on you."

"He'd have the good sense to keep his mouth shut. Some people could learn a lot from a horse."

Blas clanged a pothook against a steel rod, calling the hands to supper. That gave Hewey a welcome excuse to end the conversation, which was not going anywhere. Walking ahead of the others, he heard Tommy talking quietly to Skip. "You oughtn't to tease Uncle Hewey. He's just gettin' sort of old, is all."

Must think I'm losing my hearing, too, Hewey thought. The words stung a bit, but he supposed from Tommy's viewpoint he was a little long in the tooth. He was more than twice his nephew's age.

He lifted his bedroll down from the hoodlum wagon so he could sit on it while he ate. Tommy joined him, his own bedroll too small to provide much of a seat. Under pressure of time, Hewey had forgotten his intention of buying Tommy a protective tarp before they left Alpine. It probably wasn't going to rain anyway. It didn't often. There was not room enough left for Skip on the bedroll, so he sat on the ground and leaned back against the end of the roll for support.

The new adventure was good for Tommy's appetite. He had heaped his plate high with beef and beans and two tall sourdough biscuits. He said, "I don't know when I ever tasted better."

Skip commented, "Blas cooks good, but it gets monotonous after a while: biscuits and beef and beans, beans and beef and biscuits."

Hewey said, "It's hard to have variety when the kitchen keeps movin'. Anyway, try batchin' for a while and you'll appreciate a good cook."

A high canyon wall just west of camp blocked the setting sun so that dusk came early and stretched out awhile. With darkness and the first bright stars came a light chill, though not enough to cause Hewey to dig into his war bag for a denim jacket. He heard a horse squeal, and hooves shuffled in the corral as one of the more dominant animals bullied a timid one. Night birds called to one another from the trees. Wood crackled as it burned down into glowing coals in Blas's fire pit.

On the other side of camp, one of the Mexicans plucked at a guitar, and Aparicio Rodriguez's voice rose in a plaintive song of unrequited love and welcome death. It seemed to Hewey that most Mexican songs were melancholy at heart. Many cowboy songs as well told sad stories of dying on the range far from home, or of long-ago loves who had been left behind.

The music carried Hewey back to another time, to a summer's courtship of Spring Renfro. He asked Tommy, "Since you finished your schoolin', do you ever see Miss Renfro anymore?"

"Every time I've been over to the Lawdermilks'. She's always there."

"Has she changed any?"

"Got a little older, I guess." From the vantage point of a boy in his teens she had been old to start with, having been in her thirties when she became his teacher.

"I mean, is she still pretty?"

"I never thought of her that way. Old maids ain't supposed to be pretty, are they?"

"She's not an old maid yet. From where I sit, she's still young."

"From where you sit, I guess just about everybody looks young."

Skip Harkness was a bad influence on the boy, Hewey thought.

Tommy looked up at the stars. His voice was tinged with awe. "Ain't it beautiful out here, Uncle Hewey? I never saw the like of these mountains."

Hewey nodded. "It *is* a smilin' country."

"I can see why you never could be happy with anything but a ridin' job. It never was this pretty on the farm."

"Your mama and daddy would argue with you about that. It's not just what you see that makes somethin' pretty; it's findin' what you *want* to see."

"This is what I wanted to see, all right."

Hewey suspected it would take a while to talk Tommy into going home . . . if he even could.

4

The Circle W pleased Hewey on first sight. Most new places did, then gradually lost their luster through familiarity. One point which appealed to him was that the previous owner seemed to have shared Hewey's aversion to barbed wire. Except for a couple of horse traps, most of the ranch's hundred square miles were in one large pasture fenced only around its perimeter. It reminded him of the open-range days of recent memory, when hide-ripping wire was scarcer than rain.

Most ranchers claimed that smaller pastures were easier to work, but Hewey saw no reason why everything should be easy. A little physical exertion was good for the soul. He made an exception for opening gates.

As he had heard the story in town, Augie Wilson had put the ranch together in the late 1880s and early '90s for the eventual benefit of his two sons. Unfortunately, one had died of dysentery serving under Teddy Roosevelt in Cuba. Hewey could relate to that, for the same ailment had caused him to miss the charge up San Juan Hill. He had never so much as shot at a Spaniard. Hindsight had made him grateful for that. The Spaniards were said to have blown up the *Maine,* but none of them had done him any personal injury. Still, there was a void in his life. He wished he could have enjoyed the excitement of charging up that hill with Teddy. What a bully show it would have been!

The other Wilson son had been a sticky-fingered sort who developed a bad habit of burning his brand on other people's calves, earning him a one-way trip to the Huntsville penitentiary. Having no family member to help her run the ranch or to leave it to, Wilson's widow had chosen to sell it and spend her declining years in the comfort of Fort Davis town.

Wilson's dislike for barbed wire had been equaled by his love for the Longhorn, so the scattering of cows that retreated ahead of the horses showed the original wild Texas strain. Hewey suspected Old Man Jenkins would not wait long to bring in Hereford or Durham sires, consigning the Longhorn bulls to a packinghouse—as many as his cowboys could catch, anyway. In three or four generations, most of the old blood would be bred out. That was the trend in this new century: throw away whatever was old and traditional, grasp whatever was regarded as modern . . . fast automobiles, fast trains, electric lights that required no matches and no blowing out.

He had even seen a flying machine set down on a flat stretch of ground outside of Alpine. It looked like a cross between a kite and a prickly-pear burner. If God had intended a man to get that high in the air, He would have put feathers on him.

Tommy seemed favorably impressed by the lack of fences because he'd had to shut so many wire gates on the way here after the horses had gone through. Some were so tight that

Skip had to join forces with him to fasten them. Hewey could have done it, but he figured the boys needed the education. A seasoned cowboy knew to stay on horseback and let somebody else do most of the footwork.

Tommy said in admiration, "It's a wonderful-lookin' country."

True, its scenery was more spectacular than Upton County's. A high gray rimrock towered over the western side of the long valley like a great stone wall built to keep the barbarians out, or perhaps to keep them in, depending upon how you chose to look at it. Some of the mountains ranged from six thousand feet in altitude to more than eight, and the valley that made up most of the ranch was probably close to four, easily a thousand to fifteen hundred feet higher than the Calloway homestead. It was a high-lonesome country, sure enough.

One good thing about the altitude in Hewey's view: this region was too high for growing crops. It ought to remain safe from the plow.

A man could freeze the buttons off his shirt here on winter mornings, though that towering wall probably provided shelter against the west and northwest winds. It had been Apache country even to the time of Hewey's boyhood. He wondered how Indians had made it through January and February in nothing more than breechclout and leggings.

He need not dwell on that because he would probably move on before next winter. For now, the spring sun was pleasantly warm. Grass was turning green at its base, poised to receive the rains that usually began here in June, except in those years when they forgot to come at all. Given decent moisture, it was a great country for cattle in the summer and fall. It was fair enough through winter if the landowner avoided overgrazing and saved back enough summer forage. Spring, usually dry, could be long and challenging, but ranchers hung on to the hope that June would bring rain. Hewey could see a thunderhead building over the rimrock, probably setting the stage for an afternoon drenching.

Tommy would wish he had a tarp to shed water from his bedroll. Well, next time he would know. Life was one hard-learned lesson after another.

Letting the remuda set its own easy pace, Hewey noticed a roadrunner trotting to one side. "Smart little bird," he told Tommy. "He's lettin' the horses scare up dinner for him."

A tiny lizard, frightened into movement by the passage of the remuda, scurried away from the noise and into the path of a far deadlier hazard. In a startling dash the roadrunner overtook it, spreading its tail to brake to a quick stop. It threw up its head, and the lizard disappeared down its throat.

Skip declared, "Poor little devil didn't have a chance."

Hewey said, "It would've had better luck if it'd been too big to swallow whole. That *paisano* bird might've just grabbed it by the tail, the tail would've broke loose, and the rest of the lizard would've gotten away. They can grow a new tail, you know."

Skip was incredulous. "That story's too big to swallow whole, too."

"It's a fact. Why, I've heard the Mexicans tell about *paisanos* that raised herds of lizards like me and you would raise a herd of cattle. They wouldn't eat anything but the tails, and pretty soon the tails would grow back. Them birds didn't have to waste time huntin'. They just laid around gettin' fat and watchin' their herd grow new tails over and over, the way sheep grow a new clip of wool every time you shear them."

Tommy suppressed a grin; he had heard his uncle spin windies before. Hewey took pleasure in the quizzical expression on Skip's freckled face as the young cowboy floundered between scorn and reluctant belief. It did a green kid good to guess a little, reminding him that he didn't know everything.

Skip said, "There ain't no bird that smart." But he still wavered.

Hewey shrugged. "I never seen it for myself, of course. I'm just tellin' you what's been told to me."

Tommy observed Skip's confusion as long as he could before he let his grin break free. "Uncle Hewey, you're still the best liar I ever listened to. Better than Snort Yarnell."

Hewey smiled. Even backhanded praise was welcome, coming from his nephew.

The farther Hewey rode onto this ranch the better he liked the look of it. He appreciated that many of the cattle hoisted their tails and took to the breaks in a sturdy lope at first sight of horses and riders. That demonstrated a healthy Texas independence. Most of the calves had been left unbranded because of the probability that their ownership would change.

The long rock wall and the distant blue mountains framed the broad valley like a picture, topped by a crystal-clear sky. Wildflowers in bloom lent their colors to the green of the rising grass, and Hewey breathed deeply of their perfume.

So what if he had to patch the knees of his britches when he got settled, or dig a few thorns from his hide? A lot of folks in town would spend good money to see such as this, and he was being paid thirty dollars a month for the privilege.

For the last part of the drive Hewey freed the half-broken bronc he had been riding and saddled Biscuit, for he knew Old Man Jenkins would be watching the procession roll into ranch headquarters.

As the cottonwood trees and the ranch buildings came into view, Skip said, "Tommy, I'll bet the corral gate is shut. I'll race you to see who opens it."

"On that spavined nag? My bronc can run rings around him."

Hewey warned, "Mr. Jenkins'll teach you boys some

words you never heard before. You was hired to drive horses, not to race them."

Skip argued, "A little race never hurt nobody."

"Don't come cryin' to me if you find yourself sittin' on a street corner in Alpine with your pocket empty and your stomach talkin' to you."

He remembered, though he would not tell these boys, that he and Snort Yarnell had run many a horse race together and sometimes had lost everything but their shirts. First the boys should learn the way things ought to be. They would learn soon enough the way things actually were.

The headquarters reminded Hewey of something out of his boyhood, as if little new had been added in thirty or forty years. Though a stream ran nearby, a windmill tower stood tall to catch the wind coming up the valley or down from the rimrock to turn the wooden Eclipse fan, insurance against drought that might dry up the surface water. Whoever had first settled the place must have imported Mexican artisans, for most of the buildings were of adobe. The main house was constructed low and flat, as was an even longer structure Hewey judged to be a bunkhouse and kitchen for the hands. The main barn was of weathered wood, a stranger to paint. The corrals were of the same brush construction as most of the camps on Jenkins's J Bar, though the swinging gates were built of sawmill lumber. A couple of small sheds had adobe outer walls and were open in front.

It seemed right and proper that as much as possible be built of materials which existed in nature and close at hand. Thick adobe walls held the heat out in summer and in during winter. Hewey had been in frame houses where cold wind whistled between the boards and he could not haul enough wood to keep the place warm. He had slept outside in July and August rather than lie beneath a sheet-iron roof that trapped enough heat to keep supper biscuits warm all night.

Adobe suited him fine. He would enjoy this place for however long he stayed.

The boys' race ended prematurely, and the two came back, their horses breathing hard. Skip was looking over his shoulder. Tommy said, "Mr. Jenkins and Bige Saunders have already got the gate open."

Hewey smiled. The boys dreaded a lecture from either boss about the evils of running their horses unnecessarily. Half the basic training for a cowboy was in learning what *not* to do.

They put the horses through the gate, and Bige pushed it shut behind them. Jenkins walked up, broad shoulders hunched like he had rheumatism. Hewey could believe it, him riding all this way over the rough road in that car. Jenkins eyed Hewey's mount critically, perhaps with a little suspicion. "You were ridin' Biscuit when I last seen you, and you're ridin' him now. You sure you ain't pushin' him too hard?"

"He hardly knows he's been rode."

Blas and his swamper had pulled the chuck wagon and hoodlum wagon up close to the long adobe building and were carrying the groceries inside. At least Blas would get to cook indoors for a few days, though Hewey doubted it made much difference to him. The old vaquero enjoyed being outside except when the weather was bad. During his long years, he had probably slept more nights under the sky than under a roof. Even so, it would do his bones good not to have to be out in the rain or the chill night wind.

A couple of strangers approached from the main house. One had the look of an old cowboy. The other bore all the earmarks of a money changer. Jenkins introduced the cowboy first, probably feeling more in common with him than with the other man. "Hewey Calloway, this is Oscar Levitt. He's Mrs. Wilson's brother, here to see after her interests while we count the cattle. Mr. Petrie here, he's her lawyer. Says he don't know straight up about a cow, but he knows inside and out about transfers and deeds. He's here to keep me and Mr. Levitt honest."

"Pleased to meet you fellers," Hewey said, shaking hands with each in turn. Levitt's hands were rough as old cowhide, but his eyes were direct and honest. Petrie's hands were slick as kidskin, and his gaze barely touched Hewey's face before he turned his attention elsewhere. Hewey wondered why Jenkins even bothered to introduce Levitt and Petrie to him, for he was just a working hand here. He supposed the old man was hoping to butter him up and make him reconsider the foreman's job. Hewey thought he would enjoy staying on this place awhile, but he didn't want the weight of being a boss to interfere with his sleep.

Bige said, "Mr. Levitt's got a ranch of his own in the Guadalupes. He brought some of his crew to help with roundin' up and countin' the cows."

Hewey felt a pleasant glow at the thought of a roundup in this valley. It was the kind of work he had always liked best, for most of it was done a-horseback. He could see Jenkins's touring car parked in the shade of a big cottonwood near the main house. Peeler lay on his back, his feet extending out from beneath the running board. It seemed he was forever having to fix something on that contraption. Pity, Hewey thought, that a good horseman should waste his time messing around with an automobile. What if he was getting an extra twenty dollars a month? There had to be something wrong with an able-bodied man who would willingly pass up a riding job.

Because most of the ranch was unfenced, the roundup was conducted in the old-fashioned style of the open range. The cowboys rode a daily circle several miles in diameter and picked up all the cattle they came across. Each drive overlapped the previous day's to catch unworked stock that might have drifted into the cleaned area.

If Augie Wilson had disliked barbed wire, he had had no

prejudice against building corrals at strategic intervals to fa-
cilitate working his cattle without having to push them the
long miles to headquarters. The size and location of each
drive was calculated to bring herds to one of these sets of
corrals.

A day's gather might run from a hundred to three hundred cows, given the animals' natural instinct to graze in
clusters rather than disperse evenly over the entire range.
As the riders pushed their individual gathers into a larger
herd, a cloud of dust hovered over it, twisting and turning
in constantly changing patterns like the drifting cumulus
clouds overhead. Cows and calves separated in the move set
up a din of anxious bawling as each mother sought reunion
with her offspring and each calf frantically searched for the
proper udder to relieve its hunger. Calves that could not find
their own mothers might try to steal milk from another cow
and, more often than not, were kicked or hooked away in a
hostile manner. Maternal instincts had their limits.

Congregating cattle in bunches almost always resulted in
headbutting, horn-gouging contests between bulls routed
from their own individual domains and thrown together into
open competition for whatever females might currently be
in heat. These fights could be long and savage, for Longhorn bulls were aggressive, ready for war against any male
they considered a challenge to their dominance. Hewey had
long observed that one major problem in trying to upgrade
a herd by the introduction of more productive beef blood
was that Hereford or Durham bulls were a poor match for
the Longhorns in combat. Any Longhorns allowed to remain in the herd would claim most of the females and fight
the other bulls away.

The Longhorns did not bluff. They went into a fight ready
and willing to kill any opponent that did not turn tail and
run.

Hewey had always found it interesting to watch these
jarring contests of will, trying to guess which bull would

come out victorious. Usually, but not always, it was the largest and oldest, the most experienced, though there came a point in life when the older bull's strength and reflexes began to fail, and it was forced to yield to the younger and more vigorous. Whipped down, the older bull would eventually have to break free and run lest the younger one pierce its vitals with a sharp horn. These whipped males usually found a place at the edge of the herd, away from the others, and continued muttering empty threats to vent their frustration.

Skip Harkness took particular enjoyment in watching these bawling, bellowing battles, taking sides with one or the other of the combatants. "Hey, Hewey, bet you a dollar Old Spot yonder makes that black one run like a scalded cat."

"You better give them bulls some room. They'd knock over a locomotive if it got in their way while they're fightin'."

The most dangerous place to be was in the path of the loser when he decided to quit the battle, for usually he was in a blind panic to escape an opponent's horns. Hewey had seen them knock down full-grown cows and trample calves to death in their haste.

The daily procedure was for both Bige Saunders and Oscar Levitt to count the cattle, Bige representing the buyer and Levitt watching out for his sister's interests. Because both were experienced cattlemen, their counts never differed by more than one or two head. Only cows and bulls were tallied; the calves were thrown in with the deal. Once the day's count was finished and any differences reconciled, the cattle would be driven through a narrow chute where Hewey would use a pocketknife to bob off the long hair at the ends of their tails so they would not be counted a second time if they got caught up in another gather. As the last of the day's cows trailed out of the chute, the ground was littered with short tufts of hair, easily lifted by any breeze that swept through. The square-ended tails looked awkward, but the hair would grow out again after a while.

It came as no surprise that Jenkins ordered the Longhorn bulls to be separated from the herd and driven into a holding trap. When the counting was done, he would ship them to a Fort Worth packinghouse and replace them with whiteface bulls.

Driving them to the trap was like a foretaste of glory for Skip Harkness because every mile was punctuated by fights as the animals struggled to establish an order of dominance. The strongest might have to combat half a dozen before he proved himself the cock of the walk. Then, bloody but triumphant, he would assume his place at the head of the line. The others would fall in behind him, more or less in the order of the ranking they had won or lost in battle.

People who preached disparagingly about the violence of man in comparison to the tranquility of the animal kingdom had never watched cattle sort out the intricacies of their social structure.

When the fighting died down and the trip became dull, Skip contrived to throw together a couple of bulls that had already demonstrated their combative natures but had not yet fought each other. More often than not he was able to stir up a rousing fight.

Halfway through the roundup, Skip precipitated one of these contests as a small herd of bulls neared the ranch headquarters and the gate to the holding trap.

"Hewey," the farm boy said, "you pick your bull. I'll bet you a dollar on the other one."

Hewey declined. "Better save your money."

Skip turned to Tommy. "How about you?"

"I ain't got a dollar to spare. Bet you a quarter, though."

Hewey thought about reminding Tommy that his mother regarded gambling as the devil's snare, but there were some lessons a boy had to learn for himself. One of the young vaqueros declared, "I bet you too, Skip." Tommy and the vaquero went into whispering consultation and chose a red bull with white spots that had whipped every challenger so far.

Skip said, "My money's on the lineback. Help me throw the two of them together, Tommy."

Hewey warned, "Tommy, give them bulls plenty of room. They can hurt you."

Tommy heeded Hewey's advice, but Skip rode in among the bulls and pushed the red one up to the lead position, where the lineback, drooling, lumbered along in an ill humor, angry noises rumbling from its throat. It did not take long for the lineback to take umbrage and ram a horn against the interloper's ribs. The red bull bellowed in anger, pawed dirt and rushed the lineback. The two butted heads with a thud like a clap of thunder, then scrambled for footing while their horns locked together. One pushed as the other gave way, then stumbled and went off balance, giving ground while its opponent pushed. The rest of the bulls seemed to ignore the pair except in yielding them space.

Hewey said, "Skip, this is a fool's game. If one of them gets crippled or killed and Mr. Jenkins finds out you set up the fight . . ."

Skip said, "They'd fight anyway. They didn't need me to get them started."

The fight began going against the lineback. The pleasure in Skip's face gave way to disappointment. He moved in closer and shouted encouragement to his champion. "Get in there! You can whip him!"

Hewey yelled, "Skip, get the hell out of the way!"

The warning was too late. The lineback abruptly wheeled and broke into a dead run to escape the red bull, blind to anything in its path. And in its path was Skip Harkness.

Struck before it could react, Skip's bay bronc was bowled over by the bull's strength and weight. Skip had time only for a grunt of surprise before the lowered head slammed into him, driving a horn deep into his stomach. The lineback flung the youngster aside as if he were a rag doll.

Hewey could only murmur, "My God!"

Tommy shouted, "Skip! Look out!" But the damage was

already done. The red bull trampled Skip as it raced in close pursuit of its opponent. Skip lay on his back, trembling in shock. His shirt reddened around a large hole ripped through its front.

Hewey leaped from the saddle and hit the ground running, Tommy close behind.

Tommy cried, "Skip, are you all right?"

It was obvious he was not. Hewey brushed Tommy aside and ripped the shirt open, popping buttons. A hole in Skip's belly bubbled blood. Hewey's stomach turned over in fleeting nausea. Tommy turned away, trying not to gag.

The bay bronc rose unsteadily to its feet and staggered off, shaking itself like a dog coming out of water. It did not seem injured. Hewey saw no blood except Skip's.

In Spanish, Aparicio upbraided the vaquero who had participated in the bet. Hewey said, "That won't do any good now. Lope to the house and bring a wagon. Better still, send Mr. Jenkins's car if that driver is around."

Aparicio looked down at Skip, confirming all his fears, and spurred off in a long lope. Hewey pulled a handkerchief from his pocket. It was not clean, but this was no time to worry about niceties. He wadded it and shoved it partway into the wound, hoping to stanch the flow of blood. He wished he had a handful of flour from Blas's kitchen.

Tears trailed down Tommy's paled cheeks. "We've got to do somethin'."

"Ain't much we can do here except try to keep him from bleedin' to death." Hewey pressed down upon the handkerchief. He did not like Skip's ashen look or the way he trembled.

Tommy insisted, "Is he goin' to die?"

Hewey feared he was, but he did not want to betray that feeling to his nephew. Best to keep him hoping so long as there was any hope. There would be time enough later for grief. "Tommy, I wisht you and the boys would go on and put these bulls in the trap before they scatter. I'll stay here 'til Aparicio gets back."

Tommy's voice broke. "I oughtn't've bet with him. If he dies, it's my fault."

"You're not doin' him any good standin' here cryin'. There's a job to get done. And I don't want to hear any more about whose fault it is."

Reluctantly Tommy mounted. The Mexican hands who had gathered around Skip backed away and joined him after two made the sign of the cross. Hewey heard them discussing Skip's poor chances and was glad Tommy understood little Spanish.

Skip groaned. Hewey gently squeezed his shoulder. "You just hang and rattle, kid. Help'll be comin'."

Under his breath, he whispered a prayer for mercy on a foolish boy.

Pity and anger clashed, the anger because Skip had recklessly put himself into this predicament. It bothered Hewey's conscience that such a feeling should come upon him at a moment like this, but damn it, he had tried to teach the boys better, Skip and Tommy both. Part of the anger was at himself for not being a better teacher. Skip should not have been his responsibility, but somehow he was. Just by being around and being older, Hewey had owed him guidance that would have avoided a wreck like this.

He would acknowledge that his own life had been reckless. Too many times he had yielded to the urges of the moment without regard for what might follow. Too often he had followed impulse rather than reason, bringing grief to himself and to others around him. He could not really blame this youngster all that much. To some extent, recklessness was a trait common in the cowboy trade. It took a reckless man to get on a bronc that had every intention of throwing him off and stomping him into the ground. It took a reckless man to put a loop around a pair of sharp horns that with the least turn of bad luck could end up goring him.

He gripped Skip's hand and felt his eyes burn. "You're a good boy. Don't you be turnin' your horses back to the outfit."

Skip's hand went limp.

Hewey heard an engine. The Jenkins touring car raced across the valley toward him, bouncing over ruts and clumps of bunchgrass. It braked to a stop in a swirl of dust. Leaving the motor running, Peeler jumped from behind the steering wheel. Old Man Jenkins was slower getting out, but he moved with more alacrity than Hewey would have expected for a large man of his years.

Jenkins said, "We'll take him to town in the car. It's a lot faster than a wagon."

Skip's features were relaxed, the pain gone. Hewey covered the cowboy's face with his hat.

He had to try twice before he could bring himself to speak. "There's no use bein' in a hurry now. The kid is gone."

5

Hewey and Tommy stood together on the station platform, hats in their hands, watching two station workers slide the wooden box into the baggage car to begin its long trip back to Skip Harkness's home in East Texas. Tommy sniffled a couple of times, and something got in Hewey's eye . . . dust blown up from beneath the train more than likely. A local minister had just finished offering a prayer, generously praising the many good qualities of a young cowboy he had never known. Old Man Jenkins hunched beside the baggage wagon, supervising the loading of the coffin as if he feared the railroad people did not know how to handle the responsibility.

"That was a good lad," he told the baggage man, "and he worked for me. He deserves to be treated kindly and with respect. You can't put a value on a good lad."

You can if he's a cowboy, Hewey thought. *Twenty-five dollars a month, thirty if he's a top hand, fifty if he can drive an automobile.* Jenkins had barely known Skip's name when he was alive, but he was generous now that Skip was dead, paying the cost of sending the youngster home to be buried among his own. He was a rancher of the old tradition, feeling more kinship with the cowboys who worked for him than with the bankers who tended his wealth.

Blas Villegas and Aparicio Rodriguez stood beside Hewey and Tommy, seeing Skip off. Blas crossed himself as a railroad employee slid the door to the baggage car shut. Aparicio followed suit. The two men were of a different heritage than Skip, but they were kinsmen in their trade and their chosen way of life.

The train slowly began moving eastward, black smoke trailing. Hewey heard Tommy choke, trying to force back a fresh rush of tears.

Hewey said, "It ain't somethin' you ever get used to, seein' your friends die. But the older you get, the more it'll happen, 'til one day you look around and it's you they're sayin' words over."

"He was too young to die, Uncle Hewey."

"And too reckless to keep himself alive." Hewey said no more because he did not want Jenkins to hear. Hewey and the others had avoided telling him that Skip had brought the accident upon himself. Even an *old* man needed a few illusions.

Jenkins headed back to the Circle W in his automobile, Bige Saunders and Blas Villegas riding with him. The cowboys who had come to see Skip off would return on horseback. Tommy untied his dun, then stood beside it with his head down, making no effort to mount. He said, "Uncle Hewey, I don't know if I can go back out there. I'd keep rememberin' what happened."

"You'll remember it no matter where you're at. It's like gettin' back on a horse after he's throwed you off. Best thing is to go out yonder where it took place and look the devil square in the eye."

"But I feel like I caused it. If I hadn't bet with him, he might not've thrown those bulls together."

"He'd've done it whether you bet with him or not, so stop whippin' yourself over the shoulders like some New Mexico *penitente*. He flirted with Lady Luck once too often."

What Tommy needed was to go home, Hewey thought, and remain there where he belonged. "When the roundup is finished, I'll take you back to your folks. But for now, a good cowboy don't quit in the middle of the works and leave the boss shorthanded"

"You sayin' I'm a good cowboy?"

"I don't know many better except me and Aparicio and Snort Yarnell."

It looked for a while as if the work they had done would go for nothing. The cattle count went cleanly enough and without friction, for Jenkins and Oscar Levitt were cattlemen who understood and trusted each other. Because cattle prices had been agreed upon beforehand, lawyer Petrie had no function during the counting except to endorse the numbers as the other two called them.

The big dollars took care of themselves. It was the nickels and dimes that almost blew up the ranch sale, for there Petrie got his hands into the pot up to his elbows. Inventorying and pricing the miscellaneous items led to argument after argument over everything from the wagons and the Wilson family buggy down to the hay in the barn, the value of shovels and pitchforks, and finally the evaluation of a steel crowbar. Petrie thought it ought to be worth fifty cents. Jenkins offered two bits.

Oscar Levitt put an end to the wrangling by slamming a quarter down onto the table and shoving it toward Petrie. "There!" he declared. "I want to be gettin' home."

When the last papers were signed and the check handed over, Jenkins and Levitt watched Petrie's departure with considerable satisfaction. Jenkins declared, "If I ever need to change my brand, I may just burn a line across their ribs and call this the Crowbar Ranch."

Not until the work was done and most of the crew was preparing to return to the J Bar did Hewey tell Jenkins that he was taking Tommy home. "The boy's still grievin' about Skip. He's havin' a tough time stayin' here where it happened."

Jenkins was disappointed, but he understood. "I've buried a lot of friends and kin. It never gets no easier."

"Every time one goes, you're that much closer to bein' left by yourself."

"I been watchin' that nephew of yours. He's got the makin's. Pretty soon he'll be as good as you were in your prime."

"I'm still in my prime."

"We could argue all day about that, but I ain't got the patience. Thing is, I hate to see you-all quit. You could take the boy home to visit his folks a few days and do me a favor at the same time."

"What kind of favor?"

"You know a man named Frank Gervin?"

Hewey would not have thought of the name for twenty dollars. "Fat Gervin, in the Upton City bank? I know him."

"Is he dependable?"

"I guess you could say that. You can always depend on him to do the wrong thing."

Jenkins frowned as he pondered Hewey's appraisal. "My Fort Worth banker got me in touch with him. Gervin sold me a string of broncs."

Hewey's eyebrows lifted. "Sight unseen?"

"If you can't trust a banker, who *can* you trust? Anyway, Gervin says they come from the ranch of a man named Lawdermilk."

"Alvin Lawdermilk. He raises good stock."

"So Bige tells me. You and the boy could take a short vacation, then bring me the horses."

Hewey nodded. "I can't promise you about Tommy; he's liable to stay home." At least Hewey hoped he would. "But I'll bring you your broncs."

Jenkins wrote out checks for Hewey and Tommy. "I still need me a foreman to run this Circle W outfit. Do some thinkin' on it, won't you?"

"I've already thought on it. I just want to be a plain forty-a-month hand."

"Thought I was payin' you thirty."

"After I bring your horses, I'll be expectin' forty."

"You ought to've been a lawyer, pricin' crowbars."

They could have made the trip in two days of hard traveling, but Hewey saw no need to abuse Biscuit or Tommy's dun horse. He took his time, stopping in Fort Davis to buy grub for the trail and to give Tommy time to prowl over what remained of the old army post, from which many sorties had been sent against the Apaches, most of them finding Indians only when Indians wanted to be found.

The only town between there and Upton City would be Fort Stockton. He wanted Tommy to have a chance to see the country. If the boy could be persuaded to remain at home after this stab at independence, it would be well for him to know as much as possible of the world beyond the homestead's outer fences. They climbed out through Wild Rose Pass, where tradition had it that Apaches had ambushed travelers on the old immigrant road, then eased down away from the mountains and across the open desert.

Hewey considered venturing over to Pecos City, where he had had a roaring good time more than once, but that town was out of the way. Sister-in-law Eve would appreciate his bypassing it. Pecos had an exaggerated reputation for violence, a result of shootings in the not-so-distant past and recent confrontations between ranchers and homesteaders over possession of state lands. Not long ago one of the town's more notorious exiles, known as Deacon Jim Miller, had finished his career at the end of a rope in Oklahoma, assisted by a delegation of angry citizens. Eve would say it was not the kind of story a churchgoing boy needed to be told.

They camped a night beside Fort Stockton's Comanche Springs, where cool, sweet water gushed from the ground in a volume that always amazed Hewey. Water was in such short supply across most of West Texas that Nature seemed overly extravagant here. They could have used the likes of this around Upton City. There everybody had to dig or drill for water and could never be certain of finding it. Hewey had seen a driller strike good water, then move fifty feet to one side or the other for a second well and come up dry.

Camped near the spring was a family with an automobile. They had erected a couple of canvas tents and spread their bedrolls inside. The woman of the family and a daughter of ten or so were cooking supper over a campfire.

Tommy said, "I'd think anybody rich enough to afford a car could pay for a hotel room in town."

Hewey thought the automobile an ugly intrusion upon an otherwise pleasant pastoral scene. A wagon and horses or mules would have been more appropriate. "The runnin' of the thing would keep most people broke. You watch, them stink wagons'll have the whole country chuggin' down to the poorhouse. The only folks left outside will be them of us that never had one."

The head of the family invited Hewey and Tommy over to share their supper, but Hewey politely declined. He told Tommy, "Poor feller already has too many mouths to feed . . . a wife, four buttons and an automobile. He'll be lucky to keep a shirt on his back."

The man looked as if he might be a drummer or store-keeper or something of the sort. He certainly did not seem like anybody who could make a hand a-horseback. Pickings could be poor in this part of the country for someone who could not hold a riding job.

Tommy extended a strip of bacon over the coals on a long, sharp stick. He said, "You sure you came just to get those broncs for Mr. Jenkins? Or were you hopin' that once I got home I'd decide to stay there?"

Some boys were too smart for their own good. "I made Mr. Jenkins a promise. Anyway, I thought it'd be nice for you to visit home a few days, and your folks'd be put out with me if I let you ramble around over this country by yourself. You could get snakebit or set upon by horse thieves. Worst of all, you could get taken in by some good-lookin' wheeligo girl and left without a cent to your name."

"Them things ever happen to you?"

"I never got snakebit or robbed by horse thieves."

"I don't have enough money for a girl to pay any attention to me. Mr. Jenkins probably didn't even notice the little bit of pay I drew."

"He noticed. He can tell you to the penny just how much he's got in the bank, and he'd as soon lose blood as to spend it. That's how all them old ranchers got rich . . . Mr. Jenkins, C. C. Tarpley. They never would spend anything 'til it was a case of life and death."

"Daddy always said he respected men who knew how to hold their money together."

"I respect them, too. I just don't want to be like them. Money is made to buy things with."

"I'd like to save enough money to get me a ranch some-day like the one Mr. Jenkins just bought."

"You've already got a place, you and your daddy and mama."

"But it was them that put it together. And you. I know you've sent them money, Uncle Hewey. I want to do the same thing they did, but I want to do it myself. When I have my own place I want to know it was my doin', not somebody else's."

"That'll be hard, workin' for cowboy wages."

"Not if I save them. Not if I know where I'm goin' and what I want to do when I get there." His face went solemn. "Me and Skip, we talked a lot. He had the same kind of idea. We even talked about goin' partners so we could get there quicker. He didn't get his chance, but I'm goin' to have mine."

Hewey smiled. "I'll bet you will. If there's anything I can do to help you along the way . . ."

"You can teach me everything you know."

"There's some things your mama wouldn't approve of."

"Even those. I need to know it all."

Maybe they should have gone to Pecos City, Hewey thought. But Tommy had plenty of time to learn about the dark side. It would be better if first he knew the sunshine.

Hewey just wished somebody else would do the teaching.

He was tempted to drop in on Upton City before they went to the homestead. The thought of a drink at Dutch Schnei-der's bar brought his tongue to his lips in imagined plea-sure. But Eve's eyes would freeze him all the way to his toes if she knew he had exposed her younger son to that sort of atmosphere. Schneider was a kind and gentle man but socially tainted by the fact that his occupation was dis-pensing whiskey. It had always struck Hewey odd that womenfolks could attach more blame to those who sold it than to those who drank it. Possibly it was because their husbands, fathers and brothers were among the latter.

A long, flat-topped hill in the distance was the first landmark to show that they were approaching the Calloway homestead. They came to the field, where a soft southwest wind rustled sorghum feed nearly waist-high. Hewey said, "Looks like your daddy got the plantin' done without you."

"Probably hired Lester to help him."

"If he did, it was your daddy done most of the work."

Lester the nester boy was locally known for putting on a show of exertion while expending a minimum of effort. He was habitually the last to reach for a pick or shovel, usually after someone else had taken it up. He would manage a rueful look at the missed opportunity, but he also managed not to break a sweat unless it was in a race to dinner.

Across the field, moving toward them, a man rode a cultivator drawn by a pair of mules. Hewey had to squint. "Looks like your daddy comin' now."

Tommy tensed. Hewey suspected his nephew had been dreading the first confrontation with his parents. He had left home without a by-your-leave.

Walter halted the team at the end of the row and stepped down from the cultivator, wiping sweat from his face onto his sleeve as he walked toward the two horsemen. Every time Hewey saw his younger brother he was struck anew by the realization that the world had lost a good cowboy when Walter decided to become a stock farmer, molding his hands to fit a plow handle instead of bridle reins. He retained none of his cowboy appearance anymore. With his shapeless old hat, his patched and faded overalls and his dirt-encrusted brogans, he looked like what he was, a sunburned, wind-punished, overworked man of the soil, carrying on his gaunt shoulders the kind of heavy responsibility Hewey had always shunned. He was a man of property, certainly, but in Hewey's view property could be more a burden than a blessing.

Hewey said, "I brought back your wanderin' boy." He tried in vain to read his brother's eyes as Walter stared at his son.

Tommy dismounted from the dun horse and took a step toward his father, then stopped, not sure of himself. Hewey held his breath, wondering if the two would speak, if it might even have been a mistake to bring Tommy home.

Walter took two long strides and threw his arms around Tommy, pounding him on the back. "It's mighty good to see you, son." The voice cracked a little.

Hewey expelled the breath he had held in until his lungs ached. He let himself break into a grin.

Walter stepped back to observe his son at arm's length. "Can't see that you've growed any."

"I ain't been gone all that long."

"It seemed like a long time to us."

"How's . . . how's Mama?"

"All right. She'll be a lot better when she sees you." Walter looked at Hewey, who was just now at ease enough to dismount from Biscuit. "When she sees both of you."

I doubt she'll be all that tickled to see me, Hewey thought. Though she might or might not say so, she probably held him responsible for Tommy's leaving in the first place. She regarded Hewey's wanderlust as contagious. Her older son, Cotton, had left home to pursue a dream of finding a place in the new technological world of the automobile. He was working now in a San Angelo garage, repairing cars. Tommy could take automobiles or leave them alone, but he had some of Hewey's restless spirit, an itch to see for himself what lay on the other side of the hill.

Walter looked at the sun, still a couple of hours short of setting. "You-all go on to the house. I need to use up the daylight."

Tommy offered, "I'll take over for you. You can ride Dunny and go in with Uncle Hewey."

Hewey knew Tommy was nervous about the reception

awaiting him from his mother, though his father's welcome had been warm. Hewey was uncertain, too.

Walter understood. "No, son, when you've got a dose of medicine to take, best thing is to swallow it the quickest you can." Humor flickered in his eyes. "Besides, if she lights into anybody, it's liable to be your uncle Hewey."

Hewey winced. Walter was teasing, but he might be closer to the truth than he knew.

Walter said, "Tell her I'm liable to be late, so you-all go on and eat supper without me."

Hewey suspected his brother was glad for the excuse not to go in right now. If a storm awaited, he would be better off riding the cultivator, out of earshot.

Hewey dreaded facing Eve without Walter being on hand to give him at least a modicum of moral support. But chances were that if Walter saw she was in an ill humor he would retreat to the barn anyway and leave Hewey and Tommy to face judgment alone. Years of marriage had taught him the signs.

Looking toward the house and its three big chinaberry trees, which had grown up from saplings he had helped plant many years ago, Hewey touched his spurs gently to Biscuit's sides. His thoughts ran to San Juan Hill. He had missed that battle. He wished he could miss this one.

A little surprised, he said, "Looks like everything's been painted since I was here."

"Last fall," Tommy replied. "Our yearlin's brought more than we expected, so Daddy decided we ought to paint the house and barns before they fell down around us."

The plain box-and-strip house was white, the barn red. They had not painted the windmill tower and cypress fan, though. Surely that would not have required much extra paint. To Hewey, a well-painted windmill added a smart touch to a place, made it look up-and-coming like those on C. C. Tarpley's ranch. Maybe if they had a little paint left over he would do it himself, though ordinarily he tried to avoid work he could not do on horseback.

Aside from the paint job, he could not see that much had changed. The chicken pen had been enlarged a bit, and Walter had added a couple of corrals. It was still a nester outfit at bottom and a stranger to real prosperity, but at least it looked like Walter and Eve were finally on their way up.

Tommy and Cotton's black dog was old now, but his bark had not diminished. He trotted out from underneath the house and challenged the horses. He had always barked at Hewey, no matter how many times Hewey fed or petted him. The dog often tangled with coyotes that came snooping around the chicken pen at night. Hewey had long hoped he would run up against one with sharper teeth than his own; it would serve the dumb mutt right. But the worst that ever happened to him was an occasional unfortunate spraying by a skunk.

When Tommy stepped down the dog sniffed at him, recognized the scent and went into a wild display of joy. But when Hewey moved close, the animal barked at him.

"If I was you," he told Tommy, "I'd swap that dog for a one-eyed tomcat. You'd have the best of the trade."

They unsaddled the horses and turned them loose in a corral beside the barn. Tommy fetched oats in a bucket and poured them into a trough. Biscuit tried to edge Dunny out of the way so he could have the oats to himself, but Dunny circled the trough and took his share from the opposite side. Biscuit nipped at him, then gave up and tried simply to eat faster.

Sharing was a human concept, not contagious to horses.

Hewey put his saddle on a rack beneath a shed where no horse or mule could gnaw on it. He watched Tommy carefully rack his own saddle and hang his bridle on a hook placed on the wall for that purpose. Tommy knelt down to pet the dog.

Hewey said, "We've stalled about as long as we can."

Tommy looked toward the house with a mixture of hope and dread. "Reckon so. We'd just as well go and see what the medicine tastes like." He started forth, the dog trotting happily beside him.

Hewey saw a vague movement through the screen door and knew Eve had seen them coming. He had rather they would have surprised her, for then she would not have had time to prepare a sermon. He carefully scraped his feet in case he had stepped in something unnoticed at the barn, and held the screen open for Tommy. Ordinarily he would have waited for his nephew to do the honors, but this was no time for such deference.

"Go ahead," he said. "I'm behind you."

"Make sure you're not too far behind me."

Eve stood in the kitchen, to one side of the big Majestic iron stove. Her hands were on her hips, not a good sign in Hewey's opinion. The glare of sunlight through a window behind her obscured her face, so he could not see her expression or what was in her eyes.

Tommy's voice faltered. "I'm home, Mama."

Eve stared at her son for a moment that seemed an hour, then enveloped him in her arms. "I'm glad, son, real glad."

Hewey's shoulders slumped in relief. Right now, if he were at Schneider's bar, he could down a double shot of whiskey in one swallow.

Eve held her son at arm's length. "You look like you've grown a foot."

"Daddy didn't think I've changed at all."

"Your daddy probably had the sun in his eyes." Her own eyes blinked a lot. "At least you found your way home."

"Uncle Hewey knew the best way."

"I'm sure he was a world of help."

Hewey was not certain whether she meant it or was being sarcastic. With Eve it was often hard to tell.

She said, "You must be starved half to death, son. I'll start some supper."

"I'm fine, Mama. Me and Uncle Hewey, we've been eatin' mighty good." That was a shameful stretch of the truth. They had eaten little on the trail that could not be boiled in a can or broiled at the end of a stick. But Hewey did not contradict him. This was no time to compromise a reception that had turned out much better than he expected.

Eve turned finally to Hewey. "Thanks for bringin' him home." She smiled at him, which he thought must have taken some doing.

Hewey shrugged. "I was comin' this way anyhow."

"Bet you thought I was goin' to raise Billy Hell with both of you."

"Why, no. We knew everything was goin' to be just fine."

At the supper table, Walter asked, "You plannin' to stay, Hewey?"

Hewey dropped a third spoon of sugar into his coffee and stirred it. "Maybe a week or so. We got a job to do for Mr. Jenkins."

He explained that he was to pick up twenty broncs Fat Gervin had sold to the J Bar but that Jenkins was in no big hurry about getting them.

Walter stopped a forkful of beans halfway to his mouth. "Never knew Fat to trade in horses. But since C.C.'s health began failin', Fat's taken over just about everything C.C. owns. Reckon he's lookin' to make money everywhere he can."

Hewey snorted. "He wouldn't know a good horse if it bit him on the . . ."—he looked at Eve—"on the neck."

It was generally agreed around Upton City that if Fat Gervin had not married C. C. Tarpley's daughter and thus acquired an inside track toward someday inheriting the old man's money, he would probably be eking out a living swamping for saloons or doing something that offered similarly poor prospects. He had slouched his way to failure at everything else he had tried, including a foredoomed effort at being a cowboy.

Hewey said, "I'll ride over to Upton City tomorrow and ask Fat when he wants to deliver the broncs."

Eve was suddenly concerned. "Walter had better go with you. Every time you and Fat get close to one another, somethin' unpleasant comes of it."

"I don't see what could go wrong. This is strictly a business deal between Fat and Mr. Jenkins. All I'm doin' is carryin' the mail. Anyway, Walter's got his plowin' to do."

Eve frowned. "I just don't want to see you get into a fight with Fat."

"You ain't havin' trouble with the note on this place, are you?"

"No, we're all right now, but you never know when you may need to be on good terms with a banker."

"The only reason Fat's a banker is that C. C. Tarpley says so. But I'll watch myself. I'll bend over backwards to be nice to the son of a bitch. Beggin' your pardon . . ."

Eve pretended she had not heard. A respectable woman was not supposed to be familiar with such an expression, and to acknowledge it would be tacit admission that she was. But Hewey had heard her use it herself on occasions of stress.

He said, "I may circle by Alvin Lawdermilk's place afterwards. That might be where the broncs are at."

Eve looked him square in the eye. "It's still where Spring Renfro is at, too."

Hewey squirmed. "You don't reckon she holds it against me, leavin' the way I did? She told me herself that I ought to go."

"What else could she say? She knew you'd leave anyhow. She just tried to ease your conscience, if you had one."

"It was about the hardest thing I ever done, but it was best for both of us. I wasn't cut out to marry like Walter and turn myself into a farmer. And I couldn't drag her around from one cowpunchin' job to another."

"She would've been happy for you to keep on bein' a cowpuncher so long as you lit in one place and stayed put."

"The milk's a long time spilt, so there's no use in talkin' about it."

"No, there isn't. She's found somebody else."

Hewey looked up sharply. "Who?"

"A nice young fellow . . . widower who went to work as a foreman on Alvin's ranch after Alvin began gettin' stove-up."

"I didn't know Alvin was ailin'."

"Not ailin', exactly, just can't do all the work he used to. It comes to everybody eventually, even to fiddle-footed cowboys."

He knew that was aimed at him. "I'm doin' just fine."

"Sure you are. Those lines in your face are just sun grins. And I saw you catch at your side while you were walkin' toward the house."

Hewey did not realize he had done it. The last bronc he had broken had touched off an internal ache that kept coming back, slipping up on him when he did not expect it. But what if he did have a few miscellaneous aches and pains? He had earned every one of them fair and square.

Eve had a way of making him feel guilty even when he was as innocent as a newborn calf. It almost ruined his appetite, for he refilled his plate only once and didn't eat but six biscuits and two helpings of dried-apple cobbler.

He could not see a nickel's worth of change in Upton City, or perhaps a dime. It still fell far short of being a city despite the name. He noticed a couple of new houses, but that did not represent any wild spurt of growth, considering how long he had been gone. The only two-story building was the square stone courthouse topped by a domed cupola, tallest thing in town, taller even than the windmills that stood beside or behind almost every house. Locals liked to tell gullible city folks passing through that there were so many windmills they sucked up all the wind on slow days and left the air dead-still on the downwind side of town.

He looked toward the plain, all-business stone structure of the Tarpley Bank and Trust. He thought about going there first, but instead he angled Biscuit across to Schneider's saloon. A good stiff drink might make the sight of Fat Gervin a little less disagreeable. Once they got past discussion of the weather and wishing it would rain, he could not remember that he and Fat had ever agreed on anything of consequence. The only thing fatter than Gervin's broad butt was his head.

Hewey knew of no one who really liked Fat unless it would be his wife, and sometimes he wondered about her. Once in a while, for a moment or two, Hewey could bring himself to feel sorry for the man, but he would remember some past incident and the sympathy would disappear, leaving no trace.

A truck was parked just past the saloon. Beside it stood a familiar figure with a wrench in his hand, staring in frustration at the engine. Steam boiled into the clear air and disappeared.

Hewey shouted, "Howdy, Blue Hannigan! If it was a horse or a mule, you'd just shoot it."

The freighter looked around, recognition spreading a broad grin across his grease-smeared face. He and Hewey had worked as cowboys together years ago before Hannigan decided to marry and take on the burdens of a respectable family man. He made a show of throwing the wrench at Hewey but held on to it. "Just when I thought the day had turned about as bad as it could get, look who showed up."

Biscuit eyed Hannigan warily, still taking the wrench as a personal threat. Hannigan reached out with the other hand, covered with black grease. Hewey did not hesitate to grasp it, grease and all. He shook vigorously, for old cowboy friends were still the best of all.

Hewey said, "It's God's punishment for you takin' up with the machine age. I never saw a mule steam like that."

"I wish I'd never laid eyes on any machine more complicated than a wheelbarrow, but times change. A truck can travel a whole lot faster than mules and a wagon."

"Not when it's broke down. Maybe a drink would make things look better to you."

"Couldn't make them look no worse. You buyin', or have I got to?"

"I'll set them up. That truck probably keeps you broke, and us cowboys get paid real good."

"That ain't how I remember it." The freighter jerked his head toward the saloon. He drew back the wrench. Hewey thought for a moment he was going to throw it at the engine, but Hannigan pitched it into the bed of the truck. He was not destructive of property, especially his own.

When Hewey's eyes accustomed themselves to the dim interior of the saloon, he saw Dutch Schneider walking toward the bar from the back, where a skinny old man sat hunched over a small table, a bottle and glass in front of him.

Hewey plunked fifty cents on the bar and said, "Dutch, you got anything fit for two hardworkin' men to drink? One, anyway. I ain't sure about Blue."

"Hewey Calloway! So long I have not seen you, it wondered me if they had buried you and I had missed the funeral." Laughing, Schneider walked behind the bar and poured two shot glasses full. "For two good friends, the best in the house."

The genuineness of his welcome warmed Hewey even before he tasted the whiskey. He could not understand why some people in Upton City were always down on Schneider, who had drifted into town years ago from somewhere down in the Hill Country German settlements. He was a quiet, dignified man, much more tolerant than those who criticized him. He attended the local Baptist church on Sundays, though some of the local women whispered that they believed he was a Lutheran, or possibly even worse, a Catholic. But he ran a clean place and sold clean whiskey. That was recommendation enough for Hewey.

Hewey enjoyed the gentle burn as the drink went down, and the glow that followed it. He turned, facing toward the rear of the room. "Tell me that ain't C. C. Tarpley back yonder."

Tarpley had always been slight of build and looked as if he might have to carry rocks in his pockets to keep the wind from blowing him away. Even so, he appeared to have shrunk.

Concern came into Schneider's eyes. "It is indeed Mr. Tarpley. Often he comes here and sits. He does not drink much, he just sits. I think he waits to die."

Hewey found the concept difficult to accept. "Old C.C. never was sick a day in his life."

Hannigan said quietly, "He's sick now. I ain't sure if it's in his heart or in his head, but either way it's slowly killin' him." He leaned in as if to share a dark secret. "You remember the time Old Man Adcock and C.C. had a hell of a fight in front of the bank? Well, sir, the old man had a note comin' due on that little shop of his a couple of weeks ago and asked for an extension. C.C. said he'd do better than that. He tore up the note. Said he put more value on Adcock's friendship than on the money. No, sir, he sure ain't the C.C. we used to know."

C. C. Tarpley had his faults, but holding grudges was not one of them. He also had his virtues, but generosity was not one of those—at least it hadn't been.

Hewey asked, "What did Fat think, since he's supposed to be runnin' the bank?"

"You could hear him holler halfway across town." Hannigan chuckled, remembering. "I'd best be gettin' back to business. I've got a haul to make if I can bluff that truck into runnin'."

Hewey shook his head. "Job the spurs to it."

"Fat holds the note. I've got half a mind to turn the truck over to him, but he'd probably bust a blood vessel. I'd hate to have his dyin' on my conscience."

After Hannigan left, Hewey studied the racehorse pictures that covered the wall behind the bar. Most bars of this kind were more likely to feature pictures of women in scanty dress or no dress at all. Schneider loved horses like many old bachelors loved women, from afar. Hewey had never seen him on horseback.

He considered another drink but decided against it. Though the bronc deal was made and he had no reason to match wits with Fat Gervin, he thought it wise to have all his wits about him. Unlike his father-in-law, Fat never turned loose of a grudge, and Hewey in the past had given him grounds enough to stay mad until he was a hundred and six.

Hewey moved back to the table where the old man sat staring off into nothing, his mind far away. "C.C.?"

Tarpley looked up in surprise. "Hewey! Didn't know you was anywhere in the country." He shoved an arthritic hand forward and motioned for Hewey to take a chair.

The voice was thinner than Hewey remembered it. He had always thought C.C. looked old, but now he appeared absolutely aged. "Just got into town."

"I'll buy you a drink."

"Already had one, thanks. I'm fixin' to go see Fat . . . Frank."

When the old man was on decent terms with his son-in-law, he called him Frank. When he was on the outs, he referred to him as Fat, like everybody else.

"What you need to see Frank about? Your brother's got himself in good shape over at the bank."

Hewey explained that he was representing Morgan Jenkins, who had bought a string of broncs from Fat . . . Frank.

Tarpley seemed puzzled. "Now where would Frank get

broncs to sell? We don't raise any except what we need for our own usin' at the ranch."

"I reckon he's took up horse tradin'."

"Dangerous business, horse tradin'. It can get you in more trouble than a case of bad whiskey." His eyes were weepy, as if something in the air disagreed with him. "You lookin' for a cowpunchin' job?"

"Already got one, out in the mountains."

"Never did like the mountains. Give me the flats every time. If you fall, it ain't far down."

Hewey was hesitant to ask Tarpley what was troubling him. In the first place, it was none of Hewey's business, and the C.C. he used to know would tell him so in no uncertain terms. In the second place, he probably could not help anyway. C. C. Tarpley had always been too proud to appreciate sympathy. Tougher than whang leather, he had come to the dry Pecos River country while the departing Comanches' tracks were still fresh, cut out a goodly chunk of range for himself and held it against cattle thieves, drought, lawyers, bankers and other hazards of the ranching trade. The one thing he had not been able to beat was the long succession of calendars that changed over his desk year after year.

C.C.'s eyes bored into Hewey until Hewey felt uncomfortable. He had punched cattle for Tarpley in the past and might again if circumstances demanded it, but he would rather not. Like Jenkins, Tarpley was close with a dollar. His idea of liberality was to bring a couple of watermelons to camp a time or two during summer. That was why his canceling of Old Man Adcock's debt seemed so unlikely. He said, "I worry about you, Hewey."

"About me?"

"Life is short. I'm findin' that out for myself. I'm afraid you'll come to the end of yours and not leave anything to show for it."

"I've had a lot of experiences and made a lot of friends."

"But what'll you be leavin' behind?"

"A lot of experiences and a lot of friends."

"That don't count for much on the ledgers down at the bank."

"I don't read ledgers *now*. I sure won't be interested in them after they salt me away."

"Don't make light of it. Death ain't no small thing."

Hewey saw an opening to ask the question. "How come all this worry about dyin'? I don't imagine the angels are in a hurry to receive me or you either one."

"It's comin' whether we're ready or not, and I ain't sure it's the angels that's waitin' for us. I've got a pain in my gut, eatin' away at me. It's tellin' me to get myself ready."

"You been to a doctor?"

"These pill merchants around here? Ain't nothin' they can do when it's your time except sell you patent medicine and drain your purse."

Hewey had had his differences with Tarpley over the years, but he had always liked the old man. Though Tarpley's principal motivation had been personal enrichment, he had helped to build the country in his own perverse way. Hewey had no quarrel with people who wanted to better their own condition. In the process they often bettered the condition of others around them.

Hewey said, "Maybe if you'd go to a doctor somewhere like Kansas City or Chicago they could help you. Even Fort Worth. I always had a good time in Fort Worth."

"I don't mind so much for myself. It's my daughter I worry most about, her married to Frank Gervin. You know and I know, Hewey, he ain't no hand."

Hewey had no argument there. When it came to cattle and horses, Fat Gervin was about as useless as a fifth wheel on a wagon. "I'm afraid I can't be no help to you. Anybody who could make a hand of Fat could probably walk on water."

"Left on his own, he'll likely run through the bank and the ranch both before the grass takes hold over my grave."

Tarpley started to pour whiskey into his glass but set the

bottle back down, his attention drifting away. Hewey stood up. "I'm sorry to find you feelin' poorly, C.C. I do wish you'd go someplace and hunt up a good doctor."

Tarpley did not respond. Hewey was not sure the old man even heard him. He walked back to the bar, where Schneider was reading a newspaper. He subscribed to several. Dutch Schneider and Alvin Lawdermilk were the best-read men in the county. They could name just about every king, president and major knave on the international scene.

Hewey said, "I always thought he was too ornery to die."

Schneider looked toward Tarpley. "He still is. I think when the time comes, he will not go."

6

Hewey stopped just outside the saloon door and looked down the dirt street. Blue Hannigan still tinkered with the truck's engine, using the same bristling language he often employed against recalcitrant mules. Sometimes the mules responded and sometimes they did not. The truck remained indifferent.

Hewey turned toward the bank, resolving to state his business to Fat Gervin and get out as quickly as he could. He tried to regard it as a challenge, like riding a new bronc, for he had always found a certain exhilaration in that sort of contest. But he saw nothing exhilarating about C. C. Tarpley's son-in-law.

When he walked into the bank, he was not surprised to see that Gervin was in. The high ceilings and tall, open windows kept the stone building fairly cool, and Gervin much preferred to spend his time indoors rather than be out on the ranch, where the sun was hot and sweat labor plentiful. His desk was cluttered with paper, indicating work deferred. Fat had always believed in putting off until tomorrow that which did not absolutely have to be done today. The desk was behind a low wooden fence meant to keep the clientele from getting too close to the money.

Taking Hewey to be a potential customer, Gervin stood up, turning on his best come-spend-it-with-us smile. Recognition killed the welcome. Gervin sat down heavily, his chubby cheeks sagging, his face taking on a sour look. "You back already?"

Hewey said, "Already? I been gone four years."

"It don't seem near long enough. I know you didn't come to put money in the bank. You never had twenty dollars at one time in your life."

Gervin never had forgiven Hewey for helping Walter and Eve save their stock farm from foreclosure or for other miscellaneous indignities suffered over the years at Hewey's hands.

Hewey said, "I'm here on business for Mr. Morgan Jenkins." He fished a letter from his shirt pocket and extended it across the desk into Fat's thick hands.

Fat frowned as he read. "Says here you're to receive the horses I sold him and take them back to Alpine. How come him to trust you with this much responsibility?"

"I'm the best hand he's got."

Fat snorted. "Must be mighty hard times around Alpine. What did he tell you about the horses?"

"Said they're of Alvin Lawdermilk's raisin'."

"I told him they came from Alvin's place. When do you want to get them?"

"He's not in a hurry. Told me to have a nice visit with the folks before I go back. I'll let you know when I'm ready."

"You do that. Now, I got business to attend to." He started shuffling papers.

He hadn't looked all that busy when Hewey came in, but Hewey had no interest in staying any longer. "Then I'll mosey along. Adios, Fat."

Gervin's voice soured more. "I almost shook off that

nickname once. I ain't forgot that you're the one who hung it on me again."

It had happened so long ago, Hewey had almost forgotten. He and Walter had been working on C. C. Tarpley's ranch. Frank Gervin had been on the payroll too, but he could hardly be accused of working. The minute Tarpley was out of sight Gervin would head for the shade, look for something to eat or sweet-talk Tarpley's daughter. Hewey never had figured out what she saw in him. These days she probably wondered, too.

Fat was widely reputed to have a roving eye, though his romantic notions usually came to naught. Whatever seductive charms he might once have had he had used up in winning Tarpley's daughter and carving his initials on the Tarpley inheritance.

Hewey had used the boyhood nickname in an attempt to shame Gervin out of the kitchen and away from the shade, but it had only won him Gervin's enmity. He had no particular regrets about that. A man was known by his enemies as well as by the friends he kept. Around here it was a mark of honor to be disliked by Fat Gervin.

Hewey stepped out into the sunshine, his brief ordeal over. He looked across the street toward a store whose modest sign, almost hidden beneath gingerbread trim, read PHELPS GENERAL MERCANTILE AND SUNDRIES. Though he did not need anything, he would buy some smoking tobacco. The genial Pierson Phelps always treated him like company whether he had spending money or not, but Hewey liked to give him a little business when he could. He had spent four bits with Dutch Schneider. Pierson Phelps deserved no less.

Hewey noticed a wagon and team in front of the store but thought little of it. Farmers and ranchers around Upton City depended upon Phelps for supplies. If they were old-timers, Hewey would enjoy a chance to say howdy. If they were newcomers, he would enjoy a chance to meet them and say welcome. Nobody remained a stranger long around Hewey Calloway.

The gray-haired Phelps came out the front door, carrying a box of groceries. A tall cowboy of forty or so followed with another box, placing it in the bed of the wagon. Phelps brightened as Hewey strode casually toward him. "Look who's here. We see more of Halley's comet than we see of you, Hewey Calloway."

The cowboy seemed to know the name, for he turned abruptly to look. Hewey did not recognize him, however.

Hewey said to Phelps, "You still peddlin' grub? I thought you'd be rich by now and mayor of some big city like Midland or San Angelo, livin' in the lap of luxury."

"I decided my first million wasn't enough. I'll stay 'til I make my second." Phelps turned to the tall cowboy. "Hewey, meet Farley Neal. He's Alvin Lawdermilk's foreman."

Neal gave Hewey a firm and friendly handshake. "I've heard about you."

"Not from Fat Gervin, I hope."

"Yes, but mostly from your friends. You've got a lot of them, seems like."

Hewey tried to remember what he had heard about Alvin's new foreman. "Somebody told me Alvin's stove-up."

"Just enough that he needed somebody to take part of the load off of him. He's wrestled too many rough broncs and too many iron-jawed mules. They've caught up with him."

It wasn't just the horses and mules that had caught up with Alvin, Hewey knew; it was whiskey. "I need to go by and auger with him. Me and Alvin have had some good times together."

"He'll be tickled. He talks about you."

Phelps said, "Come on into the store, Hewey. It's warm out here in the sun."

Hewey stepped up onto the wooden sidewalk and halted in mid-stride. A thin woman in her thirties ventured into the doorway and stopped abruptly, looking at him in surprise.

Hewey's jaw dropped. Words ran through his head but would not come off his tongue. He could only stammer.

Spring Renfro seemed equally flustered, a tiny smile so quickly come and so quickly gone he was not sure he had really seen it. Her trembly voice was barely audible. "Hello, Hewey."

"Spring," he managed, then grasped for propriety. "Miss Renfro."

She usually gave people the impression of tallness, though the top of her head would barely reach Hewey's chin. Her thinness exaggerated her height.

Hewey did not know whether to step closer or turn and go. But there was no question of going. His boots seemed nailed to the sidewalk. He could only stare, warmth rushing to his face. He knew he looked like an idiot. For certain, he felt like one.

Her composure regained, she made two short steps toward him and held out her hand. Hesitantly he took it and gave her a weak handshake.

She spoke with reserve, as she might in being introduced to a stranger. "You look well, Hewey."

She looked better than well. To him, she looked wonderful. He wanted to tell her so, but all that came was "Mighty pleased to see you." An idiot could have done better, he thought.

He would have been prepared had he seen her at Alvin Lawdermilk's ranch, where she taught school for children of the Lawdermilk neighbors. He would have expected her there. But here she had taken him unawares and put him into shock.

Often on quiet nights he had thought of her when he sat beside a fire alone or when he rode in the mountains and let his mind dwell upon horseback rides they had taken together during the time he was contemplating marriage. Eventually he had reached a point where the pleasure of old memories outweighed the sense of loss they brought. He had thought he had come to an accommodation years ago with his decision to choose freedom to roam rather than the confining responsibilities of married life.

Now the years fell away in an instant, and his convictions about the rightness of old decisions lay in shambles at his feet. He stood as if hypnotized.

She seemed to wait for him to say something. When he did not, she asked, "Did you meet Farley Neal?"

Hewey nodded, his tongue stuck to the roof of his mouth.

It came to him then, something Eve had told him. She said Spring had found someone, a widower who had become foreman at the Lawdermilks'. He forcibly put down a fleeting resentment. He had given up any claim on Spring Renfro the day he bid her good-bye and rode away seeking adventure with Snort Yarnell. She had every right to happiness wherever she might find it.

He could put away the resentment but not the unexpected pain of seeing her with someone else.

She said, "Mr. Phelps, I believe we still have one box of supplies on the counter."

Hewey broke his silence. "I'll fetch it." That gave him an excuse to move away from her, to collect his wits. Perhaps by the time he came back outside he would be able to wipe that deaf-and-dumb look from his face and say something that would not sound simpleminded. He paused, both hands on the box, and squeezed his eyes shut in an effort to stop their burning. He walked back out into the sunlight, trying not to look into Spring's blue eyes but unable to help himself.

He watched Neal help her up onto the wagon seat and told himself Neal was a lucky man.

Spring looked down at Hewey. Her voice was formal. "Are you home to stay?"

He swallowed, throat dry. "No, just got a little business. Soon as it's done I'll be leavin'."

"Alvin will be disappointed if you don't visit with him before you go."

Neal said, "Glad to've met you, Hewey," and set the team into motion. Hewey could not take his eyes from the wagon until it disappeared beyond the courthouse. Spring did not look back in his direction.

Phelps finally spoke. "Mighty fine woman, Miss Renfro."

Hewey cleared his throat. "As fine as ever was."

"Farley Neal's a good man. They make a handsome couple."

"Where'd he come from?"

"He was foreman a while on C. C. Tarpley's ranch, but Fat Gervin kept tellin' him what to do. He either had to quit or whip Fat, so he left."

"Anybody who can't get along with Fat is all right with me. They fixin' to marry?"

"I've heard nothing definite, but everybody here expects that they will." Phelps squinted one eye. "You thinkin' about putting in a claim on her again?"

Hewey shoved his hands into his pockets. "If I ever had a claim, I gave it up a long time ago. You say Neal's a good man?"

"Reminds me a lot of your brother Walter . . . solid, serious, hard-workin'."

Hewey swallowed again. "Everything I never was. I reckon I'm glad for Spring." He turned away.

Phelps said, "Aren't you comin' in?"

"No, I've got to go back and talk to Fat."

He walked into the bank and made directly for Gervin's desk. Gervin looked up, displeased. "You forget somethin'?"

"No, changed my mind about a long visit. How quick can you have them broncs ready for me?"

Eve did not take the news with good grace. "Leavin'?" she demanded. She put away her sewing and faced Hewey with her hands on her hips. "What do you mean, you're leavin' the day after tomorrow? You said you and Tommy were stayin' a couple of weeks."

Hewey averted his eyes. "Fat's anxious to get rid of them broncs."

It always amazed him the way a woman could sense the truth no matter how good a liar a man thought he was. She said, "You saw Spring Renfro. Now you're afraid if you stay around you won't be able to leave her again."

Denial was useless, so Hewey did the next best thing. He sidestepped. "I didn't say Tommy was goin' with me. I figured once he got home he might decide to stay here." He had hoped so, anyway.

Tommy said, "You can't drive those ponies to Alpine by yourself. Besides, you promised to teach me all I need to know."

"I never promised no such a thing. You said that, not me."

"You didn't say you wouldn't."

"But when Skip got killed, you wanted real bad to get away from that place."

"You made me stay and face it, so I already put the worst of it behind me. I can take it now."

Eve argued, "You don't have to trail after your Uncle Hewey to God knows where. If it's a job you want, you can get one here with Alvin Lawdermilk, or even C. C. Tarpley. At least you'd be close to home."

"But that's what's the matter. I'd be too close. I need to learn to make it on my own without you and Daddy always standin' there to catch me if I fall."

"Won't Uncle Hewey be doin' the same thing?"

"He lets me fall. Says I learn more that way, and it's good for my character."

Hewey said, "If it's fallin' you want, you can do it here at home. Out yonder, them rocks are sharp and hard."

Tommy did not budge. Walter watched and listened, saying nothing. Hewey suspected he sided with his son, for he had not always been the homebound farmer he was now.

Walter could understand what drove a boy like Tommy, eager to know the world, though he would await the proper moment before saying so. Hewey could leave, but Walter had to keep on living with Eve.

She turned to Hewey, her eyes stinging. "I wish I knew what would cure that restless streak in you, because it's contagious. You gave it to my oldest son, and now Tommy's caught it."

That was not exactly the straight of it. Cotton had always been intrigued by things mechanical, so the farm could not hold him when he came to his time. He would have left with or without Hewey's influence. Tommy was different. He had always been more comfortable with a life tied to the soil and the seasons, to the grass and the animals, but he wanted a bigger bite of it than the home place could give him. He might indeed have caught some of that from his uncle, who had inherited itchy feet from his own improvident father.

Hewey suggested, "Tommy, why don't you wait 'til you get a couple more years on you? Everything'll still be out there, waitin'."

"*You* may not still be out there, the kind of life you lead."

Hewey and Tommy left the farm at sunup, cutting across country toward the C. C. Tarpley ranch, where Fat was to have the broncs ready for delivery. Eve's demeanor had been frosty, and Hewey could not blame her. He too wished Tommy would stay home. It was a burdensome thing, being saddled with responsibility for a youngster so closely kin, yet not his own.

Tommy said, "I wish we hadn't had to be in such a hurry. Daddy's lookin' tired. I was goin' to finish that south field for him."

"You could stay here awhile and go back to the ranch later." Maybe if Tommy remained a couple of weeks he would decide not to leave at all.

"I hired out to do a job of work, and I'll stick to it like you've taught me."

They were not long in reaching the outer perimeter of the Tarpley ranch, for it spread across a major portion of the county and lapped over into the next. C.C. had kept adding to it, buying out homesteaders as they finished proving up their claims on state and school lands and became legally entitled to sell. Most had not found this part of the country hospitable to the plow because rainfall was too erratic. C.C. had tried several times to buy Walter out. Walter managed to make a crop of sorts most years, but only because he watered the land with his own sweat. Had he not been grazing a herd of cows and a few brood mares on the place for extra income, he probably would not have survived, and the Tarpley range would have expanded by eight more sections.

Tommy said, "Daddy always talked like C. C. Tarpley was a hard man to work for."

"He just had his own ways, and once you learned what they were, you could get along with him all right. He never liked for a cowboy to see the sunrise through a window, or the sunset either. He wanted you out workin' as long as there was daylight to see by. But he would generally be there with you. Wasn't like some I've worked for, that sent you out and then went back to the house."

"Like Fat Gervin?"

"I can call him Fat because I'm as old as he is, and I don't owe him nothin'. You'd better call him Mr. Gervin, at least 'til your folks have their land all paid out."

"He came near gettin' it once, that time Daddy got his leg broke. If you hadn't stayed and taken Daddy's place . . . Mr. Gervin still holds a grudge against you, I think."

"His grudge goes back a long ways farther than that. When C.C. got mad he'd forget about it in a day or two. But Fat's got a memory like an elephant."

"At least he ain't dangerous. He couldn't whip an old man on crutches."

"That's what *does* make him dangerous. He'll figure some way to come at you from behind and hit you when you're not lookin'. Give me an honest fightin' man every time. If you can't whip him, you may be able to outrun him."

The Tarpley headquarters was imposing, its centerpiece a large two-story white frame house standing on a slight knoll, surrounded by tall chinaberry trees. Their upper reaches extended higher than the roof. Chinaberries also formed a circle around a nearby surface tank, nurtured by its constant supply of water. Hewey recalled that the tank was stocked with catfish, supposedly for C.C.'s own use, though he never seemed to have time to wet a hook. Fat Gervin fished there when he was certain his father-in-law was miles away.

C.C. would be content to live in an adobe bunkhouse or even a dugout, but the late Mrs. Tarpley had insisted upon having a house in town and one on the ranch, with accommodations appropriate to their station in life. C.C. had an eye toward accumulation of land, cattle and capital. His wife had an eye toward architecture and landscaping.

The ranch house had been hers to furnish and maintain as she wished, but the rest of the place was C.C.'s personal domain. A broad layout of corrals, barns and sheds had been built to his utilitarian specifications. All in all, it was a pretty place, but Hewey could not remember that he had seen it often in the full light of day. He had usually left before the sun was up and did not return until night was settling in. C.C. got his money's worth whether he was buying land or labor.

Hewey saw horses in a large corral and reined Biscuit in that direction. A cowboy arose from a seat on the step that led up into the largest barn. He hailed them and slouched out partway to meet the incoming riders. Something about the way he moved reminded Hewey of Fat, though this man would have to put on fifty or seventy-five pounds to match Gervin's weight.

"Howdy." The cowboy had a loosely rolled cigarette dangling from his lower lip and talked around it rather than take it from his mouth. His shirttail was hanging out. "I suppose you'd be Hewey Calloway?"

"I was the last time I checked. Where's Fat?"

The cowboy nodded toward the large white house. "Mr. and Mrs. Gervin are up yonder. He said for me to turn them ponies yonder over to Hewey Calloway. You got anything to show that you're really him?"

Hewey felt a little annoyed that the cowboy doubted him. Everybody this side of San Angelo knew who he was, or ought to. This puncher must have come from someplace farther east, automatically a mark against him. "Call Fat. He'll know me."

The cowboy's frown said he had rather not. "If you say you're Hewey Calloway, I reckon I'll have to take your word for it." He pointed his thumb toward the barn. "The broncs are yonderway. I suppose you're in a hurry to get them started?"

Hewey looked up. The sun was moving toward noon, and he knew Tommy would be hungry. Boys always were. At most ranches they would be invited to stay for dinner. Even a Yankee-owned outfit would offer that much hospitality, and C. C. Tarpley was no Yankee. Hewey waited for the cowboy to say something, then did it himself. "We'll line them out right after dinner."

The cowboy remembered his manners, sort of. "Yeah, I reckon you would like to eat first. We'll see if the cook can rustle up a little somethin'." He did not look like somebody C.C. would keep on the payroll for long. He was probably a Fat Gervin protégé, Hewey thought. Old C.C. *must* be sick to turn loose of things this way.

He remembered the cook, a dour little fellow who seemed as devoted to thrift as C.C. himself when it came to buying groceries for the bunkhouse kitchen. He had gone to work for the ranch after Walter and Eve had left to take up their homestead. Before, Eve had operated the bunkhouse kitchen. It was often expected of a ranch foreman's wife that she cook for the hands without extra pay beyond her husband's salary. That was one reason she held to their homeplace with such a determined grip, for there she never had to cook for anyone again except her own if she did not want to.

The food was about as Hewey remembered it and reminded him of one major reason he had left C.C.'s employ. Without canned tomatoes the cook would have been at a total loss. They seemed to be in everything except the biscuits. For dessert he offered another biscuit and watery blackstrap molasses of a cheap brand so poor that Pierson Phelps refused to handle it in his store. C.C. got it from Midland. No wonder the cook looked as if he would not weigh a hundred pounds soaking wet.

"Mighty fine dinner," Hewey lied, turning to Tommy and the cowboy. Hewey could not remember the cowboy's name, or if it had even been offered. It didn't matter. Some people were meant to be forgotten as quickly as possible. "Let's be seein' about them broncs."

He realized before he reached the corral that something was awfully wrong. He climbed up on the plank fence, looking down among the horses in disbelief. He had never seen a sorrier-looking bunch of scrubs in his life.

"These ain't what Mr. Jenkins bought," he declared, turning to challenge the cowboy. "They're supposed to be from Alvin Lawdermilk's, and Alvin wouldn't give a day's grass to such as this."

The cowboy shrugged, all innocence and puzzlement. "I wouldn't know nothin' about that. All I know is that Mr. Gervin said these are the ones you're supposed to take."

"Like hell they are! They wouldn't make good soap."

They were a mixed lot of long-tailed mustangs, a couple of ewe-necked old geldings Hewey would bet were spoiled outlaws and one black stud that bared its teeth at any animal that dared come near. "What's Fat tryin' to pull?"

"I just work here. You'll have to talk to him about that."

"I'm fixin' to do that very thing!" Angrily Hewey jumped down from the fence. The impact sent pain lancing through his knees, but he paid little attention to that or the sudden hurting in his belly. Biscuit seemed to sense his agitation, for the brown horse lifted its head high, ears and eyes alert. Hewey swung onto its back, not waiting for Tommy to catch up. He put Biscuit into a long trot.

The Gervins had a home in town, but they freely used the Tarpley house when they were at the ranch. It would be theirs anyway when C.C. passed on to glory.

Fat must have been watching through a parlor window, for he came out onto the veranda and stood there, nonchalantly picking his teeth. Hewey would bet his meal had been a lot better than the one put up by the bunkhouse cook.

Fat's wife, Ellie, a frail-appearing little woman, stood just inside the screen door. Most people in town used to regard her as pretty, but Hewey had always suspected they were influenced more by her father's money than by her features. Even granting that she was good-looking, Hewey doubted that she had inherited old C.C.'s smarts, or she would not have wasted herself on Fat Gervin. Two children peeked out from behind her long skirt.

"Fat!" Hewey shouted. "What're you tryin' to get away with?"

"What's the matter? You don't like them horses?"

"They're supposed to be young broncs of Alvin Lawdermilk's raisin'. I'll bet Alvin never laid eyes on a one of them."

"I didn't say they were of his raisin'. I said they came from his ranch, and they did. They was driven right through it." He grinned in appreciation of his own cleverness.

"There's even a stud amongst them. They were all supposed to be geldin's."

"You've got a knife, ain't you? I don't see where it's any

skin off of your nose anyway. You said yourself, you're just a hired hand. The deal was between me and Jenkins."

"But I'm here in his interests, and I sure ain't interested in takin' him them snides you've got out yonder."

"Then he'll have to send somebody else, because those horses are his. I've already got the money."

Hewey dismounted and dropped the reins, knotting his fists as he strode toward the veranda steps. "Fat, you've had a good whippin' comin' to you for a long time."

The woman and children quickly disappeared into the darkness of the hall. Gervin stepped back into the doorway, then forward again. He leveled a shotgun at Hewey. "You take one more step, Hewey Calloway, and they'll tote you away from here in a box."

Hewey stopped short, a chill in his belly. The muzzle of that shotgun looked as wide as a milk bucket.

He choked, "I ain't armed." He never carried a gun because he considered them too dangerous, especially those assumed not to be loaded. He had an old pistol in his war bag back at the Jenkins ranch, but he had not cleaned it in so long that it could have a dirt-dauber nest in its barrel for all he knew.

Fat's hands shook. Ordinarily Hewey would not consider the man dangerous, but anybody that nervous was dangerous when he had a shotgun in his hands. "I'm phonin' the sheriff that you came out here and tried to provoke a fight. Now you get back in that saddle, Hewey, and you take them horses and git. If you ain't gone in ten minutes, I'll file on you for trespass."

Hewey feared he might accidentally squeeze the trigger. "I'm goin', but I ain't forgettin'. Just because Mr. Jenkins is old don't mean he's to be trifled with. And I ain't either."

Tommy's face was two shades paler than normal. The boy had never faced a gun before. Hewey had, but repetition did not make the experience easier. He said to Fat, "I don't suppose C.C. knows anything about this."

"It's my deal, not his. Now git!" Fat made a poking motion with the shotgun.

Hewey mounted and turned away, toward the corrals.

Tommy could hardly speak. "He'd've shot you."

"Not on purpose, but Fat's subject to accidents. Anytime a man points a shotgun at you, you better tell him he's right and you're wrong. There'll come another day."

The cowboy with no name opened the corral gate and helped push the horses out into the open. Hewey saw nothing to thank him for, so he did not speak as he and Tommy rode past and lined the horses out on the trail that led toward town. He would put them in a corral at the wagon yard tonight and talk to Sheriff Wes Wheeler. He doubted Wes could do anything, but it wouldn't hurt to talk. He considered talking to C. C. Tarpley also but decided against it. The old man had too many worries already.

He did not have to look up Wheeler. Wheeler came to meet him several miles from town, a big man riding a big horse. Wheeler's back was straight as a ramrod, his manner friendly but somewhat formal. He reined up and let Hewey come the last short distance to him. He frowned as the loose horses trotted past him, Tommy trailing. "Are these what all the fuss was about?"

"Wasn't much of a fuss to it. Fat throwed a shotgun on me, and the fuss was over with. Howdy, Wes."

"Howdy yourself, Hewey." Wheeler had a deep, commanding voice that could bring a roomful of drunks to immediate attention, and a handshake that could crush bones. "Fat told me his side of it over the telephone. What's yours?"

Hewey explained about the sale. "Mr. Jenkins was given to understand that they was of Alvin Lawdermilk's raisin', but they wouldn't fool a blind man."

Wheeler gave the horses another study. "I remember these skates. A ragged-britches horse trader brought them into town from way down on the Devil's River. I wondered what Fat was goin' to do with them."

"What he done was run them in as ringers on his deal with Mr. Jenkins. Can you do somethin' about it?"

Wheeler's mouth turned downward. "I wish I could, but this is a case for the lawyers to fight over. I expect Fat was real careful how he described the horses when he wrote his letter. He's gotten awful bold since C.C. took down with his miseries."

"I'd call this theft. Grand larceny, maybe."

"I can't argue the point, but I'm a sheriff, not a judge. Mr. Jenkins'll have to get a lawyer if he wants to fight the case."

"He's got a low opinion of lawyers. If he was younger, he'd just show up with a bullwhip and make Fat come to Jesus."

"And I couldn't blame him none, but this is 1910, and that's not the way folks do things anymore."

"More's the pity. I'd be sorely tempted to do it myself if I caught him without that shotgun."

"I couldn't allow it, Hewey. It's a matter for the court."

"There's more than one kind of court, and sooner or later Fat'll come up for judgment." Hewey grimaced. "Lord, I wish I didn't have to be there when Old Man Jenkins sees these horses."

7

The horses traveled easier than Hewey expected, probably because they had been trail-broken coming up from the lower country, so he was early in reaching the outskirts of Upton City. He looked at the sun and tried to judge how much daylight he could count upon.

"Wes," he said, "I believe we'll shoot for Walter's and Eve's before me and Tommy quit for the night. We'll circle around town."

That would probably spare the feelings of housewives who had freshly washed clothing hanging on their lines. Even a small band of horses could stir a lot of dust. They would also rouse up the town dogs and perhaps result in a stampede. There was no limit to the damage twenty frightened broncs could do.

Wheeler said, "I'll help you." Some of the complaints would surely be brought to him, so he was saving himself some aggravation.

If anyone should ask, Hewey would say he was simply trying to make all the miles he could, but the principal reason for avoiding town was that he did not want everybody to see this string of third-rate horseflesh and know how badly Fat had snookered him and his boss.

When they cleared the far edge of town Wheeler reined up. "I'll bid you adios, Hewey. Ain't no tellin' what crimes have been committed in my absence."

Hewey nodded toward the horses. "This one was bad enough."

"I wish there was more I could do. Nothin' would tickle me better than to have Fat be a guest in my jailhouse. But don't you do somethin' that'll put *you* in there. Or that boy yonder." He jerked a thumb toward Tommy.

Hewey said, "I've been a guest in a few jailhouses, but Eve would never let me hear the end of it if Tommy was to be locked up with me. Right now all I intend to do is deliver these horses . . . such as they are."

He got to watching the stud in particular, for the black displayed signs of antisocial behavior that bordered on the criminal, biting, kicking at every other horse it could reach. It even took a notion to charge at Biscuit, and Hewey had to beat it off with the doubled end of his rope. He strongly considered leaving the stud behind and telling Jenkins it had gotten away, like the bull he and Skip Harkness had released. But that would be a dirty trick to play on anybody whose good mares took up with this sorry excuse for crow bait.

Just at dusk Hewey saw the familiar homestead and loped ahead to open a corral gate. Walter spotted him coming and reached the gate first. "Thought you might not come back by," he said.

"I hope Eve has got over bein' provoked at me. I been tastin' her biscuits ever since we left C.C.'s place."

"She gets mad easy, but she don't hold it long."

Tommy brought the horses in. Hewey observed his brother's expression as the horses passed by him and through the open gate. Walter did not have to say anything. His frown told it all.

Hewey said quickly, "Fat has run a sandy on us."

Walter latched the gate. "If those are of Alvin's raisin', I'll eat your hat."

"My hat is safe, but I don't know about my job. I been thinkin' about lookin' for work over in the Guadalupes anyway."

Eve was more cordial than Hewey had thought she might be. She hugged her son and gave Hewey a greeting that was civil enough, though not what he would call enthusiastic. She said, "You-all have got plenty of time to wash before supper." She pointed that remark especially at Hewey.

Tommy was eager to tell her about the day. "We had some excitement over at Mr. Tarpley's. Fat . . . Mr. Gervin . . . he aimed a shotgun at Uncle Hewey."

Eve's mouth fell open. Hewey tried to explain what Fat had done, but all she heard was that a shotgun had been pointed in her son's general direction. "Hewey Calloway, it's bad enough that you've lured him away to wander around like a gypsy. Now you've come close to gettin' him killed."

"You know Fat Gervin. He ain't goin' to kill anybody. He's full of wind, and I'll bet that shotgun wasn't even loaded."

He knew better, for he had been shaken all the way to his

toes looking into that wide, dark muzzle. But surely the Lord made allowances when a man lied to a woman for her own good.

She burned the biscuits, always a sign that she had lapsed into a bad humor.

After breakfast Tommy stood in the kitchen doorway, a leftover biscuit wedged in his teeth, and fidgeted to be on his way while Eve handed him a sack of food and repeated the previous day's instructions and admonitions. Giving Hewey a distrusting look, she warned, "Don't you do everything your uncle Hewey does. Use your head and don't let him get you hurt."

Hewey said, "Tommy's levelheaded. Like as not he'll be lookin' after me more than I'll be lookin' after him."

"That is exactly what I'm afraid of."

Tommy finished the biscuit and peered into the sack to see what his mother had fixed for him. "Mama, I'm grown, almost."

"I want to see you live to get grown. It's a wonder to me that your uncle Hewey has survived this long."

Hewey said, "Caution and clean livin' is what has done it." He swung into the saddle. "We'd better be startin'. It's a long ways to Alpine."

As Hewey had expected, Old Man Jenkins's reaction to the horses was not pleasant to watch. He feared at first his employer would burst a blood vessel, the way the veins rose in his neck.

Hewey said, "I talked to the sheriff. He said there wasn't nothin' he could do. Said you'd ought to get you a lawyer."

"I don't trust lawyers, and from now on I ain't trustin' bankers, either. Since you knew him, why didn't you warn me about Frank Gervin?"

"I did. I said all you could be sure of was that he would do the wrong thing. Anyway, you'd already made the deal."

Jenkins stewed, studying the horses corraled at the J Bar

headquarters after a three-day walk and trot from Upton City.

Hewey offered, "At least we got them here in good shape. Didn't lose a one."

"Might've been better if you'd lost them all. Especially that one yonder." He pointed to the black stud. "Acts like he's been on locoweed."

"He needed a good cuttin' and didn't get it."

"We'll do it when the almanac says the signs are right. 'Til then, watch out for him. He'll hurt somebody."

Hewey had never liked castrating studs, but in this case he would consider it a privilege. "You goin' to do anything about Fat Gervin?"

"I paid seventy-five dollars a head. That's fifteen hundred dollars for twenty head. Takin' him to court would cost me that much or more, and it'd all go into the lawyers' pockets." Jenkins's eyes took on a wicked gleam. "But there's a Mexican *curandera* woman over in town that claims she can put a curse on anybody she wants to. She put one on me once, and I never had so much bad luck at one time in my life. I'll see what she can do about Frank Gervin."

Hewey would have favored something more direct, but it was Jenkins's money. "If she can put a curse on people, reckon she could turn it the other way around and do somebody some good?"

"I'll ask her. You got anybody in mind?"

"Old C. C. Tarpley. Considerin' the sort of man he is, he ain't a bad feller. He needs all the help he can get."

"I'll talk to her, but you'd do better with a preacher." Jenkins watched Tommy unsaddle his dun and begin brushing him down. "I wasn't sure you'd bring the boy back with you."

"I hinted every way I knew how for him to stay home, but he's bound and determined to learn the trade. Says he wants a ranch of his own someday."

"He's got a good spirit, and there's a lot he can learn from you."

"I didn't set out to be no teacher."

"For forty dollars a month you can add that to your job." Jenkins turned his attention back to the horses. "They ain't much, but I'd like you and the boy to take them down to the Circle W. Maybe the hands can teach these skates a little somethin'. Then I can resell them and recover some of my investment."

"What you want us to do after we've made delivery?"

"Stay there. The crew's brandin' calves, and you'll be a right smart of help." Jenkins squinted one eye again. Hewey had learned that was a sign he had something on his mind, sometimes good but more often not. "Since you couldn't see your way clear to take the foreman's job I offered you down there, I've hired another man. Name's Ralph Underhill. You'll report to him."

Hewey nodded. For forty dollars he didn't much mind who he reported to.

Jenkins added, "I've made it clear to him that I don't want you ridin' any broncs."

Hewey protested, "You know I can do anything them boys can, and make a better job of it."

"Dammit, Hewey, I know how old you are even if you've forgot. These broncs are for Aparicio and the younger hands."

Hewey felt a spasm of insubordination coming on. "Next thing, you'll be tellin' me to swamp for Blas around the wagon."

"There's plenty of cow work you can do better than most. Ain't no call for you do it ridin' a bronc." Jenkins turned away, then came back. "Underhill's a top hand with horses and cattle, but he don't get along with men too good. You'll find him a little on the touchy side."

Old Man Jenkins was touchy. *Anybody he regards as touchy must be a bearcat sure enough*, Hewey thought.

He wished Bige Saunders could be foreman at the Circle W, but Jenkins needed him here on the home place.

Jenkins's auto driver, Peeler, had stood off to one side, eyeing the newly arrived horses with silent disapproval. He wore jodhpurs and tall lace-up boots, which Hewey thought looked plumb disgraceful on a cowboy. After Jenkins walked away, Peeler sidled over. "Looks like you and Mr. Jenkins took a skinnin'."

"It was his money."

"But it'd be your skin if you had to ride any of them outlaws. The whole outfit would be ahead if you'd drive these snides up onto the rimrock and jump them off."

Hewey had had the same thought. "I'm tempted, but I never killed a horse in my life, no matter how much they deserved it."

"Had you rather have these horses on your conscience, or some poor cowpuncher?"

"Neither one. But I *would* like to tie Fat Gervin to that black stud and turn him loose on the side of a mountain. I could sell tickets to every man, woman and child in Upton City."

"It's horses like these that convinced me I'd rather be drivin' an automobile." Peeler rolled a cigarette and offered the sack to Hewey. Hewey accepted with a nod. Peeler said, "You want one more piece of advice?"

Hewey knew he was going to get it whether he asked for it or not. "Can't hurt none."

"Don't forget what Mr. Jenkins said about Ralph Underhill. He's got sore toes on both feet. Even his mama probably didn't like him much."

"I get along fine with most people."

"Ralph Underhill ain't most people. Me and him almost came to a knuckle-bustin' before he went down to the ranch. We would've if it hadn't been for Mr. Jenkins."

"I'll tiptoe when I'm around him. Got to set a good example for Tommy."

The only good news he had heard since arriving with the horses was that Blas Villegas was at the lower ranch, cooking for the hands while they branded the J Bar on Jenkins's newly acquired calf crop. Branding could not be done at the time the cows were being counted because ownership had not been legally transferred. The deal could have collapsed, as it almost did over the value of a crowbar. Because he had bought the rights to the Circle W brand along with the cattle, Jenkins would not have to change brands on the older animals. Attrition would gradually phase out the Circle W.

Trailing had become almost routine for the horses, so all but the black stud gave Hewey and Tommy little trouble. It often tried to pick a fight and kept the other horses in fear except for one wiry little paint, short of leg and shorter of patience. After feeling the sting of sharp teeth, the squealing paint landed a solid kick to the stud's belly where it would inflict the most pain. Afterward the black was selective in its bullying and kept a wary eye on the paint.

Ordinarily Hewey had a low opinion of paint horses, but he decided this one had special virtues. He said, "I'd like to set Fat Gervin behind that kickin' paint and see how fast he could dodge."

Tommy grinned, savoring the image. "Mama would say revenge is a mean and hollow thing."

"But thinkin' about it is like music to the mind."

It was good not to have to open any more pasture gates once they were inside the Circle W's perimeter fence. The horses acted as if they sensed that the journey was almost over, and even the stud settled down to purposeful traveling. Hewey let Tommy lope ahead to open the corral gate. He contented himself to stay behind the horses at a slower pace, for jolting across rough ground had stirred a pain in his side. That seemed to be happening a lot lately.

As the horses began filing through the opening, Hewey gave his attention to a horseman who had stationed himself on the opposite side from Tommy to make sure none doubled back. The rider sat rigidly, one hand on his hip, his attitude that of a man who controlled all creation. Even before the introductions, Hewey decided this was the new foreman, Ralph Underhill.

His surmise was confirmed by a challenging tone of voice as the man ordered Tommy to shut the gate, then rode up to Hewey. "I thought you were supposed to be bringin' me a string of horses."

The attitude rankled Hewey. "They ain't burros."

"I've seen burros that looked better. You pick these yourself?"

"I'm not any happier about them than you are. Mr. Jenkins made a deal with a four-flusher, and this is what he got."

The man frowned. "I'm guessin' you'd be Hewey Calloway."

"That'd be a right fair guess."

"Mr. Jenkins told me you'd be comin' along with some broncs, though he didn't expect you quite so soon. Said you was takin' a little vacation."

"It don't take me long to vacate."

"You won't get any vacation here. This is a workin' outfit."

Hewey sensed that Underhill had a mad on about something. He supposed it was the poor quality of the horseflesh, which was understandable, but there wasn't any point in taking his frustrations out on Hewey.

Underhill didn't take them out on Hewey alone. He hollered harshly at Tommy, who remained at the gate afoot, awaiting instruction. "Hey, button, don't just stand there with your thumb in your butt. See them boys brandin' calves in that corral yonder? Fall in there and see if you can be some help."

Chastened, Tommy swung quickly into the saddle and rode away in a long trot.

Hewey felt a prickling along his backside. "You got no call to talk to the boy thataway. He's my nephew."

"I don't care if he's the Prince of Wales. If he works here, he *works* here."

Hewey felt a streak of rebellion coming on. He saw Blas Villegas's chuck wagon standing idle beneath the trees. Blas would be cooking in the bunkhouse kitchen as long as they were at headquarters. "It's been a long ride. I'm goin' for some of Blas's coffee."

"You can drink coffee when everybody else gets to drink coffee." Underhill pointed at the horses. "Go in there and show me what you brought."

Underhill gave orders the way Hewey remembered army sergeants doing it. A thoughtful ranch foreman would usually be more subtle in exerting his authority, framing his orders in the form of a request rather than a command. Hewey said a crisp and exaggerated "Yes, sir," the way he had addressed officers in the Spanish war. It was a way of telling Underhill he was two sizes too big for his britches. Underhill got the message, for his face turned red.

Hewey liked the Circle W, but his stay was likely to be short if this was the way he and Tommy were going to be treated.

Underhill pointed his chin at Biscuit. "Is that your own horse or the company's?"

"He belongs to me."

"Most places I've been, they don't allow private horses eatin' company feed."

"Mr. Jenkins has never had any objections." *I wonder if he's like this with everybody or if I'm a special case*, Hewey thought.

Underhill accepted the situation but not in good grace. "If he sees fit to allow it, it's his ranch and his feed. But if it was up to me . . ." He did not finish. He proceeded through the gate and left it for Hewey to close. He walked toward the horses, most of which faced around to watch him suspiciously. A man afoot in a corral had never been good news to them. The stud bared its teeth.

Hewey said, "I'd keep an eye on that one."

Underhill must have heard, but he made no response. He walked directly toward the black. It backed its ears and made a bluffing start in his direction, paused, then came forward again with serious intent. Underhill stood his ground, waiting until the stud was almost upon him, then shouted loudly and slapped his hat across its nose. Startled, the black pawed at him, missed, then turned and ran back into the bunch, eyes rolling. It looked as confused as when the paint kicked it in the belly.

At least the son of a bitch is not afraid of horses, Hewey thought. It took nerve to stand and call a bluff like that. *I'll give him a little time before I haul off and punch him in the nose.*

Underhill walked among the horses, which drew to one side or the other at his approach, all giving him their full attention. He studied them one by one. Hewey suspected when he was done he could probably turn away and give a pretty good description of each animal without looking back. He had the marks of a horseman, even if he was a son of a bitch.

Underhill said, "You can tell by the saddle marks that most of them have been ridden before, or ridden at. They're mostly outlaws and knotheads. But we'll stake some of them after supper like they were all young broncs. Might be somethin' we can salvage."

"It'll be like tryin' to find a ripe peach in a barrel of rotten apples," Hewey said. "But we can try."

"We?" The wrinkles went deeper in Underhill's face. "Mr. Jenkins gave me strict orders that you're not supposed to ride any broncs. Seems like you're some kind of privileged character."

So that *was it,* Hewey thought. Underhill resented his being considered a special case.

"Mr. Jenkins has a notion I'm gettin' a little too much age on me to ride the rough string anymore. But what he don't see he don't need to know, and what he don't know won't hurt him. I'll do my share of the ridin' along with everybody else."

Underhill shook his head. "When I work for a man, I do what he tells me. These broncs are for the *young* hands."

Hewey wanted to argue the point, but he had already lost that argument with Jenkins, and it was clear that once Underhill took a stand, wild horses could not drag him from it. Hewey had never understood such stubborn people. He said, "I'll ride broncs if I'm a mind to."

"Do and I'll fire you."

"Try to fire me and I'll quit."

Underhill turned to face him. "Looks like me and you ain't goin' to get along very good."

"Sure looks like."

"Mr. Jenkins says you're a top hand, so I'll try and put up with you for a little while. Maybe we can come to an accommodation."

"Ask anybody. They'll tell you I've always had a smilin' disposition."

Underhill peered closely at him, and Hewey tried to force a smile. Underhill stalked through the gate and left it open. Hewey hurried to close it so the horses would not get out.

He sensed that even in silence, Underhill had had the last word. Almost, anyway. Hewey walked up to the bunkhouse to get that cup of coffee.

While he sat at the long table, the cup in his hand, he questioned Blas about the new foreman. Blas shrugged, evasive. "He is a boss. I have had many bosses. He is not the worst."

"How do you get along with him?"

"I do as I am told." He left unstated the fact that as a Mexican working for gringo bosses, he had always done as he was told. That was the key to survival.

Hewey said, "He seems to have a burr under his blanket. Maybe a bunch of them."

"It is said that his wife left him and took their child. That is a hard thing for a man to bear."

"She probably had reason enough."

It occurred to Hewey that he did not know if Blas had ever even had a wife. He had accepted Blas for what he had become, a wagon cook, and had never asked questions about his past. Feeling guilty, he asked now, for he realized that the old man's friendship was important to him.

Blas said, "Once, in Chihuahua. She was the daughter of a farmer, a *campesino*. The fever came, and she died."

"I'm sorry."

"It was a very long time ago. It is hard even to remember her face. I try to see her in my mind, and I cannot. It would be an old face now, so perhaps it is as well."

Hewey stared into the cup. He found it easy to conjure up Spring Renfro's face in all its detail. It was hard to imagine that someday he might not be able to. "You ever still miss her?"

Blas stared across the room at nothing in particular. "Sometimes at night, when I am dreaming, she comes and lies beside me. I can feel her body, but in the darkness I cannot see her face." He turned back to Hewey. "At least I have something to remember. What have you to remember, Hooey?"

Hewey had never spoken of Spring to anyone here. "A lot of country, a lot of horses, a lot of good times."

"But there should be more. For every man there should at least be one woman."

The remnant of coffee had become cold in the cup. Hewey walked to the door and flung it out onto the ground. He put the cup in Blas's tub. "I reckon the boys may need some help with the brandin'."

Blas said, "At night, when you dream, is that all you can dream of, the branding?"

"No, sometimes it's horses."

Aparicio was roping calves by the heels and dragging

them toward the branding-iron fire. Tommy was partnering with one of the young Mexican hands to throw the calves down as Aparicio brought them by, then hold them still for branding.

Aparicio motioned as Hewey climbed over the fence rather than walk all the way down to the gate. He would sooner ride a mile than walk a hundred yards. "My arm is tired, Hooey. Would you like to heel for a while?"

Anybody could flank calves or wield the hot irons, but not everyone was good at roping heels in a branding pen. As Aparicio handed the reins to him, Hewey glanced toward Underhill. The foreman was watching. Hewey promised himself he would make every loop a good one, and he roped at least twenty calves before he missed one. By then Underhill was no longer paying attention, or appeared not to be.

At last Hewey searched through the calves, his loop ready, but found none still unbranded. Underhill counted the bloody-edged pieces of ear notched from every calf. That tally jibed with the one he had taken before the calves were branded. "All done," he announced.

Hewey could have told him so. He felt as if Underhill was checking up on him. They turned the calves into a larger pen with their mothers to allow them time to pair before being released back into the open. The bawling was loud but more pleasant to Hewey's ears than a lot of human conversation he had heard lately.

Tommy dusted himself off. "I'm sure ready to put away some of Blas's cookin'."

Underhill said, "Before anybody stops for supper, we'll stake out some of these broncs."

The job consisted of roping the new arrivals, earing them down and in a few cases even throwing them to the ground to get a hackamore over their heads. Horsebackers then led them to a stretch of open ground, where a scattering of heavy logs and a couple of big wagon wheels awaited. Most resisted the lead rope, so the riders had to wrap the long hackamore reins around their saddle horns and half lead, half drag the broncs.

Hewey saw that Tommy was eyeing the black stud with misgivings. He said, "You're still a little short in the britches to be handlin' one like that. He's for somebody like Aparicio."

The black seemed to go out of its head when the rope tightened around its neck. It fought wildly, threshing like a fish on a line, even falling on its side, hooves flailing. After it scrambled to its feet, Hewey worked his way up the rope and grabbed the ears, dodging as the bronc tried to paw him.

"Put the hackamore on him, Tommy." All the time Tommy and Hewey struggled, the stud squealed and kicked. It landed a glancing blow against Tommy's leg, and Tommy fell. Hewey feared the black would stomp the boy, so he bit down on the left ear to give the animal something else to think about. He knew he would be spitting horsehair from now until supper.

Tommy got to his feet and finished knotting the hackamore. Hewey stepped away quickly so a hoof would not strike him. He took a firm grip on the long rein. "Go bring Biscuit."

Tommy limped as he hurried to fetch Hewey's brown horse.

Underhill had been watching while he hackamored the paint that had given the black a dose of humility. "I'll give you this, Calloway: you know what you're doin'."

"I didn't just start yesterday."

"Or twenty years ago, either. You better let one of these young hands wrestle with that black."

"I've got him under control."

The stud tried to shake Hewey loose. Hewey bit down on its ear again, venting on the horse the resentment Underhill had roused in him. Turning loose, he mounted Biscuit and wrapped the long hackamore rein around his saddle horn. "Come on, damn you!"

In response to the tugging of the rope, the stud bared its teeth and charged. Biscuit dodged, almost unseating Hewey but causing the black to stumble and fall.

"You're makin' things rough on yourself," Hewey growled. "But sometimes the worst things that happen to us are the things we do to ourselves." As the black regained its feet, Hewey put Biscuit into a trot that did not allow slack enough for a fight. Instead the stud pulled back on the rein in a contest of wills. Biscuit plodded ahead, the black hopping unwillingly on braced legs.

Hewey chose a heavy log that lay a safe distance from where the other broncs were being staked. Tommy rode along behind, ready to help.

Hewey said, "When I get down, you take Biscuit and lead him out of the way. I'll tie this outlaw."

He expected the black to run at him once he was afoot, so the sudden lunge did not surprise him. He jumped to one side and jerked on the long rein, bracing it around his hip. While the black floundered, Hewey wrapped the end of the rope around the log and took a quick half hitch. He stepped back out of the way as the black ran at him again. The log's weight brought the bronc up short at the end of the rein, almost throwing it off its feet.

Hewey watched in satisfaction as the black transferred its frustrations and began trying to drag the log to death. Each run moved it only a few inches.

"Time you've jerked that thing around for an hour or two," Hewey said, "you're liable to be about half civilized."

The stud fought its head, trying in vain to free itself from the tyranny of the hackamore.

Tommy watched with doubt. "Reckon he'll tame down?"

"There's only one thing he'll ever be fit for, and that's a bar of soap. It'd probably blister the hide off of anybody who used it."

Underhill finished tying the paint to a log. He came over to look at the black.

Hewey said, "Luckiest thing that could happen would be if he fell over that log and broke a leg."

Underhill shook his head. "Mr. Jenkins spent good money for that skate, so it's up to us to try to make somethin' of him." He turned to Tommy. "You think you can ride him?"

Tommy swallowed. "I don't know."

Hewey quickly put in, "He's just a boy. He's got no business on a loco outlaw like this."

"He's bein' paid a man's wages. He'll do a man's work." Underhill rode away.

Hewey felt a rising dread as he studied Tommy. "I sure wish you'd stayed home."

8

Tired though he was, Hewey did not sleep much. He lay on his cot, staring at the moonlight through the narrow bunkhouse window, listening to others snore. He had heard Tommy turn several times and guessed that his nephew was awake too, thinking about that outlaw black. Tommy had broken broncs for Alvin Lawdermilk, but Alvin didn't raise any like the loco devil hitched to a log out on the flat.

Underhill had not exactly said he would order Tommy to ride the stud, but the implication had been plain enough.

It's on account of me, Hewey thought. *Underhill doesn't like me, so he's taking it out on Tommy. And he's liable to get the boy hurt bad.*

Hewey would send his nephew packing home tomorrow if he could, but he knew Tommy would refuse to go, fearing it would look as if he were running away. Hewey would not leave under those circumstances either, and Tommy was trying to model himself after his uncle.

Why can't he model after somebody else, like his daddy?

Or even Old C. C. Tarpley? After some consideration he eliminated Tarpley.

He could slip out yonder right now, shoot that stud in the belly and tell God it died of colic. But Hewey had not fired his pistol in a long time. The barrel might be rusted enough to blow up in his hand. He was not even sure he had any cartridges in his war bag. He felt about guns much the same way he felt about posthole diggers; they were simply a working tool that he took no pleasure in. Besides, as he had told Peeler, he had never killed a horse in his life. The thought repulsed him.

In any case, Underhill was likely to want to see the stud remain staked for several days before it was saddled. A lot of things could happen in that length of time.

Hewey tried to think what they might be and how he might help them along, but no good ideas reared up and showed themselves.

The branding continued, and each evening the hands staked broncs to spend the night contemplating the authority of the long rope rein that tethered them. The animals were freed each morning to water and to graze under the loose supervision of a young Mexican horse jingler. Spoiled though they were from previous misuse, most seemed to show an educated respect after a couple of days. Their noses were sore from the hackamore's stern discipline, imposed each time they resisted being prisoner to log or wagon wheel.

The stud, however, remained unbent. Though the hackamore had burned a raw sore across its nose, the black fought like a caged cat each time it was caught and led to the log.

Underhill watched each day's struggle without comment. The fourth evening, the branding was finished earlier than usual. Peeler had driven Old Man Jenkins out in his touring car to see how the work was progressing. Underhill announced, "Them broncs've had time enough to learn that the rope is boss. We'll start ridin' them this evenin'."

Hewey thought he was applying the word *we* a little loosely. It was not a foreman's job to ride raw broncs; it was his place to see that the others did. Underhill assigned them, starting by giving Aparicio Rodriguez the paint. It might never be a good cow horse, but Hewey was willing to forgive its shortcomings out of respect for the way it stood up for its rights against the black stud.

The stud was the last to be assigned. Underhill turned toward Tommy, but his gaze settled upon Hewey as he spoke. "They tell me your uncle was a real bronc stomper in his day. Reckon it runs in the blood?"

Hewey listened for a trace of malice.

Tommy was hesitant in answering. "I don't know."

"Then we'll have to find out. If you can handle that stud, you ought to be able to handle anything that comes along."

Hewey was not in the habit of arguing with foremen, but this was a time to make an exception. "You know this boy ain't ready to ride a horse like that. He'd be a handful even for me or Aparicio."

"You're out, and I've already given Aparicio his mount. It's time to see if this boy can pull his weight."

Tommy's words were strong, but Hewey heard doubt in his voice. "I can do it, Uncle Hewey."

Underhill grunted with satisfaction. "You heard him yourself." He walked away, putting an end to argument. Hewey stared after him in frustration, trying to decide which to do first, fight him or quit.

Tommy said, "Would you help me saddle him, Uncle Hewey?"

Dread stirred like acid in Hewey's stomach. "It'd be smarter to roll our beddin' and leave here right now."

"But we're not goin' to." Tommy's voice had picked up determination. "We're not goin' to let some old bronc scare us."

"He scares me."

"Daddy always said it's best to spit in the eye of whatever scares you and go ahead with what you have to do."

That had usually been Hewey's philosophy, though circumstances from time to time had caused him to back away and rethink his principles. "Your daddy may not've taken a good look at that black stud."

Aparicio was the first to saddle and ride. The paint gave him a creditable fight but was no match for the vaquero's skill. After a few jumps, the paint began to race around the corral. Clearly it had been ridden before but perhaps had been given up as a bad job by someone who lacked Aparicio's touch. The cowboy let the horse run until it was lathered with sweat, then force-reined it to left and right until the paint surrendered. A couple more cowboys rode their broncs, one being thrown but immediately getting back on and staying until the horse quit bucking.

Underhill jerked a thumb in Tommy's direction. "Let's see what you can do."

The black fought so hard that Hewey had to rope it by its forefeet and trip it, then tie up one foot while the horse was down. Even on three feet the squealing stud was formidable, lunging against the rope, eyes rolling and nostrils flaring as Tommy kept trying to place the saddle blanket on its back. It attempted to paw first Tommy, then Hewey, falling each time but showing no sign that it had learned anything.

Hewey grumbled, "This horse is crazy as a bedbug."

They managed finally to get Tommy's saddle on. While Hewey gripped the black's ears, Tommy attempted to fit his left foot into the stirrup.

Hewey did not know how the stud managed it on three feet, but it kicked Tommy on the hip and sent him spinning back, falling in the dirt.

"That settles it," he declared. "Tommy ain't ridin' this loco son of a bitch. Aparicio, grab ahold of him."

Tommy had ridden a bronc once for Skip Harkness, who was no kin. Hewey would ride this one for his nephew.

The vaquero took Hewey's place, holding the ears, biting down on one as the black kicked at Hewey and grazed his leg. Hewey gritted his teeth against a flash of pain and grabbed for the bouncing stirrup. He shoved his foot into it and grasped the horn, swinging up, leaning forward to off-set the pull if the bronc should suddenly surge ahead before he was firmly set. He considered keeping his hold on the horn, but he let pride prevail over prudence. A real bronc stomper did not grab leather. The black lunged forward, nearly falling.

Old Man Jenkins's stern voice boomed from outside the fence. "Hewey Calloway, what the hell do you think you're doin'?"

Hewey saw no reason to answer. Jenkins had eyes to see.

"All right, Aparicio, untie his foot."

The vaquero loosened the rope and scrambled out of the way. Loosing a furious sound that reminded Hewey of the bull he and Skip had brought down, the stud seemed to twist halfway around in midair and come down at a ninety-degree angle from where it had started. The impact of hooves against the ground jammed Hewey's teeth together so hard he feared some might shatter. The bronc bawled in fury.

Before Hewey could regain his balance the black was in the air again, repeating the twisting motion. Hewey tried to anticipate and counter the move, but he seemed always a second behind. He felt his head twisting and thought he could imagine how a chicken felt as its neck was wrung. He knew he showed daylight between his seat and the saddle. He tightened the grip of his knees and tried to con-template the virtues of a nice soft job in town.

He saw the fence coming at him and realized the bronc was going to strike it a glancing blow. He could do nothing to protect himself from the impact. His right knee seemed to explode as it smacked against a post. The shock set Hewey's head to reeling. He forgot about pride and grabbed the saddle horn, trying to steady himself. He was sure the pounding had broken something loose inside—his lungs, his liver . . . he had no idea what. He hurt like he had never hurt in his life.

The black made another high jump but somehow failed to land solidly. The legs buckled, and it slammed down hard on its right side, pinning the already-injured knee. The horse rolled half over, threshing to find its feet. The saddle horn punched against Hewey's ribs. He felt as if he were sinking into a deep pit of agony.

A thousand bright suns circled around him. The black scrambled to get up. Instinctively Hewey's hand found the horn again. He heard the shouts of the cowboys, but the only voice that came through clearly was Aparicio's. "Jump, Hooey! Jump!"

He felt the stud surge ahead, then slam hard against the fence. The force of the sudden stop hurled Hewey forward. He smashed against the fence and fell away. The back of his head slammed against the ground. For a panicked moment he wondered where the bronc was, but he could not see. He feared the strike of the hooves, or perhaps having his foot caught in the stirrup so that he would be dragged around the corral.

Strong hands tugged at him, pulling him away from the fence, but he could not find the faces through the brilliance of all those whirling suns. He fought for breath and tasted the sticky salt of blood on his lips. He wanted to cry out but could not muster the voice. He heard a weak groan and knew it came from somewhere deep inside.

He heard Underhill's voice. "I believe that crazy bronc broke his neck."

Whose neck? Hewey wondered. *Mine or his?*

Old Man Jenkins's voice said, "We ought to've shot that outlaw. Now we won't have to."

The black's neck, then. But Hewey felt as if it might be his own as well. He hurt from his feet to the top of his head. He tried to move his hands, but his left did not respond. The sharp pain told him the arm was broken. So was every other bone in his body, for all he could tell.

Jenkins said, "Damn it, I've kept tellin' him one of these broncs would kill him someday. Salinas, ride to the bunkhouse and tell Peeler to fetch that automobile down here. Spur like hell."

Hewey lapsed into semiconsciousness, though he was aware when they lifted him from the ground. He heard Jenkins's voice. "Gentle with him, boys. If he's got any broken ribs, they might punch a hole in his lungs."

A sharp pain pierced his left side, and his arm felt as if it were wrenching itself loose from his shoulder. He was vaguely aware of being carried and of the misery that compounded with every stride.

Tommy's anxious voice demanded, "You don't reckon he's goin' to die?"

Hewey had wondered now and again how death must feel. At this point he thought it might come as a relief. But amid all those whirling flashes of light he glimpsed Tommy's face, beseeching him to live.

He drifted off somewhere far away and remained there awhile in some vague sort of limbo. He was only dimly conscious of the automobile's roar.

Jenkins said, "Ease him into the backseat, boys. Careful. Ain't no tellin' what all may be broke."

Tommy said, "He's my uncle. I want to go with him."

Jenkins replied, "All right. You may have to hold him down if the pain really hits him. I think he's got a busted arm and leg, and maybe some ribs. His innards may be a mess, too."

Aparicio said, *"Mala suerte.* He is a good one, that Hooey."

"Was," Jenkins said. "If he lives, he won't ever be the same again." His voice darkened with regret. "He was a great cowboy in his day. I wish he'd quit while he was still in one piece."

Peeler said, "You sure that stud is dead? If he ain't, I'll cut his damned throat."

Somebody replied, "A hundred years from now he won't be any deader."

Tommy sat on the edge of the backseat, beside Hewey. He pleaded, "Don't you die, Uncle Hewey. Don't you die on me like Skip did."

The starting of the trip was a nightmare of agony, the automobile jolting unmercifully on the rough trail that passed for a road. Hewey awakened sufficiently to know that he lay stretched out on the backseat, his legs bent because the car was not wide enough to accommodate the length of his body. Tommy perched precariously beside him, insurance against Hewey's rolling off the seat. Jenkins sat in front beside Peeler.

He heard Jenkins complain, "A good forty-dollar cowboy busted to hell by a bronc that wasn't worth twenty. Why does this bad luck always happen to me?"

Peeler said, "Maybe Doc Evans can fix him up."

"You can patch an old shirt, but it'll just be an old shirt with patches on it. Maybe someday I'll learn to fire every cowboy as soon as he turns thirty."

Hewey wanted to protest that he wasn't as old as Jenkins made out, but he could not muster voice except for an occasional groan. He was not even sure that what he was hearing was real. All kinds of images ran through his mind like a magic lantern show gone berserk. Some were memories, but some were hallucinations, flitting dreams and nightmares prompted by the pain. He heard Tommy tell him, "You oughtn't to've done it. I could've handled him."

Hewey wanted to say he doubted it, but he could not form the words. Gradually consciousness fell away, and with it much of the hurting. Through a haze he saw Tommy leaning protectively over him. Strangely, his nephew seemed to change, to grow younger and smaller. He was as Hewey remembered him from four years ago, when Tommy had bid him a tearful good-bye and said, "You'll be back, won't you, Uncle Hewey? You ain't goin' to let some old bronc kill you?"

Maybe he had. Maybe he *had* let that black stud kill him.

Hewey realized that the pain was draining away from him. Everything that had hurt so terribly was going numb. Gradually he began feeling warm and safe and comfortable, as if he were floating free on a soft cushion of air or a gentle south wind. A sense of euphoria came over him, a sense of peace so total that he could compare it with nothing in his experience. He knew in some deep corner of his subconscious that it was a dream, but it seemed much more than a dream. It was as real as life.

I'm dying, he told himself, and wondered that the thought brought him no fear. He found himself welcoming it.

Faces came to him, dear faces out of his past—his mother, whom he barely remembered because she had died so young, and his father, who had never quite found his way. He wanted to call to them but had no voice. They seemed to want to speak to him but made no move to come closer. They faded as in a twilight mist, and in their place came his old sidekick Grady Welch, flashing a wide, happy grin that had been his trademark. He and Snort Yarnell had been a pair to draw to, so much alike they could have been brothers. Grady waved and turned to mount a black horse that appeared out of nowhere.

A horse like the one that got me, Hewey thought. He saw that the horse had four stocking feet, like the one that had stomped Grady to death. Hewey tried to shout a warning, to tell Grady not to get on him, but he still had no voice. Grady and the horse drifted away into the same twilight mist that had taken Hewey's mother and father. Hewey was alone.

He wanted to follow, for the mist seemed friendly like an easy April rain, but he could not move. The warm glow enveloped him once more, and he would have been content to remain in its embrace forever.

He felt as if someone were tugging on his arm, trying to pull him back toward the darkness. He resisted, for he did not want to go back. He did not want to leave this cradle of peace, but the tugging was insistent.

He saw Spring Renfro. She held his hand, bidding him to follow her, but the direction was wrong. It led back to the pain. She smiled with reassurance, and it was the smile she had shown him the day he first met her, long ago. He tried to pull away from her grip, for death seemed preferable to the agony. Sadness came into her blue eyes, the sadness he had seen the day she had released him from his promise so he might ride away once again, a free spirit seeking a place that did not exist and perhaps had never existed, where time would stand still and he would always be twenty years old.

In her eyes he saw what those four years of freedom had cost him, for now she belonged to another. She gave him a faint smile that seemed to say good-bye, and a terrible loneliness settled upon him. He reached for her, but she was gone back into the mist from which the vision had come. He tried to call to her, but he could summon no voice.

The regret lasted only a moment, for he settled again into the peace of this strange place into which he had drifted. He did not want to leave.

He felt himself being pulled away once more and fought to remain where he was. He had never realized how easy it would be to accept death when it came with the faces of his mother and father and good old Grady Welch. But the hand he could not see kept pulling him away against his will.

"Let me go!" he shouted in his mind. "It's better where I am."

He saw a face forming in the mist, and it was his nephew's. Tears welled in Tommy's eyes. He held firmly to Hewey's right hand. "Hang on, Uncle Hewey. Don't you die and leave me."

Hewey wanted to tell him, *I did die, and you pulled me back. I wanted to stay there, but you wouldn't let me.*

The misery returned, strong as before, and told him he was still alive. Tears stung his eyes and warmed his face as they trickled down.

Alive. But alive for what?

The sun was down, and darkness came. At times the weak headlights caused Peeler to let the automobile stray from the poorly defined road. He sped along, almost high-centering the car a couple of times lurching through cement-hard ruts left after the drying-up of a mud puddle. A particularly severe jolt sent a shock coursing through Hewey and caused him to lapse into unconsciousness again.

Spring Renfro came back to him, telling him he was going to be all right. He reached toward her, but he could not find her. She had disappeared into a gray haze, gone with a man named Farley Neal.

Hewey had but little concept of the time spent on the road to Alpine. He was aware of Tommy jumping out to open gates, but he had no idea how many there were. He realized the car had come to a stop, and he heard Peeler pounding on a door, calling for Dr. Evans. Hewey cried out as they picked him up and carried him inside. The next thing he knew he was lying on a bed, his boots and clothes off, and the doctor was feeling his arms and legs, trying to locate broken bones. He caught the unpleasant odor of medicines and disinfectant.

Hewey cried out again as hands searched down his right leg.

Evans asked, "Is that where it hurts?"

Miraculously, it seemed, Hewey could speak. "It hurts every place there is."

"That knee looks bad."

"I can't raise my left arm."

"It's broken. Didn't anybody ever tell you that riding broncs is a job for the young?"

They had, often, and Hewey's stock reply had been that whenever a man had a sitting-down job he should hang on to it. But that did not seem funny now. Nothing seemed funny now.

Jenkins said, "He done some talkin' out of his head. From what he was sayin', I'm afraid he's probably tore up inside, too."

The doctor's face was grave. "I can wrap his ribs and his knee. I can put a cast on his arm. But as to internal injuries, they will either heal themselves or they won't. I am afraid they are beyond any abilities of mine."

Jenkins said, "Do what you can. He's been a good hand, even if sometimes he hasn't got the judgment God gave a jackrabbit."

Hewey was not too far out of it to grasp what Jenkins was implying. *He's been a good hand. Been!* Like it was all over with. Like he really had died.

He tried to raise up but fell back. Somewhere inside, something was badly wrong.

Tommy bent over him. "You'd better lay still, Uncle Hewey."

Hewey squeezed his eyes shut, as if that would block off the pain. He felt tears burning. Crying like a baby . . . hell of a thing for a grown man.

When the worst of it was past, he managed a weak voice. "Did they say that black stud is dead?"

"Broke his neck when he hit the fence."

"I almost wish he'd broken mine, too. Seems like he broke everything else." Hewey remembered the brief period of peace, when death had come to him like a friend and had taken away the pain. It still seemed as if he should be able to reach out and grasp it and leave this suffering behind.

The doctor told Tommy, "Son, you'd better wait out in the front room. I'm going to set his arm, and it won't be something a boy would want to watch." To Peeler he said, "Would you mind helping me?"

Tommy said, "I'll be close by, Uncle Hewey. If you need anything, just holler."

Hewey would holler, all right. He would holler like hell when they set that arm.

The work done, Dr. Evans brought something in a glass. "Drink this. It should dull your senses and help you sleep."

"Is it whiskey?" Cold sweat running down his face and burning his eyes, Hewey would give a week's pay for a double shot of bourbon or rye. He would even settle for tequila.

"Not quite, but it should have some of the same effect."

It certainly was not whiskey, Hewey found as soon as he gulped it down. The worst rotgut he had ever tasted was ambrosia in comparison. But in a while he felt more at ease and dropped off to sleep. When he opened his eyes, daylight through the window made him close them again quickly.

He heard Tommy's voice. "You awake, Uncle Hewey?"

"I ain't even sure I'm alive." He knew he must be, however. A dead man wouldn't hurt so much. His ribs were wrapped tightly. He moved his right arm, then tried to move his left but found it in a cast, tightly bound. His right leg was immobilized. It felt as if it weighed a hundred pounds. Trying to lift it sent pain lancing through his body.

"I've roped and tied cattle that wasn't as helpless as this."

"I wish you'd had more faith in me. You wouldn't be here if you hadn't taken it on yourself to try and ride my bronc."

Hewey thought he detected a touch of resentment. "I was afraid he'd hurt you."

"I'm younger than you are, and not near as brittle. Now we'll never know if I could've ridden him."

"You'd've wound up where I'm at."

"Maybe, maybe not." Tommy turned to stare out the window. "I can't be mad at you, seein' you layin' here all busted up. You thought you were doin' what was right for me."

"I promised your folks I'd look out for you."

"You sure did that, all right. Now I'm feelin' guilty because you got yourself tore up takin' my place."

"There's no cause for you to feel guilty about anything. I didn't give you time to have a say about it." Hewey tried again to raise up but could not. "Besides, I'll be back amongst them before you know it."

"That's not the way the doctor talks. For a while he wasn't even sure you'd live."

"Ain't the first time some horse busted my arm. I was always a quick healer."

"You weren't always this old."

Dr. Evans heard their voices. He walked into the room carrying a steaming cup. Though Hewey had always enjoyed coffee, he found the aroma strangely nauseating. "I don't believe I can handle any coffee."

"It's mine, not yours. A man in your condition shouldn't be drinking coffee." The doctor swallowed what remained in the cup. "At least you seem to have gotten some sleep. That's more than your nephew did. He sat up in this room all night."

It was Hewey's turn for guilt. "Wasn't no need in that. Boy his age needs his rest."

"I dozed some," Tommy said. "That big chair is pretty comfortable."

Evans felt Hewey's forehead, then stuck a thermometer in his mouth. "Feeling any better?"

Hewey could not answer without biting down on the glass and risking a mouthful of mercury. He was not certain what he would say anyway. He knew only that it would be hard to pick out one place that hurt worse than another.

Tommy said, "I wish I could let Mama and Daddy know."

The doctor said, "You could telephone them."

"They don't have a telephone. It costs too much to run a line. But there's one in the sheriff's office. I could tell Wes Wheeler."

When the doctor removed the thermometer, Hewey protested, "Ain't no need gettin' your folks all upset. I'll be back at the ranch in a few days."

Frowning in disagreement, the doctor turned to Tommy. "Have you ever talked on a telephone?"

"No, sir, never was any reason to before."

"Then I'd better ring Central for you. It's a complicated business, talking long distance."

"I'd sure be obliged, sir."

Walter and Eve had brought the boy up to have good manners, Hewey thought. He wished they had taught him not to get people unnecessarily excited over something that time would heal.

Though the telephone was two rooms away, Hewey could hear the doctor's and Tommy's voices clearly, for they had to shout to be heard. Tommy sounded nervous, not just because of the message but because he had never talked on a telephone before. Hewey had done it a couple of times, though he never had quite trusted the contraption. There was something unnatural about carrying on a conversation with somebody miles away, somebody you couldn't see.

Tommy came back. "Mr. Wheeler said tell you to hurry up and get well. Said he'd ride out this mornin' to tell Mama and Daddy."

"It's a waste of a public servant's time and a burden on the taxpayers."

"How much tax have you ever paid, Uncle Hewey?"

"A right smart of whiskey tax, I expect."

Later in the day—he judged it to be around noon—a booming voice awakened him from a light doze. Blinking the sleep from his eyes, he saw a tall, lanky, slightly stooped figure standing in the doorway, hat crushed in his big hands. A false smile revealed a gold tooth.

The voice declared, "Hewey Calloway, you've got awful lazy in your old age, layin' in bed plumb to noontime."

"Snort Yarnell! I thought I was in the midst of a nightmare, but it's turned out real. What're you doin' in town this time of the day? Get fired again?"

"I ain't been fired in my life. I always quit before they got the chance." Though he forced himself to grin broadly, Snort could not control the anxiety in his eyes. "I hear you finally found a bronc too tough for you to handle. I'll go out and ride him for you."

"That won't be hard to do. He's dead."

"Probably died of fright, knowin' I'd be comin' to turn him wrong side out. You ain't goin' to be in here long, are you? I've got plans for the two of us."

"Plans?" Snort always had plans. Most of them led to calamity of one sort or another.

"Figured we'd go down into Mexico this fall and buy us a bunch of raw broncs real cheap. We could spend the winter ridin' them, then bring them north in the spring to sell. Our pockets would jingle like a wagonload of trace chains."

"Last time we went to Mexico we were lucky to get out of there with a horse apiece and the saddles to put on them."

"That was on account of bad tequila. This time we won't drink nothin' but the best." Snort laughed, but Hewey sensed that the laughter was as fake as the gold tooth. That notion about Mexico had probably just popped into his head as a way of making conversation. There was not a career politician in the Austin statehouse who could outlie Snort Yarnell.

But Hewey was not exactly an amateur at the game. "I'd sort of figured we might go down into South Texas and rope outlaw steers out of the brush this winter. Them ranchers down there pay pretty good for clearin' the mossyhorns out of their pastures."

"That sounds like fun, too. We'll take Tommy with us and show him what *real* cowpunchin' is like. Think you'll be able to ride in a few days?"

"Why not? May need somebody to help me onto my horse at first, 'til this bum knee heals a little, but once I'm in the saddle I'll be as good as I ever was."

"All right, old pardner, I'll be lookin' in on you again." Snort turned to go but stopped in the doorway, his head down. He twisted the hat in his hands before turning and coming back. His eyes brimmed with tears.

"Damn it all, Hewey, who are we lyin' to? That doctor says you'll be lucky if you ever get back on a horse again. Your cowboyin' days are over with."

Tommy was dismayed. "Snort, you shouldn't . . ."

Hewey tried to say the doctor was wrong, that he would be out of this bed and riding again in no time. But his throat tightened up so that he could not speak.

Snort placed a strong hand on Hewey's good shoulder and squeezed. "Best friends I ever had in this world was you and Old Grady Welch. Grady's gone, and now you . . . Damn it all, life just ain't fair." He cleared his throat. "I promise you ain't goin' to ever need for nothin', old pardner. Anything you want, just let me know. Old Snort'll be here before you can draw a second breath."

A tear on his cheek, Snort turned quickly and strode out of the room. Tommy spoke to him as he started out the front door, but Snort gave him no answer.

Damn that doctor, getting Snort all upset for nothing. Of course I'm going to ride again. I'll keep cowboying 'til I'm a hundred years old and get myself killed by a jealous husband.

Hewey turned his head away from the door. His throat felt as if he were about to choke, and his eyes burned like fire. He supposed it was the fumes from all that medicine in the doctor's cabinet.

9

Old Man Jenkins came that afternoon. Peeler trailed behind him in his jodhpurs and lace-up boots, offering no more than a quiet "Howdy" so long as his employer was there.

Jenkins sat beside Hewey's bed. "By rights I ought not to pay none of your expenses. You got yourself hurt doin' exactly what I told you not to. But I've always had a generous heart. I'll go halves with you."

"I hate to put you to all that expense."

"I've arranged for you to be moved to a boardin'house soon as you're able. It'll be some cheaper. This old quack charges like his place was the Menger Hotel in San Antone."

"I figure to be back at the ranch pretty quick."

Jenkins's eyes showed strong doubt, but he made no direct comment. "By rights it's Frank Gervin who ought to pay the bills, foistin' off that bunch of snides on us. But I sicced the *curandera* woman on him. She claims she can give him a case of the itch, at least. Maybe even the piles." Jenkins arose to leave. "The next place you work, I hope you follow orders better than you did for me."

By that, Hewey assumed he was out of a job. Well, he had been out of a job many times but had never had much trouble finding someplace to work. There was always call for a good cowpuncher. Soon as he knitted a little he might take Biscuit up into the Guadalupes, as pretty a country as he had ever seen. Tommy too, if the boy wanted to go. They would have their pick of places to work.

Peeler had been so quiet, Hewey had almost forgotten he was still there. The chauffeur moved nearer the bed and gazed down on Hewey with sympathy. "I wish there was somethin' I could do for you."

"There is. Next time you go to the ranch, tell Aparicio and

the boys I'd be obliged if they'd look after Biscuit for a couple of weeks 'til I'm in shape to come and get him."

Peeler looked at him askance. "A couple of weeks? Don't you know how bad you're hurt?"

"I've been hurt worse than this fallin' off a wood-haulin' wagon."

Peeler carefully gathered his words. "You're not goin' to want to hear this, but I wouldn't be honest if I didn't say it. While you're layin' here you'd best be thinkin' about what you'll do from now on. Your wild-ridin' days are over. Even a gentle horse like Biscuit may be too much for you. But you've got to keep on livin'. You'd better start figurin' on how you're goin' to do it."

He did not wait to hear Hewey's protests that this was just a temporary setback, that he would soon be making a hand again.

Hewey stared in frustration at the open door through which Peeler had gone. He made a fist with his right hand, for he could barely move the fingers on his left. He would have thought everybody knew him better than that, already giving up on him when it hadn't even been twenty-four hours since his little accident. It would take more than a crazy black stud to set him permanently on the ground.

Tommy came into the room. "Need anything?"

"I need for everybody to quit tellin' me what a hopeless wreck I am. I've had toothaches hurt me worse than this." His left arm and his right leg both pulsed with pain, and each time he moved he felt as if someone were running a sword through his lungs. He moved no more than he had to.

Tommy did not answer. Hewey changed the subject. "You'd better be findin' a way to get back to the ranch. You ain't been fired too, have you?"

"I'm stayin' here to look after you."

"The doctor's supposed to be doin' that, and at considerable expense, the way Old Man Jenkins tells it. If you're goin'to be a cowboy, you'd better be out there cowboyin'."

Tommy's face was sad. "I had no idea it was goin'to be like this. First Skip, then you."

"The cowboy life ain't all roses. It sticks a thorn in you from time to time."

"Home looks a lot better to me than it used to. But right now the main job I've got is takin' care of you."

"I always took care of myself."

"Let's see you walk to the toilet."

"You know I can't do that."

"Then there's no use in us talkin' any more about it." Tommy looked into a water pitcher on a small table beside Hewey's bed. "I'll go pump some fresh water for you."

"A stiff drink of whiskey is what I need."

He knew he would not get it, not until he was out of this place and away from the doctor's close scrutiny. He had been looking at a pair of crutches leaning in a corner, propped between a medicine cabinet and the wall. He had never used any before, but it stood to reason that a man who could ride broncs should be able to master a pair of crutches. He imagined the surprise he would see on bystanders' faces when he entered the saloon and bellied up to the bar with an arm and a leg wrapped like Christmas packages. They would know then that Hewey Calloway was made of sterner stuff than they had given him credit for.

He appraised the distance. He would be unable to put weight on his right leg, but he could hop on his left, holding on to the bed partway, then the table and finally the medicine cabinet.

The first step was to get out of the bed. That, he reasoned, might be the hardest part, for he had lain here since last night, hardly changing position. His body would be stiff, resisting movement. He tried sitting up, but he immediately fell back on his pillow, stricken by an internal wrenching so intense that it left him in a cold sweat and breathing hard. He rested a bit until the pain subsided, then decided to try a different way. Carefully he slid his left leg to the edge of the bed and dragged the bound leg after it. He swung both legs off, twisting his body around to a ninety-degree angle without his back losing contact with the mattress. The left leg bent normally at the knee, but the bound right leg extended straight out, stiff as if splinted between boards. He gritted his teeth.

The really hard part would come now, raising his upper body off the mattress. He had little control over his left hand, but with his right he gripped the edge of the mattress and pulled himself to a sitting position so quickly that he was up before the pain had time to register. It came with such a blinding force that he bit his tongue to keep from crying out, and he almost fainted. The room seemed to swing back and forth like a pendulum. Nausea brought his breakfast up into his throat, burning hard, and he thought he would lose it.

Gradually the dizziness diminished, and with it much of the hurting. He felt sweat, cold and clammy, running down his face, tickling his chest. But he was still sitting up. He wished Old Man Jenkins could see him, and Peeler and Snort.

When he thought he was steady enough, he eased forward until his left foot touched the floor. He tested his weight on it and decided it would hold him. The right leg remained stiff and useless, but he could hold the edge of the bed with his right hand. He pushed himself the final inches to clear the mattress and was standing on his left foot. Holding to the edge of the bed for balance, he made the first hop.

The internal pain came roaring back. This time he could not help crying out. Nausea came upon him again in a rush, and with it the dizziness. He could not hold on to the bed. He fell forward, unable to help himself. He struck the floor on his stomach, then his face. Most of the breath gusted from his lungs, and his nose smarted as if a fist had struck him. He felt he was still falling, far into some bottomless black hole.

Tommy hurried into the room. "Uncle Hewey!"

The doctor was only a few steps behind. "Come, son, help me lift him back onto the bed. Careful. He may have undone everything we did for him."

Hewey had never felt agony more intense. All the bright suns he had seen yesterday came back, spinning as wildly as before. He had but a fingernail hold on consciousness.

The doctor's voice was angry. "He thinks he's a bronc rider, and he can't even stay on a bed. We may have to tie him like a horse."

Hewey tried to explain that he was trying to reach the crutches, but he was just mumbling. He could not even understand himself. The doctor felt over his leg and his arm, then his ribs and his chest. Hewey groaned at his touch.

Evans told Tommy, "These old cowboys get to thinking they're made of rawhide. They're more like eggshells, and nobody ever put Humpty Dumpty back together again."

Hewey spent a miserable night, all of yesterday's pain reawakened and intensified. Trying to get out of bed too early had been a mistake, a lesson learned the hard way like so many others in his life. But if he had not tried, he would not know.

The doctor took the precaution of removing the crutches to another room. "I should have done this in the first place. You don't leave candy in front of a child and expect him not to eat any."

If Hewey had felt better he might have taken offense, but a few disparaging words carried no sting compared to the injuries imposed upon him by that black stud. He lay half awake, half dreaming much of the night, trying to conjure up appropriate measures of vengeance against Fat Gervin but finding none that seemed devilish enough to fit the crime. The one or two that came closest would probably result in his taking a trip to the Huntsville penitentiary, much too far from cow country.

At least Tommy did not spend a second night sitting up in a chair. The doctor admired the boy's loyalty but had arranged for him to sleep and eat in a nearby boardinghouse. Nevertheless, Tommy was at his uncle's side soon after sunup, asking how he felt.

"A whole lot better," Hewey lied. "That medicine is doin' me a world of good." In fact, when the doctor was not looking he had poured much of it into a bottle provided for him to empty his bladder. If a medicine had to taste bad to do a man any good, this one ought to cure everything from warts to double pneumonia.

He still judged distances by the length of time it would take to travel them on horseback. Though he had ridden in automobiles several times, he never had gotten used to the notion that they could carry people as far in an hour as a good horse might go in the better part of a day. He was not surprised that Walter and Eve showed up, but he was amazed that they arrived so soon. He would have thought they would come in a wagon, the way they usually traveled.

Walter said, "Alvin Lawdermilk brought us in his automobile."

"Alvin's got him an automobile?" Alvin had always been a horseman and had preached mightily against the motorcar. First Blue Hannigan and now Alvin Lawdermilk. "The world's changin' too fast."

Walter said, "We came all this way and didn't have to fix but four flats. That's some travelin'."

Eve hesitantly took Hewey's right hand after seeing that it was not injured. "Tommy says you're in this shape on account of him."

"I'm in this shape on account of Fat Gervin."

"When we asked you to look out for Tommy, we didn't mean for it to come to this."

"He was a little put out with me for not lettin' him ride that bronc, but I was afraid he didn't have a chance."

Eve blinked away tears. "Damn you, Hewey Calloway, you're the most aggravatin'man I ever knew."

She took Hewey by surprise. "How do you figure that?"

"You do the most thoughtless things sometimes without givin' any consideration to the consequences, and you make me mad enough to want to shoot you. Then you do somethin' like this and make me want to hug your neck. I would, but I don't know where all you're busted."

"I'd appreciate the hug. What I'd appreciate a lot more would be for you-all to take me away from here. I'm damned tired of this bed."

Walter shook his head. "The doctor says you'll be on your back for some time yet."

"If I had Biscuit here, I'd saddle up and ride off right now." He knew better, but he did not want them thinking of him as an invalid. They would want to start doing things for him, and he had always been most comfortable doing for himself.

Walter said, "Alvin's waitin' in the next room. He's anxious to see you."

Hewey warmed with pleasure at the thought of seeing his old friend and sometime employer. He had intended to stop by Alvin's place for a visit when he and Tommy went to Upton City to receive the broncs from Fat, but his unexpected encounter with Spring Renfro had gotten in the way. "Good old Alvin. I wonder if he's ever got any better lookin'."

"Judge for yourself," Walter said, and went to fetch him.

Alvin grinned like a new cat in a barnful of mice, his false teeth a little too large, his pudgy face a little too red. He looked older than Hewey remembered him, though he lacked a lot being as old as Jenkins or C. C. Tarpley. People had said Alvin had to slow down, which was the reason he had employed a ranch foreman to help ease the burden of labor and responsibility. His longtime love for good whiskey probably bore much of the fault.

Hewey grasped Alvin's hand. "Did you bring me a drink?"

Alvin winked at Eve. "Eve drank it all up on the way here."

She made a fist as if to punch him.

Alvin said, "But soon's you get out of that bed we'll make up for lost time. About four years' worth."

"Four years is a lot of whiskey."

"We won't drink it all at once. We'll spread it out over a couple of days."

Eve said, "You know you've stopped drinkin', Alvin. You've been quit for two years."

Alvin looked about as if to see who might be listening. "What did you have to go and say that for? You'll ruin my reputation."

Hewey made a halfhearted grin, trying to play along with their joking, though he did not find it funny. He remembered when Alvin used to hide bottles from his wife, Cora, all over the ranch so he would never be without. If he really had quit after having loved whiskey so much, that was another indication he was slipping.

Damn it, why do my friends have to get old while I've got my back turned?

Alvin said, "Everybody back home is anxious about you . . . Cora, even her mother."

Hewey believed what he said about Cora, but not his comment about Cora's mother. Old Lady Faversham never had liked Hewey, but then, she didn't like her son-in-law either. Hewey waited for Alvin to mention someone else. When he did not, Hewey asked, "How's Miss Renfro?"

Alvin said, "You can ask her yourself." He turned and beckoned.

A shadow moved through the doorway, almost hidden behind Walter and Eve and Alvin. Spring Renfro stepped around them. She gave him only a thin and fleeting smile, but it was like someone had lit up all the lights in the house.

"I'm sorry to see you like this, Hewey."

He pulled up the sheet to cover his shoulders. "I feel fine. Just a bruise here and there." He reached for her hand, but she was not close enough. Even so, the sight of the teacher was like a tonic to him. Some might regard her as a spinster and even say she was plain, but each man's standard of "pretty" was a personal matter. She could probably still have her pick of Upton County bachelors, age forty and over, and there were a good many of them. Hadn't somebody told him she and Alvin's foreman—what was his name?—had been seeing one another?

"I sure didn't expect you to come, Spring . . . Miss Renfro. But I'm glad you did. I can already feel the hurt fadin' away."

Spring's lips tightened as she stared at him. "I . . . everybody's been very concerned about you."

"You don't have to be. I'll be up from here in a few days." He looked at Alvin. "I'm out of a job. Reckon you've got one for me? I wouldn't ask for full pay. I know it'll be a month or two before I can do anything heavy."

The fun went out of Alvin's eyes. His gaze drifted to where the sheet covered the bound arm and leg. "Sure, Hewey. You'll be as good as new in no time, and there's always more work than we can get around to."

His words were confident, but their tone said they were empty. Alvin could not see the future as Hewey chose to see it. He saw only a crippled-up cowboy. He had seen a lot of them in his time.

But Hewey had no intention of remaining this way. He would be as good as he had ever been . . . better, even, because every year he lived made him a little smarter.

Hewey's visitors stayed a couple of hours, the talk rambling around like a blind sheep over subjects of little or no interest to Hewey. He only half listened to most of it, putting in a word here and there. He concentrated his attention on Spring. He remembered with pleasure the summer they had come to know one another, and with regret the promises spoken, promises broken.

Four years. It seemed not half so long since they had talked of buying the Barcroft homestead and settling down together to a life of farming. But Hewey had been too restless to walk long behind a plow. Spring had released him, and he had ridden away to seek new country, hoping to find a place where life would remain as it had been in his youth, never changing, never making him feel like a stranger lost and passed up by time, trapped in a world he no longer understood.

Surely somewhere there must be such a place. Maybe he would find it in the Guadalupes, when he was well.

There was no question of the visitors returning home that evening, for the drive from Upton City had killed most of the day. They took rooms in the hotel. That was enough to tell Hewey his brother and sister-in-law were coming up in the world. In earlier times when they had to be in town overnight they carried their bedrolls and put up in a wagon yard.

They came again after breakfast. Hewey talked with everyone, but his gaze remained mostly on Spring.

Alvin took a watch from his pocket. "I hate to bust up a good party, but we'd better start if we're to get home before dark. No tellin' how many flats we may have to stop and fix."

Eve tried to talk Tommy into going home with them, but Tommy declined. "I need to stay and watch out for Uncle Hewey. Anyway, my horse is still at the Circle W."

Hewey said, "I can take care of myself. I'll be up and out of here in a week or two, and I'll get our horses."

Tommy had a stubbornness in his eyes that Hewey had often seen in his mother's. When Eve got that look, not even an earthquake could shake her. "I'm stayin'."

Alvin, Walter and Eve said their good-byes and walked out with Tommy, leaving Spring alone for a private moment with Hewey. She gripped Hewey's hand, as if on impulse, then quickly released it. "Please do whatever the doctor tells you."

"Can't do much else as long as I'm layin' here. But I won't be here long." He wished she had held on to his hand, but she had moved back a step. He got an inkling of the hurt he had caused her, the hurt she must still be feeling. "How about you, Spring? Are you happy?"

"I'm making a living."

"But are you happy?"

"It depends on what you consider happy. I guess I am. Are you?"

"I was. Thought I was, anyway, 'til this happened to me." He struggled for the words. "Everybody tells me Farley Neal is a good man."

She was a moment in answering. "He is."

"You-all plannin' on gettin' married?"

The question took her by surprise. "Would it bother you?"

"I've got no right to be bothered. I went off and left you a long time ago."

"It was a decision we made together. If you'd stayed you'd have had to change too much, and you weren't ready for that."

"I still ain't changed. Not much, anyway."

"If you did, you wouldn't be Hewey Calloway." She reached as if to take his hand again but changed her mind. Before he could say anything more, she was gone.

He stared at the empty doorway, remembering the way she looked, the way she talked, her gentle fragrance, and he pondered the imponderable price of freedom.

He hated the crutch. Though it gave him limited mobility, it was unwieldy and kept threatening to throw him to the floor. Because of his broken arm, he could use only one. That kept him off balance. Each step aroused sharp protest somewhere inside, so he ventured out of the room only to take advantage of the doctor's indoor plumbing at the end of the hall. Tommy was usually there to support him, but Hewey made him stop at the bathroom door. Some activities were meant to be private.

Peeler visited every day that he was not driving Old Man Jenkins somewhere. Blas Villegas and Aparicio Rodriguez dropped in once. Aparicio said little, but Hewey could read the thought in his eyes: *This could have happened to me. It still might.* Blas said, "Maybeso now you will learn to cook, like me."

"One day of my cookin' and the whole outfit would up and quit. No, I'll stick to punchin' cows."

Jenkins did not appear. Hewey asked the doctor about him.

The doctor said, "He inquires after you almost every day, but he won't come by. I think you trouble his conscience."

"But not enough for him to pay all my doctor bills."

"The age of miracles is past."

It bothered Hewey that Snort Yarnell had not visited him again. He assumed at first that Snort was in a distant camp on the Slash R and could not come to town. Then Tommy told him he had bumped into Snort on the street. Snort had asked about Hewey, then hurried away.

That he had not come by to visit hurt almost as much as the broken arm and the bum knee.

About a week after the accident Dr. Evans said Hewey was doing well enough to be moved to the boardinghouse where Tommy was staying. He brought a wheelchair. "It's too far to walk on that crutch. Tommy can push you over there in five minutes."

Hewey took an instant disliking to the chair. Among other things, it reminded him of Old Lady Faversham. She could walk when she wanted to, but she favored a wheelchair because it was a way of seeing to it that others waited upon her. "Can't we hold off 'til dark so everybody won't be lookin' at me? I don't want them all thinkin' I'm a cripple."

"They might as well get used to seeing you as you are."

"I don't intend to stay this way. The healin' is just takin' a little more time than I expected."

"You'd better get used to the idea, Hewey. I don't know to what extent you will eventually recover, but I can tell you this: you'll never be the same as you were."

"Bet you."

Getting out of bed and into the wheelchair involved considerable internal pain, but the embarrassment of being watched by strangers was almost as bad. Hewey kept his head down and his hat low as Tommy pushed him along. They had almost reached the boardinghouse when Hewey's eye caught a familiar figure on the opposite side of the street. Tommy said, "There's Snort Yarnell."

Snort stopped to look, and for a moment he seemed about to hurry away. Instead, he reluctantly crossed the street, pausing to let a wagon go by.

"Howdy, Hewey." His subdued voice sounded guilty as if he had been caught sipping whiskey in church.

"What you been doin' that you couldn't come to see me?"

"I wanted to, God knows I did. But I couldn't bring myself to look at you in this shape."

"I won't be like this for long. Tommy says he saw you a couple of days ago. You must have an easy boss if he lets you hang around town."

"Ain't with the Slash R anymore. I quit."

Hewey was not overly surprised. It had not been in Snort's nature to stay with one job long enough to wear out a pair of pants, but Hewey had thought he might have found a home at the Slash R. Even someone restless as Snort needed to light in one place eventually.

"What're you goin' to do now?"

"Got me a job here in town. Night watchman."

Hewey could hardly believe. "Walkin' around in the dark, jinglin' keys and checkin' doors? That don't sound like a job for Snort Yarnell."

"I hate to admit it, Hewey, but seein' you the other day scared the hell out of me."

"Why? That was nothin' compared to the time you saw a horse stomp Old Grady Welch to death."

"But that was years ago, and we're older now. After seein' you I went back out to the ranch, took a look at them owl-headed broncs and got the shakes so bad I couldn't hold a cup of coffee. I asked for my time."

"You'll get over it. Me and you'll be ridin' the rough string together before the snow flies."

Snort's voice cracked. "Ain't you figured it out yet? You ain't ever ridin' the rough string again. Neither am I. It's a fool's game, and we sat at the table too long."

Hewey stared at Snort's back as the cowboy's long legs carried him quickly away.

Tommy seemed shaken. "I never thought I'd see Snort Yarnell boogered over anything. You reckon he's right?"

"You can't pay attention to what Snort says. He changes his mind a lot oftener than he changes his socks." But Hewey had a cold feeling in the pit of his stomach. He tried to dismiss it as foolishness, but it would not go away. His broken arm hurt, and his knee, and something inside. He tried to roll a cigarette, but his hands shook and he spilled his tobacco.

Damn that Snort! Whatever he's got is contagious, and he's given it to me.

The boardinghouse room he shared with Tommy was on the ground floor so he did not have to contend with the stairs, though getting up the two steps to the front porch was a challenge. Because of that, he did not try to venture beyond the porch the first three days. He gradually learned to manipulate the crutch with some dexterity.

He could see an improvement in his right knee when the doctor unwrapped it. Most of the angry red was gone, the blue was fading, and the external damage was healing over.

The knee remained stiff, however. He could not straighten the leg.

He said, "This *will* keep gettin' better, won't it?"

The doctor said, "That knee took a lot of punishment. It's like a twisted hinge. You hammer it out the best you can, but it may bind and never work again quite the way it did when it was new."

"You're tellin'me I could have a gimpy leg from now on?"

"It's a mark of your trade. How many *old* cowboys do you know that don't limp or walk with a cane? The body can take only so much."

"What about my arm?"

"It may never be strong again, but at least the elbow is intact."

Hewey resisted the doctor's appraisal. "Maybe you just ain't run onto a patient as determined as I am."

"Keep that attitude. Determination may be better than any medicine I can give you."

But determination and faith both began to flag. Each morning when he arose, Hewey sat on the edge of the bed and tried straightening the right leg. He attempted to convince himself that it was getting better every day, but after five or six days he realized that any improvement was marginal or perhaps even imaginary. At least the knee was giving him less pain day by day. He could put a little weight on it. The doctor said perhaps soon he could discard the crutch and get along on a cane.

The day came when he told Tommy, "I want to go to the wagon yard and take a look at Biscuit." Aparicio had brought the brown and Tommy's dun to town.

Tommy eyed the crutch with misgivings. "It's a good ways down there."

"Fine. I need to get as far away from this place as I can."

He shrugged off Tommy's attempt to help him down the porch steps. "Let's see how good I can do on my own."

The knee hurt less than he expected, though he felt a

sharp pain inside. Whatever had shaken loose was still floating around. It was only a couple of blocks from the boardinghouse to the wagon yard, but it felt like a mile. Sweat ran down his face by the time he got there, and the breeze was cool blowing through the wet spots in his shirt.

Tommy said, "You better sit down awhile."

"Been sittin' too long already. The only place I want to sit down is in a saddle."

He whistled, and Biscuit ambled up to the fence. Hewey rubbed the horse's nose, then moved through the wooden gate. Biscuit watched suspiciously, for Hewey's movements were strange to him, and he took the crutch as a potential threat. Hewey talked softly, whistling under his breath until the horse ventured up to nuzzle him, hoping for some kind of handout. Hewey patted him and rubbed his good right hand up and down the brown neck. His eyes burned a little. Cooped up indoors so long, he was not used to this bright sunlight.

He told Tommy, "Saddle him for me."

Tommy protested, "Uncle Hewey, you can't."

"Saddle him."

Tommy fetched a bridle, then led Biscuit to where the saddle had been placed on a wooden rack. "You oughtn't to do this."

Hewey knew he could not mount from the ground. "There's a hay bale on the ground yonder. Lead him over there."

Hewey had some difficulty in stepping up onto the bale, but the crutch gave him leverage. Tommy led the horse up close. Hewey handed him the crutch. Gripping the horn with his right hand, he made a little hop, fitting his left foot into the stirrup and swinging the stiff right leg up and over the saddle. It extended awkwardly out to one side. He could not bring it in close enough to touch the stirrup. The effort set the knee to throbbing. But Hewey was in the saddle; that was the important thing.

"Come on, Biscuit, let's mosey a little."

He set Biscuit into a walk, then a trot out into the large corral. Almost immediately Hewey had to slow him back to a walk, for his knee felt as if it were afire, and the internal pain was like a sword thrust between his ribs. Nauseous, he leaned out to one side, expecting to vomit.

Tommy saw his distress. "I tried to tell you." He came running, bringing the crutch. "Let me help you down."

"I can make it by myself." But Hewey quickly found that he could not. He had to lean heavily on Tommy for support to dismount.

He fitted the crutch under his right arm and felt cold sweat breaking on his face. The nausea was slow to pass.

Biscuit seemed confused. Hewey patted him on the neck. "It ain't your fault, old friend."

Tommy's voice was quiet and sympathetic. "I'll unsaddle him for you while you rest awhile. Then we'll go back to the boardin'house."

Hewey dropped down on the bale of hay, his shoulders slumped. He watched while Tommy removed the saddle, blanket and bridle and fed Biscuit some oats out of a barrel.

All the discouraging words he had heard from Snort and Peeler and the doctor seemed to be shouting in his ears.

What if they were right? What if he never could ride again?

He bowed his head so Tommy could not see him drag a sleeve across his eyes.

10

Hewey sat in a wicker chair on the front porch of the boardinghouse, absently tapping the end of a cane against the wooden floor as he gazed morosely out into the street. He observed people going about their end-of-the-day business as if the world were not skewed off its proper axis and they had never heard of such a thing as an outlawed black stud.

Tommy sat sideways on the top step, leaning against a post and positioned so he could watch his uncle, his guileless eyes full of concern. He had remained close after the incident at the wagon yard. "Uncle Hewey, you ain't taken a decent meal in three days. Ain't slept much either."

"It's hard to sleep good when you've had the slats kicked out from under you."

Hewey had not summoned the nerve to go back to the wagon yard, much as he wanted to. Seeing Biscuit, knowing he could not ride him, would only renew the bitter disappointment.

Tommy said, "It ain't healthy, sittin' around here mopin' and spendin' money you ain't got. You'd be better off at home with the folks. How about me telephonin' Alvin or Wes Wheeler?"

"They got more important things to do than drive all this way for a cripple who ain't in shape to do anything for anybody."

"You've done a lot of good things for a lot of people."

"That was before. I ain't worth much to anybody now."

"You're worth a lot to me, and Mama and Daddy. And to Miss Renfro too, I'll bet."

"Miss Renfro and Alvin's foreman have got an understandin', or so I heard."

"She came all the way here to see you."

Hewey did not feel like putting up with Tommy's pestering. "I wish you'd go down to the wagon yard and make sure they fed Biscuit this evenin'."

"I fed him myself, remember? He's gettin' fat, standin' in that pen. He's liable to try and throw you off the next time you get on him."

The next time. Hewey wondered when the next time would come, or if it would ever be.

"Well, go see if he's got enough water. The worst thing that can happen to an animal is to run out of water."

He knew Tommy was not fooled; Hewey was trying to get rid of him for a while. Tommy pushed to his feet. "I'll go see if they need help puttin' out hay for the night." He had been doing some work around the wagon yard to pay for the two horses' keep.

As Tommy started up the street a chugging noise made him stop and look back. He returned to the edge of the porch. "I think that truck yonder is Blue Hannigan's."

Hewey had not reconciled himself to the thought of Blue Hannigan retiring some of his freight wagons for a truck. It was like surrendering and taking up the enemy's flag.

The truck pulled to a shuddering stop in front of the boardinghouse, its engine clattering before it shut down. Hewey expected to see one of Hannigan's drivers, but Blue Hannigan himself stepped to the ground. He extracted a wad of tobacco from his mouth and dropped it in the dirt before starting toward the porch.

"Damn if this ain't a sight to behold, Hewey Calloway in a rockin' chair. Ain't you ashamed of yourself, lollin' around in idleness while there's still daylight left?"

He walked up onto the porch and extended his hand.

Hewey said, "No more ashamed than you ought to be, turnin' good mules out to pasture and scarin' horses off the road with that stinkin' contraption."

"At least it hasn't throwed me off and stomped on me." Hannigan's forced smile faded as he stepped back to give Hewey a deep-frowning once-over. "You look better than I expected, goin' by what I heard. Can you navigate with that cane?"

"Fair, but I couldn't even footrace Fat Gervin." He enjoyed a moment's fantasy of outrunning Fat and administering a few good cane licks to that broad backside. He tried to flex his left arm, but the cast would not give. "I don't know how much it'll bend when the doctor finally cuts this thing off."

"Time and patience, Hewey."

"Worst thing is somethin' busted loose inside. The doctor says he can patch up an arm and a leg, but he can't do much for my vitals."

Blue blurted, "How would you like to go home?"

Home had always been whatever ranch he was working for, and at the moment he was unemployed. "I don't have a home except for Walter and Eve's place, and that's theirs, not mine."

"I brought a load of freight, and it's too late to start home tonight. I've got room for a passenger if you'd like to go back with me in the mornin'."

Tommy had come up to join them on the porch. "Why don't you, Uncle Hewey? I can take the horses home."

"By yourself? I'd never stop catchin' hell from your mama."

"I can handle it, like I could've handled that black stud."

"But what use would I be to anybody? What could I do besides maybe swat flies?"

"What're you doin' *here*? At least we wouldn't be runnin' up a board bill."

Hannigan put in, "He makes sense, even if he *is* kin to you. Maybe you'll heal faster, bein' amongst family and the people that know you best."

The thought set Hewey's skin to prickling. This was an eye-filling country to be in, surrounded by the rock-crowned peaks of the Davis Mountains, but even a mountain got old when watched too long from a rocking chair.

"I won't be able to get out and open gates for you."

"Any gates get in our way, we'll just bust through them."

Hewey found Tommy nodding hopefully. The boy had grown up a lot in a short time, and he was ready to go home. "All right, Tommy, but don't you tarry along the road, and be sure you go way around Pecos City. It's too rough for a farm boy."

Hewey tried to look stoic while the doctor carefully unwrapped his knee, though it remained sore enough to make him grit his teeth. The surface appeared to have healed over fairly well. "Bend it a little and let's see what happens. Slow and careful now."

Hewey tried, cautiously. The knee felt as if he had jammed a hot coal into the joint.

Evans said, "I don't know how much more it will improve. I'll rewrap it, and you'd best abuse it as little as possible until the healing is complete."

"What about my arm?"

"That cast had better stay on it another month."

"It itches under there like a nest of lice have found a home."

"That is altogether possible."

Hewey could not tell when the doctor was joking with him, for his face never changed. The only hint of a smile was a slight twitching at one end of his gray moustache.

"Doc, I'm obliged to you for takin' such good care of me. I'll start payin' you soon as I'm able to work again."

"Don't you worry about that. Jenkins is paying me."

"Only half. He said half the expense is mine."

"That's what he thinks. But I quoted his share at double my normal rates."

"Is that honest?"

"Of course not. Do you think cowboys are the only liars in the world? One of the first things a young doctor learns is how to look regretful when he asks a well-heeled patient for twice what the treatment is worth." He motioned that he was finished. "Let me know how you get along." He put the bandage roll back in a cabinet. "And do me a favor, will you?"

"What's that?"

"Leave the broncs to the young men. Their bones knit better."

Hannigan and Snort Yarnell waited for him on the porch rather than go inside. Snort swore that the smell of medicine made him sick, and the only cure he had found was whiskey. When he had money or his companions did, he took a lot of curing. He walked with Hannigan and Hewey to the truck, which he eyed with silent disapproval.

Hewey said, "You won't last another week on that night-watchman's job. You'll be bustin' broncs again before I get this cast off my arm."

"I wouldn't want to take your money, not that you've got any. I know how Old Man Jenkins pays." Snort's eyes watered a little. "I do hate to see you leave here in this shape. I've got half a mind to go along and see that you're took care of."

"Don't worry, I can't afford to die. I'm too broke to bury."

Snort gave him a grip that threatened to put Hewey's right hand in a cast along with his left arm, then helped him up into the truck. "Don't you let Blue run you off in a ditch. Them trucks is dangerous."

Hannigan picked his way along a crooked old wagon trail to which rubber tires were still something new, out beyond the Glass Mountains, then across the dry greasewood flats toward Fort Stockton. The truck was rough even on an average stretch, and the jolting was severe in places where wind had blown out the ruts or where they crossed over deeply worn cattle trails. Hewey ached inside, but he would not complain. Now and again when a relatively smooth surface presented itself, Hannigan would step on the accelerator and push the truck to twenty or twenty-five miles an hour. The speed almost took Hewey's breath away.

Hannigan said, "I've owned many a good mule in my time, but I never had one that could go like this."

Hewey remembered Hannigan's frustration with this

truck on the street in Upton City. "When a mule acted up, though, you could kick it in the belly. Kick this thing and all you'll get is a broken foot."

The freighter said, "What would you think about drivin' one of these things?"

"I think I'd rather have *both* legs broke." Hewey frowned. "Are you serious, or just makin' talk?"

"Just makin' talk right now, but someday when you've healed up as much as you're goin' to, I might get serious. Like them or not, these trucks are a comin' thing. I took a look at the wall a couple of years ago and saw the handwritin' all over it. The day'll come when you'll stand at the road and see a car or a truck pass by every ten or fifteen minutes. Horses and mules are fixin' to go the way of the buffalo."

It was a sobering thought, one Hewey did not tolerate for long. "Nope, these gasoline buggies are a big thing right now, but they'll fade out like chin whiskers when everybody's had a bellyful of tryin' to keep them runnin'. There'll always be horses and mules."

Hannigan shook his head. "Even Alvin Lawdermilk sees what's comin'. He's sellin' off a lot of his mares and increasin' his cow herd to take up the slack. Ain't you read about the big oil booms over in East Texas? It's on account of everybody needin' gasoline."

"I heard those oil fields stink worse than a den of polecats."

"Not if they belong to you. They smell like money."

"But I don't own one. I've always been happy just bein' a cowpuncher."

"If that leg don't straighten up, and that arm, you may not be a cowpuncher anymore. What you goin' to do then?"

Hewey swallowed hard. He did not want to admit how many nights he had lain awake wondering the same thing. He certainly did not care to start driving a truck. He fell back on one of Eve's favorite sayings when doubt intruded. "The Lord will provide."

"The Lord generally provides best to those that help theirselves."

Late in the afternoon, Hannigan pulled into Upton City. He had repaired three flat tires along the way, which he said was not bad for the distance. Hewey figured it would have taken three days to make the same mileage on horseback if one did not want to punish the mount. But time had seldom been of premium value to him. He had rather have made the trip on Biscuit.

Hannigan said, "I need to stop by the office and see if the roof has fallen in. Then I'll take you on out to Walter's."

A sinking sun had turned the clouds to gold low on the western horizon. If Hannigan drove out to the place now, he would finish the trip in the dark. Hewey said, "It's late, and I've already put you to too much trouble as it is. I'll tote my bedroll down to the wagon yard."

"I ain't keen on drivin' after dark, so I won't argue with you. There's a cot in my office that don't get used much. It's better than any at the wagon yard, and free."

Free sounded good to Hewey in his present financially stressed condition. "I ain't quite flat busted. I'll set you up to supper down at the chili joint. It's little enough to pay for the ride home."

Hannigan's schedule was so erratic that his wife never put anything in the oven until she saw him coming. "It's a deal."

Hewey fumbled his tarp-covered roll down from the bed of the truck with his right arm, making a grab with the fingertips that stuck out from the cast on his broken left arm. He dropped it. Hannigan said, "Let me." He picked up the roll by the rope that bound it.

Hewey said, "Damn if I ain't come down in the world. Can't even handle my own bedroll."

Leaning on the cane, he followed Hannigan up onto the narrow porch. Out back was a complex of corrals that used to be home to a considerable aggregation of horses and mules when all the freighting was done by wagon. Now only a few remained, milling around wooden racks piled high with hay. Hewey saw a new sheet-iron garage, and in front of it a couple of barrels with pumps attached to dispense gasoline and oil. At the distance he could not actually smell them, but he imagined he did.

Hannigan had surrendered to the new times. It seemed to Hewey that most people had. Regret gripped him, then turned into something akin to grief at an old friend's funeral. The world he had known—the world in which he had been at home—was slipping away from him piece by piece.

What he called a chili joint was actually more than that, though it had not always been. It had begun as a hole-in-the-wall café started by a one-time wagon cook who decided he wanted to spend the rest of his nights sleeping under a roof instead of a tarp. Now it was operated by a couple of widows who had little experience with the open range but knew their way around a wood range. Though their fare was lacking in fancy appearance, it compensated in flavor and generous quantity. *Fancy* was all right for city folks, but *filling* was what a cowboy wanted. And Hewey was hungry. He and Hannigan had made their noon meal, such as it was, on cold biscuits, bacon and coffee boiled in a black pot Hannigan carried in the bed of the truck.

The two middle-aged women bustled about in the kitchen. One had a daughter who might be eighteen or twenty— Hewey had difficulty in guessing the ages of people that young. She waited the tables, taking orders from the customers and from the two older women. In Hewey's view she was pretty as a speckled pup, slender where she ought to be and plump in the right places, but he suspected she might be a little lacking in smarts. She seemed to have to be told everything twice.

Hewey remembered one of the older women and her husband, who had been only moderately successful as a farmer. In Hewey's view he had worked himself to death trying to make crops on land better suited for grass.

The widow came out of the kitchen to sympathize with Hewey. "I hope you'll soon be back to your old self."

Hannigan said, "I don't know if we want him that way or not. There was things about his old self that needed improvement."

"One thing I ain't done," Hewey responded, "I ain't surrendered to trucks and automobiles."

The girl brought out two platters with steak, gravy and fried potatoes. "Maybe you won't mind surrenderin' to this."

Hewey took up his knife and fork and quickly capitulated. Even Blas Villegas did not cook this well.

Hannigan watched Hewey cut into the steak, swabbing each piece in the gravy. He told the women, "If Hewey ever decides to give up his bachelor ways, he's liable to come lookin' for one of you."

The farmer's widow said, "As I recall, there was talk a few years ago that he might be about to jump over the broomstick with that schoolteacher, Miss Renfro."

Hewey swallowed and laid down his fork. "I figured everybody had forgotten."

Hannigan said, "In a small town, everybody knows everything and nobody forgets nothin'."

"It was best for her that it didn't happen. I wouldn't've been no catch."

The conversation dampened his appetite; then Fat Gervin came into the restaurant and finished it. Gervin stopped just inside the door to grin at the girl. "Howdy, sweetness." Embarrassed, she looked away.

Her mother called from the kitchen door, "Annabelle, you come in here and start a new pot of coffee. I'll wait on Mr. Gervin."

Relieved, the girl hurried into the kitchen.

For the first time, Gervin saw Hewey. He seemed about to turn and leave, then changed his mind and walked with heavy steps to the table where Hewey and Hannigan sat.

"Hadn't heard you was back in town."

Hewey was about to say he had just arrived, but a stubborn streak cut off the words. He didn't have to explain a damned thing to the likes of Fat Gervin.

Gervin stared at the cast on Hewey's left arm and the bulge in his trousers leg caused by the heavy bandage on his knee. "Somebody told me you ain't the bronc stomper you used to be. Looks like they was right."

In spite of himself, Hewey said grittily, "It was that loco black stud you palmed off on Old Man Jenkins."

Hewey thought he could see gloating in Gervin's eyes, though perhaps it was imagination. Gervin asked, "How did the old man like them horses?"

Hewey decided there was no reason he should be the only one here with worries on his mind. Fat Gervin deserved a few. "He throwed a ring-tailed fit. Last time I saw him, his Fort Worth lawyers were gettin'ready to file a lawsuit against you." Fort Worth lawyers had a reputation for being among the toughest in Texas, unless it might be the ones in Galveston. But those were too far away to carry much weight here.

Gervin's smile died a sudden death. "A lawsuit?"

There was no use in settling for a small lie when a big one would do so much more good. "His lawyers said you pulled a fraud on him and he ought to be able to collect at least fifty thousand dollars. Maybe a hundred."

Gervin gripped the back of a chair, his heavy jaw sagging. "A hundred thousand dollars?"

"Plus lawyers' fees."

Doubt came into Gervin's eyes. "They can't do that."

"Mr. Jenkins has got the same lawyers that almost throwed the T&P Railroad into bankruptcy."

Arms folded, the woman said with exaggerated politeness, "We've got a nice table for you in the corner, Mr. Gervin."

Gervin turned and walked out, dragging his feet. The woman went to the window and stared after him, puzzled but not disappointed over his abrupt departure. She said,

"I never saw such a shameless flirt. It's a good thing all the young ladies around here know him for what he is. And him a married man with two young'uns."

To Hewey, how Fat Gervin had wooed and won C. C. Tarpley's daughter was a mystery as profound as the afterlife.

Hannigan held back a laugh until Gervin was well out of sight. "I'll swear, Hewey, you're still the best straight-faced liar in West Texas. Fat won't get a bit of sleep tonight."

Hewey should have felt a surge of triumph, but anger came instead, and a sharp pain in his side. "I ain't had a good night's sleep since that black stud did this to me. That stud and Fat Gervin."

He did not seem likely to sleep well tonight either. He lighted a lamp, then spread his blankets and sat on the steel cot in the back of Hannigan's office to roll a cigarette. He shifted his weight as the frame's sharp edge bit into his legs. He had found no way to be completely comfortable, whether sitting or lying down. He was tired from the trip, but the anger Gervin aroused had swept away any sleepiness he might have felt. He was wide awake and itching to move.

The cigarette was bitter, its smoke burning his eyes. He took a couple of unsatisfactory drags on it, then tossed it into a metal can filled with ashes to catch cigarette butts and tobacco juice. Tobacco had not tasted right to him since the accident.

He limped out the door and looked down the street. He saw lamplight in Dutch Schneider's saloon. A drink couldn't hurt, and it might even help a little.

The little German was dismayed to see Hewey's condition. He expressed his regrets. Hewey saw a couple of cowboys at the bar, men he did not know. At a table toward the rear, C. C. Tarpley was hunched alone, as he had been the last time Hewey had seen him. He saw Hewey and beckoned.

Hewey asked Schneider, "Is C.C. doin' any better?"

Schneider shook his head. "About the same. Always he was a fighter. Now the fight is gone, and he only sits, sipping a little whiskey."

"I know how he feels. I'll go back and jaw with him a bit."

Tarpley gave Hewey the same study that the Dutchman had. Hewey knew the sympathy in his voice was genuine. "I heard tell you got busted up. I'm sorry."

"It's what I always got paid such high wages for."

"Sit down and have a drink. We can share miseries."

Hewey pulled out a chair and stretched his good leg. The other would not bend. "You ever gone and seen a doctor, C.C.?"

"I don't need a doctor to tell me I ain't long for this world. He'd charge me for information I already know."

Hewey pondered the logic in that. If C.C. died, the money he saved would do him no good . . . unless he figured on taking it with him. If anybody could do that, it would be C.C. "Maybe whatever's wrong with you can be fixed."

"Can what's wrong with you be fixed?"

"I wish I knew." Hewey did not like admitting to his doubts, but there were times when they bore down on him like the chill of a cold winter norther. They came now as he stared into the melancholy of the old man's eyes.

Tarpley said, "I was like you once, wilder than a March hare. Rode anything with hair on it and roped anything that'd run. Came a time, though, when I had to start doin' my ridin' in a buggy. Hated it at first, 'til I figured out I could hire men to do the things I couldn't do for myself, and I could concentrate on puttin' my ranch and my bank together."

"I ain't a rancher or a banker."

"I wasn't either, then, but I learned there's bigger and better things to do than ride broncs and rope wild stock. Gettin' stove-up was the best thing that ever happened to me." Tarpley's voice dropped, and his eyes were bleak. "Now that I got all that stuff put together, what's fixin' to happen to it?"

"You've got a daughter, and she's got a couple of young'uns. It'll go to them."

"Time them kids get grown, there won't be nothin' left of it. That son-in-law of mine is just waitin' for me to cross over Jordan, then he'll run through it like a drunken mule skinner. Some gold-diggin' woman'll flare a skirt and show him an ankle, and he'll be gone. Fat Gervin ain't got the judgment God gave a goose."

Hewey doubted that Tarpley knew of the swindle Gervin had run on Old Man Jenkins. He saw no reason to burden his already troubled mind by telling him.

Tarpley said, "If I knew just when I was goin' to die, I might go shoot Fat on my last day. We could make the trip to hell together."

With a little luck, Hewey thought, some affronted father or husband might beat Tarpley to that pleasure. Most women shied away from Fat like quail from a bird hound and giggled behind his back, but a few would probably be impressed by the wealth he was in line to inherit. "You could put it in your will that Fat ain't to have anything to do with anything."

"But I've already made the mistake of lettin' him pretty well take over the bank and the everyday runnin' of the ranch. And whether I like it or not, he's my daughter's husband and the daddy of my grandkids."

Hewey shrugged. "Looks to me like the only choice you've got is to be stubborn and outlive him. You used to be a fighter, C.C. I can't see you just givin' up."

"Are you any better? You used to be full of piss and vinegar. Now you've got a look about you like a whipped dog, with your tail between your legs."

They sat in silence, together but each alone, agonizing over his individual troubles. Schneider came over to see if their glasses needed refilling, but they did not, so he

retreated quietly, careful not to disturb their solitary delib-
erations.

The whiskey made Hewey's stomach uneasy. He decided
he had had enough. Staring into the old rancher's sallow
face only depressed him. He stood up to go.

"I do wish you'd see a doctor, C.C."

The old man did not answer, and Hewey did not push
him. He said, "Good night." Tarpley did not reply.

Hewey slept fitfully and was up before good daylight, boiling coffee in a can on top of a wood heater in Hannigan's
office. Hannigan came along about sunup and invited Hewey
down to his house for breakfast, but Hewey begged off. His
stomach was none too stable. He had not drunk much last
night at Schneider's, so he blamed his problem on his brief
encounter with Fat Gervin, author of his difficulties.

Hannigan was gone awhile, then came back. He cranked
the truck motor, but it would not start. He used mule-skinner
language on it to no effect.

"Told you," Hewey said. "You oughtn't to've sold the
mules."

"It probably needs a rest after goin' to Alpine and back.
My other truck's out on a trip. Looks like I won't be gettin'
you out to Walter and Eve's today."

"No hurry. I'd be nothin' but a burden to them anyway."
Perhaps someone would come to town from over in the direction of Walter's, and Hewey could get a ride home in a
wagon or buggy. If not today, maybe tomorrow. Time didn't
mean much when a man couldn't do anything useful with it.

Hannigan still had a couple of wagons and a load of
freight to haul in them, but they were going in the wrong
direction. Hannigan said, "Make yourself to home. You're
welcome to stay here as long as you want to."

Hewey had no wish to impose upon hospitality. As soon
as Hannigan and a driver left with the wagons, he began
looking around for something practical to do. The office had

not been cleaned in a while. Hannigan's wife probably figured she had chores enough in keeping their house clean.
Hewey found an old rag and wiped dust from shelves and
cabinets. Then he took a broom from the corner and began
sweeping the floor. His impairments made him awkward,
and he knew the effects of his labor would be short-lived.
As soon as the wind arose, dust from the street and corrals
would blow in through the open windows and door. At least
when Hannigan came back he would find new dust instead
of old.

"Ah, Hewey," said a voice in the doorway. Turning,
Hewey saw Schneider, the saloonkeeper. "It is a good thing
you are doing. If a job you are looking for, there is more of
the same at my place of business."

Hewey felt a little embarrassed, being caught with a
broom in his hand. "I've drunk a saloon dry a time or two,
but I've never swamped one out. And I've never herded
sheep." He did not know which job would be the most
humiliating.

Schneider said one of Hannigan's trucks was supposed
to have brought him a supply of whiskey from the railroad
at Midland. They looked around but did not find it.

"Blue said he had a truck out. It must be bringin' your
whiskey." Hewey explained that he needed a ride to Walter's. "If anybody comes in from that direction, I wish you'd
tell them. I don't want to impose on Blue any longer than I
have to."

"He does not mind. He is your friend, and I am your
friend, too. Come visit my place as long as you wish."

Hewey warmed with gratitude. He had never had much
money in his pockets, but he had never lacked for friends.
Fat Gervin had access to C. C. Tarpley's bottomless bank
account, but he had no real friends. Hewey would not trade
places with him for all the money he could load upon both
of Blue Hannigan's trucks.

"I'm obliged to you, Dutch. Maybe it's time I learned how to swamp out a saloon. Then about the only thing I can say I've never done is to herd sheep."

After Schneider left, Hewey walked down to Pierson Phelps's store and told Phelps about his need for a ride if anybody came to town from that direction. Phelps expressed concern about Hewey's injuries. Hewey said, "I'll be as good as new pretty soon, and maybe a little smarter." His voice sounded hollow, for he felt he was lying to himself as well as to Phelps.

Phelps said, "I hope you'll be smart enough to quit ridin' those bad broncs."

Schneider kept a pot of coffee in the saloon and urged it upon his customers when he felt they had had enough of his other merchandise. Hewey had rarely seen him drink anything other than coffee. Schneider contended that whiskey was made to sell, not to drink.

Hewey accepted his invitation to a cup of coffee, then asked where Schneider kept the broom. After a mild protest, the Dutchman handed him one from his storeroom. It probably pained the man more to watch Hewey work than to do it himself, but Hewey persevered until he swept the dust out the front door. Then he went back to the storeroom and began cleaning it, too.

He heard a familiar voice from inside the saloon. At the storeroom door, he saw Fat Gervin buying two bottles of bourbon to take to the ranch with him. Gervin spotted Hewey, standing with the broom in his good hand. Surprise faded to a look of satisfaction. "You've finally found a job that fits you, Hewey Calloway."

Hewey's skin prickled. He wanted to say, *You're the son of a bitch that put me here*, but he bit back the words.

He had always been generous with whatever little money he had. Often he had lent it to down-on-their-luck friends and strangers without worrying about getting it back. But

Fat Gervin owed him, and sometime, the good Lord willing, that self-important gentleman would pay up.

"If I was you, Fat, I'd be off to Fort Worth or someplace, findin' me some lawyers like Old Man Jenkins has got."

Gervin said, "I don't believe that lawsuit business. You're just hoorawin' me." But his eyes revealed doubt.

I've got him on his left foot, Hewey thought. *And I'm going to keep him there.*

11

For lack of something constructive to do, Hewey was lying on the cot with his right arm over his eyes in Hannigan's office when a tall man walked in. "Didn't mean to wake you up," the intruder apologized.

"Wasn't asleep," Hewey said, though he had been napping, compensating for another restless night spent mostly awake.

"You may not remember me. I'm Farley Neal. Mr. Phelps told me you're needin' a ride."

Hewey blinked sleep from his eyes. He recognized the man who it was said was keeping company with Spring Renfro. He arose and shook Neal's hand. "I do remember you." He could not have forgotten. He gave Neal a long study, wondering how serious he really was about Spring.

"I've got a wagon, and I'm goin' to Alvin Lawdermilk's this afternoon. Somebody can carry you on over to your brother's place in the mornin'."

Hewey had reservations about riding with Neal, but he did not want to remain in town, either. "You sure it won't put you out none?"

"I've been stranded myself, and somebody always came along."

He seemed genuine enough, though Hewey kept a few

reservations just in case. "I'll leave Blue a note." At Hannigan's paper-strewn rolltop desk he found a pencil advertising the Fort Worth stockyards and scrawled a few lines on a ruled tablet. "I don't like for people to worry about me. Blue's got troubles enough of his own."

Neal helped Hewey roll his bed, though Hewey would rather have done it for himself. He was not keen on getting in Neal's debt. He was indebted to too many people already for favors he might never be able to repay. Neal tied the roll and carried it outside. Hewey dragged his saddle, blanket and bridle until Neal came back to take them from him.

Two young horses hitched to the wagon appeared to be in training. Alvin Lawdermilk had long made a business of raising and training horses and mules for the saddle or for harness.

Neal said, "You don't need to worry about them runnin' away and spillin' you. They're pretty well broke."

"I'm pleased to hear that." A wreck could undo all the healing he had accomplished and add to the damage.

Neal gave him a boost up, not loosing his hold until Hewey was safely set on the wagon seat. Hewey thanked him and tapped his cane gently against the sideboard. "Never thought I'd ever need three legs to get around."

"Things happen no matter how careful we try to be. It's nobody's fault."

Hewey saw Fat Gervin climbing into a red automobile in front of the bank and figured he had bought it with his father-in-law's money. Resentment warmed him, but he said, "No, it's nobody's fault."

He studied Neal, trying to find something about him to dislike. As Neal took hold of the leather lines, Hewey saw that he had big workingman's hands similar to his own, rough and calloused. One knuckle was knocked down like Hewey's, probably the result of an accident suffered in the line of duty. His face was lined with the marks of living, of working in the sun. His gray eyes were crow-tracked at the corners and had a way of looking straight at Hewey, un-flinching, yet making no judgment.

Hewey took him to be just what he appeared, a cowboy through and through. He could find no reason not to like him, apart from the fact that he was keeping company with Spring Renfro.

The road to the Lawdermilks' was long. Neal seemed to sense that Hewey did not feel like talking much, and he did not push him for conversation. Hewey felt more at ease riding on the wagon seat than in Hannigan's truck. Even when one of the horses broke wind, the smell suited him better than the odor of gasoline.

He wanted to ask about Spring, but he was a long time in gathering the nerve. Instead he asked, "How's everybody out at Alvin's? Is Julio Valdez still there?"

"Julio's the top horse and mule man, after Alvin himself."

"He always was. How do you get along with Old Lady Faversham?" Hewey regarded Alvin's vindictive mother-in-law as being a few bricks shy of a full load, a woman who could find fault in Jesus Christ.

"I get along with her just fine. For some reason she seems to like me."

"I'm glad she likes somebody. She used to pray for light-nin' to strike me and Alvin both." Hewey fretted awhile before he asked, "And Miss Renfro?"

"A fine lady. But you know that."

"I do for a fact."

Neal stopped the team at a fence line. Hewey apologized for being unable to climb down and open the gate.

Neal said, "I'd have to open it anyway if I was by myself, and I'm pleased to have the company." He handed the lines to Hewey. "Reckon you can drive them through after I open the gate?"

Hewey took the reins in his right hand and flexed the stiff fingers of his left, which protruded beyond the cast at the first joint. He did not want to admit to any doubt about his ability to handle the green team, though that doubt was substantial. "Nothin' to it."

He eased the team through the open gate. Though one of the young horses began acting up, Hewey kept a firm grip on the reins and brought the pair to a stop. His right hand was slick with sweat, but he felt a sense of minor victory. So far as he could remember offhand, it was the first substantial challenge he had met and mastered since his big bronc wreck.

He handed the lines back to Neal and rubbed his sweaty hand against his trousers. "Like I said, nothin' to it."

The horses surged against the harness. Silent a while, Neal finally said, "Spring tells me you and her once came close to marryin'."

"She told you about that?"

"We don't have any secrets. I've told her all about my first wife. Ada was a good woman, patient and kind, a lot like Spring. Saw most things the same way. She was . . ." Neal's voice thinned, and he looked away. However long it had been, it was obvious that he still grieved a little.

Hewey said, "People say you and Spring may marry up."

"Everybody's talked about it but us. How would you feel if we did?"

Hewey had to be honest. "I don't know."

"Do you feel like you still have some claim on her?"

"No claim. I don't reckon I ever did have. But to be honest, I still think about her a lot. Sometimes I wish . . ." He felt his hand sweating on the cane: "I wouldn't blame you none if you put me off right here and let me walk back to town."

"I wouldn't deserve her if I did a thing like that. I can understand you still thinkin' about her. After my wife died, I roamed around a long time tryin' to find someplace I belonged. Then I met Spring. She'd come close to marryin' once even before she knew you, but the poor feller died in Cuba durin' the war. Did you know about that?"

"She told me."

"She made me feel like I'd finally found a home. I expect it was that way for you, too."

"For a while, 'til the old ways got the best of me and I thought I just had to leave."

"I had the travelin' fever once. Finally got over it. Have you?"

Hewey rubbed his hand against the bandaged knee, which ached from the jolting of the wagon. "I don't know. Maybe. That crazy black stud may have put the fire plumb out."

Hewey had worked for Alvin Lawdermilk for short periods, so the ranch headquarters was like a second home to him. It was comforting to see it ahead as they passed through the final pasture gate. Several goats, unafraid, clustered at the roadside and watched like kids at a parade. A burro stubbornly stood its ground in the middle of the road and would not move until Neal got down from the wagon and threatened it with a stick.

The place appeared but little changed from the last time Hewey had seen it except that a modest new house had been constructed to one side of the sprawling single-story one that was home to Alvin, Cora and Cora's mother. Hewey surmised that the smaller house had been put up for Neal, who could not be expected to sleep in the combination bunkhouse and toolshed indefinitely, though Julio Valdez had done it for years.

The small schoolhouse had a fresh coat of white paint that gleamed in the sunlight like vanilla frosting on a cake. There Spring taught children from several miles around because town was too far away. To their regret, Alvin and Cora Lawdermilk had never had children of their own, so they had built the country schoolhouse on their place that they might enjoy the sight and sound of others' sons and daughters. Spring lived in a corner room of the L-shaped Lawdermilk house and took her meals with the family.

Hewey was not sure if school was out for the summer,

but certainly it must be out for the day because the sun was almost down. He watched the white building nevertheless, hoping he might see her step outside at any moment.

A screeching peacock heralded the wagon's approach, and a couple of blue-gray guinea hens trotted out of its way in a fluttering panic. The Lawdermilk headquarters had always been something of a menagerie. Whatever the species—beast, fowl or fish—if it was not carnivorous and would survive here, Alvin had it. It was Noah's ark without the water.

Julio Valdez heard the trace chains and came out of the barn as the wagon passed on its way to the big house. He shouted a greeting and trotted alongside, extending his hand. "Hey, Hooey, you come to stay?"

"Just the night, Hooley. Ain't caught you a *señorita* yet?"

"They run too fast for me."

Alvin Lawdermilk strode onto the broad porch of the big house, a jolly smile breaking across his ruddy face. "Well, looky what just dragged in. Couldn't stay away from Cora's cookin', could you, Hewey?"

"Been tastin' it in my dreams."

Alvin helped him down and hollered for his wife. "Cora, put another plate on the table. Better make it a platter. Look who's come for supper."

Hewey had noticed a telephone line strung above the barbed-wire fence that paralleled the wagon road. Alvin had a telephone now, but Hewey doubted that he needed a phone to talk to anyone within less than two miles. His voice would carry that far.

Cora came out onto the porch, wiping her hands on a white apron edged with lace. There had always been something of gentle elegance about Cora Lawdermilk, even when she and Alvin had started their married life thirty-something years ago in an unpainted one-room shack. She had spent those years guiding and cajoling her husband past his various weaknesses, the worst being whiskey and cussing, so that they might not be parted in the hereafter. If Alvin had truly quit drinking, as was claimed, the hereafter seemed secure. He was in other ways an upright citizen, a substantial rancher who his neighbors repeatedly re-elected to be a county commissioner. Everybody in the community would turn out for his funeral someday. Hewey hoped that was still years in the future.

Cora already knew of Hewey's injuries, but even so she seemed dismayed. She was the caring kind of woman who would bandage a sparrow's broken wing and raise dogie calves on a bottle. "Alvin, you help him up the steps and into the house so we can feed him. There's nothin' like good solid food to hurry the healin' process."

The screen door was bumped open, and a heavyset woman pushed onto the porch in a wheelchair, her gray hair atangle, her voice belligerent. "I can't hear myself think for all the commotion." Her accusing eyes lighted upon Hewey and did not soften as they took in the cast and the bandaged knee. "Some people are like a bad penny. They keep comin' back."

"Mother!" Cora admonished her.

Hewey could not remember anybody ever shutting Old Lady Faversham up before she had her say. "First cowboy I ever saw that was bound up tight enough to suit me. He ain't in no condition to be a danger to poor weak womenfolk."

No matter how well Alvin had provided for her daughter in later years, Mrs. Faversham had never forgiven him for having been a poor man at the start. She had always felt that Cora had settled for too little in marrying him. She had become equally protective toward Spring Renfro, fearful that some lusty rakehell might despoil her innocence.

Hewey had always felt a little guilty in the old woman's presence whether or not he had done anything to feel guilty about. "I'll just be spendin' the night and movin' on, Mrs. Faversham."

She raked him up and down with what the vaqueros out at the J Bar would call an evil eye. "Been many a young maiden's life ruined in just one night. But I reckon you're not in a shape to do much damage."

Her eyes softened as Farley Neal came up onto the porch, carrying groceries in his arms.

Anybody that old woman likes has got to have something wrong with him, Hewey thought But for the life of him he had not seen it, and he had been looking.

Hewey used the cane to hold the screen door open for Neal, who had both hands full. Cora said, "Go on in, Hewey. You know where the washpan is, on the back porch."

Washing one-handed, he dried his face on a towel and cast the pan of water out into the yard, scattering several chickens and a guinea hen that had been pecking around in the dirt. He walked back through the hall into the dining room.

There stood Spring Renfro, blue eyes wide. He had taken her by surprise. She brought both hands up to her face. "Hewey! I thought you were still in Alpine."

"I left," he said, realizing how silly that sounded. Of course he had left, if he was here.

She stared at him for a long, quiet moment. Once the surprise was gone, her eyes guarded whatever thoughts lay behind them. She said, "You're looking better than when I saw you last."

He wanted to say, *You've always looked good*. But all he managed was "Pleased to see you again."

She came closer, looking at his arm. "I hope it's knitting all right." Her voice was neutral, with the kind of general solicitude she might have given to anyone, even a stranger.

He wished for more. "If itchin' means knittin', it is."

"It's good to see you at home, Hewey."

"I ain't home yet."

"You're among friends anywhere you go. You're always at home." She gave him the smallest of smiles, finally, and Hewey melted.

Old Lady Faversham wheeled her chair down the hall and

stopped in the doorway to the dining room, shocked at see-ing the two together. "Farley Neal, you better get yourself in here. A wolf is after your lamb!"

It had been Lawdermilk family custom to gather around the piano in the parlor at night and sing while Cora or Spring played. Hewey's singing was more appropriate for night guard at the edge of a cattle herd than for a parlor, so he kept his voice low. Spring's clear soprano carried the mel-ody in perfect pitch, and Hewey thought Neal's smooth bari-tone would serve well in a church choir. The two made pleasant harmony together. Much too pleasant, Hewey felt.

Old Lady Faversham had a strong voice better served in yelling than in singing. She could not carry a tune in a milk bucket.

Cora said, "I haven't had a chance to buy any new sheet music in a while, Hewey. Surely you have learned a few new songs."

He had, but they would not do for a family parlor. "I'm afraid I don't have much ear for music."

"But you've got big eyes for a nice-lookin' woman," said Mrs. Faversham, her gaze switching to Spring, then back to Hewey.

Hewey felt his face flush. If Spring had any reaction, he could not see it.

Eventually the piano went silent and the conversation began to lag. Old Lady Faversham slumped in her wheel-chair, mercifully quiet, her eyes closed. Alvin yawned, and Cora laid down the knitting that had occupied her hands. Hewey reluctantly pushed himself to his feet, leaning heavily upon his cane.

"It's high time I let you-all get your rest." He turned to Spring. "You've got school to teach tomorrow."

"School's out for the summer," she said. "But it *is* late."

"I'll be takin' my bedroll out to the toolshed."

Neal said, "There's an extra bed in my house. No need to wake up Julio."

A house would be more comfortable than the shed, though Hewey wondered that Neal was being so kind to him. Perhaps he was trying to make a good showing for Spring. Hewey saw nothing wrong with that so long as it got him a good bed. "I'm obliged."

Spring said, "Be careful on the steps, Hewey. Help him, Farley."

Hewey appreciated her concern, though it rankled that she had to see him this way, unable to take care of himself without help the way he used to do.

Damn you again, Fat Gervin.

He and Neal said their good nights and walked to the smaller house, which Hewey assumed would be Neal's and Spring's together if they married. Just inside the door Neal struck a match and lighted a lamp. The house still had a new-lumber smell and the faint odor of recent painting. Hewey recognized a couple of pieces of furniture as having come from the Lawdermilk parlor. The rest appeared new but plain and utilitarian.

He said, "High livin' for a cowpuncher."

"I'd've settled for much less, but Cora insisted. She wanted it to be nice for Spring . . . if things go that way."

"They will, won't they?"

A tone of doubt crept into the slow answer. "I was fig-urin' they would." He looked at Hewey, then turned away. "I'm not sure now."

Hewey wondered what he meant by that.

Neal showed him a spare bed in a small room off the kitchen. Hewey tried to keep his eyes closed, hoping to bring on sleep, but he kept opening them, looking at moonlight reflected from the window. He was as wide awake as if it were the middle of the day. He thought a long time about how he must look to everybody, especially Spring, hobbling around on one leg and a cane, one arm useless except for limited movement of the fingers.

The doctor had told him to keep the knee tightly bound at least a couple more weeks, but now of a sudden the binding seemed oppressively heavy and hot and restrictive. He flung the thin covers aside and sat up on the edge of the bed. He had cut off the right leg of his long underwear above the knee to accommodate the binding. Even then it had been difficult to pull the shortened underwear and his pants on over the bulge of cloth.

With no light except what came through the window, he found the knot the doctor had tied in the gauze covering. He could not untie it with his fingers, so he cut it with his knife and began to unwrap the binding, slowly and carefully at first, then quickly, wanting to be done with it.

When the cloth lay like spaghetti on the floor he cautiously tried flexing the knee. It moved, though stiffly, like a tight hinge badly in need of oiling. With the movement came pain like a knifepoint punching into the joint. He worked for several minutes, improving the flexibility, though he could not straighten the leg completely. When he had worked up enough confidence he reached for his cane and stood, putting his weight first upon his left foot, then increasing it slowly on the right.

He found himself shivering and realized he was sweating profusely. A night breeze through the window was chilly upon his skin. He wanted to close it but feared he would wake Neal. He raised the tip of the cane from the floor and tested his full weight on the leg. He found he could stand, even if shakily. When he tried to walk, however, the leg gave way with a stabbing pain. He caught himself on the cane, stopping a fall, but the impact made a loud thump. It had almost been another disaster like his first attempt to walk on a crutch. He felt dizzy and sat back on the edge of the bed.

A match flared, lighting Neal in his underwear. "Are you hurt?"

Hewey's face warmed with embarrassment. "My feelin's are shot to hell. I think I'm all right otherwise." He felt like ten kinds of a fool.

The flame curled the match down near the end, burning Neal's fingers. He quickly dropped it and struck another, lighting a lamp on a small bureau. He touched his tongue to the burned fingertips. "You weren't supposed to take the wrappin' off so soon, were you?"

"That doctor doesn't know how helpless I feel when people have to take care of me like a baby. I'm a grown man."

"Let me look at that knee." Neal knelt, gently probing it with his fingers. The joint remained sore, but the surface looked almost normal except for a reddish scar.

He said, "Let's see how far you can bend it."

Hewey showed him. "It won't straighten all the way."

"It's been bound hard and fast. You have to expect it to be stiff at first."

Hewey felt a rush of disappointment that left him empty and a little angry. "If I was a horse they'd shoot me."

"A horse and a man ain't the same."

"They are in some ways. When a horse gets too old or too stove-up to use, you shoot him or turn him out to pasture. I ain't ready for the pasture."

Neal smiled. "Surely you don't want me to shoot you."

"No, but if the chance comes my way, I may shoot Fat Gervin."

"Want me to help you rewrap the knee?"

"No, I'll leave it like it is. That doctor's way off in Alpine. I won't tell him if you won't."

Hewey managed a little sleep, once he forced down his disappointment. He awoke to the crowing of a rooster and the neighing of a horse in a corral, letting everybody know it was time to feed.

The knee felt lighter with the binding off. Hewey tried bending it again. At first it was tighter than when he went back to bed, but after a few attempts he got it to flex as far as it had last night. He tried standing on it without the cane, though he held to the bedstead as a precaution. After a few tentative steps he decided he could not throw away the cane as he had thrown away the binding, not for a while.

Peeking into the room where Neal had slept, he found the bed made and the man gone. Through the open window floated the distant sound of conversation from the corrals. In the early morning light, he could see Neal and Alvin forking hay to horses and mules. Julio was probably milking the Jersey cows.

I ought to be out there helping, he thought, feeling guilty for having slept almost to sunup, but he knew he would be more a liability than an asset. Some of last night's anger revived.

He limped to the barn, leaning on the cane, his eyes squinted against the first bright sliver of sunrise on the horizon. Alvin hollered, "Sleepin' late, ain't you, Hewey? The Bible speaks hard against sloth."

Hewey tried to think of an appropriate rejoinder, but none came. He was not in a joking mood. He guessed that Alvin and Neal had close to thirty young horses and mules in the big corral. These would be in training for riding or working to wagons or plows. Alvin no longer broke them himself. He farmed them out to various young bronc riders such as Tommy Calloway to be ridden several times, wearing the rough edges off so they were ready to start their real lessons administered by Alvin, Julio and, Hewey supposed, Neal. Hewey had rough-broken a good many himself in times past, turning them over to Alvin to be honed into useful shape.

As always, Alvin picked out favorites for special treatment. He moved close to a young red roan and caught a handful of mane high up on the neck. He led it out to the fence where Hewey stood. It walked along obedient as a pup. "I wisht you'd look at this colt. Smarter'n my mother-in-law and ten times easier to get along with. If you ever get tired of Biscuit, this one would make you a good hand. He already watches a cow like a cat watches a mouse."

"Me and Biscuit are figurin' on gettin' old together . . . someday." The rate he was going, Hewey thought darkly, he might have little use anymore even for Biscuit, much less a young colt.

Alvin patted the colt on the neck and let it go. He unlatched the gate and came outside, waiting for Neal. Julio walked up from the milking pen, carrying a pail in each hand.

Alvin said, "We'll eat breakfast, then I'll take you over to Walter's and Eve's in my automobile."

"I hate to pull you away from your work."

"Farley and Julio do most of the work anyhow. I'm gettin' too stove-up. Comes a time when we all have to settle for less than we used to."

Hewey sensed that Alvin was not just speaking about himself.

Through breakfast Hewey sat across the table from Spring. He stole glances, trying not to be obvious, and often found her staring at him. She would avert her eyes, hiding her judgment, whatever that might be. Neither said much. Old Lady Faversham held the floor through most of the meal anyway, talking about the hardships women had to endure living in an uncivilized environment, not the least of them the ingratitude of their men. That train of thought led her to a lecture about the faithlessness of cowboys.

After breakfast Alvin asked, "Cora, how would you and Spring like to go with us? You-all ain't had much chance to visit with Eve lately."

Cora begged off, saying she had too much work stacked up. She said, "Spring, why don't you go? You could return those dress patterns I borrowed from her and take her some of the preserves we put up last week."

Spring seemed caught in a bind. She glanced at Hewey,

then at Neal. His nod told her it was all right to go, but his eyes wished she would not. She shook her head, not looking at Hewey. "There is a lot of work to be done. Perhaps another day."

Hewey stared at the ground in regret. He had much to apologize to her for if he ever got the chance, and if he could work up the nerve. Likely as not it was too late anyway. The time for apology had been four years ago.

Alvin went to start the automobile and back it out of the hay shed where it was kept safe from the weather. Shortly the roar of the engine told Hewey that Alvin had pulled the car up to the front of the house. He gave Spring one more quick glance. "I'll go fetch my roll," he said, and left as hurriedly as the cane would allow.

He heard Old Lady Faversham behind him, telling Spring she had made the right decision. "I don't blame you, not wantin' to go with Alvin and that fiddle-footed cowpuncher. His kind are a dime a dozen and badly overpriced."

Neal came into the little house as Hewey finished tying his bedroll. "I'll carry that for you," he offered.

Hewey said, "It wasn't my idea to invite her in the first place. She belongs to you."

"She doesn't *belong* to anybody. She's a free woman."

Hewey wondered if the man wasn't too good to be real. "Lots of old boys I've known wouldn't have so much trust."

Regret pinched Neal's eyes. "I didn't always have. I was young and green and a little jealous when I married. Kept a tight rein on Ada when there wasn't any reason for it. I realized that after I lost her, and I didn't like myself much." He hoisted Hewey's bedroll over his shoulder. "I wouldn't want Spring to look back years from now and have regrets on my account."

You're the right man for her, Hewey thought. But the thought was too painful to speak aloud.

Cora gave him several messages to take to Eve. Hewey assured her he would deliver them, though he knew he would forget most of them before he got there. For the hell of it he waved good-bye to Old Lady Faversham, who sat in her wheelchair on the porch. She did not respond. She was not there to wish him farewell but simply to be certain that he left.

Spring and Neal stood side by side. Neal nodded at Hewey, and Spring made a weak smile that carried a hint of sadness. Hewey forced himself to look away, facing forward. The automobile backfired, and Alvin came within inches of running over a flustered peacock that contested him for the right-of-way and yielded just in time. Alvin laughed. "Them peacocks belong to my mother-in-law. When she ain't screechin', they are."

Though getting in and out of the car was a struggle, Hewey insisted upon opening and closing the gates. The wooden ones were little challenge, but the tight wire gates were almost more than he could handle. Alvin was sensitive enough to Hewey's pride that he let him wrestle them alone, though it must have taken all the patience he could muster not to get out and take over. Alvin would never be a good poker player; whatever he was thinking showed in his face, and his pity was apparent.

It only made Hewey feel worse. "Sometimes I almost wish that stud had killed me instead of leavin' me in this shape, havin' to depend on everybody."

Alvin frowned. "Have you talked to the Lord about it?"

"Pray? I've prayed for other people, but it always seemed selfish to do it for myself."

"Not when you've got a real need. The Lord generally answers, though not always like you hope for. You remember how fond I always was of whiskey? It got to a point that I was sick a lot of the time, so me and the Lord had a long talk about it. Well, I done the talkin', but I could tell He was listenin', because pretty soon it got to where it tasted so bad to me that I didn't want it anymore.

"When He takes things away from us, He usually gives

us somethin' in trade. We lose the energy we had when we were young, but He gives us more wisdom. And as He takes away our ability to do one thing or another, He also takes away most of the want-to so we can be content with what we've got left."

"I ain't content with the way I am, and I don't intend to settle for it."

"Fine. The Lord loves a man who won't give up tryin'."

"It wasn't the Lord that put me in this shape; it was Fat Gervin. Be damned if I'll let him win."

Alvin nodded approval. "You're gettin' mad, and that's good. As long as you're mad, you'll keep fightin'. But when you go as far as the Lord intends for you to, you'll have to make your peace and be glad for what you've still got."

"What *have* I got? The shape I'm in, I'll do well to swamp out Dutch Schneider's saloon."

"You told me Morgan Jenkins offered you a job as foreman. You wouldn't have to ride no rough horses to do that."

"I couldn't take care of a ranch afoot."

"The wheel has been around for thousands of years. Every buggy and buckboard has got four of them."

Hewey noticed dust rising to the south. Alvin pinched his eyes almost shut, trying to see through the haze. "Looks like horses runnin'. You don't reckon somebody's rustlin' a bunch of my stock? I ain't got a gun with me."

Hewey doubted that Alvin had ever pulled a gun on anybody in his life. It was not his style. He was a peacemaker, like Walter.

Rustling had become rare in this big country because the horse had not been born that could outrun a sheriff's telephone calls. In these vast distances a thief would have to travel far and hard to remove himself from harm's way.

Alvin left the road and set the car bouncing across the open pasture. Hewey held tightly with his good hand to keep from being tossed around in the seat. He could only imagine what this jarring might do to his innards.

When they were close enough that Alvin could see the horses clearly, he braked to a slow stop, relieved.

"They ain't mine. I wouldn't allow any on my place as sorry as them."

Two riders were driving a remuda of thirty or so runty-looking Mexican ponies. A horseman with his shirttail hanging out reined toward the car. Hewey recognized the no-name cowboy he had met on the C. C. Tarpley ranch.

Alvin shouted, "Where you goin' with them broomtails?"

The cowboy's clothes were dirty, and he had several days' growth of whiskers, showing he had been on the trail. "We're takin' them to Mr. Gervin for delivery to a buyer. They come from down on the Pecos."

Alvin said, "It'd be a lot easier to take them along the road than to cut across my ranch."

"It was Mr. Gervin's orders to bring them this way. We'll be off your place before they have a chance to eat much of your grass. Adios." The cowboy spurred off after the horses.

Alvin said, "Now, why would Fat give an order like that?"

"So he could tell a buyer that they came from your ranch and not exactly be lyin' about it." Hewey explained about the bunch Gervin had sold to Old Man Jenkins under false pretenses.

Alvin swore. "The duplicitous son of a bitch!"

Hewey was surprised to hear such language come from Alvin. He didn't used to say words like *duplicitous*.

12

The sound of an automobile was still so uncommon in the countryside that it brought out everyone within hearing distance to see who was coming or going. Walter appeared in the door of the toolshed, and Eve stood on the step in front of her kitchen, shading her eyes with her hand. The black dog trotted to meet the car, barking all the way.

Out in the field, someone halted a team and turned to look. Hewey could not be sure at the distance, but he supposed this was Lester the nester boy, hired on a day basis to help Walter with his crops. Lester never lacked for excuses to halt work. Hewey would bet a dollar that he would leave the mules standing and come all the way to the house to find out who had arrived, though it was none of his business.

Eve waited for the dust to settle after Alvin braked to a stop; then she walked to the car. "Hewey! We didn't expect to see you home so soon. Is anything the matter? Are you all right? Where's Tommy?"

That was a lot of questions, and Hewey lumped the answers together. "I'm doin' fair to middlin', and Tommy ought to be along in a day or two. He's bringin' our horses."

"That boy? All by himself?"

"By the time I was his age I'd seen all of Texas and half of hell." Lately he had seen the other half.

Alvin asked, "How long 'til dinner?"

Eve said, "If I'd known you-all were comin' I'd've killed the old red rooster. I'm afraid you'll have to settle for mutton stew."

"Mutton?" Hewey demanded.

"Didn't Tommy tell you that Walter bought us a flock of sheep? They pay better than cattle when we can keep the coyotes off of them."

A bad taste came into Hewey's mouth, as if he had been chewing tobacco. He had boasted to Dutch Schneider that there were two things he had never done: swamp out a saloon and herd sheep. He had then proceeded to sweep Schneider's floor. Now he might find himself herding sheep.

Stove-up and not worth his beans, he could sink no lower, it seemed.

As Hewey stepped out of the car, bracing himself on the

cane, the old dog moved up close and barked at him. It never had accepted him as a member of the family.

Hewey had to limp all the way around the car before he could satisfy Walter that he was not a total invalid. Alvin declared, "He's gettin' pretty good with that cane. Before long you'll have to run to keep up with him."

Alvin was trying to make him feel better, but his solicitude only sharpened Hewey's sense of being less than whole.

Lester stopped twenty feet short of the car and stared without speaking. It was just as well; Hewey could not remember ever hearing him say anything worth listening to. Lester welcomed any chance to get away from the plow a while. Sooner or later, Hewey figured, he would wangle himself a job at the courthouse. Things there moved at about his chosen speed.

Hewey said, "Lester, would you mind takin' my bedroll to the barn? I'll be sleepin' down there."

Eve said, "You'll do no such of a thing, Hewey. You'll sleep in the boys' room like kinfolks, not in the barn like a hired hand . . ."—she turned severe eyes toward Lester— "one that's fixin' to get fired if he doesn't go back to the field and do a little work."

Walter said, "Now, Eve . . ." Walter's peacemaker trait was often called upon when things did not go Eve's way.

Lester turned and started toward the field in a trot, though he soon slowed to a walk, and he climbed over the fence rather than take the trouble to open a heavy gate.

"That boy's poor mother," Eve lamented, "I can imagine the tribulations he's put her through."

Though he was a brother-in-law rather than a wayward son, Hewey had given Eve more than her share of tribulation over the years. He said, "Soon as I get this cast off my arm and my knee is a little more limber, you can send Lester home."

Eve said, "You wouldn't be in that shape if you hadn't tried to spare Tommy from gettin' hurt. You're here to rest,

Hewey Calloway, and you'll do it if I have to tie you to a rockin' chair."

Alvin asked again, "How long 'til dinner?"

After three days Hewey feared he would wear a hole through the seat of the rocking chair. He was restless to be up and doing something, even if it was wrong. The dog's barking gave him reason to arise and hobble to the door.

"Looks like Tommy's comin'," he told Eve, then went outside. He was halfway to the barn when he heard the screen door slam as Eve came out to look for her son.

Tommy was not alone. Long before he could see the face, Hewey knew the rider. He could usually recognize his friends at a distance by the way they sat on their horses, and no one rode with quite the same easy slouch as Snort Yarnell. Hewey was not sure whether to whoop for joy or give in to dread. With Snort, there was never any knowing.

Tommy was riding his own dun horse, leading Biscuit on a long rope knotted so it would not choke. As soon as Tommy released him, Biscuit headed straight for the feed trough; he knew exactly where it was.

Hewey said to Tommy, "You're kind of careless who you let ride with you."

Snort grinned at Hewey, showing his gold tooth in full glory. "You still gimpin' around, tryin' for sympathy?"

"What happened to that night watchman's job? They catch you openin' the bar after hours?"

"Me and a runny-nosed constable had a little set-to. It was his fault, not mine, but you know how narrow-minded them small-town John Laws can be. After a few nights of walkin' the streets, I decided I'd rather take my chances on bein' killed by a horse than die of boredom."

Snort's grin died, and he looked Hewey up and down with a sober eye. "We've come to help you get well, me and Tommy. We're goin' to work you and make you exercise 'til that arm and leg move better than the day you was born."

"It's more likely you'll kill me, if I don't kill you first." Hewey turned back to Tommy. "You took your sweet time gettin' home."

A hint of guilt came into Tommy's face. Hewey noticed a bruise on his cheekbone. "Snort had to go by Pecos City to see a man about a horse."

"I warned you to take roundance on Pecos. It's too lively a town for a boy your age."

"It sure was lively after Snort got there. We had to leave in kind of a hurry."

Snort was all innocence. "It was their fault. They ain't as friendly anymore as them old-timey Pecos folks used to be."

Eve was walking out from the house. Hewey cautioned Tommy, "I wouldn't say anything to your mother about Pecos. She might run us all off."

Eve hugged her son, then stepped back to examine the bruise. Quickly Tommy said, "Dunny spooked at a rabbit and caught me off guard. I took a fall."

Somebody's been teaching that boy to lie, Hewey thought. He gave Snort an accusing look.

He doubted that Eve was taken in. She had seen through windies told by far better liars than Tommy. Her voice had a crisp edge of suspicion as she asked Snort, "You *are* stayin' for supper, I suppose?" It was less an invitation than an expression of resignation.

Snort was notoriously unreliable. He might stay a month, or he might ride away in ten minutes without saying a word. Hewey hoped he didn't stay a month. Eve would be chewing up nails and spitting them out long before then.

Snort said, "Eve, the angels in heaven could take lessons from you. I'll be here for supper tonight and many more after that. Poor old Hewey needs my help."

Eve frowned. "God had better help us all."

After she returned to the house, Snort poured oats in a trough for his horse and dropped the bucket back into the barrel from which it had come. "First thing we got to do,

Hewey, is cut that cast off of your arm. How do you expect to move your elbow with it all trussed up thataway?"

Hewey had been toying with the same notion. His leg had not collapsed when he unwrapped his knee. It was becoming a little more flexible every day, though he could not straighten it fully. He could even take a few rabbit-hopping steps without the cane. "Since when have you been practicin' medicine?"

Snort said, "I've doctored many a horse. In your case there can't be much difference."

Gratitude made tears come into Hewey's eyes. "You don't know how much it means to me, Snort, you comin' all the way back here to try and help."

Snort's face went dead serious. "You're my friend, Hewey. I've moved around a lot and rode with a lot of good fellers, but I ain't ever had many real close friends. Mainly there was just you and Old Grady Welch. I lost Grady. Time we got to him, there wasn't a thing I could do to help him. In Alpine, I was sore afraid I was fixin' to lose you, too."

"I'm figurin' on bein' around for a long time yet."

"And I'm here to help you."

At the supper table, Lester the nester boy listened with mouth hanging open as Snort told stories. Some contained a grain or two of truth, though not enough to hurt them much.

When Snort paused to poke half a biscuit into his mouth, Tommy told Hewey, "Mr. Jenkins asked about you. Said he was sorry you left without sayin' good-bye. He wanted to proposition you again about that foreman's job at the Circle W."

"He hired him a foreman."

"Seems like him and Mr. Underhill got in an argument over the way to handle those broncs he got from Fat Gervin."

Eve corrected him. "*Mr.* Gervin."

"Mr. Fat Gervin. Anyway, Mr. Underhill left, and Mr. Jenkins needs a foreman."

Hewey felt a stirring of interest. The Circle W was as pleasurable as any place he had ever worked, situated in a valley with sheltering mountains on either side, a clear creek meandering unhurriedly down the length of it, and not too many fences or gates. It was far enough from town that a man wouldn't be bothered by a lot of uninvited company.

"I can't think of a place I'd rather go if I was inclined to take on the responsibility and if I wasn't busted up like an eggshell. I can't even ride a horse."

Snort argued, "What responsibility? You just tell the boys what you want done and they do it. A foreman don't even have to ride a horse. I've worked for several that rode around in a buggy like they owned the bank. Even had somebody hitch up their team. It's like havin' a gravy bowl that don't ever run dry."

With Snort around, it would need to be an awfully deep bowl, Hewey thought, watching him take another helping of mutton stew. Snort probably didn't recognize what it was, for he had a cowboy's unreasoning prejudice against sheep and everything associated with them.

Hewey said, "I don't know that I could give orders and stand back, and the shape I'm in, I couldn't do much else."

After supper Snort jerked his head toward the door. "Come on out to the barn with me, Hewey. We'll do somethin' about the cast on your arm."

Eve protested, "That time Walter broke his leg, we had to leave the cast on for three months."

Snort assured her, "An arm heals faster than a leg."

Hewey wondered where that piece of wisdom came from. Probably out of Snort's imagination. But he was ready to shed the cast anyway. It itched as if a nest of wood ants had hatched under it, and it gave off a smell that reminded him of a dead mule.

Snort rummaged among Walter's tools. Cotton had been methodical, making sure every piece of equipment had its proper place and was returned to it immediately after use.

When Cotton left home to seek his own way working on automobiles, that sense of good order went with him. Snort said, "Walter's bound to have a set of hoof trimmers around here someplace."

He found them and began to nip at the edges of the cast, breaking it away one small piece at a time. Hewey winced, for Snort's twisting and straining made the arm hurt. Hewey was almost ready at one point to call a halt, but by then half the cast was in shreds, and he saw no choice except to go ahead. Both men had worked up a healthy sweat, Snort through exertion and Hewey through fighting pain. Snort stopped to roll a cigarette. He offered it to Hewey.

Hewey said, "I've quit. Since the accident they've got to where they taste like cow chips." Not only could he no longer work as he used to, but one of the simplest of his pleasures had abandoned him as well.

"Never tasted a cow chip," Snort said, "so I wouldn't know."

Tommy and Lester had come to the barn and watched in silence as Snort methodically demolished the cast, passing the elbow and working along the upper arm. Finally he pulled the last of it away. The rough barn floor was littered with bits of plaster and cloth.

Hewey carefully felt the arm. It still hurt to the touch where the bone had been broken just above the elbow. "Looks sort of crooked, don't it?"

Snort shrugged. "Nobody'll see it. Your sleeve'll cover it up." Snort had one leg twisted and scarred from an argument with a horse. He maintained that it still worked all right, even if it looked like a bear had chewed on it. A cowboy hadn't graduated to the top ranks until he was marked up some.

Hewey tried working the elbow. Like the knee, it resisted. The arm bent only a little.

Snort said, "You need to squirt some axle grease in there."

Lester was awed. "You reckon that'd work?"

Tommy elbowed him. "Don't you know when Snort's kiddin'?"

"It makes sense to me."

Snort gripped Hewey's arm above and below the elbow and tried to force it to bend. Hewey hollered out and jerked free. He rubbed the arm in an attempt to smother the fire Snort's abuse had aroused. "If that's the way you've doctored horses, you probably had to shoot them afterwards."

"Some of them got well. Your arm is goin' to take a lot of work."

That night Hewey lay in bed awake, the arm throbbing so hard from the strain that tears forced their way through his clenched eyelids. He was bitterly disappointed that it had not healed straight, that it seemed so weak. He kept trying to work it, but the elbow moved only a little, and every attempt was like dipping the arm in hot coals.

He had been resisting what Alvin had suggested. Now, through the pain, he whispered a prayer.

Hewey paused from hoeing weeds in Eve's garden to wipe sweat from his face. Snort leaned on a fence post and rolled a cigarette. He hollered, "Don't stop now. You need to keep workin' if you're goin' to free up them joints."

Hewey considered breaking the hoe handle across Snort's head, but that would probably violate some stupid law passed by city folks who had no idea of the emergencies that might arise in the countryside. He looked out into the field, where Walter and Tommy were working. Lester the nester boy had gone home.

Hewey said, "There's weeds enough here for both of us."

"You're the one that needs the exercise. Just keep doin' what you're doin'. I think I'll go see if there's any coffee left from breakfast."

Snort entered the frame house. Shortly Eve came out,

walking to the garden, her arms folded. She looked back over her shoulder, a frown set deeply. "You reckon Snort has got a tapeworm?"

"Nothin' about Snort would surprise me."

"I asked him if he was hungry. He said no, he just wanted a cup of coffee. Then he mixed half a pound of butter into a plateful of molasses and started swabbin' it up with cold biscuits. I never saw a skinny man who could eat so much. How much longer does he figure on stayin' here?"

"He ain't said, but I'm wishin' he'd take a notion to leave. Every day for two weeks it's been 'bend that arm, work that leg,' over and over. And when he gets tired he sics Tommy on me. He's about wore me down to a nub."

"They say absence makes the heart grow fonder. I would sure like to get a lot fonder of Snort Yarnell. I guess he's done you some good here, but in the long run he's a bad influence. He'll try and lead you back to the wanderin' ways you and him shared for all those years."

"Snort's a good old boy at heart. He don't mean any harm."

"Take a real hard look at him. He's got nothin', he's got nobody. He drifts from one place to another. God knows what he's lookin' for. I doubt Snort knows himself."

"He seems happy enough."

"It's all a show. He's lonely and miserable, and he tries to cover it up with bluster and hooraw. You've been enough like him that it scares me half to death. He'll never change, Hewey, but you can. You just have to make up your mind. It wouldn't hurt you to call on the Lord for help."

"I already have," he admitted. "And maybe He heard me. See my cane hangin' on the fence yonder?"

She suddenly realized. "You're walkin' without it."

"Can't hold a cane and a hoe both at the same time."

Eve was so pleased she kissed him on the cheek. "Mind what I said about Snort. The world's not big enough to hold two like him."

When she returned to the house, he noticed that Biscuit had walked up to the garden fence and stood there, watching. Hewey laid down the hoe and limped over to the horse, which stood still while Hewey rubbed and patted its neck. "You're gettin' fat, old boy. All them oats and no work. But I don't know what I can do about it." Tommy had been riding the horse a little, though not enough to wear off much weight.

Biscuit turned his head, pointing his ears toward the road. An automobile was coming. Hewey said, "It's a disgrace for company to catch a cowboy with a hoe in his hand. But it'd be worse if I was herdin' Walter's sheep." He patted the horse once more and turned away, propping the hoe against the fence and picking up his cane.

The car was Alvin's. Snort came out of the house, eating a biscuit. He walked to the garden to join Hewey. "Just because we've got a little company don't mean you need to quit work. Ain't nobody except Alvin and his womenfolks."

Spring was in the backseat, behind Alvin and Cora. Hewey glanced down at his clothes, dirty from the garden work. He tried to brush some of the dust away, but he did little more than move it around. He felt awkward about going out to greet Spring, but it would be even more awkward if he avoided her. Every time he saw her, old emotions began to stir, regret for old decisions still painful though they had seemed right.

Snort sensed his indecision. "Careful, *compadre*. You got away once by the skin of your teeth. You may not be that lucky again."

Hewey limped to the car, tipping his dusty hat to the women and shaking Alvin's hand. Alvin said, "Farley Neal and Julio are behind us a ways. They're bringin' a set of green-broke ponies for Tommy to work to the harness."

Walter and Tommy had seen the car and were on their way in from the field. Eve hugged Cora and Spring. "Everybody come on into the house. I'll make us a fresh pot of coffee." She gave Hewey a quick, furtive nod that told him to join Spring. "You too, Hewey."

Hewey said, "I still got a lot of work to do." Reluctantly he pulled away from Spring and the others, earning a reproachful frown from Eve. Spring's face was without expression; he could not tell what she was thinking. He returned to the garden, Snort walking with him.

Snort said, "You done right, not goin' in the house. Womenfolks are always workin'and schemin' to get somebody hitched up. They can't stand to see a man stay free."

"They never got *you* hitched up."

"And they won't. There ain't no bigger threat to a man's freedom than a good woman. Once they set a hook in him, he's a fish on a line. The kind of women I like don't ask for much, a few dollars and a little of your time. They smile when they see you comin' and they smile when you go. No tears and no regrets."

Hewey nodded. It sounded good if he didn't examine it closely. "But someday you'll be old and all by yourself, and even your money won't make them smile at you."

"I don't figure on ever gettin' old. I'll just turn into a gray mule and go around kickin' the people I don't like."

Hewey retrieved his hoe and chopped a few more weeds. Snort sidled up to him and elbowed him in the ribs. "Look out. She's comin'."

Hewey turned. Spring was at the garden gate. The sight of her stirred a warm feeling.

Her voice was pleasant enough, though her smile was tentative. "Are you going to work all day?"

"The weeds are tryin'to take Eve's garden. And I need the exercise to get my joints limbered."

Snort said, "I been workin' real hard on him. Want to get him back to where he was before that bronc messed him up."

Hewey sensed that Spring wished to talk but did not feel free while Snort stood there. He said, "Snort, you look like a man that needs a cup of coffee, or somethin'."

"I had my coffee already." He caught on. "Oh! Sure, reckon I do." He made his misgivings plain as he moved toward the garden gate, looking back. "Don't you forget what I told you about them good women."

Spring gave Hewey a quizzical look. Hewey shrugged. "Don't pay no attention. Half the time Snort don't know what he's sayin'."

When Snort was out of hearing, Spring nodded toward Hewey's cane hanging from the top wire of the fence. "It appears you're making good progress if you don't need that cane all the time. I'm pleased for you, Hewey."

"It's Snort's doin', mostly. He keeps workin' me 'til I'm about ready to bust him with an ax handle."

Biscuit remained near the garden fence, grazing. Spring said, "Are you riding your horse yet?"

"Ain't tried. It hurt too much the last time."

"Perhaps it's just as well. As soon as you could ride you would probably be wanting to leave again."

He thought he detected a faint edge of resentment but hoped it was his imagination. It had been four years, and anyway, she had told him it was all right for him to go. He hoed a few more weeds, waiting for her to say something else to give him some gauge of her feelings.

She said, "This may all have happened for a reason. It may be a way of turning your life around and setting you off on a new road."

"I liked the road I was on, and my life the way it was."

"How well I remember."

"Look at me, all busted up, can't do an honest day's work. What am I worth to anybody?"

"You're worth a lot to Walter and Eve and Tommy."

He hoped she might add *And to me*, but she did not. He was not sure how he would react if she had. Four years ago he had shut a gate and locked it behind him.

She asked, "So, what next, Hewey? What do you do now?"

"Ain't much I *can* do. Cowpunchin' was the only life I ever knew or cared to know. I may not be able to do it any-more."

"You have to accept that some things may never be the same. There've been changes in what you can do, but there doesn't have to be any change in what you *are*."

"And what is that?"

"You're a good and decent man at heart. Alvin once said you're an eagle on the wing. That's why I let you ride away, because I couldn't bear to tie up an eagle or put it in a cage. You're still the eagle you always were."

"I'm afraid I got my wings clipped."

"But I think your eyes are still on the sky, Hewey. And my feet are still on the ground."

She walked back to the house. Hewey kept hoeing the same weed over and over.

Neal and Julio brought the young horses. Hewey saw the eagerness in Tommy's face at the challenge of training them, and he felt a glow of envy. At least Eve wouldn't have to worry about her son leaving again for a while. He had some-thing to stay for.

Hewey stood outside the corral, looking in. Neal came around and stood beside him, saying nothing at first. Hewey decided one of them had to speak. "Good-lookin' set of horses. Ain't nobody raises better ones than Alvin."

Neal blurted, "I'm goin' to ask her to marry me."

Hewey flinched as if Neal had hit him in the stomach. He forced a smile, but it was thin as water. "I think she'll say yes."

"Maybe she will. Again, maybe she won't."

"Why wouldn't she?"

"Afraid, maybe. She's been hurt in the past."

Hewey gripped the fence so hard that his knuckles ached. "I reckon I know about that." As badly as it pained him, he had to say, "I think you're the right man for her. I wish you luck."

Neal walked to the house alone. Hewey leaned against a post, trying to think of what he should have said to Spring, though it had already been too late . . . four years late.

The two horsebackers left soon after dinner so they could get back to the Lawdermilk place in time for the chores. Alvin, Cora and Spring stayed until mid-afternoon. Hewey remained in the garden for the most part.

Spring made no attempt to be alone with him again, but he was acutely conscious that her gaze followed him when he was in sight. As the visitors prepared to go, she turned to Hewey. "Keep trying. You can do it." She got into the car and did not look at him again.

Eve was keenly watching them both. Once she had pushed hard to make a match between the two, hoping to crowd Hewey into giving up his wandering ways and setting a more stable example for her sons. Watching the automobile pull away, she moved close to Hewey. "You know Spring's concerned about you."

"She's concerned about everybody. She's got a good heart."

"And it could've been yours." She went back into the house.

Snort jerked his head. "Let's go, Hewey. There's still a-plenty of weeds in that garden, and you need to be workin' them muscles."

Instead, Hewey looked for his nephew. "Tommy, I wisht you'd go catch up Biscuit for me."

Tommy's eyes lighted like the Fourth of July. "You goin' to ride him?"

"I'm goin' to try damned hard."

Snort said, "It took you long enough to make up your mind. Or was it that schoolteacher done it?"

Tommy saddled Biscuit and led him out of the corral. He

said, "You ain't been on him in a while, so he's fat and frisky. I'd better ride him around a little first."

"The day somebody has to top out my own horse for me is the day I go lookin' for a night watchman's job." He gave Snort a challenging look.

Snort winced. "You goin' to hold that over my head the rest of my life? Just stepped off of the trail one time . . . just once . . ."

Hewey started slowly, patting the horse on the neck, rubbing its ears.

Snort declared, "If you're goin' to do it, do it!"

Hewey hung his cane on the fence. Carefully he lifted his left foot to the stirrup, which forced him to put all his weight on the injured right leg. He gritted his teeth against expected pain, but it was milder than he thought. Tommy's eyes were wide with anticipation. Walter had caught on to what was happening and had come from the milking pen to watch.

Hewey said, "Tommy, you're young and innocent, and the Lord'll listen to you. Talk to Him for me."

"I already have."

Hewey gripped the saddle horn and pulled himself up. The right leg was still stiff, and he dragged it across Biscuit's rump. A less gentle horse might have jumped. Hewey sought the stirrup with his right foot, found it and slid it in past the toes. The leg felt as if it were still bound. He could not bring it tightly against the horse's ribs as he did with his left, and a small ache began in the knee. But these negatives were minor considerations against a much more important fact: he was in the saddle.

Tommy whooped for joy. Walter stood beside his son, an arm around Tommy's shoulder. Snort Yarnell grinned in satisfaction, as if it were all his doing.

Hewey rode Biscuit in a wide circle, walking him at first, then putting him into an easy trot. He hurt in several places; there was no getting around that. But he was riding.

Eve came out onto the kitchen step to watch. Hewey saw her lift the hem of her apron and dab it against her eyes.

After a while his side began to ache, and he knew he had done all he should for the day. But he would ride again to-morrow, and the day after. It would get better. It had to.

He felt like shouting as he slid down from the saddle, avoiding too much weight on the right leg. He patted Biscuit again and handed the reins to Tommy. "Unsaddle him for me, will you? And give him a double bait of oats."

Tommy had a smile a yard wide. "Sure thing, Uncle Hewey."

Walter pumped Hewey's hand, and Snort slapped him on the back so hard that Hewey thought he would lose his breath. Walter said, "Let's go to the house. I think we could all use some coffee."

Hewey retrieved the cane from the fence. He took a couple of steps on it, then detoured over to the woodpile. He pitched the cane onto the top of the chopped stove wood and limped back to join Walter and Snort.

"I don't believe I'll need that thing anymore."

13

Hewey was half a mile from the house, riding Biscuit along-side Snort Yarnell, when he recognized the open-topped automobile making its way along the wagon road from town. "That's Old Man Jenkins's car. Wonder what he could want?"

"More money. Them old ranchers are always after more money, like they ain't already got most of it corraled."

Hewey put Biscuit into a stiff trot. The jarring touched off an internal ache so slight that Hewey was able to ignore it. The pain had diminished gradually, day by day. He was confident it would soon be gone entirely if he did not do something foolish and undo the progress he had made.

He waved his hat to be certain he was seen. Peeler eased the car to a stop in front of the house and took off his goggles as Hewey and Snort approached. Beaming, Jenkins hollered, "I wisht you'd look at Hewey Calloway on horseback. I expected to see you rockin' your life away on the front porch."

"I wore out that rockin' chair in about a week," Hewey replied, dismounting slowly to shake hands with both men. He still had to be careful how he moved, for his right knee remained tricky. He had limited mobility in his left arm.

Jenkins said, "Then I reckon you're ready to go back to work."

Hewey sobered quickly. "It's better, but it ain't that good. I'm afraid I've rode my last bronc."

Snort eyed Peeler with misgivings. "I remember you. You're the gink that spurred our outlaw bronc to a standstill and cleaned out us Slash R boys."

Peeler grinned. "And you're the man that drank the rest of us under the table. Hard to forget a feller with that kind of talent."

Eve came out of the kitchen, and Hewey introduced her to the two visitors. He said, "You-all go on into the house. I'll unsaddle Biscuit and be along in a minute."

Snort reached for the reins. "I'll unsaddle him. I expect Mr. Jenkins came here to talk to you."

It still made Hewey uncomfortable to let someone else saddle and unsaddle his horse for him, though Tommy had been doing it lately. "I'm obliged," he said, and motioned for Jenkins and Peeler to precede him into the house. Eve set three coffee cups on the table and poured them full in silent invitation.

Jenkins looked Hewey over before he seated himself. "I'm tickled to see you doin' so much better. I've had you on my conscience, seein' as you got hurt workin' for me."

"Wasn't your fault. I got hurt on account of Fat Gervin."

"It was my ranch and my horse. If you've been concerned

about your doctor bill, don't be. I paid my half and yours, too."

"I'm obliged." Hewey wanted to smile but didn't. Dr. Evans had been a big winner on this deal. "Did you manage to get rid of them broncs Fat sold you?"

Jenkins scowled. "Only a couple of them. It appears I'm stuck with the rest. Buyers come and take a look, and they leave so fast their shirttails don't touch them 'til they're back on the road. Blas may have to learn how to cook horsemeat and make it taste like steak."

"I wish there was a way you could make Fat Gervin eat them." For whatever satisfaction it might give the old man, he described the lie he had told Gervin about Jenkins planning to sic a battery of Fort Worth lawyers on him. "It's thin comfort, but at least I worried him for a little while."

Not long enough, however, for evidently Gervin had pulled the same swindle on someone else. Hewey told about the day he and Alvin found two Tarpley cowboys driving a remuda across the Lawdermilk ranch so Gervin could trade on the good reputation of Alvin's horses and palm off some scrubs he had bought cheaply down on the Pecos. "I'd bet he's usin' the Tarpley bank's money, but the bank ain't gettin' none of the profit. Poor old C.C. ain't been in any shape to keep an eye on things lately."

He described Tarpley and the old man's troubles. "You'd like C.C., Mr. Jenkins. You and him have got a lot in common."

Both were highly ambitious and tight with a dollar, though this was not unusual among ranchers of their generation. Without those traits they might not have endured and prospered through the harsh challenges of the early years. Hewey was not critical. He understood the men and the drive that compelled them, though he did not share it.

He said, "It'll be a poorer country when C.C. is gone. Fat Gervin ain't fit to polish the old man's boots."

"Gervin!" It sounded like a cussword, the way Jenkins said it. "It's not so much the money. I've lost that much through a hole in my pocket. It's the principle of the thing, lettin' him skin me that way. I shot a man once for stealin' horses, but at least he was honest after his own fashion. He never claimed to be anything but a horse thief."

Eve kept staring at Peeler with poorly hidden curiosity. He must have looked like some foreign being to her, wearing a duster, cap and goggles, jodhpurs and tall lace-up boots. Hewey decided not to tell her he was just a reformed bronc rider. Like as not she would start pointing to him as a potential model for Hewey's own reformation.

Jenkins said, "Looks like all I can do with them broncs is load them on a train and ship them to the Fort Worth stockyards. They ought to fetch a little somethin' for soap, but they won't bring back what I've got in them."

Hewey sympathized. "It's a pity you can't sell them back to the man you bought them from." A glimmering of an idea began forming. "Or maybe you could."

"To Frank Gervin? He wouldn't take them back. I'll bet he's been laughin' up his sleeve ever since he sold them to me."

"There ain't any use appealin' to Fat's good nature. He ain't got one. But maybe we can appeal to his greed."

"How?"

"I've got the first stirrin's of a notion." Hewey arose and looked out the window toward the corral where Snort was helping Tommy and Walter unhitch a raw team Tommy had been working to a wagon. After a minute he turned to stare at Peeler. "Eve, what does Peeler look like to you?"

Eve was caught off balance. "What kind of question is that?"

"If you was to bump into him in town, lookin' like he looks right now, what would you think he was?"

"He looks like a gentleman, of course, dressed for a drive in an automobile."

"Would you figure him for a man of means?"

"How else could he have an automobile? We sure don't have one."

Hewey grinned at Peeler. "How are you at catchin' fish?"

"I've hooked a few in my day."

"With a little luck you may hook the fattest fish you ever saw."

The two automobiles moved along slowly, a couple of hundred yards in front of seventeen horses driven by Tommy, Snort Yarnell and two J Bar vaqueros. As they came to a wire gate, Hewey could see the windmill towers of Upton City half a mile ahead. He turned in the seat of Alvin Lawdermilk's car and motioned for Peeler to pull Jenkins's automobile up beside him. Aparicio Rodriguez left his place behind the band of horses and loped ahead to open the gate.

Hewey climbed out of Alvin's car. He had to speak loudly to be heard over the roar of the two engines. "Mr. Jenkins, you'd better get in the car with us. Wouldn't do for Fat to see you and Peeler together."

Jenkins left his own automobile, moving over to the backseat of Alvin's.

Hewey said, "Now, Peeler, we'll let you go on into town ahead of us. You won't have any trouble spottin' the bank. If a red car is parked alongside it, you'll know Fat is there."

Peeler nodded. They had been over this already.

"Now, you're a rich cotton merchant from Dallas. You've just bought a big ranch, and you need a bunch of horses for your hands to ride. You're puttin' all your trust in him to find you some."

Peeler mumbled impatiently, for he already had it memorized. "And my name is Smith."

"Smith, Jones . . . whatever you want it to be. Tell him

you're willin' to pay up to a hundred dollars a head. No, better make it a hundred and twenty-five. Mr. Jenkins deserves some profit on this deal."

"And a little commission for you?"

"I don't care about any commission. I just want to see Fat Gervin get his comeuppance. We'll wait at Dutch Schneider's saloon. It's up to you to set the hook, then me and Mr. Jenkins'll try and pull in the fish."

Tommy, Snort and one vaquero pushed the horses through the open gate. Aparicio stood holding it, waiting for the automobiles to pass. Peeler drove through first, Alvin following. Aparicio closed the gate and set his mount into a lope to catch up.

Jenkins said, "If we put this over, I owe them boys a bottle of whiskey apiece. You too, Mr. Lawdermilk."

Hewey said, "Alvin has reformed. But I reckon he'd take a bottle and give it to his friends. How long've we been friends, Alvin?"

Alvin muttered some kind of reply. Hewey suspected his reformation had more to do with Cora than with health or religion.

Tommy and Snort took the lead, guiding the vaqueros to the Upton City wagon yard. Hewey told Alvin, "In case Fat might be lookin' out the window, maybe we ought to pull this car in on the back side of the barn."

Alvin remained far enough behind the remuda to avoid the dust. He stopped and let the motor run while the four riders penned the horses in a large lot. Hewey could not see the bank from here, which meant that Fat should not be able to see them, either. Alvin parked the car at the side of the large red barn.

Snort was explaining to the liveryman that the horses belonged to Mr. Jenkins of the J Bar at Alpine. Jenkins took over the negotiations. He said, "Just throw them a little hay. Not too much. They ain't worth much."

The liveryman grumbled, "Ain't no horses goin' to be

worth much if everybody keeps buyin' them damned automobiles. Looks like I may have to turn this place into a garage."

Hewey heard a commotion in a corral back of the barn.
Two men were trying to saddle a sorrel bronc, and it was
giving them a fight. This was the kind of show Hewey had
always enjoyed watching, but somehow it put a cold feeling
in the pit of his stomach. He watched as one of the punchers eared the pony down and the other mounted. Turned
loose, the bronc pitched hard. Hewey wanted to look away
but could not. He seemed unable to move, fascinated like a
bird watching a snake.

It became obvious that the rider would not remain in the
saddle for long. Hewey held his breath. It seemed the cowboy was suspended in midair for a whole minute before he
came down like a sack of bran. The sound of impact was
physically painful to Hewey. He could not breathe until he
saw the cowboy get up and dust himself off. At least he was
not hurt.

Only then could Hewey bring himself to turn away, shaking as if a cold norther had just blown in.

Tommy asked, "You all right?"

"I'm fine. For a minute there it was like watchin' myself
and that black stud. I used to love a good bronc ride. Now
just watchin' it gave me a chill."

Alvin Lawdermilk said, "It's like I told you. You lose the
ability, then you lose the want-to."

They walked out the front of the barn. At the far end of
the street stood the bank. Peeler had parked Jenkins's car
beside it.

Jenkins said, "Looks like we've got some time to kill. If
you gentlemen won't mind, I'll set everybody up to a drink."

Snort said, "Bad as I hate to . . . the saloon's right down
thisaway." He led out.

Aparicio had misgivings. "It may be that we are not welcome, Raul and me."

Some saloons did not allow Mexicans or blacks, but Hewey assured him, "Dutch Schneider ain't got an ounce of prejudice in his body." He looked at Tommy. "Except for underage boys. You'd best take you a sody water and stay real quiet."

Schneider came from behind the bar to shake hands with the men as Hewey introduced them. He was as cordial to the Mexicans as to Old Man Jenkins. He seemed surprised to see Alvin Lawdermilk. "It is a long time since you were here to visit me, Alvin."

"I took the pledge."

"That is good. How better it would be if more did the same." Though it went against the business he was in, Schneider could safely make that statement because the pledge was more often honored in the breach than in the keeping among male citizens of Upton City.

Schneider carried glasses and a bottle to a table large enough for all seven. Like Tommy, Alvin settled for a soda water. Cora should be proud of him, Hewey thought, though Old Lady Faversham would no doubt find fault somewhere. She would be terribly disappointed if she were someday to enter the pearly gates and find her son-in-law there ahead of her.

Snort was already on his third drink when a thin figure appeared in the doorway, stopping to squint and accustom his eyes to the darkness of the interior. C. C. Tarpley spotted Hewey and hollered from the door. "Hewey Calloway! I thought I saw you comin' into town a while ago." He strode with a strong step toward the table. His back was straight, his eyes alive and cheerful.

Hewey was taken aback. The last time he had seen C.C., the old man looked ready for the graveyard. Hewey stood up and extended his hand. "You're lookin' real good, C.C."

"I finally decided to take your advice. I went to Fort Worth and let a couple of doctors look me over from my head to my toenails. They said the only thing wrong with me is that I've got a stomach ulcer."

"That's all, an ulcer?"

"That's it. Said I been sittin' around worryin' too much instead of gettin' busy and grabbin' ahold. I need to cut out the whiskey and drink lots of milk. Trouble is, I've got five thousand cows on that ranch and not a one of them I could pen up and milk. You reckon Walter's got a Jersey cow he'd sell?"

"He's got a heifer fixin' to freshen. I'm sure he'd let you have her at a fair price."

"Price is no object, as long as it's not too high."

"I'm sure glad to hear the good news, C.C."

"I owe it all to you, Hewey. The doctors said if I'll take care of myself there's no reason I can't live another ten, maybe twenty years."

"I'll bet Fat was tickled to hear that."

The irony went over C.C.'s head. "Frank didn't seem as cheered up as I thought. I suspect he don't believe them doctors. He'll believe, though, when I grab ahold again out at the ranch, and I'm goin' to take a bigger hand in the bank, too."

"He'll be real tickled," Hewey said.

C.C. paid for a round of drinks for the crowd, though he did not take one for himself. "I'm headed for the ranch," he declared. "Ridin' out in Blue Hannigan's truck with a load of horse feed. There's a couple of Fat's hired hands badly in need of a firin', and I feel just good enough to do it."

He had been gone only a few minutes when Hewey heard an automobile pull up outside. Peeler walked in, pushing his goggles up. Hewey met him halfway. "How'd it go?"

Peeler looked as if he had won a big pot at poker. "If anybody asks you, you're addressin' Mr. Percival Smith, a rich cotton trader from Dallas, who's got more money than he knows what to do with and is willin' to spend a wad of it on horses."

Hewey asked, "You think Fat bit on it?"

"Ever watch a wolf grab a rabbit? I could see the cash register workin' in his eyes. I told him I'd find me a boardin'-house and be around town for two or three days."

Hewey said, "We'd best give Fat a little time. If we go over and brace him too quick he's liable to smell a badger game."

Jenkins frowned in Snort Yarnell's direction, his voice a little sarcastic. "I don't suppose your friend Yarnell would object if I bought him another drink?" Snort was two drinks ahead of everybody else and working on another. "I'm gettin' curious. I wonder how much it'd take to fill him up?"

Peeler shook his head. "You don't want to find out."

Hewey's skin prickled with impatience, but he forced himself to wait for what he guessed was half an hour. Peeler still had half of his first and only drink, for he had to drive. Snort had drunk enough for Peeler's share and Alvin's as well. He seemed lost in a far-off solitary world of his own, half humming, half singing a raucous ditty that could get a Baptist thrown out of his church, though that was no hazard for Snort.

The song was happy, but Snort's expression was melancholy. Even with a crowd around him, Snort was somehow alone.

He was always alone, Hewey realized. He had lived his life that way, drifting like a cottonwood leaf on the vagaries of the wind. He reached out for friendship, yet always left for new country before people could come too close. He had many acquaintances but few real friends. It came to Hewey as a sudden revelation that Snort was getting old, too old to continue much longer the kind of life he had led. Hard as he might fight it, trying to live young and loud and reckless, the years were pressing down on him. One day he would look in a mirror and see himself as he truly was.

Perhaps he already had, and that was why he looked sad. *Maybe I ain't far behind you,* Hewey thought. A chill ran through him, like the chill he had felt watching the bronc ride.

He asked Jenkins, "You ready to go take Fat's temperature?"

He looked back once at Snort before he left the saloon. Snort had his head down as if he were half asleep. He sat at the edge of the group, but his chair was pulled back a little, not quite in the circle with the others. He was talking to himself, talking about Grady Welch and the way he died. Nobody seemed to be listening to him.

Hewey and Jenkins crossed the street and walked toward the bank that had C. C. Tarpley's name prominently carved across its stone front. Blue Hannigan leaned against a truck parked a little short of the door, a load of feed stacked on its bed. As Hewey and Jenkins neared, Hannigan stepped free and held up his hand, gesturing for them to stop. He looked pleased.

"C.C. is readin' the gospel to Fat. You wouldn't want to disturb a good sermon."

Hewey heard Tarpley's voice inside, loud and commanding. "I'm fixin' to get to the bottom of this, Fat." He never called his son-in-law Fat to his face except when he was provoked. "Now, I want them books brought up-to-date, and I don't mean some time next week. I'll be back from the ranch tomorrow, and they'd better be ready."

Gervin's meek voice answered, "Yes, sir."

Tarpley burst out of the bank with a strong stride that said he was in full charge. He saw Hewey and Jenkins and seemed to feel that an explanation was in order. "Sometimes you've got to hit a mule over the head to get its attention. You-all got business in the bank?"

Hewey said, "We just need to talk to Fat about a horse."

"I don't think he knows which end eats grass, but I'll teach him if it takes me twenty years." He turned to Hannigan. "Ready to go, Blue?"

"Ready and rarin'." Hannigan winked at Hewey.

As the truck pulled away, Hewey said, "Now, that's the C.C. I used to know."

He motioned for Jenkins to precede him into the bank, which he thought was appropriate in view of the fact that Jenkins was much the oldest. It did not matter that he had the most money.

Fat Gervin sat at his desk, his head low. His chubby face was even redder than usual, for he had taken a dressing-down from his father-in-law in front of two harried, underpaid bank employees who probably enjoyed every minute of it. He looked like a man who had just been run over by a team of mules. Glancing up, he saw Hewey first.

"Hewey Calloway, what do you want?"

"I want to introduce you to Mr. Morgan Jenkins of Alpine, Texas. He's the man who's fixin' to sue you for a hundred thousand dollars."

Jenkins suddenly had Gervin's full attention. "You the man I sold them horses to?"

Jenkins took a cue from Hewey and drew himself up like an officer commanding a firing squad. "I am, and I have come here for satisfaction."

"I sold you them horses in good faith. I don't see where you got anything to sue me for."

Hewey reminded him, "You said they came from Alvin Lawdermilk's ranch. All they did was cross over it."

"A technicality. I didn't claim that Alvin raised them."

Jenkins charged, "But you wrote the letter in such a way as to deliberately mislead me. It's a federal offense to use the mails to defraud. I intend to lodge a complaint with the post office. And sue you besides." He looked at Hewey. "For two hundred thousand dollars."

Hewey took pleasure in the old man's audacity. "You never saw so many lawyers in one bunch as Mr. Jenkins has got."

Cornered, Gervin turned both palms upward as if to say he was helpless. "I got troubles enough right here in the bank. Them horses are way out yonder at Alpine. I don't know what I can do."

Hewey said, "The horses are here, down at the wagon yard. We're givin' you a chance to buy them back before the lawyers get into it. You know what a mess they can make."

It took a moment for the information to soak in on Gervin. His expression made a gradual transition from despair to hope to greed. "They're here? Well, now, that does alter circumstances. It just so happens . . ." He caught himself and did not finish.

Hewey suspected he had been about to say he had a ready and willing buyer but realized that information was best kept to himself.

A calculating look came into Gervin's eyes. "I've always wanted to be fair. If I was to buy them ponies back from you for the same price you paid for them, that ought to set things right. It was fifty dollars a head, wasn't it?"

Jenkins said, "It was seventy-five, and you know it."

Reluctantly Gervin said, "Seventy-five, then."

"But I got a lot of labor and expense in them broncs, and a big doctor bill besides." He motioned toward Hewey. "One of them outlaws ran into a fence and broke its neck. It'll take a hundred a head to square the deal."

"How many head?"

"Seventeen. I sold two."

Gervin tried to look displeased, but his eyes gave him away. Peeler had told him he would pay a hundred and twenty-five dollars. Hewey could see him mentally multiplying twenty-five dollars times seventeen, his potential profit.

Hewey tried to do it himself and came up with four hundred and seventy-five. That didn't seem right, but he had rarely had occasion to tally up large sums.

Jenkins said, "Deal."

Gervin put down a satisfied smile. "I'll write you a check."

"No check. Cash."

Frowning over the imposition, Gervin walked into the open vault and returned with a handful of greenbacks. He counted out seventeen hundred dollars. "I'll want you to sign a receipt."

Jenkins counted the money for himself.

The teller moved up cautiously to Gervin's side. "You'll need to make a note for that cash, Mr. Gervin. Mr. Tarpley will insist on knowing where it went."

"I'll have the cash back in the vault long before he comes in tomorrow."

Jenkins said, "Mr. Gervin, I'll call off my lawyers. I'm glad we got our account settled."

"So am I. Come again."

Jenkins muttered, "When the sun rises up out of the west."

Walking back toward the saloon, Hewey said, "I guess I've settled my account with him too, as much as I ever will."

"I'd love to see his face when he goes lookin' for Peeler and can't find him."

Hewey smiled over an imagined confrontation. "Even more, I'd like to be there when he tries to account to C.C. for that seventeen hundred dollars."

"That would be a show worth stayin' for, but I'd best be gettin' out of town. When he catches on, he's liable to put the sheriff on me and Peeler."

"Wes Wheeler's the law. You don't need to worry about him."

Before they entered the saloon, Jenkins pulled out the roll of bills he had received from Gervin. "I wouldn't have got it done if it hadn't been for you, Hewey. I feel like I owe you a commission." He peeled off a hundred dollars, considered a moment, then said, "Aw, what the hell!" and peeled off a hundred more.

Hewey debated about accepting. "It was worth it to see Fat put up a tree." But he considered his financially embarrassed condition and took the money.

Jenkins said, "I'm still needin' a foreman for the Circle W. Looks to me like you're healed well enough to take on the job."

"I doubt I can do rough work anymore. I'll never wrestle wild cattle again. I won't be able to ride anything but gentle horses, and maybe not all of them, either."

"It's time you learn the difference between a cow*boy* and a cow*man*. A foreman can point out what's to be done and let the younger hands do it. If he can't ride a horse, he can ride in a buggy. He uses his head and lets the others use their hands and their backs. You've got a head on your shoulders, Hewey. You showed that when you figured out how to snooker Fat Gervin."

Hewey rubbed his neck, wondering. He had never liked having to answer for anything or anybody except himself.

From inside the saloon came Snort's voice, telling again in painful, tearful detail all the facts about Grady Welch's sudden death and how hard it was to lose a good friend when he had so few. The words came slowly and badly slurred. Listening, Hewey felt the chill again.

He said, "I'm afraid Snort's pretty far gone."

Jenkins frowned. "He doesn't know where he's at or where he's goin'. I'd hate to see you wind up like him, Hewey. There's too many lost souls in this world already."

"I'll bet Snort would enjoy workin' at the Circle W."

"He's a good cowboy, but he's not foreman material. You could be."

Hewey reached deep inside for courage. "If I was to go, I'd want to take Snort with me. Aparicio, too. And I'd like to have Blas Villegas there to cook for the hands."

"Blas? The boys at the J Bar would kick like hell over losin' him. But all right, he's yours."

Something inside told Hewey to turn and run, but he stood his ground. "You sure you're ready to take a gamble on me?"

"If you're ready to take a gamble on yourself. Me; I think it's a cinch bet."

Hewey's hand trembled, for self-doubts remained strong, but he steadied it enough to hold it out and shake with Jenkins. "Deal."

Snort, Tommy and the Mexican hands had left their horses at the wagon yard. Hewey got the group together and started them walking in that direction, Tommy holding Snort's arm to keep him from weaving off into the street. A heavy figure moved ahead of them, also going toward the wagon yard. Fat Gervin was on his way to look at the horses he had bought, the ones he expected to turn a nice profit for him.

Jenkins climbed into his automobile while Peeler cranked the engine. Gervin turned to look as the car pulled away from the front of the saloon. He started to wave, but his hand froze in midair. Hewey wondered who he recognized first, Peeler or Jenkins, and how long it took him to realize they were working together.

Gervin staggered back a step. His body seemed to sag. He stared into the dust until the automobile passed out of sight around the livery barn. He slumped onto the edge of the wooden sidewalk, his arms hanging limp.

Most people called him Frank to his face. Only a few who had no tact or had nothing to lose called him Fat where he could hear it.

Walking by him, Hewey said, "It's been a pleasure to do business with you, Fat."

14

Hewey had to pull his hat down tight to keep from losing it, for Alvin must have been driving all of twenty miles an hour. In an earlier time, Hewey might have suspected he had been drinking.

Alvin said, "It's been a good day." He knew Hewey had accepted Jenkins's offer. "I know you're anxious to tell Walter and Eve about it, but I need to go by my place first."

"The news'll keep, I guess." Hewey was still surprised at himself for accepting the job. Now he faced the awesome responsibility of living up to his promise.

Alvin said, "I suppose you've thought this all out and you're sure what you want to do?"

"Hell no, I ain't sure. The whole notion scares me plumb to death. The only thing I'm certain of is that I don't want to end up like Snort."

"Nobody ought to ever end up like Snort."

"I wonder what Spring . . . Miss Renfro'll think about me bucklin' down to be a foreman?"

"Only way to find out is to tell her."

Hewey chewed on his lip. "If all this had happened to me four years ago, things might've turned out different. I might not've gone off and left her."

"Maybe it's not too late."

"I'm afraid it may be. Farley Neal told me he was fixin' to ask her to marry him."

Alvin chewed on his thoughts for several silent moments. "How much money have you got, Hewey?"

"Mr. Jenkins gave me two hundred dollars. Except for what I had in my pocket, that's about it."

"Some people don't have near that much to start a new life on. Of course, a bachelor don't need much . . . a change of clothes now and again, a little tobacco and whiskey money." He gave Hewey a speculative look and nearly ran out of the road ruts. "A married man, now, that's different."

"It takes two to get married."

"And one of them has got to do the askin'." Alvin gave Hewey another long look and this time let the car run off into the pasture. He had to turn the wheel hard to pull back into the ruts. "The worst she can do is tell you no."

Hewey's mouth went dry, yet he felt cold sweat breaking on his face. "Farley Neal is the better man for her."

"I don't doubt that, but you'll never know for sure that he's her choice unless you ask her yourself."

"You think I've got a chance?"

"What would I know about women? I'm just an old horse and mule man."

Alvin scattered the peacocks as he drove into the yard. Old Lady Faversham sat in her wheelchair on the porch. She was shouting something at Alvin, but the engine noise drowned out the words, which Hewey considered a blessing. Dust drifted up onto the porch, and she raised a lace handkerchief to her face. Hewey looked for remorse in Alvin's pudgy face but saw no sign of it.

Cora came out onto the porch. Alvin said, "I'll bet Cora'll bake you a cake when she hears about your new job."

Hewey doubted he could eat it, as nervous as he felt. The sound of voices drew his attention toward the barn, where Farley Neal and Julio were hitching a raw team to a sledge for training to the harness. Hewey watched a minute, wondering if Farley had asked her yet. "That's a good man yonder."

"Yes, and so are you, Hewey. If you're goin' to ask her, be damned certain you mean it this time. Be sure you won't be changin' your mind again and ridin' away without her."

Hewey walked up the steps, taking off his hat for Cora and nodding a silent greeting to Mrs. Faversham. Cora responded with warmth, but her mother only stared. He asked, "Is Spring here?"

Cora said, "She's in the parlor, Hewey. I'll take you."

Alvin caught his wife's arm. "Hewey knows the way."

Hewey opened the screen door and walked into the hall. The parlor was to the right, but he hesitated, twisting his hat out of shape in an effort to calm his shaking hands. He swallowed hard and entered the room. Spring sat with hoop and needles, crocheting. She smiled. "Hello, Hewey. Did you accomplish what you set out to do?"

"Better than we had any reason to hope. I doubt that Fat Gervin gets any sleep tonight."

"Nothing can pay for the harm he's caused you."

"What's done can't be undone. I've made up my mind to live with it and do the best I can."

"You'll do fine. You always did, after your fashion."

"Gettin' hurt myself has made me realize the hurt I caused you a long time ago. I wish I could undo that."

"As you said, what's done can't be undone."

"Just the same, if we'd married like we planned, look where we'd be now. We'd have us a farm of our own. We'd be somebody."

"And you'd be miserable, trying to make a farmer of yourself. You were a cowboy. You still are."

"That black bronc fixed it to where I can't be the kind of cowboy I was. But I'm about to try my hand at bein' a foreman. It pays better, even if it ain't as much fun." He told her about accepting the offer from Morgan Jenkins.

She said, "You can do it if you set your mind on it."

"The Circle W's a pretty place, in a wide valley with mountains all around . . . about the smilin'est country I ever saw. I wish you could see it."

She put down the crochet work. "That sounds like an invitation."

Flustered, he said, "I guess it is." He searched her face for a sign of acceptance but did not see it. He felt as if the floor were sagging beneath his feet. His weakened leg must be giving way, he thought.

She said, "If I didn't know you better, I might even think it was a proposal."

He meant it to be, in his own awkward way. He waited for her to say more, but she did not. She turned her eyes away from him. Disheartened, he took that for an answer.

He said, "All the way from town I wondered how I could get up the nerve to ask you, and I've done a poor job of it. I'm just a stove-up cowpuncher workin' for wages. You'll be a lot better off with Farley Neal." Breath came hard, for his throat had tightened to the point of choking him. Turning, he walked out the door to the hallway, then onto the porch.

Alvin and Cora looked at him in surprise over his quick retreat. Twisting the hat in his hands again, Hewey said, "Alvin, if you don't mind, I wish you'd take me over to Walter's right now."

Disappointment came into Alvin's eyes. "Sure, if that's what you want." He turned to Cora. "I may be late for supper."

Hewey walked to the car, his head down. He heard Old Lady Faversham say with satisfaction, "Good riddance if you ask me." He felt his eyes burn.

Footsteps told him Alvin was coming, so he opened the car door and took his seat.

He was startled by Spring's voice. "You didn't give me time to answer." She was standing beside the automobile.

"You didn't have to say anything. I saw the answer in your eyes."

"If you thought you saw doubt there, you were right. I haven't forgotten how close we came once, and how hard it was to see you leave. I wouldn't want to go through that again."

"With Farley, you won't have to."

"He asked me, and I told him no. I like Farley very much, but I don't love him."

Hewey took a deep breath. "You don't?"

"I've loved only two men in my life. One went to the war in Cuba and died. The other . . . just went. How do I know you wouldn't go again, Hewey?"

"I'm four years older, and I hope I'm four years smarter. I went off the last time lookin' for somethin' . . . I didn't know what."

"But you didn't find it?"

"If it was ever there, it's gone."

"What if some morning you wake up and the wind calls you, and you decide to go again?"

"I'm not claimin' it'll be easy. There'll be times it'll be tough. I'm liable to need help."

"You'll have Snort Yarnell."

"Most of the time Snort doesn't even know how to help himself. If you'll go with me, Spring, I'll never leave you again. Never."

Eyes shining, she reached over and clasped her fingers around his hand. "Then tell me about that smiling country."

He got out of the car and took her in his arms.

On the porch Old Lady Faversham cried, "Cora, do somethin'. A fox is loose amongst the chickens!"

Preacher Averill closed the Bible and smiled. "What the Lord hath joined together, let no man put asunder. Now, Hewey, you may kiss the bride. And if you don't, I'm fixin' to."

The wedding ceremony was conducted on the big porch of the Lawdermilk house to accommodate as many as possible of the couple's family and friends. A considerable overflow watched from the yard. About the only person Hewey could think of who had not shown up for the event, other than Fat Gervin, was Old Lady Faversham. Alvin said she was in her room, down with the vapors.

Music from Cora's piano came through the open parlor windows, and a gentle south breeze brought the pleasant prospect of barbecue from an open pit which Julio Valdez tended past the yard fence.

Though it was custom and his right, Hewey was shy about kissing Spring in front of so many, so he gave her a quick peck and an unspoken promise of better when nobody was watching.

Alvin was first in line to kiss the bride and pump Hewey's hand. Walter and Eve were next. Eve hugged Spring, then Hewey. She said in a shaky voice, "I'd almost come to the givin'-up point. This goes to show the power of prayer." Tommy was behind his parents, followed by Blue Hannigan and his wife.

Snort Yarnell kept almost at arm's length from Spring, taking her hand cautiously as if it were an eggshell. Eyes sorrowful, he turned to Hewey. "I never thought you'd do it, old pardner. First Old Grady and now you."

"But I ain't dead."

Snort cast a furtive glance back at Spring. "You might as well be. Things ain't goin' to be the same."

"Everything changes. You know you've got a job with me out yonder in the mountains."

"I'll be there. Got to go get a little drunk first, and I sure do dread it."

C. C. Tarpley had a strong grip for a man so recently given up to die. "Hewey, I owe you more than I can ever pay, but I brought you a gift." He handed Hewey a pocket watch. "Bought it in Midland. Cost me three dollars."

"You're a way too generous, C.C. I don't know what to say."

"Ain't no need to say anything. I've carried it myself for the past year or so. It keeps good time."

Merchant Pierson Phelps and Dutch Schneider had come out from town together. Phelps gave Spring a bolt of fine cloth, enough to make several dresses. Schneider brought a bottle of champagne. "Save it for when it is just the two of you alone."

Sheriff Wes Wheeler did not kiss the bride, but he took off his hat and bowed as he squeezed her fingers. "I hope, ma'am, that you can keep him out of jail."

"I shall make every effort, Mr. Wheeler. Between Mr. Jenkins and myself, we'll try to keep him too busy to get into any trouble."

Morgan Jenkins and his driver came along in their turn. Jenkins said, "Sorry I can't stay for the barbecue and other doin's, Hewey, but me and Peeler have got to get started if we're to make Alpine by dark." He pointed toward a new black buggy beside the picket fence. "That's yours to use on the ranch, but don't feel like you've got to be in any hurry about gettin' there. The day after tomorrow would be soon enough." He reconsidered. "Aw, take a little longer if you want to. Them cattle won't be runnin' off."

Alvin Lawdermilk had given the couple a pair of matched grays for the buggy. They trotted westward along the wagon road at an easy pace. Hewey said, "I thought we'd make camp at the Pecos River tonight."

He and Spring had spent their wedding night at the Lawdermilks', a poor place for privacy, especially when it seemed half the men in Upton County showed up to steal the bride and then give the couple a joyous and noisy shivaree that lasted until almost daylight. There had seemed little point in going to bed, and Hewey had not.

He held the reins in his right hand and took Spring's hand in his left. "Every time I saw you, I wanted to ask you to take me back, but I was scared to death you'd turn me down. I was ready to promise you just about anything."

"And I was afraid you were going to ask me and I couldn't say no 'til you *did* promise me just about everything."

"We've got a lot of lost time to make up for."

"We have the rest of our lives to do it."

"I feel kind of bad about Farley Neal, though."

"He's a fine man. He'll find someone, or someone will find him."

Jenkins and Peeler had taken most of Spring's boxes and her trunk in their automobile, leaving only the immediate necessities to be carried in the buggy. Hewey glanced at a basket just behind the seat. "Cora put enough barbecue and fried chicken in there to last us a week if we decided to stretch the trip that long."

Spring leaned to kiss him, her lips soft and warm. She rested her head against his shoulder and said, "We've spent four years getting this far. I'm not in a hurry to reach the ranch."

He put his injured left arm around her. It did not even hurt. "I'm not either," he said, and pulled the team down to a walk.